M000205104

Full Bone Moon

G. Cameron Fuller

Woodland Press, LLC

For Jon,
Hope you enjoy the
thrill ride.
With chills,
Geoff
2011

© Copyright 2011, G. Cameron Fuller
ISBN 978-0-9829937-9-8

All rights reserved. The Morgantown in this book is purely fictional and bears only passing resemblance to the author's actual hometown of Morgantown, West Virginia. Specifically, the information about the fictional Morgantown's founder, Haskell Morgan, was completely invented for the novel by the author. The real Morgantown was founded by Zackquill Morgan, the son of Morgan Morgan, in the 1770s, and none of the information about Haskell Morgan is true. All characters appearing in this work are fictitious. Any resemblance to real persons, living or dead, is purely co-incidental. No part of this publication may be reproduced, stored in a retrieval system, or transmitted in any form or by any means - electronic, mechanical, photocopying, recording, or otherwise, without the prior written permission of the publisher. Contact the publisher by sending an email to woodlandpressllc@mac.com.

PUBLISHED BY
Woodland Press, LLC
Chapmanville, West Virginia
Printed In The United States of America

SAN: 254-9999

G. CAMERON FULLER demonstrates an adroitness with language rarely seen in suspense and mystery novels and sets the bar higher for us all. Crafted by a terrific new voice in fiction, *Full Bone Moon*'s pacing, characterization, and settings are all wonderfully well wrought. In fact, Fuller's terrifying tale sneaks up on you and reveals itself as the best fiction I've read in years. Extremely talented work.

— Robert W. Walker, author of *City for Ransom*, *Children of Salem*, and *Titanic 2012*

Full Bone Moon is a bona fide gut-wrencher. Dark, smart, and quite honestly impossible to put down at three o'clock in the morning! G. Cameron Fuller shows us this gritty tale through the light of a full bone moon...and dares us to blink.

— Michael Knost, Bram Stoker Award-Winner and editor of *Writers Workshop of Horror*, *Legends of the Mountain State*, *Specters in Coal Dust* and *The Mothman Files*

Woodland Press, LLC

Table of Contents

I

"In the woods"

Preface
Early Friday evening, August 27: Full Moon

Shannon Green turned and walked backwards slowly, her thumb out. Her left hand held her backpack, arm swinging loosely. If she was going to make it home in time for dinner, she had to hitch, and this was the route she'd most likely get a ride. The college students always thumbed from here. She faced traffic—the student union to her left, the full moon rising above it in the daylight sky, Woodburn Circle with its clock tower off to her right: 5:30. Shannon could see the hills in the distance, behind the tower, hazy with the humidity of late summer.

Track practice had gone late, but Shannon had taken her time showering, then smoked her daily cigarette with Staci and Elisa. Although the semester had just started, she was already settling into a routine. Two out of the three practices a week, Shannon took an hour after that was all her own. She didn't exactly avoid going home so much as not get around to it. It allowed her a certain distance from her parents. She was glad that hitchhiking was coming back, once again becoming common. On college campuses, at least. Her parents said it was dangerous, but they were *so* last century.

Ever since she'd started working as a nurses' aide—Tuesday and Thursday afternoons, plus two shifts on the weekends—Shannon felt less and less like being at home. She earned money as well as school credits from her job, and she'd be graduating at the end of this semester. . . . Children and parents spent their time at home, not independent young women. At least it seemed that way to Shannon.

Evening traffic drifted by. Occasionally a car stopped, students piled in and rode off. She kept backpedaling gradually away from the standing hitchhikers. Shannon felt out of place among the college students, like they all knew each other, like she was the only stranger there. She imagined they all looked at her and thought, High School Kid. But she took it in stride, part of the problem of growing up in a university town, even in West Virginia.

She started down the section of road that looped around the base of the small hill. She flicked her brown hair loose from her collar and shook her head, squinting into the westering sun.

The car had gone a little ways past her before she realized it was stopping. Because of its tinted windows, Shannon could only see a shadow of the driver inside, probably a rich kid with indulgent parents. She hoped he wasn't a jerk; a lot of the ones who picked up female hitchhikers were, and she didn't want to ride with another grabby guy like last week.

She opened the door and hesitated, suddenly doubting the driver was a student. Too old. He didn't look at her, but stared straight ahead, both hands gripping the wheel. Shannon saw his forearms: thick, dark hair, heavy muscles that seemed to bulge in all the wrong places. She almost didn't get in the car, suddenly sure she shouldn't get in the car, but then grew aware of the traffic backing up and became embarrassed. She got in the car.

"Hiya," she said. "Thanks for stopping."

Silence.

"Great day, huh?"

The car started to move again. The man didn't say anything and still did not look at her. The way he held the steering wheel—both hands, grip firm and constant—unnerved her. The man's physical *presence* also bothered her. His head was set too far forward, she thought at first, before she noticed that his back was round, almost hunched, as thoroughly muscled under his white button-down as the forearms that seemed to sprout from the partially rolled-up sleeves.

She shouldn't have gotten into this car.

She tried to sound cheerful, chatty. "I'm going up past Austin's Grocery there. On the way to the hospital."

It seemed like the man grunted, but she might have imagined that. Shannon had hitched enough to know that some people only stopped to give you a ride, they didn't want to talk. It didn't mean anything. They just weren't talkers. She folded her hands in her lap, a formal action that said, I'll just sit here, mister. No talk.

At the light, the car turned and started up the hill. She watched the close-set houses pass the window. Once, those were family homes for glass factory workers, now gutted and cut into student apartments. But they all still had porches, and small TGIF parties were beginning to gather on some. Music. Beers.

At the intersection near the top of the hill, they stopped at the light. Shannon almost got out even though her house was still a quarter mile away. She was looking out the passenger window, wondering if this car had a way that the driver could keep a passenger from unlocking her door, when he spoke. "You shouldn't hitchhike, you know. It's dangerous."

Shannon tensed, startled; his voice was an almost whisper. She turned toward him. His eyes were deep-set. The sweep of his forehead was smooth, but where his eyebrows drew together, the skin rippled.

"It's okay in town, I think." Her voice sounded frightened, which surprised her—she didn't feel frightened. Not exactly. Well, sort of.

"No." He shook his head. She thought he looked sad. His hands never left the steering wheel. "Not really. It just *seems* that way."

She should get out of the car now. If she could. But she didn't try, frozen by his stare. She remembered what she had heard about snakes and the birds they ate. How it happened.

". . . don't believe this at your age, but you could be killed." Shannon hadn't heard the beginning of his sentence. He kept staring and she couldn't look away. "Remember those girls a few years ago? Mared Malarik and Karen Ferrell?" he said.

She didn't know what he was talking about. Seemed like his spidery whispers came and went like waves. Only his eyes were constant.

". . . six years ago. . . picked up down by the Met Theater . . . the evening . . . full moon . . . full *bone* moon. . ."

The streetlight changed to green. She'd missed most of what he'd said.

"It's green," she said. She stared at the light. She still couldn't reach for the door handle. The car didn't move.

"The police found the girls south of town, in the woods. They never found the heads."

That snapped her out of it. She clawed at the lock, but it wouldn't give. Even as she did, the dark-haired man floored it and the car shot forward, tires screaming, leaving blackened patches. "I'm not finished!"

It was the first thing he'd said that wasn't a whisper. It was a roar.

Shannon scrunched down in her seat, hunched against the door.

"The guy they put in jail—Clawson—he was an idiot. He never did it." The dark-haired man was whispering again, his eyes fixed on the road, driving too fast around the curves. "He was in Philadelphia at the time."

They neared the turn-off to Shannon's house, her parents' house. "Let me off here," she managed to say, her voice thin, weblike. The car didn't slow down.

"You shouldn't hitchhike," the dark-haired man said.

1
Sunday evening, September 26: Full Moon

Amelia Samosky never had much trouble getting rides. She hitched whenever her schedule got a little tight, and she'd never waited more than fifteen minutes for someone to stop—as long as she hitched in the daylight, when the drivers would have plenty of chance to see how she looked. They were bound to stop then.

Even though it was Sunday, Mel was supposed to meet Carla and Louise later that night; they were going out drinking—Rocky's, then Mr. Sam's, then on to Grand Central Station for dancing. Everything would go great if she could get a ride quick.

She started to walk backwards, standing straighter, very conscious of her tight jeans and long legs. She was sure—the way that some people were sure that black cats meant bad luck—she was sure she would get a ride soon.

In less than five minutes, Mel smiled as the car stopped for her. She opened the door.

*   *   *

The phone was ringing. From somewhere far away. It rang and rang. The sound brought Alexandra back, echoes of her dream dissipating into smaller and smaller waves, scattered by the ringing phone.

She was laying on her side in the bed, facing her husband, her cheek snuggled deep in the pillow. She didn't even open her eyes. Jerry wasn't going to answer it; they both knew it was most likely one of her patients. Without looking, she threw her arm behind her, groping for the phone she'd left on the nightstand.

"Yeah-hello," she said, almost one word.

"Doctor?" A scratchy, male voice. Alexandra recognized it.

"Yes?" She scooted up the sheet to lean against the headboard. "I'm here."

A long pause, filled with slow, even breathing. Alexandra waited, but no words came, just the ragged breathing. She had gotten to bed late and didn't have the patience for this tonight. "What is it this time? Talk to me."

The breath caught abruptly. *The way it happens with some old people,* Alex thought. *When they're about to say something.*

"Doctor. It's happening, again."

The voice brought her up short. Different than usual. The hair on the back of her neck stood up. "What's happened?"

"Just remember, I warned you about this possibility." He seemed to

7

struggle to form the words, as if he were drunk.

"Hypnotic regression is not—"

"Soon it will be two, Doctor," the voice interrupted. "It's already happening." Abruptly, the voice became sharp. "It's too late to stop the next one, but stop what you are doing, or more people are going to die. You're in over your head, but it's not too late. Stop now. You won't hear from me again."

"But there's never been any—" Alexandra was interrupted again, this time by a dial tone. Just as well. She had started to say there had never been any reported side effects of the kind he had alluded to in his earlier calls, but that would have sounded weak.

She fell back against her pillow, drained, face turned to the ceiling. She felt sick to her stomach. The way he said those three words—*It's happening, again*— uninflected, a sense of infinite, empty distance, like he was speaking from the other side of the moon. She had been frightened this time.

She drew herself deeper under the covers. There had been danger in that voice, and she remembered that her dream had left the same impression of danger. . . . Or was she confusing the two?

What did he mean, "more people are going to die"? Alexandra tried to make sense out of that. The only deaths lately in Morgantown were either from old age or car accidents, the usual. Oh! and one drowning back in June. She couldn't tie any of them to anything to do with her patients. Still, it chilled her. The man must know something she didn't. Or he was just crazy. But despite her logic, she kept coming back to that voice, and the words, *It's happening, again.*

*   *   *

The color of the blue lights that flickered against the leaves and trunks of the trees that night has no natural equivalent. Water is never that color. Neither is the sky, especially not in the West Virginia hills, where the sky is most often grey, or the wispy white of humidity. The blue flashing that lit the forest clearing is peculiar to the lights on police cars.

Four cars were parked around a clearing in the woods, headlights pointed inwards. They'd come by the old fire road, rutted deeply and rarely used. The forms of the six policeman in the middle of the clearing were lit blue by the emergency lights and yellow-white by the headlights. Four other people, two policemen and two civilians, stood at the rim of the clearing, near the edge of darkness.

The low murmurings of human voices didn't carry far in that three AM night, but the intermittent crackling of police radios seemed awfully loud.

The smell of rotting meat.

The two officers who stood off to the side were interviewing the two civilians, a man and a woman. The woman's face was streaked with mascara; she stared at the ground and answered questions in single syllables. The man clenched his jaws slowly and deliberately, and his eyes darted around the darknesses that the police lights didn't reach.

Two of the six policemen in the clearing were walking carefully in concentric circles, looking at the ground. Weeds, sticks, dirt. Whatever clues had been there seemed to have disappeared sometime in the—what? Two weeks? Three? Four?

Two others were also examining the ground very slowly, but in the straight line that led from the center of the clearing toward their vehicles. They were making sure the path the stretcher would take was empty of evidence.

Unlike the other four, the two in the center of the clearing weren't in uniform. They were standing still, looking down at the headless body. Bags under their eyes, they both looked as if they had just gotten up.

"Aww, Darnell," said the younger of the two, not taking his eyes off the body that lay at their feet. His gaze kept returning to the stump of her neck, all the dried blood there and on her shoulders. He'd never seen a headless body before, and his brain kept telling him it was a mannequin. "We ain't gonna find nothin' here. Dogs already got to her."

"Dogs didn't take the head." Detective Darnell Watts dispassionately took in the details: face-down, left arm—missing from the elbow down—stretched above where her head should have been, right arm perpendicular to the torso, brown twine still tied around the wrist. The hand still had flesh and skin, the arm had only bits of either. The ground for three or four feet around the body was stained dark, probably from blood. Even time hadn't eliminated it completely. She had been decapitated here, where she lay. When they lifted her, they would no doubt see her blouse stained almost black from lying in her own blood.

The legs of the corpse bent sharply at the knees and splayed, the soles of the feet pointed off to the right. Most of the skin was still present from the ankles down, frayed and scattered on the legs above. The same twine around the ankles.

The skin and muscles on the back were still there, down to the bottom of the ribs. Below that was the nearly bare spine, packed dirt visible on either side. The skin on the upper back that had not decayed or been picked at by small and large animals was covered with shallow, parallel slices, about an eighth of an inch apart. Greyish-purple in the flashlight.

There, at the edge of the weeds. Two small fragments of bone reflected the flashlight. Detective Watts stepped toward them and crouched. Three more bone fragments just beyond, bits of a young woman's skull, picked clean by insects.

Crime scene would be busy until well into the morning. They might even find a bullet deeper in the woods.

He turned his attention to the five small areas around the body that had been swept clean, down to the bare dirt. They were about the size of a pack of cigarettes laid flat, or a man's fist. Beside each was a deep hole in the earth; stakes had been driven in there, deeply, solidly.

One bare spot was just inches from where the victim's head should have been. The other four were evenly spaced, more or less where the victim's hands and feet would have been if she had laid spread-eagled. If they were connected by lines, they would have formed a star.

The detective knelt and looked at them closer, squinting. The edges of growth that surrounded the clear places caused shadows in the bad light. The effect made it hard to see. He licked the tips of the first two fingers on his right hand and felt around the spot near the head. The gritty texture of dirt. Then he touched something smooth, a small, rounded bead of smooth. He picked it up, held it up to the light of the headlights.

Wax. Red wax. Detective Watts pursed his lips. He stood again, looked at the junior detective, rubbing the wax between the thumb and forefinger of his right hand.

"There's still a lot here, Dale. More than enough. Get on the horn there and see what's keeping the crime scene guys. Then make sure the first perimeter is secure."

Dale headed for the cruiser. The couple who had discovered the body was being shepherded toward another cruiser. The woman was sobbing.

2
Monday morning, September 27

Michael Chase padded barefoot onto his porch. The sun was rising behind him, beginning to cause shadows. Cigarette and coffee in hand, shoulders bunched against the cold, he pulled his robe closer. He dragged on his cigarette, stared out at the neighborhood. His head was empty.

The air was thick with fog, the kind he knew would burn off and leave a clear, but cool, September day. Shadows of telephone poles slanted across the street, into the yard directly opposite his. The house was on a corner, a T intersection, the fence wrapped around. There was only a thin shadow from the section that started down the hill. Chase had never known what the fence was there to keep out, or keep in. Everything cast slight shadows: the pine tree one yard over, the cars parked on both streets. The tomato stakes in the yard next door, stark against the turned earth.

Parts of a dream he'd had the night before came back to him, bits and images: a man's silhouette suddenly standing in Chase's bedroom, picking up the sleeve of a shirt that lay across his dresser. "What material is this made of, Mr. Chase?" the stranger had asked, then he'd picked up another shirt: "And this?" The man bounced a small crystal globe in his hand as he talked. Gradually, Chase became aware of a woman's screams from somewhere far away. Next came his own voice speaking to him, a sense that he might be speaking aloud, in his sleep. "What are *you* made of, Michael Chase!" He struggled to wake up, tried to figure out if he were shouting, as it seemed to him in the dream. At one point he believed he had awakened, only to discover that he had not.

It'd been an odd dream, not all that extraordinary, but there was something. . . *familiar* about it. He couldn't place what, though. The only remarkable thing was that he didn't usually have dreams on a night when he'd been drinking. Or he didn't remember them, if he did. He took a long drag on his cigarette, remembering that this was his version of a hangover. He also recalled the empty bottle of whiskey that lay on its side on the kitchen table, just inside the door, next to a large ashtray overflowing with the butts of his Basics.

He squinted into the brightening sky, high and clear above the mist, which had changed from a light blue almost to a white. The moon was setting, pale and bulging, just then resting on the hillcrests a few miles away. His cigarette was done, and he pinched it between his fingers, put the butt in his robe pocket. There was something he was forgetting.

The night before, he'd been trying to work on a feature his editor had assigned about a Ph.D. candidate at the med school who had petitioned the county for permission to exhume the bones of Haskell Morgan, the man who had founded Morgantown and died in the 1840s. Morgan had been a flamboyant character: visionary, woodsman, friend of the local Indian tribes, scourge of local Christian missionaries, famous according to some people, notorious to others.

The doctor-to-be believed that contemporary reports of Morgan's erratic behavior were due to an advanced case of syphilis. That rumor had been floating around Morgantown forever, probably since Morgan's time. The academic wanted to run biochemical tests to determine if it was true. Local passions had been aroused, many people very against using Morgan's "mortal remains" in that way.

Some of the townspeople thought of Morgan as a hero, conveniently forgetting the tales of his rants at town meetings and church gatherings, his disappearances into the woods for months at a time, his claim that he'd been visited repeatedly by God Himself. Those people wanted to erect a statue to honor a "noble, self-sacrificing gentleman who founded Morgantown as an important port along the Monongahela River."

Very selective memories these folks have. The way Chase recalled it, Morgan had wanted to found a renegade religious sect as far from meddling civilization as possible, where Europeans and Indians could co-exist.

Ho-hum. The assignment bored Chase, and he was having a hard time finishing it. Actually, he was having a hard time *starting* it. He usually liked writing science articles. He had a flair for explaining scientific things so that anyone could understand them, and he generally liked to do it. But this time, he just couldn't get going.

He'd done all the research but couldn't come up with a decent angle. The article would have to be about more than the molecular biology being practiced at West Virginia University hospital. The science would have to be addressed, but the controversy was mostly about exhuming the bones of the city founder. The essence of the article was political as much as scientific. Chase hated newspaper politics, always a cartoonish portrayal of real human interactions.

He pulled a cigarette out of the pocket of his robe, lit it, coughed twice. *Not yet the hack of the hopelessly addicted,* he told himself. But he knew he was lying.

The whole project bored him so thoroughly.

He drew on his cigarette.

Truth was, he wasn't enjoying anything these days. A couple of years ago, he would have just said the heck with it and gone down to the Omega for some beers. Beer always used to make his periodic lack of interest in life more tolerable. He hardly ever drank these days; all he could do for his moods was wait them out.

And what was he forgetting?

Two years earlier Chase's editor had given him better assignments. He had kept an eye on state and local politics for the *Herald-Dispatch,* and he'd always gotten the most interesting crime stories, such as they were in this small university town encamped in the northern West Virginia hills. Of course, that had all changed after the Clawson episode. Which still burned him.

He went back into his kitchen for more coffee. Once inside, he headed for the sink, stopped in mid-stride, staring into the living room. A massive figure lay sprawled on the couch, one arm hanging off, forearm resting on the floor, head tilted back, mouth open. The big man was snoring fitfully.

Crap. That's what I was forgetting. Shango.

Shango was passed out on his couch.

3
Monday morning, September 27

Unlike most people, Chase never got hangovers—headaches and a body so sensitive that it hurt when the heart beat, all that stuff he'd heard friends complain about—instead, what he got was stupid. Which was fitting, considering how hangovers happened.

He shook his head, rubbed one hand slowly from forehead to chin, and looked at Shango. He had the urge to pinch himself, like he still needed help to wake up. Instead, he re-filled the kettle with water and put it on to boil. *Coffee. I need more coffee.*

Shango had shown up the night before at midnight, just when Chase was cursing his computer screen, trying to arrange his notes into some kind of coherent story. Shango had pounded at the door, startling Chase, hammering as if Chase lived in a three-story house instead of a three-room apartment. He'd known immediately who it was.

Most of the time, when someone showed up unannounced when Chase was working, especially at that time of night, he met them at the door, mumbling something like, "Yeah, yeah. Well, sorry. I'm in the middle of something." They would leave and he'd close the door, feeling guilty for his anti-social impulses.

He'd done just that to Shango before, and probably would again, but not this time. He needed diversion, and Shango was good for that—an easy excuse to get away from that stupid story. He'd flicked on the porch light and the pounding stopped, and he threw the door open, pleased to see Shango blinking back the sudden flood of bright light.

"What is wrong with you!" Chase shouted. "Think I live in a bloody mansion!"

Shango shielded his eyes from the bare porch bulb. "I come bearing gifts, Bwana." He held out a bottle of Henry McKenna whiskey. No bag, just a bare bottle. A third of it gone. Chase eyed the bottle but didn't reach for it or step back from the door.

Shango shook it a little. "Take it or leave it."

Chase took the bottle, swirled the contents. He turned toward the cupboards. "Glass or pottery?"

"Cup. Give me cup." Shango stepped into the kitchen, swung the clear plastic bag he was carrying in his other hand onto the table. It landed with a thunk and the sound of rattling plastic.

Chase motioned vaguely for Shango to have a seat. He poured whiskey into two small blue ceramic cups, set them on the tabletop, and took the other chair. He glanced at Shango's huge hand as it surrounded the cup. Chase was a little over six feet, but Shango was one of the few people who made him feel like a half-grown teenager sitting next to an adult.

After a moment of silence, during which they both swirled the liquid in their cups, Chase said, "So, what's up?" He looked at the bag on the table—cheap cardboard chessboard inside, the hollow plastic pieces.

"I know you got a stereo here somewhere. What's your latest kick?" Shango asked.

Chase got up, eager to share what he had been listening to lately: James McMurtry, *Paint by Numbers*. He'd discovered it by accident, as he did with most of his music. He also knew Shango would probably hate it. He tapped in the play order so that the first song was, *It's a Small Town*.

He watched Shango grimace. "What is this crap? Country?"

"Just listen, city boy."

Shango smiled, feral and toothy. "Naw, Bwana. You ain't from around here. You're as much of a city boy as I am." He drained the cup in one swallow, poured himself some more. Chase wondered how much whisky it would take to make a man of that bulk drunk. He probably weighed 225, 250. Far above Chase's 180.

Shango took the board out of the bag and dumped the pieces out on the table. "I need a chess partner," he said. He began to set them up. He locked eyes with Chase. "I think I should be black."

"You need a party partner that's not as stupid as the ones you usually hang out with," Chase said. He moved the white pieces onto the appropriate squares.

In the two years since they'd met, Shango had been a constant mystery, and Chase couldn't resist a mystery. Shango was homeless and mostly stayed in Bartelby House, a local shelter. But he refused to look for a job. "What do I need a job for?" Shango would say. "I already work for Sister Brendan. She's okay, for a nun."

Chase figured Shango put in 30 hours a week at the Christian Help Center, all without pay—unloading shipments, arranging inventory, helping clients. God knew where Shango got his money—Chase sure didn't want to—but he refused to take any cash from the government. He did say something once about liking to gamble and had offered to show Chase some card-counting tricks.

He claimed to have been both a guard and an inmate at Rikers, which was where he learned to play chess. "There wasn't nothing else to do but play chess, twelve hours a day, eight days a week." He was proud of his chess game. Chase had played him often enough to see why.

He'd known then he was in for a long night. Shango would want to play chess and talk, play chess and drink whiskey. Chase would lose and lose, and get drunker and drunker while he heard grim stories about the first Gulf War, Shango's three tours of duty, and the way dying "towelheads" sucked spastically for breath. He would see Shango's snorting re-enactment of those scenes. If they got drunk enough, Shango would show the scars on his belly that he had gotten when an IED exploded a little too nearby, and the one on his side where he said he was knifed.

Chase had heard all of it before, but always with new details: revealing, illustrative, important in some way. He couldn't count on Shango for the truth, but always for a good story.

Chase moved the king's bishop pawn forward one square, to cover the king's pawn he had moved to the center of the board.

Shango laughed. He could barely keep his hand from moving to his pieces too fast.

It was going to be a long night.

As the morning coffee water built toward a boil, Chase thought about what he'd read on Bing Bites the day before. He often checked Bing Bites for weird news stories, and yesterday he'd read about how groundwater picks up fragments of ancient and long-dead micro-organisms when it filters through rocks. When water heats up, those pre-Cambrian organisms began to reform, the heat reassembling them into replicas of the creatures they'd once been, not alive, but not dead: tiny pre-historic zombies. When the water boiled, they disintegrated. Chase wondered if this was true.

While he waited, he flipped on the computer in his living room. He didn't worry about waking Shango. Why bother? The man had beat him four straight games of chess.

He called up the *Dispatch* website. He logged in, hit the link to AP, and searched "West Virginia." As it searched, he glanced at Shango on the couch. No movement.

The search stopped and the headline told him that their junior senator, the former governor, had managed to secure some pork for the state. *More jobs. Yeehaw.* Chase's irreverent streak popped up at the worst times. A lot of people needed those jobs; he knew a few who did—Shango one of them, even though he refused to look—and he saw others outside the Social Security office every time he went in to work.

He came across another story: *Unidentified Body Found.* He skimmed the text.

... The body was located in a forest clearing off Interstate 79, near Morgantown, West Virginia. ... The victim, either in her late teens or early twenties according to officials, was found face down, her hands bound, although a police spokesman said it is not clear whether or not this was caused by the action of forest animals. ...

The sentence made Chase laugh. He tried to picture squirrels tying a person up. Raccoons must have done it, he decided. *Their tiny hands are more agile.*

The kettle in the other room whistled urgently, but Chase stared at the computer screen, unseeing. He had just laughed at the careless writing in an article about a murdered girl. What *was* he made of?

The water kettle kept whistling.

He shook himself, a shudder that ran the length of his spine and curled his toes into the carpet. Maybe he should make himself an egg—eating was the best thing for a hangover—a nice over-easy egg, the yolk all runny and ready to be soaked up by bread, a "Best Ever Breakfast" as someone he once knew—but couldn't quite remember, an old girlfriend perhaps—had called it. Then he remembered that his sister had called them *bloody eggs*; "That yellow is the egg's blood," she'd never failed to point out.

Chase suddenly wasn't hungry anymore. He made coffee and took a shower instead. As he walked through the living room on his way out the door, he kicked the couch hard, jarring the sleeping Shango.

"Get up, slug. I'm going to work."

Shango just grunted. Chase left for work.

4

Monday morning, September 27

Maria Redmann looked up sharply from the morning paper when her son came into the kitchen. He'd startled her. Her nerves were a little frayed, but she managed a smile for Adrian.

"Hi, hon," she said.

He dropped his backpack on the floor just inside the doorway. She was surprised that not only was he up, it looked like he was all ready to be on his way to school. He headed for the refrigerator.

"You're moving awful early," she said as he opened the refrigerator door and bent over, peering inside.

"Yeah, Mom," he said without looking back. He reached in, moved a few things around. "Hey, what happened to that pizza?"

"I'm sorry. Your father and I finished it off last night. There's some eggs in there."

"Nah." He straightened and turned around, holding the gallon milk jug. He twisted off the cap.

Maria knew what he was about to do. "Adrian Allen! Don't you dare. You get a glass for that." Her voice sounded harsher than she meant it, but Adrian just grimaced and stepped to the cupboards. He looked like his father when he made that face, although it occurred to her now that Adrian might turn out even more handsome than Don. "So what's up?"

Adrian's brow furrowed as he looked at her over his full glass of milk, like he didn't understand what she was saying. She wished he didn't have to assert his independence by acting stupid. She rephrased her question.

"Why are you ready to go so early?"

Adrian spoke after draining the last of the milk from a glass. "I'm gonna walk today, Mom. Gotta get going." He filled the glass again.

Maria felt a pain in her stomach, almost as if he had hit her there. She felt rejected. Usually, she gave him a ride to the high school after Don had gone off to work. It was something they'd started a couple of years ago, when Adrian first started going to the big high school across town. She'd drop him off, then drive downtown and open her shop. She enjoyed the time with him.

"See ya, Mom." Adrian scooped up his pack by the straps and left the kitchen.

"Bye." By the time she spoke, he was gone. Maria sighed and laid the paper down on the table. Even though he was only seventeen, it felt to her like he was already out of the house, out of her life. Danielle hadn't been like that at all; she'd never really pulled away, not like Adrian was doing. Even though Danielle was in college now, and had her own apartment across town, she still called home and came for dinner every so often. Adrian made Maria feel unwanted. She even wondered whether he'd ever really loved her. . . .

She sighed again, this time exasperated with herself, trying to pull herself together. There—she was doing it again. Thinking Like a Victim, Alex called it. Thinking Like a Loser was what Maria called it, one of her bad habits that came up like a weed in every one of her sessions with Alex.

"You've got to unlearn those patterns, Maria," Alex would say to her when she brought it up. "It isn't just unproductive and. . . not useful, it's negative. It pulls you down. It undercuts all the other aspects of therapy that you're doing so well in."

Maria would apologize and compliment Alex's advice; Alex would laugh and wave her hand dismissively. "There you go again," she'd say, as if it were a minor backsliding. "Acknowledge it, forget it, and start fresh. We do enough looking back." Then she would sit forward in her seat and say something like, "How's the shop doing?"

Alex was right, of course. There was no reason for Maria to feel rejected by her son. It was all part of what had been going on with him for the last year. Early in the fall, he'd started having her drop him off at the graveyard near the school, rather than right at the front gate. She'd believed at first he was ashamed of her, but after she saw other mothers doing the same thing, she realized it was just something teenagers did. Too cool to ride the bus, but also too cool to be seen getting out of their parents' car.

It's so silly the kinds of emotional hoops we make ourselves jump through, she thought. She wouldn't have thought that three years before, when she first began seeing Alex. The psychiatrist had helped Maria look at herself a little more rationally and see that the kinds of insecurities she felt were to be expected, hardly major problems.

Alex also gave Maria strength in other ways. When Maria first told Alex she'd always wanted to own her own business, Alex had urged her to go for it. "Danielle's on her own, and Adrian's in high school. It's time you did something just for you."

So Maria opened the children's toy store on High Street, the main drag in downtown Morgantown, a few months later. *Chuckles* was small, but big enough to give her something constructive to do, big enough to display the items she thought children really wanted and needed to be able to get in this town. Happy toys with wind-up motors, bright colors, and plenty of lights. *Chuckles* also offered a wide selection of nonviolent, sneakily educational games. And plenty of rubber creepy-crawlers.

Of course, she'd had major confidence problems during the first year.

Don hadn't helped much. Although most of the time he was supportive and loving, in this he was dismissive, referring to the shop as "your little mid-life project." It was like he didn't want her to succeed. Alex had helped her through that period, too. "Maria, you've got everything you need. You're smart, you've got retail experience, a bookkeeping degree, you know what kids want, and what's good for them."

Maria laughed. "Yeah, I can see it now. Ten years from now, when you've finally got it through my head that it's okay to be assertive, I'll barge right into Don's office and stamp my foot. I'll say, 'I *told* you I could do it.' And he'll look down at his papers and mutter something like, 'Sure, honey. Guess I was wrong. Anything else?'"

Alex said nothing. Maria suddenly noticed Alex's still watchfulness and quieted abruptly. Maybe she had laughed a little too hard. The rest of the session had gone okay, but she'd finally touched on something important she needed to look at. Don had never—would never—actively prevent her from pursuing her desires, not the way her grandfather used to do, but that was what Maria feared.

"Maria?" Don's voice snapped her out of her reverie. "You okay?" He set down his briefcase softly, as if he were afraid of startling her.

"Yeah, honey. Sorry. I'm fine. I'm just thinking about how much I have to do today."

He leaned over and kissed her forehead. "You were staring into space. Your mouth was open." He looked worried.

"No, I'm fine, dear," Maria said, even though she wasn't so sure. Something had been bothering her lately, that was certain. Over the last couple of days, she'd begun to figure out what it was. Good thing she had an appointment with Alex today; Alex would help her sort it out. "I think I'm going downtown a little early. Get some things done."

"I was just worried about you. You had a restless night," her husband said as she stood up. "Did you sleep okay?"

Maria's lips tightened as she tried to remember. "Yeah, yeah. I slept fine."

"You know I worry about that old fold-out thing," Don said. He made a half-hearted chuckle. "It's not the most comfortable mattress."

"That's for sure." Maria laughed, but she wasn't so clear about it. She remembered going to bed early, about ten, but she didn't remember moving to the foldout in her study. She must have been very tired and very restless. "That mattress is the pits. Talk about lumps! I'm sore all over."

Don laughed again and she could tell he was convinced she was okay, at least for now. He picked up his briefcase and walked toward the door. "Have a good day, honey."

"I will." She kissed him on the cheek.

She watched through the kitchen window as Don's sedan backed out. She looked at her car, standing alone in the driveway. It was new, a small boldness she was proud of. She was pleased that she had been assertive enough to hold out for the color she wanted. To go with her name. Alex had been pleased, too. "A symbol of healing," she had called it.

Maria went into the living room, picked up her purse, and left the house.

5
Monday morning, September 27

Alexandra Heyden glanced at her watch as she walked through the living room on her way to the kitchen: 8:25. She was running late. Her mind shied away from the reason she'd overslept, the phone call she'd gotten, the phrase, *It's happening, again.*

She thought instead about how she wouldn't have very long to sit with her husband in the breakfast nook just off the kitchen. No time to look out the window at the wet fall grass, no time to watch the birds flit in the trees on the edge of the forest that ran up to within a hundred feet of the house. Just some quick espresso, then off to her first appointment, at 9:15.

Jerry was already in the kitchen, reading the morning paper. He lowered it and looked up when she came in. "Coffee's been waiting for you, hon."

She smiled her thanks, even though he hadn't needed to tell her: The musky scent signaled coffee dark and rich and strong enough to jump-start her day. She poured herself a small cup, not a demitasse, bigger than was probably appropriate for espresso, but good coffee was one of the sinful pleasures she and Jerry shared. She slid onto the bench opposite her husband.

The paper still lowered, Jerry stared at her as she sipped. Neither of them said anything for a while, all eye-contact, no speech. Looking at her husband like this—his slight smile and laughing eyes, like he was waiting for something surprising and inevitable to happen—Alexandra could never contain herself for long.

"What?" she said, with a laugh.

"Well," he said, pointedly smoothing the paper. "Are you going to fess up or what?"

"To what?" she said, looking down at the coffee that swirled in her cup.

"Whatever's been bugging you lately."

"Nothing's been bugging me." She glanced out the window.

"Good," Jerry said. "Good. I'm glad it's just my imagination."

He lifted the paper as if he were going to go back to reading it. She knew he wasn't being sarcastic, he was just willing to let it lie until she was ready to go into it. He was so patient. It wouldn't do to leave him hanging like this. She touched his hand with her fingertips: *Wait, I've changed my mind.*

"I guess I've just been rethinking things," she said. "I'm not sure how much good I'm doing."

Jerry smiled. "You question yourself every six months or so, and every time I have to—"

"I know, I know." She held up her hand, palm out. "You give The

Speech. 'There aren't enough people working with child abuse as it is, and no one else even *considers* the multiple personality disorders that sometimes result.' Und so weiter."

She smiled; she really did value that speech.

"No, this is different. There has been something lately. . . I guess I just wish there were a way to get to the people who *cause* the problems. I wish there were some way to prosecute. . ." She trailed off, thinking of the man who had called the night before.

This man had called her three times—no, four times in all. Always at night, always anonymous. He obviously knew she was a psychiatrist, but she was certain that he wasn't one of her patients. She would have remembered that voice.

He'd first called about two and a half months ago. He wouldn't say who he was, but he expressed concern for her patients, so she listened. She dismissed the first call as being from a quack with an interest in psychology. He was articulate and apparently well educated, but still a quack. Probably he'd seen that article on her in the *Dispatch* and gotten some minor obsession going. Harmless enough. After he'd called her a couple more times, she wasn't so sure.

At first, he'd been fairly talkative, as if he were trying to get something important across to her. He'd also been polite, although condescending.

"Doctor Heyden, you know this as well as I do. You're poking around in things you really don't understand," he had said. When she'd tried to object, to point out the years of research and experience that had gone into her branch of psychiatry, he'd cut her off with a small hissing sound: "You think a few decades of timid exploration constitutes *experience?*" He actually seemed to find that amusing.

The caller got more direct the second time:

"Suppose your explorations bring past abuses to the surface, closer to having a direct impact on behavior. Suppose the adult who was abused as a child becomes an abusive parent because you brought everything to the surface. What would that make you?"

"That's not the way it works," she had said.

"Are you sure of that, Doctor?"

She hesitated before answering. The truth was, she wasn't really so sure, not all the time at least. Before she could think of anything to say, he hung up.

The third call had been worse:

"You are going to cause many people a great deal of trouble, Doctor. You should quit while you're ahead."

"Look, I've had about enough of your nonsense." She hadn't slept well lately and this anonymous call in the middle of the night. . . Her usual diplomatic front had dropped away. "What are you getting at?"

He'd hung up on her. She thought about it later, lying awake next to her husband, looking toward the ceiling. One clear thought, the kind that only comes when one is absolutely exhausted but can't sleep: He was referring to a particular patient of hers, and only one. She didn't know which one, but she would ask him about it when he called again. If he called again. He hadn't, until last night.

She blew the steam off her espresso and sipped at it, conscious of Jerome staring at her. She looked out the window toward the forest.

Jerry leaned forward in his seat. "It was him again last night, wasn't it?"

She fidgeted on the bench. "He knows something, Jer. He's not just a crazy person. At least not totally." She picked at a hangnail on her left thumb, peeled it back. Blood. "He makes some good points. Sometimes."

"Hon, you *do* make a difference. Look, your patients don't repeat the cycle. They don't abuse their own children. That's important. You're stopping the Wheel of Karma and that's heroic in itself."

"My clients are the heroes," she said, but her tone was flat. She forced a smile. "Do you know how silly you sound when you say things like Wheel of Karma? How many venture capitalists do you think speak New Age?"

He snorted and looked down. "More than you might think. All my clients care about is an investment counselor who makes them money. They don't care what else I talk about."

6
Monday morning, September 27

Detective Darnell Watts was clenching his teeth, trying to control his temper. His doctor had told him over and over that screaming at people was not good for his blood pressure. Instead, he spoke quietly and firmly into the phone. "We need whatever prints you got, and we need them by about two hours ago. I want to know who this girl was. And I want it A.S.A.P."

He waited a little more, jaw muscles straining. First he'd been called out to a murder scene at three in the morning, then he found exactly what he never wanted to see again, not even in his worst nightmare. Now after being up all night, he had to deal with this half-wit medical examiner. He would have had that spineless smartass removed months ago, if it was up to him.

"I don't *care* how long she was out there. Just get me a print I can use." *The man wasn't fit to be a janitor.* Watts longed for the old medical examiner, the one who'd retired the year before. That man had gone out of his way to be collinsative. "Yes, we found the bullet! But did she shoot herself? Can you tell?"

He listened briefly as the ME made excuses, thinking more about trying to keep from yelling than about what the man was saying. Finally, he could bear no more: "So the splatter pattern's inconclusive. You think I don't know that? That's none of your business anyway. What about those cuts? What made—?"

The ME interrupted him. Watts waited, counted to ten. "I *know* the soft tissue's gone! Was there any evidence of puncture trauma in the thoracic—?"

He waited some more as the ME sputtered indignation. Finally, he cut it off again. "You're right. I shouldn't talk to you that way, but look, here's the bottom line, John. The FBI's coming into this now."

He paused, listening.

"I don't know why! They're here, that's all. My rearend is in the sling, and yours will be too. We can't afford any screwups. I want that report on my desk this afternoon."

He hung up the phone without waiting to hear what the man had to say.

He looked at his watch; it was only 9:00 and already the day had turned to crap. He grunted as he stood up from his desk. Darned indigestion. Darned ulcers. He wished Elaine was here to pull the files for him, but she wouldn't arrive for another half hour, and he had things he wanted to add. Already this case was sounding too familiar for comfort. Just one headless body this time, but. . .

That God-forsaken Clawson thing just wouldn't go away.

7
Middle of Monday morning, September 27

Chase hit the 'save' command on his computer and leaned back. It had been a productive morning for a Monday, despite the debauchery of the night before. Back when he drank regularly, it used to happen that way for him sometimes. The morning after too much booze would start out hazy and confused, but once he focused on the writing, it would really flow. He looked up at one of the four large wall clocks that hung on the four walls of the large newsroom: 11:30.

Chase had already thrown together the fluff piece on a cancer fundraiser that the publisher's wife wanted for tomorrow's edition. Five hundred words, appropriately upbeat and rah-rah, and Chase hated it. Partly because he disliked writing that kind of article—he never *read* that kind of article—but mostly because he disliked the publisher's wife.

The newsroom was nearing the end of what Chase thought of as the Mid-morning Dead Zone. By nine o'clock, most everyone who was going to come for the dayshift was already there. Usually this was fourteen or so people, even with the last round of cutbacks. The main newsroom seemed to get larger the fewer reporters it housed.

The Dead Zone was the time of highest productivity. People were still waking up, slurping coffee, scarfing doughnuts, hunched over their keyboards, without the urge to socialize. Even though the big room had no walls or partitions, they were all in their own worlds. The clickety-click of computer keyboards, quieted by the carpeting and covered walls of the newsroom, was the most common sound for long stretches of the Mid-morning Dead Zone. This morning, the place was made even more surreal by Chase's hungover perceptions.

He'd been able to wrap up the feature on the fake ID business in Morgantown that the Lifestyles editor wanted for the Thursday pull-out. Not a bad piece, either. One operation—basically two kids working their way through their undergraduate years—had allowed him to come to their apartment where they'd shown him their camera equipment, their light table, their laminating machine. Chase gave them $45, and they set to making a driver's license that showed him to be 42 years old.

As they worked, one of them confided to Chase that "the overhead is killing us. Once we get these machines paid for, we'll be raking it in." Chase thought it sounded like the kid was repeating something he'd overheard; the kid confided that his father, identified in the article as "a businessman in the southern part of the state," was the operator and primary shareholder in one of the state's largest construction firms.

Two hours later and Chase had a new driver's license and the meat of his article. The ID was well done, too, although very few people would believe he was 42, ten years over his real age. A photo of the license was going to be published with the article.

Chase poked at his keyboard to connect to the mainframe. Ever since The Beast had been installed, all the reporters had been having problems. Periodically, the system bombed, causing everyone who was connected to lose some of what they'd been working on. If too many people were logged in at the same time—or even a few people running extensive file searches—The Beast was deadly slow, couldn't even keep up with the slowest typist. Chase avoided all that by disconnecting while he worked.

His computer dinged at him: ENTER USERNAME.

Chase typed, MCHASE, hit the *enter* key.

Almost immediately, the computer beeped. ENTER PASSWORD.

Chase typed HYEENA, and he was in. Misspelling his password was one of the simplest ways to prevent someone from guessing it. Not that anyone would have been likely to guess *hyena*, unless they had somehow known that Chase used the names of wild animals as his passwords. As his own little joke to himself, he always picked an animal that was symbolic of his current official status at the paper.

Lately, he was a scavenger, a scruffy outcast, and the connotations of *laughing hyena* were preferable to the ones of his other choice, *jackal*. Over the years he'd been *leoperd*, *jagwar*, *condoor*, *badjerr*, *pakrat*, and many others. He'd thought about *chmpanzee* and *platapus*, but he only had seven letters to work with. Since everyone had to change passwords every three months, Chase had decided to move to sea creatures next.

Chase saved the cancer fundraiser piece to the main file server, dropped it into the copy room's electronic folder. He was glad to be rid of it. Mrs. Loughery had specifically requested that he write the piece, saying he was the best they had, and she wanted well-written PR for the event she was planning. He found it a little galling that she'd requested him even though she knew he disliked her.

He'd had quite a run-in with his editor over her last year, and since he couldn't be demoted any lower than he already was, he'd almost lost his job over it. He'd known while he was gathering evidence against her that he wouldn't be allowed to run the story. Not only did her husband own the paper, Mrs. Loughery was—in addition to being charming and allegedly witty—very popular in the Morgantown area. Mrs. Loughery of Mothers Against Drunk Driving, Mrs. Loughery of DARE to Keep Kids Off Drugs, Mrs. Loughery the cocaine addict. Chase had nothing in particular against coke-sniffers, but he didn't much like hypocrites. Especially high-profile hypocrites.

He didn't think much of Mr. Loughery, either. The way the man mixed his newspaper business and his political ambitions smelled distinctly of sulfur. Particular stories were demanded, others were vetoed—all according to Loughery's personal or political whims. No way to run a newspaper. *Ahh, what's a peon to do?* he thought.

Once he'd saved the fake ID story to the network file server, Chase was about to disconnect and take a break—this would be an ideal time to go outside and have a smoke, his first since getting to work—when he remembered the AP story he'd seen that morning. A murder, and an ugly one apparently, just north of town. Waters must have assigned someone to the story by now. Maybe some poking around on the network would prove interesting.

If Chase were assigning the story, he'd give it to Adams, that new hotshot from Ohio University. He was an intense kid, and the few times Chase had spoken with him, he'd been impressed with Adams's subtle mind. Adams was interested in crime reporting, and this would be perfect to get him broken in.

Which meant Waters had probably given the story to Dumont.

He logged off the network, but stayed connected. His eyes searched the room to make sure Dumont wasn't around. If he was, his screen would show a message saying that someone else was trying to connect under his name.

The screen blinked. ENTER USERNAME.

Chase always felt a little sneaky, snooping around like this, but that never stopped him. Snooping was what reporters were supposed to do. He typed, TDUMONT, hit *enter.*

ENTER PASSWORD.

Chase thought for a moment. Theodore Edward Dumont III was 34 years old, had a wife and three kids, and used his full name whenever he could, just to impress people. Eddie, as Chase referred to him when he wanted to be annoying, chose passwords on the basis of how easy they were to remember. Eddie didn't know to choose a 'world'—as Chase had with his world of animal names—from which to pick a password. The worst thing—the least secure—was to pick passwords directly related to one's life, which is what Dumont *always* did.

At one point, his password consisted of his initials, TED. Then it was his wife's name, LINDA. One by one he'd used the kids' names, THEO, ALEX, and LISA. Then the family pets: FURBALL, TIGER, and HOBBES. Then ELM, the street he lived on.

Chase sat back, staring off in the direction of the clock on the wall to his right. Himself, his wife, his kids, his pets—what next?

Chase sat forward and typed, BRONCO. Dumont's file list came on-screen, and Chase smiled. Dumont's wife had gotten a new car about a month ago.

He looked at Dumont's file list. There was only one that had been worked on today: UNIDENTIFIED. He called it up. It was headed, *Notes On The Murder.* Eddie always capitalized every word in the titles of his notes, as if everything was of the utmost importance.

Chase began to read.

8

Middle of Monday morning, September 27

It didn't take Chase long to review the file because there wasn't much there. Dumont had essentially just typed in key information from the AP story. At least he'd cleared up the ambiguous wording of the original. After typing the notes, Eddie would have called down to the Public Safety Building to find out what jurisdiction the case was in. That's where he'd be right now.

Chase worked a little differently. He picked up the phone, punched in the number of the local AP Bureau Chief, Paul Jacobs. He was more than the Bureau Chief; he was the whole bureau. The phone rang seven times.

"Yeah," was the gruff answer. Jacobs sounded irritated, or more likely, sleepy.

"Hey, Paul. It's Chase."

"Oh, hi."

"Sounds like I woke you."

Jacobs sighed. Chase had a mental picture of Jacobs sitting up straighter, trying to wake up. When he spoke again, he sounded more alert. "Yeah, didn't get much sleep last night."

"Don't want to keep you. There's just a couple things maybe you could help me out with."

Silence at the other end. Jacobs didn't normally say anything unless there was some reason to. Chase liked that about him. He forged ahead.

"You must have covered that murder last night. I assume you went out to the scene?" Jacobs slept with a police scanner next to his bed, something that Chase used to do when he covered crime.

"Yeah, sure."

"Who has jurisdiction?"

"City. It was out on that mountain near Exit Seven."

"The area they annexed last summer?"

"Yeah. That's it."

"Can you tell me anything more than what was in the story?"

There was a long pause. "Like what?"

"I'm just looking for some background right now."

Another pause.

"You can't print it, and you didn't hear it from me."

"Sure."

Jacobs seemed to come alive, his voice louder. "Hey, wait a sec. Since when are you on this kind of thing again?"

"I'm not. I just finished what I needed to do today, and I'm curious."

"Uh-huh." It didn't sound like Jacobs believed him.

"It was just that reading your stuff on the wire, something sounded funny. Like there was more to it than what was in the story. Now you say that you do know something, but it can't be official. What gives?"

"Who's working on the story for you guys?"

"Dumont."

"Ah," Jacobs said, as if that explained it. Chase knew that Jacobs knew that if there was a hidden buried treasure, Dumont would look for it in a tree. "Okay, it's like this. Got there, they were about to take her away, so I didn't get to see much. They had already taken the people who found her down to the station, and they wouldn't tell me who they were, so I didn't get to talk to them."

"People? How many?"

"A couple. Young lovers. Probably gone out there to. . . you know. . . in the woods after the bars closed. You can get their names from the report, if they let you see it."

Chase already knew that, and there wasn't a chance they'd let him see the report. He let it pass.

"What about the body?"

"There wasn't much left of it. Been outside too long. Made me wonder how she could have been out there for so long without anybody stumbling over her."

"Vehicle access though? These lovers—"

"Yeah, no problem. Should have been found weeks ago, but she wasn't. Who knows. She was cut up pretty bad. I've—" Jacobs was silent for a second. "I've never seen anything that bad." He coughed. "Stunk something awful."

"The story said she was bound at the wrists." He resisted the urge to tease Jacobs about the sloppy writing; it wasn't the time.

"Actually, she had twine tied around one wrist and both ankles. The lower part of the other arm was missing."

Chase winced. It did sound bad. "Were her ankles tied together?"

"Nah. They just asked me to write it like that. You know."

"Yeah." Chase did know. The police often asked reporters not to be accurate about certain small details, or to distort them so that they could be used in court or to match up with a confession. Reporters were usually obliging, as long as the details had no impact on the truth of the story in the larger sense.

"Was Watts out there?"

"Sure. He was the primary."

"Well, thanks, Paul. Thanks a lot. I'll see what I can do about getting Dumont pointed in the right direction on this."

"That's not all of it. You're not gonna like this, Chase." He paused. Chase was about to say something, urge him to continue, when Jacobs said, "Her head was gone, just like those two before. Malarik and Ferrell."

Chase grimaced. That's what he'd feared. It hadn't been in the newspaper story, but the other details had sounded similar. One body this time instead of two, but otherwise. . . After a second, he said, "Thanks, Paul."

He'd have a little talk with Eddie, but he had a feeling Eddie wouldn't much listen. He'd have to make his own visit to the gang down at Public Safety as soon as he had the chance.

9
Early Monday afternoon, September 27

Maria was taking inventory in the back room. Sort of. It was the middle of the quarter, so she really didn't need the complete inventory the tax people would want. This was in-house inventory. Still, she was being as precise as she could.

One of the dozens of books she'd read about small business management had said that McDonald's was so thorough they even counted straws, and that was one of the keys to their success: Control the inventory and you control cash flow and product turnover.

Maria was having some trouble focusing, however. Her mind kept drifting. She tried to get an accurate count of the dinosaur soap, the Beatrice Potter books, the rubber spiders and snakes, tried to keep away from. . . other things. But it was hard. Maria put the clipboard down and rubbed her temples. She wished she didn't have such thoughts. She wished she knew what they meant.

For several weeks, she had been having. . . urges. It seemed like everywhere she went, she saw some man she found very attractive. The distinguished-looking gentleman in the bank last week. That tall fellow who'd held the door for her at the grocery the next day. The dark-haired doctor that came in the shop the other day to buy his daughter a birthday gift. Maria had never even looked at another man in all her twenty years of marriage to Don, and now she saw them everywhere!

She already knew what Alex would say: "It's okay, Maria. Every woman has those thoughts from time to time. They're alright as long as you don't act on them." Which was exactly why Maria was worried; she just might act on them. Why else did she feel the irresistible urge to rent an apartment for herself, a place that almost no one—certainly not Don—would know about. She'd never had any secrets from Don, not ones this big anyway. What would Alex say about that?

She also wondered what Alex would say when Maria told her that every one of those men she was having sexual feelings for was old enough to be her father. Or her grandfather, for that matter. What did that mean? Maria had *never* been attracted to older men. Don was even 14 months younger. Alex would probably say something about father figures and self-esteem. And she might be right. . . .

She heard the silver bell that hung over the shop doorway tinkle. She started to go see who it was, but she heard Katie's voice. "It's okay, boss! Just me!" Maria smiled. She liked being called *Boss*.

She enjoyed the days when Katie didn't have class and was able to work. A grad student in geography, Katie was a little older than the undergrad type

Maria had expected to hire, a more settled and dependable employee than she'd hoped for. She was glad Katie liked the job and had no plans to leave before she got her masters.

Over the last year, Katie became more like a friend than an employee, in some ways the closest friend Maria'd ever had. Maria decided a few days ago that Katie would be the only one—besides maybe Alex. . . maybe—who would know about the apartment. And that was out of necessity.

Katie walked into the back room. She was holding a small key ring with a couple of keys on it, shaking them so they jangled. "Everything went great. Place is nice. Here you go." Katie tossed the keys to Maria, who caught them in her left hand. "You sure you don't want to tell me what the apartment is for, Boss?"

Maria gave a little shake of her head and her eyebrows knitted together for a second. Then her forehead smoothed and she smiled easily. "No, no, Katie. Sorry. Now, you just mind your own beeswax."

Katie's knowing smile. "As if I didn't know already. You get me to rent a place on High Street for you, so nobody sees you doing it, you think I can't figure out what's going on?" She winked. "What's his name?"

Maria ignored the question; she didn't know how else to handle it. Younger women today were sometimes more upfront than Maria was comfortable with. It was probably a good thing, for them at least, but sometimes it made Maria uneasy. She didn't know how to deal with it except to change the subject.

She glanced at her right wrist. It was almost time for her appointment with Alex. Might as well go ahead and go. She handed Katie the clipboard. "Would you finish up for me? This whole section is done," she said, indicating the set of shelves to her right. "I'm sorry, but I haven't had lunch yet and I've got my appointment in about an hour. You know."

"Sure thing," Katie said, smiling conspiratorially. "Enjoy," she said to Maria's retreating back.

Maria pushed out onto the street. It would be good to go see Alex. Maria needed her right now, before things went too far. But first she had to stop off at the post office, and. . . Wasn't there something else she needed to do?

10
Early Monday afternoon, September 27

Alexandra looked at the time on her cell, wondering when or if her next appointment would show. The woman had a somewhat spotty record lately. Nowadays, Alex generally charged whether the client showed up or not, something it had taken Jerry quite a bit of talking to convince her to do.

"Look," he had said one morning over espresso and eggs. "What we're talking about is your time. If they don't show, that still takes up the hour you could've been doing something else with."

"But I haven't done anything for them. How can I make them pay for something they haven't received?"

Jerry slapped his forehead in an exaggerated gee-what-a-moron-I-am gesture. "Your clients are not paying for your education or your—nearly infinite—wisdom. That's not what they're buying. They're paying for your *time.* They're paying you to be there when they say they want you. If they don't show, that's their choice."

"Okay, okay. I get what you're saying." She'd looked out the window, across the yard, toward the trees. "I don't have to like the way it works, though." She sighed: her husband, the financial consultant.

She stared out her window at the parking lot, black asphalt, the slanting rays of the afternoon sun making windshields sparkle. She adjusted the papers on her desk without looking at them.

Clinical psychiatry could be so unrewarding, and if she'd gone into any normal branch, it might be even less so. Maybe those little gains her clients saw—"Oh, now I can tell my husband why I can never answer emails!"— should sustain her through the periodic crises. But they didn't get her through the times when she felt something more should be done, even though she had no idea what it was. Days like that took a real effort to remember why she was doing what she was doing: her overwhelming curiosity about what it is to be human, her encompassing desire to help.

Whenever she felt doubt, she remembered her college boyfriend, Craig: "No, baby, I'd never go to a psychiatrist. They think they know what a person is and what a person's capable of. They make like they want to help you, but all they really do is cripple you. They teach you to walk by breaking your wings."

A vivid metaphor, but she'd thought him naive. Craig had contempt for science and fancied himself a poet of some sort. She'd thought that romantic at the time, but later on, long after he was out of her life, she realized she'd never seen a single poem.

"We are but angels, baby," Craig would say when he was feeling full of himself. "We are here to do whatever we do—hopefully, we can make things better."

When she was feeling her most cynical, Jerome reminded her of Craig, with his New Age talk, his mysticism. But basically Jer was a hard realist. He couldn't be so successful as a financial advisor otherwise. Buddhist teachings only *sounded* like New Age vagueness; ultimately, there was a lot more substance to them.

Now and then, she wondered what had ever happened to Craig. Where was he now?

This is getting me nowhere, she thought. *Frustration turns me inward.*

She stood up and paced.

Alexandra learned from a college friend who had multiple sclerosis, with its coming-and-going paralysis, what it was like relearning to walk over and over again. Now she felt that way with every client she encountered: Each time, she wondered about child abuse and split personalities and responsibilities and the limits of the human spirit. She wondered about behavior that psychology couldn't explain satisfactorily, about forces and causes that were not easy to pin down. And she constantly doubted she was discovering anything useful.

That doubt was what her midnight caller seemed to sense and explore so adeptly. She remembered the voice that had come in the dark hours of that morning, *It's happening, again.* A shiver ran up her spine.

Alex looked out the window of her seventh-story office: the parking lot, the small cars below, a tiny figure got out of a red car and headed for the front doors. Beyond that, a grassy hill, formed no doubt by the bulldozers that had done the excavations for this building. The hill had that unnatural, carpeted look. Beyond the hill, far beyond, lay the Appalachians. The Allegheny Ridge.

This is the oldest mountain range in the world, she thought. She'd heard that, anyway. *When you're outside, if you're very quiet, you can feel it.* There was something hostile—No, not hostile, but worse, *indifferent*—about the Appalachians. Humans were nothing to these mountains, and she had always thought of them as magnifying human experience: for better and for worse.

She shook her head and blinked, as if trying to wake up. Living with Jerry had gotten her thinking fuzzy, mystical thoughts. Silly nonsense.

But right then she felt the darkness, the cycle of violence: Abuse begat abuse, murder begat murder. She could do nothing about it. She shook her head again, spastically this time, half-shiver, half-shake.

Her phone buzzed. She punched the button sharply, and her secretary's voice came over. "Maria Redmann here to see you, Doctor."

"He used to make me go blindfolded," Maria was saying. "I didn't want to, but I didn't have any choice."

"Maria, you've got to think back now. Why exactly would he do that to you?" Alexandra had her patient under a light hypnosis, not enough so she would be immersed in the experience, but enough so she remembered things she might not have consciously recalled.

"He said it would make me stronger. Make me better than other people. He said that if I learned to see without my eyes, then I would know things other people didn't know."

"Like what?"

"I don't *know*. I'm sorry." She shrugged to emphasize the point. "He used to have me blindfolded for two or three days, until just before my parents picked me up. I . . . " Maria choked up, sniffled. "I didn't know *why* he was. . ." She stopped.

Alexandra watched without saying anything. Three minutes can be a long time.

Maria continued, but her voice had changed: "It was fun. Playing like I was blind."

Alexandra noted the flat inflection, the voice seemed to come from a distance. Like the call last night—*It's happening, again*—from the dark side of the moon.

Alexandra caught her breath and settled her voice. "Let's go into how you felt at the time," she said smoothly, soothingly, exactly the way she'd been taught. "Go into what you talked about before. You said something about a bowl?"

Maria twisted in her seat. She writhed as if she were being burned, but couldn't get up. "No," she said weakly. "Don't make me."

Alexandra was faced with a decision then. Maria had come to her to learn the source of her growing ambivalence toward her husband, her continuing to love and nurture her children. They had uncovered much together, much that Maria had been able to take away and apply, much that she had found useful. Was it time to stop before she clipped Maria's wings?

No. There was an imminent breakthrough. This was it. Alexandra still had faith in the methods she'd been taught, despite her coming-and-going doubts.

"I want you to tell me. First we have to take another step, a deeper step into. . . ."

11
Thursday afternoon, September 30

The Public Safety Building seemed busier than Chase remembered it. He held the door for two suits on their way out. "They'll go for it," the woman was saying. "They have twice as many rape cases as this time last—" "And 75% are open-and-shut, including this one," the man interrupted. "Roberts'll never accept. . ."

The pair kept walking and passed out of Chase's hearing. They hadn't even acknowledged his presence. Public Defenders, from the sound of it, talking about a plea bargain. Chase used to recognize all the criminal lawyers, back when he was in and out of this building like it was a second home, but there was a big turnover in this college town, since law grads tended to use the PD office as a rèsumè builder. He doubted he'd recognize half of them now.

Three days since he'd spoken with Jacobs about the murder, and this was the first chance he'd had to get down here. He wasn't even sure what he was going to do. Half-baked impulses—he mostly knew that the article on Morgan was still to be done, was due in three days, in fact, and he couldn't stand the thought of working on it. Especially not now. He was too curious about this murder thing. Maybe the police had discovered something in those three days. If so, someone at the paper had to find out what it was; God knew Mr. Eddie Dumont wouldn't do it.

Once inside the building, he ignored the information desk in the main lobby and the desk where people could pay their tickets, and turned left down the corridor to the door marked, *Police Department Central*. At least that was where it used to be. Same dumb name, too. It reminded him of a bad TV series. "Hey, I know!" he imagined someone saying back when this building was first built. "Let's use the one from *Rod Sharp, Private Eye*. That's a cool show. It's about LA."

Chase was only half-surprised to see Elaine still working the reception desk. She had wanted to move to a city—any city, as long as it was a long way away from here—for as long as he'd known her. As far as he knew, she'd never made any concrete plans, just vague dreams of being in a band that hit the big time. She looked up as he neared the counter, blinked twice before he saw recognition on her face.

"Do I look that old, Elaine?" He smiled and held out his hand, palm down.

"Chase, jeez, how you been?" She grasped his hand, seemed glad to see him, maybe almost as glad as he was to see her. He'd been afraid his connections had dried up entirely. Even if most of them had, Elaine was about the best he could have hoped for: She knew everything that went on around the station.

"Not bad, kid, not bad. I see you aren't in New York."

Elaine grimaced. "Tell me about it. I'm not even playing out these days. I mostly just go watch bands and stand around all night telling myself how much better I am."

Elaine never was all that precise with her choice of words. He knew exactly what she meant, but he couldn't help mentally converting her spoken words to printed ones, and seeing the ambiguity that would be in the literal transcription. *Better than what?*

"Listen," he said. "I'm sort of working on something that I think you might be able to help me out with." He paused. He wanted to see her reaction.

"What do I know about Mrs. Loughery's coke habit?" She grinned at him. When Elaine was teasing, it always came across as a challenge. A mean edge to her, and he liked that.

Chase leaned forward, putting his face closer to hers. "This isn't about some dizzy rich lady's chemical desires." His lips smiled, but his eyes didn't. He winked instead.

Elaine laughed again, and began to straighten some papers. "You look like crap, Chase. Don't you sleep?"

"I've been staying up a lot lately, worrying about what I'm going to get my editor for Christmas." Chase hadn't realized the lack of sleep showed so clearly. Come to think of it, he really hadn't been sleeping very well for the last month. He suddenly remembered what had been so familiar to him about that dream he'd had the other night—a similar one he'd had about a month ago. Same figure, same content, same screams. "Did you catch my series on longwall mining safety techniques? Fascinating stuff."

"You know I don't read that junk. The only thing I read of yours anymore is the odd restaurant review. And I emphasize *odd*, jack. The way I figure it, you've been drinking again."

Chase didn't say anything. He let her comment lie there in the silence. She would think he felt insulted and keep talking.

"I thought you didn't work the crime beat anymore," she said. *Bingo,* he thought. "I miss you around here, Chase. What are you working on that I could have anything for you?"

"It's about this murder."

Her face suddenly went flat, all expression drained out of it. She resumed playing with the papers on her desk. "Uh-huh?"

"How come the news didn't say anything about the girl being cut up?"

"I don't know how you know that, Chase, but I know you. I guess there are about a couple dozen cops you could've gotten that from." She adjusted the papers on her desk some more. "I'm not supposed to know either, but I do. She was. Cut up, I mean."

"Had she been in the woods long?"

Elaine waited a moment before she spoke. "No. The autopsy's not back, but I hear she was only out there a day or two at most." She paused. Chase wondered if she was lying or if she just didn't know. "Look, Chase. I can't be the way I used to. I didn't used to think I'd be around here long." She looked down; he decided she was lying.

"That's okay, Lainy, no problem. How about one more question? Just to give me something to go on?" When she didn't say anything, he went on. "Why's the official line that she wasn't carved at all? And why didn't anyone mention her head was missing?"

Elaine looked up at that. "It was? I never heard anything about that."

Maybe she didn't know after all.

12

Thursday afternoon, September 30

Chase saw the same old round and red face when Watts looked up from his desk. The same gin blossoms, too, except there were more of them.

"Darnell." Chase advanced with his hand outstretched. "Good to see ya."

In Chase's opinion, Detective Darnell Watts was a solid, if somewhat uninspired, detective. Like a bulldog who wouldn't let go. In some ways, Watts had been Chase's best asset on the force when push came to shove on the Clawson thing. They'd had a couple of drinks while Chase scoped him out. For a while, Chase had admired him. He never would have figured Watts would wither under the scrutiny of a superior officer. Especially not Captain Braxton, now Chief Braxton, over whom Watts had fifteen years' seniority. Watts had done a complete turnaround suddenly, insisting that Clawson had done the murders.

"What are you doing here?" Watts didn't move, didn't even put down his papers.

"I've missed you, you old walrus."

"Kiss off."

"Really. Don't you miss the old days?"

"Get out of my office."

"I can't do that, Darnell, old salt. I need to ask you a few questions."

"I don't know anything about the Loughery woman's coke habit."

Chase shook his head. *Is that the only thing they talk about around here?* He hadn't even been allowed to run that story. The one decent thing he'd come up with on the society beat, and Waters had killed it. And that was months ago.

Chase sat on the edge of Watts's desk. He would have to move fast on Watts, keep him off balance. The man was never known for his brains. "I need to talk to you about the murder. I understand you've been assigned to the case."

"Get off my desk."

Chase ignored him. "So far, all I've got is that the woman was cut up pretty bad."

"Who told you that? Get off my desk."

"Common knowledge, buddy. Oh, and I heard her head was missing."

Watts looked at him sharply.

"Thing is," Chase went on, "since you're the Man on this case, I hope you're going back over the Clawson incident. Might help."

"The Clawson file is closed, Chase. You know that better than anybody.

42

Now get off my desk!"

Watts was too tense; it was clear that the connection between this new case and the old one had occurred to him, too. That was all Chase was likely to get right now. Time to switch tactics.

"I'm sorry. You're probably right. This might be a copycat, but the Clawson thing is all over. Finished. Done. Didn't mean to upset you." Chase got off the desk and started for the door.

"Chase. What were you talking to Elaine about just now?"

Don't miss a thing, do ya? "That puffhead? She's not too bright, but if you watch the way she. . . uh. . . Don't know if you've noticed lately, but she's got these sexy. . ." This wasn't working too well; Watts didn't go for any of Chase's leads. "Some of us have hormones after thirty, Watts. In case you hadn't noticed."

Chase was almost out the door when he stopped and turned, half-facing Watts. "One thing. You know who the young woman was yet? Or how long she'd been there?"

Watts watched him for a moment before speaking. His jaw muscles flexed; he opened his mouth, considered, reconsidered, then spoke. "Laana Anders. A WVU student. She was reported missing a month ago."

"Could you spell that?" Watts did, and Chase memorized it.

"Thanks." Chase started to back out of the door.

"Chase!"

He stopped. "Yeah?"

"I assume your sources told you what not to print."

"No worries, mate," Chase said in a fake Australian accent. "Secret's safe with me. Thanks again."

Chase watched Watts watch him as he backed out the door. Watts didn't even blink. *Just like a lizard,* Chase thought as he pulled the door closed.

Chase was going out the front door of the safety building when he noticed Chief Braxton walking up the front steps, two at a time. Someone else was with her: a man in a dark suit, a white shirt and black tie, a leather briefcase. Shiny black shoes.

Well, well. Lookee here, Chase thought.

Chief Carol Braxton stopped, blinked twice. The man with the shiny shoes also stopped. Chase smiled at her, the smile of one familiar to another, ignoring the presence of Shiny Black Shoes. Then he turned a blank face to the man.

"Uh. . . Michael Chase," Chief Braxton said. "What brings you here?"

Chase smiled again, this time with a sort of perverse pleasure at her hesitancy. "Chief Braxton," he said, nodding at her, never taking his eyes off the man in the suit. "Aren't you going to introduce me to your FBI friend?"

"FBI?" Carol Braxton laughed easily. "Chase, allow me to introduce you to Morton Collins, mayor of Clovis, California. He's touring the east to look at mass transit alternatives. He's in town to see our Rapid Transit System."

The man nodded to Chase curtly, neither smiling nor offering his hand. He didn't seem to care one way or the other about the introduction. There was no way this Collins guy was a politician. Chase laughed, short and barking, as full of derision as he could make it. He was disappointed. Carol never did lie too well. It was a wonder she ever managed to become Chief of Police.

13
Thursday afternoon, September 30

Detective Watts didn't like it. He didn't like any of it. He hadn't expected to be involved in this kind of thing. He closed and locked his desk drawers, getting ready to leave for the day. It was one of the few things he enjoyed about this shift, the fact that he got off at three in the afternoon, as long as there was nothing more he could do that day. It was nice getting done when most people were still at work, walking the downtown streets a little. Like the old days. . .

He opened a desk drawer and exchanged his service revolver for his own private sidearm. He slipped it into his shoulder holster.

Too bad he didn't have time to wander around downtown. He could use a walk to clear his head. He *knew* this murder couldn't possibly have been committed by the same man that killed those other two girls, Malrick and Feral, or whatever their names were, but Chase could make this investigation especially tricky. The man couldn't be trusted to play along, to get along and go along. No loyalties, as far as Watts could see. Something about him made you think he'd poke the President of the United States in the eye, just to see what would happen.

Watts chuckled at his own wit. Sometimes he surprised himself. He pulled his office door closed behind him, made sure it was locked, started down the hall toward the lobby. He nodded at Elaine on his way out.

He hit the sidewalk thinking that there was some other problem about Chase, something that he hadn't yet remembered. There was something Watts had found likable about Chase, ever since—or despite the fact—they'd worked closely on the Clawson case. Something was familiar about him from the beginning.

Watts made a small clucking sound with his tongue, tsking himself for forgetting something. His mother used to do that, the same tsk-tsk. . . What made Chase likable? He was an arrogant, annoying SOB.

Watts turned toward Joyce's, the bar where he was supposed to meet Agent Collins. He wasn't looking forward to it. When he'd been introduced to Collins earlier, he'd thought the man was probably a real prick. But he was part of the same team. They were all Family; orders were orders.

That was it! Family! Chase reminded Watts of his uncle George, the one who had first approached a 19-year-old Watts, fresh out of high school, to join the Family. George wasn't really an uncle, but Watts had always called him that. He was around a lot for the year after Watts's mother had. . . died. That period had been hard on him: the teenage son of a suicide.

Watts remembered sliding onto that stool next to his uncle at the bar.

45

He'd ordered a rum and coke, the bartender bringing it, George insisting on paying for it.

There was a long silence between them.

"If it's our family's thing," young Watts said at last—he paused, frowned, trying to come up with the right question. "Why isn't Dad a part of it?"

"Who says he's not?"

Watts remembered shaking his head, disbelieving. "He woulda said something. Or Mom woulda."

His uncle watched him steadily. A long silence. Then, he laughed and said, "You think too hard, junior. You're gonna hurt yourself. You're mother did that, too. Look where it got her."

But Watts was insistent; he ignored the hurtful comment. He was sure he was onto something: "If this is so great, why didn't Mom— Why hasn't Dad ever said anything?"

Uncle George laughed again. "Your mom wouldn't have nothing to do with it. She didn't know spit." He glanced in the bartender's direction to make sure he wasn't looking. What Watts remembered most about what followed was Uncle's grip on his shoulder, the way he had gasped as his uncle's fingers dug into his flesh. He'd never felt a grip like that.

Uncle George was tugging him off the barstool.

"Let's go over here, kid. We can talk better that way."

George drew him over to a table in the corner. He sat Watts down in a chair and looked down at him. He patted Watts's cheeks with both hands.

"The first thing you have to learn, baby boy, is how to be subtle. How to be quiet." He patted Watts's cheeks again—hard—to make his point. "Don't talk about this in front of *anybody.*"

Then Uncle George had laughed again. Watts remembered the shiver of his spine when he heard the laugh, a huge laugh, full of mirth and disdain. Filled with an intelligence and superiority that scared the nineteen-year-old Watts.

It was the memory of that irreverent intelligence that reminded him of Chase. It frightened him.

The last thing he did before he stepped into the bar to meet Collins was touch the .45 automatic in his shoulder holster, just to make sure it was there.

14
Thursday afternoon, September 30

The quality of the light in West Virginia is very different in the early fall than in the late summer. One of the ways that autumn distinguishes itself from summer: the sunrays slant sharper, their illumination crisper. In that light, every form is bold; the eye sees the edges of objects first.

In wooded areas, the leaves stand apart from one another, each with a life of its own, light-green on their undersides, darker on top. Certain buildings on the West Virginia University campus are covered with ornate, hand-carved stone reliefs that leap out from their facades, ivy twining around the gothic letters and curly-cues. The hands of the high clock tower that presides over Woodburn Circle develop shadows.

Now that hitchhiking was coming back, with a vengeance, the students usually hitchhiked along the road across from Woodburn Circle, at the center of campus. They were out there seven days a week, practically 24 hours a day, with backpacks, satchels, briefcases. They were going to Towers, the freshman dorm, or up the hill into Sunnyside, or up the other hill, toward the stadium. They could see the hills from Woodburn Circle, the hills that were covered with trees—oaks, elms, locust, some pine—the hills that cast their shadows over Woodburn Circle.

A woman backpedaled, with her thumb out. The setting sun was bright on her face. The shadows of the hills hadn't even reached her knees. She smiled at the passing cars, flicked back her red hair occasionally, hoping for a ride. In many ways, she was like the young woman who had been there the Sunday before, the night of the full moon.

Only this time, a different car stopped.

15
Thursday night, September 30

Michael Chase was in a funk. *The mayor of Clovis! Not!* he thought. *That was lame, Carol, very lame.* He put his empty beer glass down on the bar a little harder than he meant to. A couple too many beers.

Carol should have known better than to lie to him, of all people. It had ticked him off. Out of proportion, probably. And alcohol had a way of blowing things up beyond where they should be.

He'd checked her story out. Called from the office. The mayor of Clovis was Linda Gonzalez. Which made sense. Clovis was a farm town, just outside of Fresno, and Mexicans had held an unfortunate monopoly on stoop-and-grunt farm labor in California for a hundred and fifty years. Carol must have known he would check, so why bother to lie? Plus, she knew that Chase had gone to school in Fresno, and would have to know that the people of Clovis weren't likely to elect someone named Collins to be their mayor. What was it about this thing? First Watts, then Carol; why the secrecy?

"I think that's about it for me, Cory. Thanks." He tucked a couple of dollars into the bartender's tip jar.

"Thank you, Chase. Good to see you again," Cory said, but he barely looked up from his closing duties, wiping down the back bar.

Chase groaned as he stood up, tendons cracking. It wasn't even his story. He'd managed to corner Dumont late that afternoon, back at the paper. It provided some amusement, but it really wasn't his business.

"You haven't even talked to Watts in the last few days?" he'd asked Dumont, whom he'd buttonholed in the hallway.

"What for? I called him several times that day. Watts said not to call him back for at least a week. Said they wouldn't have anything until then."

"You believed that?" Chase rolled his eyes. "They *always* say that." He sighed. "Where were you all afternoon? I figured you'd gone down there." Chase didn't *know* that Dumont had been out of the office, since he hadn't been there himself, but Dumont had used the 'big story' excuse to get out of the office before.

"I— Lisa had a recital that— Linda had to be down at the center, so I had to—"

"Oh, screw it, Eddie. Doesn't matter. But there should be a followup article, that's what I'm telling you. Tell me something, what was the victim's name? Do you have any idea?"

"Ummm—"

"Laana Anders."

"You know that for sure?"

"L-A-A-N-A A-N-D-E-R-S."

It didn't really matter what Chase said to Dumont. The only man Eddie answered to was Bill Waters. Still, Chase took a perverse pleasure in watching pretentious people squirm. And maybe, just maybe, he could get the reporter pointed in the same direction as the story.

Chase left the Omega, headed out the alley the restaurant was on, toward High Street. Once he was there, he stopped. He decided it was better not to drive, considering the condition he was in. It was only a twenty-minute walk, and it would clear his head.

16
Thursday night, September 30

Maria Redmann squirmed her cheek a little deeper against her husband's chest, her toes curling under the sheets. He wanted to talk, but she just wanted to smell the smell of him. It made her feel warm and secure.

"How'd your appointment go the other day?" Don Redmann asked.

"Oh, fine, honey," she murmured. His chest hairs were tickling her nose.

"What did you guys talk about?"

"The usual." Truth was, Maria couldn't actually remember at first what her and Alex had talked about beyond the opening pleasantries. Then suddenly, she remembered Alex had put her under, for the first time in God knows how long. After the session, Maria had rushed out, feeling much better, eager to get back to the shop. She wasn't really sure *what* they had talked about, but she'd felt much relieved. Unburdened. Oh well, she'd find out the specifics in a few days.

"Aren't you going to answer me? You didn't hear any of that."

"I'm sorry. I must have drifted off. What did you say?"

"Basically, I said I've been worried about you is all. I want to know what's been going on."

"I'm tired, honey. That's all. Things at the shop are taking a lot of my attention. I'm sorry." Maria lay her hand and forearm across her husband's chest and stroked it gently.

"Well, Mar, I have to say you worry me sometimes lately," Don Redmann said. "You've been acting—" But Maria didn't hear the rest. She was already asleep.

17
Thursday night, September 30

Chase turned right onto Madison Avenue, the street he lived on, glad that he'd walked home. He felt energized, awake again. Maybe he could even get some work done on that Morgan article. The thing was due way too soon.

He suddenly stopped short, seeing that the lights in his apartment were on. He crossed the street, stepped onto the sidewalk. He stopped again. He could feel it: There was someone inside his house. He walked up the steps to his porch carefully. He made sure to put his feet down only near the side of each step, worried that the porch steps would creak. At the top, he paused. Listened.

Music. Someone was definitely in there.

He tried the door, and it was unlocked. It opened easily.

Shango was sitting at his kitchen table, in the midst of pouring some bourbon into the same ceramic cup he drank out of Monday night. His eyes were on the chessboard, the pieces arrayed as if in the middle of a game. Chase felt his shoulders sag; he'd been holding his breath.

"Have a seat," Shango said, without looking up.

"What are you doing here?"

Shango grinned, but still didn't look at him. "Scare you?"

Chase stepped into the kitchen. "How'd you get in my house?" He was sure he'd left it locked.

"I didn't break anything. You really should find some quieter way to come up those steps, if you're all that worried about it." Shango tilted his head toward the kitchen door. "Stepping to the sides don't stop them from creaking, and the pace still sounds like you."

"Screw you," Chase said as he grabbed a cup. He sat down and pushed it toward Shango. "Gimme a drink."

Shango poured and Chase drained the drink in one gulp. "Long day," he gasped as he set the cup down.

Shango looked at the empty cup, then at Chase, then back at the cup. "How 'bout some more?" He held the open bottle tilted near the cup.

"Hit me," Chase said, tapping the edge of the cup with his right forefinger. He got a cigarette out while the whiskey tumbled in. He sipped it this time.

Shango waited, still holding the whiskey bottle, one eyebrow raised.

"What the heck are you doing here?" Chase said at last.

"No reason," was the answer. "I just had a feeling you'd need someone to talk to."

Chase eyed him skeptically. "You're not going to tell me now that you people have some kind of second sight."

Shango laughed. "No, I'm going to tell you that you went to the police station today. Sounds like you're really tore up about this murder."

Chase narrowed his eyes. "Well, you brought the booze, at least," he said at last.

"You know," Shango said, gesturing vaguely over his shoulder. "It only takes twenty minutes or so to walk to the Big Bird from here."

18
Thursday night, September 30

Alexandra put her head in her hands for a moment, her elbows resting on her desk. She was so tired, but she'd tried and there was no way she was going to get to sleep anytime soon. Finally, she'd gotten out of bed, kissed Jer on the cheek and whispered that she'd be in her study. He had just mumbled something incoherent.

She'd gone over it and over it, and still not reached a conclusion: *It's happening, again.* She didn't have a clue who the caller was, or what he had been getting at. The mystery had moved from a curiosity to an urgency the morning Jerry had pointed out the article in the *Herald-Dispatch*, two days after the phone call.

"You see this, Alex?"

It was on the front page of the metro section. She read the two-paragraph story slowly, with a growing sense of anxiety. When she finished, she kept staring at the page, not seeing anything.

"Yeah, I kinda wondered about that, too," Jer had said.

Now, sitting in the dark in her study, Alex felt the urgency. Her mother's grandfather clock tocked loudly in the corner. It would chime twelve soon.

She thought of that voice, the infinite distance that she hadn't heard the first three calls, but had been so much a part of the voice that night. *It's happening, again.* It implied that it had happened before. If the voice and the article were connected, it was the 'before' victim that the police had found. Was there another one out there? Another body?

Or was the caller referring to a process that had culminated in a killing, and was now beginning again. Was there another murder that might happen, maybe, probably, but some time in the future? Was it a process that could yet be stopped?

And what in heaven's name does it have to do with me! Alexandra was upset, angry, scared. She rubbed her hands over her face, pulling her head back. She should probably go back to bed, but she couldn't let it go that easily. Once she had ahold of a thought, nothing could shake her loose. *Not even me.*

It was pointless to call the police, since she had nothing for them to go on. Or was it? Maybe they could tap her phone. If he called again—he said he wouldn't, but he might—if they had a tap on, they could figure out where he was calling from. They could figure out who he was, why he was calling her.

She smiled, a burden eased. There was an action she could take. Might not lead to anything, but better than thinking in circles. *Besides,* she thought, rising. *It would be interesting to meet the man behind that voice.*

19
Thursday night, September 30

"I didn't know you drank like this," Chase said as Shango poured himself another shot. "I've consumed more alcohol the last couple times I saw you than in the last month." He and Shango were on their fourth round.

Chase had a sudden flash of the dream he'd had the other night, when he went to bed drunk—the long-armed silhouette of a man bouncing a crystal globe in his hand—and the last time he had that dream, a month before. He'd gone to bed drunk that night, too. The only two nights drunk, the same dream. He wondered if it would happen again tonight. He hoped not; the dream was disquieting.

"Anything to get high, Bwana." He drained the shot glass.

Chase shook his head; the man defied nature. He must be closing in on fifty, since he fought in the Gulf War 20 years earlier, at the end of his third tour with the Army. When they'd first met, ten years earlier, before he knew how long Shango had been in the Army, he'd figured Shango to be in his early thirties. If he'd been drinking and partying since he was a teenager, as he claimed, he should look like he was about 80. Once, when Chase asked him about it, Shango said, "You ever notice how Native Americans all look younger than they are, until one day they wake up and BOOM!, they're a hundred and ten."

"You're not an Indian."

"Almost all the Africans in America are at least a third Native American."

Like so much that Shango said, Chase didn't know whether to believe it or not, but it had seemed as good an explanation as any. He drained his cup, too, slammed it on the table.

"Where were we?"

"You sure you don't want to play chess?" Shango asked, pouring another round.

Chase shook his head. No way he wanted to get beat up on the chessboard twice in one week.

"Why do you think she lied to you?" Shango drained his cup again.

"Slow down, would you? I can't keep up." Chase drained his shot, made a sour face.

"Then just stay out of my way, lightweight." More whiskey chugalugged into both cups.

Chase left his on the table. Things were already a little fuzzy around the edges.

"A couple of things bug me about that," he said. "Why would she try such a lame fib? It couldn't get her anywhere. She must have known I would check it out."

"What's the FBI doing on this anyway? It's none of their business." This time, Shango was sipping.

"That's the other thing. It was a local murder. The victim's family lives just south of here. Fairmont. Not even out of state. Why the federal interest? What do they know they're not telling?"

When he didn't hear an answer, Chase looked over at Shango, watched a grin spread across his face. He could see that Shango wasn't even listening. "What's up?"

Shango was nodding, the cup to his lips. "Your Carol chick did you a favor."

"She's not a *chick*. She's the chief of police. What are you talking about?"

"Exactly. She's the chief of police and the old friend of the disgraced ace reporter. She's been told by the FBI this case is on the QT, but it don't sit well. Maybe she just don't like being told what to do by a fed. Then you happen along. How does she mess with the feebees without breaking her word?"

Now Chase was smiling. Broadly. Carol hadn't lied to him after all.

Shango said, "That's one smart chick." The admiration in his voice was plain. "How'd you let her get away, Chase?"

"Pour," Chase said, pointing at his empty cup.

20
Thursday night, September 30

Carol Braxton lay on her bed on top of the bedspread, propped up on some pillows, her knees bent, a yellow legal pad resting against her thighs, chewing on the pen in her hand. Papers were spread out around her. The case was only three days old and already there was a blizzard of paperwork. As case administrator, it was her job to cull through it and try to put it in some kind of order. Not easy in a case like this.

That afternoon, Watts had requested the case officer position, in addition to his field supervisor and detective sergeant responsibilities. When she said it might not be a good idea, he said, "You've got enough to do as it is, Chief. Coordinating this and laisoning with the feebees. Not to mention all the regular stuff. I've got to do most of the reports anyway. It'd be easy for me to keep all this together."

It made some sense, but she just didn't feel right about letting Watts oversee this case. There was tragedy here, something beyond the ordinary sickness and sorrow that surrounds a murder. Something that had to do with her. Somehow.

She'd decided that even if she had to work 18-hour days, she wanted to keep a tight rein on this operation. She didn't want any screwups. Not only were the feds watching like hawks, for reasons that weren't clear, but she had a feeling this was going to be a bad one. And the correspondences to the Clawson case had her on edge. If Chase had been right all along, the wrong man was in jail and the real killer had taken another victim. Even if Clawson *hadn't* killed Malarik and Ferrell, their murders were still a single incident. But the murder of Anders would make it appear to be the work of a serial killer. Or a copycat. Either way, there might be more to come.

She chewed on her pen and stared at the calendar on the wall across from her bed. The photo for September was a line of Mennonite horse buggies on a dirt road in rural Virginia. A white, two-story farm house sat in the upper right on the scene, beyond the road. The images that Carol focused on were the backs of the black buggies—five of them, the smallest receding in the distance—and the modern, international-orange caution-triangles affixed to each one. *Anachronisms. . .*

She wished that she'd been able to find enough uninterrupted time to organize this at the office, but it just hadn't been possible. Too much going on. The investigation already had about a dozen people, and all of them required her attention for one reason or another. So she had to do it after work, at home, exactly where she didn't want to be thinking about a murdered young woman.

In the past, though, Carol had found that if she plunged into the paperwork, and as long as she stayed away from the crime-scene photos, it was possible to keep reality at bay. The detailed forms broke down the event's immediacy into a series of questions—*Was there writing or drawing at the crime scene?*, *Abnormalities of the teeth (check all that apply)*, *Was the body bound?*—if she lost herself among the trees, she usually didn't see the forest.

The photograph of the murdered Anders girl lying in the woods abruptly came to mind. Without a head. She'd have to be a little more careful with her analogies.

It was still too early for the creation of a full file index, but she had begun notes toward one on the yellow pad—body recovery site, evidence log, victim identification, known associates, etc.—putting a check beside each file that had already been started.

After organizing her list, she read over it, checking off those she had forgotten on the first pass. *A decent start,* she thought as she scanned down the list. She had reports from the field supervisor, the evidence officer, the assisting patrolmen. All the foundation blocks were in place. They had lucked out on the quick ID of the victim and the easy traceability of her associates.

They'd been less lucky with the evidence log, the vehicle and the related crime reports: Nothing had turned up so far except some bone fragments and the .45 caliber bullet. One bullet wasn't much to go on, although it would be helpful in prosecution. Carol reminded herself it had only been three days since the body was discovered.

She froze, her jaw muscles clenching her teeth on the end of the pen. Why hadn't the body been discovered earlier? It had been out there, fairly accessible, for nearly a month. There was something to follow up on. Some information that was missing, some awareness that was not falling into place. Either the body had not been there the whole time, or something had kept people away from that clearing. The evidence of scavenging seemed to suggest the latter, but that begged the question: What had kept people away? She filed it away for later.

She barely glanced at the names of the various files that would have to be filled in later, the ones listed under *Suspect Information*. The lack of information only depressed her. Instead, she set the legal pad aside and dug into the 25-page questionnaire for her own records, cc/the FBI. Better to get it started now, even if there was a lot she couldn't fill out yet.

"1. Date form completed:"

That one was easy enough. She wrote today's date in pencil.

"2. Reporting Agencies' State ID# (leave blank):"

Okay, she thought. *No problem.*

The next sixteen questions were like the first two: addresses, names, time parameters, and so forth. At the top of the second page, the Incident Classification section started. The first question asked for a generalized assessment of the crime. There were thirty choices, ranging from #1, *Domestic violence*, to #30, *Unable to determine*.

Some of the categories were out of the question: *Arson* and *Sniper*, for instance. There were a lot of them she couldn't rule out, like *Rape* or *Other, sex-related* or *Revenge, Robbery, Drug related, Financial gain*, but that kind of evidence would take time. The category that caught her eye was #21: *Cult (ritualistic)*. Wasn't red wax found at the scene?

She dug through the papers until she found Detective Watts's report, glanced through it. Nothing. Where had she seen that? She rifled through the papers again, coming up with the report of Dale Gatsky, one of the assisting patrolmen. There it was: "Several beads of red wax were found in each of the five small circular cleared areas that surrounded the body, as indicated on attached chart #2."

Sure enough.

Why didn't Watts mention the wax?

21
Very early Friday morning, October 1

By nearly one in the morning, Chase and Shango had killed more than half the whiskey. Chase had to make an effort to focus across the table. Shango was on a roll, waving his cup and gesturing with his free hand as he spoke.

"That was not a personal killing. I don't think he even knew her. You go to kill somebody you know, if there's a good reason for it, it's just"—he held his cup as if it were the barrel of a pistol, sighted down it—"BOOM!! Dead meat."

Chase held up his hand. "Whoa. Hold on."

Shango leaned forward over the table, his jaw thrust forward. "I *know* what I'm talking about."

"I'm sure you do, big guy, but I don't. Slow down."

Shango settled back in his chair, clenched his jaws. Relaxed them. "Okay, it's like this. Unless this chick had some bad enemies—I mean *really bad*, people who hated her with every breath they took—then whoever killed her didn't know her. Not very well, anyway."

"How do you get that?"

Shango turned his head, a pantomime of looking around the room to see where Chase's brain had gone. "Think about it," he said. "Say you're really angry with someone. They've stolen your woman, or. . . ripped off your computer." Chase was amused by Shango's search for an appropriate analogy.

"So you decide to kill them. What do you do? You just wait somewhere, maybe in the back of their car or something, and when they come out in the morning, you sit up and BOOM!! in the back of the head. Or you stab them in the back of the neck." He tilted his head forward. "Right here, where the spine connects to the skull." He snapped his fingers. "Instant. Or maybe you wrap piano wire around—"

"Okay, okay."

"But you don't tie them up and slice and dice 'em and *then* shoot them. Doesn't make any sense."

He was right, it didn't. Unless there was a lot of anger involved. Chase gestured for Shango to continue.

"Okay. So it had to be somebody who *really hated* this woman. He wanted to hurt her *bad.*"

"But not necessarily her personally."

"No. I mean, yes. Right. She was his enemy in some way. He thought she was anyway."

"You keep saying *he.*"

"Women don't do this kind of thing."

Chase wanted to object, but he really couldn't. Women killed, and there had even been a few women serial killers, but not many. And for the most part, they didn't torture like that, they just hit them in the head with a hammer or whatever. Usually poison. Even the FBI started by assuming a killer was probably male. Generally, a white male in his late twenties to mid-thirties.

Chase narrowed his eyes, looked inward, trying hard to remember something. If the FBI—

"Enemy! is the key here." Shango's shouted *Enemy!* drove whatever connection Chase was about to make away from his mind. Maybe later. . .

"He saw her as his enemy. I've seen some of what was left after the towelheads went over some of our people. They hated us. Our boys did it, too." He paused, looked at Chase. "Although, mostly, it was the white guys that were into that."

Chase knew Shango was baiting him. He let it pass. "So you're saying that the killer saw her as some kind of enemy."

"Probably because she was a female." He shrugged. "A lot of guys are like that. They see women as their enemy. They fear, they hate, they might even kill. I could see it."

Chase didn't like it. It was probably true, but it was too simple. "What about the self-inflicted killshot?"

Shango shrugged again. "He gives her a choice. More cutting, or you can end it right now. Here's the gun."

"And the head—"

"A trophy."

It did make sense. Maybe the simplicity was what it had going for it. "So where does that leave us?"

"Nowhere, Bwana. At least not till it happens again."

Chase sat very still. That was probably the truest thing that Shango had said all night. It *was* going to happen again. He knew it in his bones. And since Laana Anders's murder had taken place a month ago, maybe it already had.

22
Early Friday morning, October 1

The Stravinsky plays loudly, so loud that it is probably annoying the down-stairs neighbors. Devon knows that the composer's discordant tones make people uneasy; that is what they were written to do. Move people. Disturb them, to whatever end: the joy that rends and reshapes, the sorrow that rips and scares. He loves Stravinsky for that ability. But it is late, and the neighbors might complain. He uses the remote to turn the CD down, but only after the movement has ended.

He slaps the back of his hand against the newspaper he holds. The weight around his wrist *thunks* against the edge of the table, tearing the paper slightly. It is a few days old, but he has kept it. He needs to keep the event in mind. He needs to constantly think about it and its causes.

He re-reads:

> . . . in a forest clearing off Interstate 79, near Morgantown, West Vir-
> ginia . . . found face down, her hands bound, although a police
> spokesman said it was not clear whether or not this was caused by
> the action of forest animals. . . .

He stands abruptly and begins pacing, hands clasped behind his back, his biceps flexing the weights that hang around his wrists. His dark hair is tousled, wild. He is careful not to let his feet clump too loudly against the floorboards, like they usually do when he wears the ankle-weights. That both-ers the people downstairs as much as loud Stravinsky. He is not particularly concerned with the serenity of his neighbors, but he does not want to draw the attention of the authorities. Not yet anyway.

With the volume of the CD lower, he can hear the crackle and hiss of his police scanner. It had also been on the night they discovered the body. Devon shakes his head as he paces, grimacing. He had expected them to find the body much sooner than they did, even though he had often found that the police did not live up to his expectations.

The few efficacious police officers that Devon has known seemed to have been good *in spite* of their training. Police training must hobble their minds in some way. He should look into that more thoroughly, try to pinpoint the prob-lem. He chuckles at the thought of Devon Lancaster providing the police with information that could improve their job readiness.

He paces faster. When he walks, he is most aware of the curved spine and the too-short legs that have always handicapped him, helped make him what he is today. He holds his hands behind his back to keep at bay the images of his knuckles scraping the ground. Even though they do not. It is a self-image problem that he has never completely been able to purge, not even in his time among the Afghanis. He often sees the reactions in the eyes of others when they meet him for the first time.

The scanner hisses and pops.

The police cannot be as blind as they seem. He would like to think that they have something more to go on than what the newsbrief seems to imply. They must have asked the reporter to withhold pertinent information. Although he would like it not to be so, he decides that the police are, indeed, fools.

Were they being as foolish as they—and the prosecutor, and the jury—proved to be on the Clawson case? He knows that if things had gone just a little differently, he might have been the one incarcerated. Briefly, he wonders how The Clod is doing in prison. He knows what happens to convicted rapists, child molesters. He knows The Clod cannot stand up straight under such treatment. *Someone should stab the poor fellow. Really, it would be better that way.*

He should check on who is handling the investigation. Probably Watts. He hopes he will not have to help, but he suspects he will have to give a few deliberate pointers before this is over.

Back on the table, the police scanner blinks, spits static. "Unit 5 to 523 Arlington Avenue. Signal 12. Other units converging."

Devon snorts derisively. *These guys really are small town cops. Domestic dispute, and they dispatch multiple units. Some slope smacking his wife around. Maybe she is screaming, throwing things at him. Maybe both of them are screaming. The neighbors call in. Pathetic. Pathetic lives and puny, pathetic outbursts.*

The scanner crackles again: "Unit 5 on the scene."

And what will you do? he thinks. *You guys do not have a clue. You will arrest the guy, the loser. Maybe. Maybe not. You will impugn the wife, imply that she is weak, or dirty, or that she deserves it. Or all three. The whole thing will start again.*

He shakes his head, almost feeling pity for the whole situation. Not so much for the wife, or even her useless and destructive husband, but more for the police. It is out of his hands. When he smiles, large canine teeth show.

He figures that it is safe enough to turn the scanner off for a while. Since it took them a month to find the first body, it is unlikely they will find the new one in the next hour or so. Besides, it is about time to get started.

In the center of the room, he grasps the edge of the throw-rug and easily pulls it and the hand-carved oak endtable that sits on it over next to the wall. He barely glances at the circle that the rug had covered, the circle he painted, with the symbols at the five points of the star.

He chants the opening ceremonial in his head as he continues to ready himself. He walks over to the closet—a *chifforobe*, more properly—the free-standing one that has traveled all over the world with him. He takes off the wrist-weights, then the ones on the ankles, lays them side-by-side on the hardwood floor. Then he takes off his clothes. He must enter the circle naked. But he must approach it clothed; he selects one of the sanctified robes from the chifforobe. He chooses the red one.

He takes his long, slender, double-bladed ceremonial dagger—sheathed—from its holder in the chifforobe. He is fond of that knife, having made it himself sixteen years ago. All those layers of iron, all that pounding. . .

He turns toward the circle, making sure to keep the sheathed blade pointing down and away from him.

Even before he enters the circle, he thinks he hears screams. He pauses, more alert. It must be his imagination. The deaths are powerful, but they are not powerful enough to carry so far, not without ceremonial amplification. He should not hear the screams until the cycle is complete.

He places the dagger on the floor, outside the circle, at the northern tip of the star. Stands and straightens and shrugs off the robe, letting it float noiselessly to the floor.

He picks up the knife, slips its straight blade out of the sheath, steps into the circle.

Holding the knife in both hands, he raises it high above his head, arms straight, the tip of the blade pointing to the ceiling and slightly forward, says the first word of the incantation: "Ator!"

He draws the knife down diagonally, down and to his right until it points toward the floor and away from him. He visualizes the bright white line of light that emerges from the tip of the blade as it moves through the air, connecting the two points: "Malkuth!"

He draws it up again, visualizing the white line of light, across his body, until his arms are extended and level with his left shoulder, stopping at the third point of the star: "Ve-Gevurah!"

He swings the blade straight across, parallel to the floor, pointed away from him . . .

23
Monday afternoon, October 4

Chief Carol Braxton sighed and tossed the file onto her desk, thinking that it was still too thin. The summaries of the investigation's various files still only amounted to some 25 pages. Not enough was happening.

She leaned forward in her chair and rested her chin on her thumbs. It had been nine days since Laana Anders's body was found. Nine days and Watts still didn't have anything. That wasn't like him. Usually he generated mountains of paperwork, whether he had something new or not. Privately, she'd always believed that he did that to give the impression he was working hard, slogging his way up the stream of investigation. It wasn't deceitful; he was trying to give the impression of hard work to himself as much as anyone else. It was an expression of his work ethic, and she'd watched him do it many times, on many cases, using dogged pursuit of details as a substitute for imagination and intelligence.

On the simple cases—which was most of them—it paid off eventually: if you turn over enough stones, you're bound to find ants under one of them. But she doubted that this would prove to be a simple case. She spun slowly in her chair until she could look out the window at the parking lot of the Public Safety building.

It was too dark outside for 10 AM: The wind was picking up, the leaves on the trees that sat around the parking lot were beginning to whip. A storm was brewing.

Detective Watts had added little of any consequence to the files since the first few days. He'd interviewed Laana's parents—the father was a manager at the Sears store at the mall, the family fairly well off. He'd spoken with Laana's brother and sister, her neighbors. He had conversations with several of her instructors, her friends at the university, both female and male, and so on, and so on: all the usual people. The last person to see her—the last one they could locate anyway—said she was hitching over near Woodburn Circle at about 5:30 on the night before she was reported missing.

Accounts of the victim were remarkably consistent. Laana's parents and siblings described essentially the same person as her college friends and professors had. A junior in college, majoring in marketing. Outgoing, friendly, well liked: No one seemed to think badly of her. Doing well in classes, attractive. Nobody had any idea who might have wanted to do this to her.

Even the small discrepancies that emerged were hardly surprising. Her girlfriends knew that Laana liked to party on the weekends, while the parents hadn't mentioned that. One of the ex-boyfriends mentioned that Laana liked to smoke pot occasionally, but that only happened at big parties. If anything, that was *additional* rather than *inconsistent* with the Laana Anders her parents described. Detective Watts judged her involvement with drugs to be no more extensive than some other college students, and less than many. No lead there.

Laana sounded like the sort of person that Carol would have disdained back in college—well-to-do, Laana hung out with the fraternity/sorority set. Carol would have dismissed her as frivolous. "In college for an MRS" was the phrase. Age had softened Carol's judgments—Laana sounded like a nice young woman.

The consistency of the accounts was good news for the police, in a way, since this case didn't need any unnecessary complications. Unfortunately, it also left them with little to go on. Nothing, in fact. Not a darn thing.

Abruptly, large raindrops started to strike the office window. Carol stood up, began to pace about her office. While Watts had come up with nothing so far, he had done solid police work. She couldn't really fault him for it. Maybe there *was* nothing to go on. It was very possible. Still, the thin file nagged at her.

Granted, their own M.E.'s report was lame at best, but where was the FBI's report? Their man—Theron Davies—came a couple days after the body turned up. He probed, photographed, took samples, did a few simple tests. Most of the major tests, though, he had to send back to Washington to be done. Now it was nearly a week, and she still didn't have that report on her desk.

At the time, Carol had again cursed the poor town/gown relations; she knew they had the necessary equipment out at the med school, if only they would let the police rent it. She suggested to Collins that they try, but he'd thought that foolish: "Chief Braxton, I must impress on you the need for absolute secrecy in this case," he'd said.

That really stuck in her craw. Why were the feebees so concerned with secrecy in this case? She'd done some speculating, but had come up with nothing concrete. Collins avoided explanations, and she was left in the dark. "I'll keep out of your hair," he'd said. "But you understand that when we come in, we're in charge."

Carol knew there was no such hard-and-fast rule as that, and she'd never known the FBI to try to take over a case like that. She hadn't said anything to him—let the man believe what he wanted to—but she'd be darned before she'd relinquish control of this one. No matter why the FBI was in town. Collins had to answer to his people, and Carol had to answer to hers.

The FBI's ME did demonstrate exactly how inadequate their own medical examiner was. Granted, John was new to the job, but he'd postulated that the wounds were made "either with a single blade drawn across the skin in several, closely spaced cutting motions, or, more likely, with a single instrument that was fitted with multiple blades, evenly spaced."

"Nonsense," Dr. Davies had said as he examined them. "These wounds were created with a kris."

"Excuse me?" Carol had heard the word before, but wasn't sure where, or what kind of blade it was.

"A kris," he said slowly and a little too loud, as if he were speaking to a slightly deaf person with a mental handicap. "A dagger or short sword with a wavy, double-edged blade," he said, speaking as if from a dictionary. "It's from Malaysia. Most often used in ceremonial killings in this country. If you draw it at an angle"—he demonstrated by pulling his pen just so above the corpse of Laana Anders—"you get this kind of parallel cutting. We'll take particle samples to be sure."

"What about a decapitation? Can a kris do that?

"Something heavier. An axe or machete. Maybe a butcher's cleaver." Dr. Davies wasn't looking at her as he said it. He was bent over the body, caressing the edges of the wounds with a thin, pointed, wooden instrument. Carol couldn't help the thought—it *did* look like he was caressing the putrefied flesh.

Carol paced, thought, paced some more. She went to the window and stared out. Fierce rain lashed it, the splatter of hard raindrops. Where was Dr. Davies's report? She couldn't shake the feeling that Watts was up to something.

It smells funny, she thought, remembering that Chase had been very fond of that phrase. "A key reporter's instinct," he called it. She first heard him use it during the Clawson case. Well, it was also a key cop's instinct, and Carol felt its insistence now. The case smelled funny. The Anders murder was *like* the murders of Malarik and Ferrell, but different. One instead of two. And neither Malarik nor Ferrell had been bound at any time. Not quite the same. Could this have been done by another person? Or by the same killer, a man who had learned from previous mistakes?

She turned back to her desk. She looked at the thin file on Laana Anders that lay there on the desktop calendar. She looked at the other item, the one that caused her even more worry. She looked at the photo of the pretty WVU student whose disappearance had been reported six days before.

24
Monday afternoon, October 4

Chase looked up from his computer to see his editor—Dave "Wanker" Waters—cutting across the newsroom, headed straight for him. *Uh-oh.* His eyes cast about the big newsroom, looking for a way out. He wanted to hide under his desk or bolt for the door, but it was no use: Deer in the headlights. He hit *save* and waited. That was the problem in these big open rooms with no partitions: Nowhere to hide.

A couple of years ago, Waters had read some ancient copy of *Organizational Management* and decided that the partitions in the newsroom had to go. After he told the senior staffers about his decision, Chase looked up the article in the library: "Partitions encourage an insular, self-protective attitude among employees. Such an attitude is incompatible with a smoothly functioning team that puts the best interests of the organization before those of its individual members." The article was published in 1989.

On the same trip to the library, Chase had looked up another article about partitions in the July 2001 issue of *Organizational Management:* "Properly placed partitions have been shown to increase productivity and employee satisfaction." The current theory was that workers needed a sense of having their own private or at least semi-private space, in order to do their best work. Providing an unwalled *public space* in addition to the *privacy* of partitioned cubicles was the way to go.

Chase had been amazed that these people got paid for such research, but that was the way of it. He'd brought his objections to Waters's attention, but was rebuffed. *So it goes!* he'd thought. The 21st century *Dispatch* lurched toward the 20th century.

"Chase! Where are you on the Morgan story?" Waters asked before he'd even reached Chase's desk. Another problem: The lack of partitions allowed management to embarrass the grunts.

"Can we talk about this in your office?"

"No, we can't." At 6'5", Waters towered over Chase's desk. He tapped the surface of it for emphasis. "Is it going to be in *this* Sunday's edition? Or have you screwed up again."

Chase had the urge to say he story itself was messed up, but he knew that wasn't true. He was the one screwing up. The story was one that readers—especially townies—would want to see. Waters had already given him an extra week, something Chase had rarely requested.

He'd managed to get every other assignment done in the past ten days, everything from a report on the new Japanese restaurant out on Route 7 to the big fraternity party that was scheduled for the weekend. But he was not able to come up with an angle for the Morgan story. He still had some kind of block.

"Bill," Chase said, "is there any kind of way we could extend this for one more week? I've got a lot going, but it's just not working. It sounds forced."

Waters assumed the appearance of thinking. Chase had been around him enough to know that it was just a game. He already had a backup in mind; he just wanted to be sure of where he was at.

"Okay, Chase. I think we can do that. But, absolutely, positively, *without fail,* this has to be in next Sunday's edition."

"That's Sunday the, uh. . ." Chase referred to his calendar. "The 17th."

Waters hesitated. *Probably wondering if he's being tricked,* Chase thought. "Yeah, that's right," Waters said finally.

"No problem, chief," Chase said.

As Waters walked away, Chase thought about how much he missed the crime beat, about being stuck writing boring feature articles on topics he didn't care about. For the first time, he felt like he wasn't in temporary exile, but in a hellish, permanent limbo, and these words occurred to him: *I hate my job.*

25
Monday afternoon, October 4

Alexandra eyed her client warily. The man in the chair across her desk was picking at his fingers, more and more absorbed by the state of his cuticles. She'd seen him do it before. For him, this was a bad sign.

"Let's ease it forward a few years," she said in a mirror-smooth voice. "Now you are seven. You're at your birthday party, Jimmy. What do you see?"

Jimmy didn't say anything. He continued to pick at his fingers, his head turned down. Abruptly his head shot up, stiff neck, alert. His eyes darted around the room wildly, unseeing. They stopped, fixed to his left.

"She's here," he said. The voice was high, childlike.

"Who's here, Jimmy?"

"Momma." He brought his left hand up to his mouth, clamped his teeth over his thumb.

"Who else is in the room?" Alexandra was desperate to redirect his attention.

"No one," he said. Almost a whisper. "Please, Momma," he said, half-whimper, half-plea.

"Okay," Alexandra said. "We don't have to go into that one right now. Why don't we—"

"Where are my friends, Momma?" James—Jimmy—was abject. He started biting his fingers. Not his cuticles, he bit the tips of his fingers—*hard*.

She'd touched on something big. She'd taken her client back to his seventh birthday party because numerous allusions to it had crept into his out-of-hypnosis therapy. He didn't remember the party consciously, but clearly he was repressing something that had happened at the party. But she hadn't counted on the strength of the experience. Taking him back there had been a mistake.

"Jimmy! Stop now!"

He didn't seem to hear her. His teeth sunk into his thumb; they drew blood.

"Momma! I really didn't mean—"

Alexandra was out of her chair, walking quickly around her desk.

"—It wasn't my—"

Before Alexandra could get to him, James was slapping himself in the face with his left hand; at the same time, he was trying to cover his head with his right arm. The blows smacked loudly in the office, his screaming even louder:

"No, Momma, please! I didn't—"

He continued to swat at his own head with one hand while trying to ward off the blows with the other. Alexandra grabbed at the swatting hand, which ripped out of her grip, smacked his head a couple more times.

She was saying, "James. . . Listen to my voice. . . . James. . . Now we come to the end of this. . . ." trying to keep her tone as calm and quiet as she could, trying to bring him out of this memory while she wrestled for control of his attacking arm.

But he was much stronger than her. His arm pulled again and again out of her grip. His fingernails raked at his cheeks. She screamed for her assistant, who she knew was just on the other side of the door.

"Donna! Demerol, 25 ccs! *Now!*" she screamed.

Alexandra struggled with her patient to keep him from hurting himself further. He was too strong. She was fighting a losing battle. Scant seconds later, just in time, Donna charged in with a loaded hypo. She jammed it into his upper arm.

A moment and he slowed, his left arm still tugging toward his head but held at the wrist by Alexandra's grip. There would be no more hitting.

Alexandra relaxed as her patient slumped down into the chair. She felt her shoulders sag, the emergency situation over. *This is getting to be too much,* she thought. *That's twice in two weeks. It's not supposed to be like this.*

"Let's get him into the other room," Alexandra said to Donna. She gripped him under the arms, let Donna take the feet. Together, they managed to struggle his prostrate body into the side room, where he could sleep it off.

"Thanks, Donna," she said as they left the room. James was sprawled on the cot; everything would be okay.

"That's what I'm here for," Donna shrugged, nonchalant as always. Alexandra very much appreciated her unflappable quality. Especially at times like these.

Back in her office, Alexandra sank into her desk-chair. Donna had been equally unflappable last week when Alexandra had problems with Maria Redmann. Alexandra rubbed her face with both hands, remembering.

Maria had been talking about her grandfather's abusive behavior and had finally gotten around to what Alexandra suspected was the most traumatic moment:

"It was fun," Maria said. "Playing like I was blind."

Her voice went flat and seemed to come from a distance.

"Let's go into how you felt at the time," she said. "Go into what you talked about before. You said something about a bowl?"

Maria twisted in her seat. She writhed as if she were being burned, but couldn't get up. "No," she said weakly. "Don't make me."

Alexandra pressed on: "I want you to tell me." She took Maria into deeper hypnosis. No deeper than they'd explored before, but deeper than she'd expected of this session. Maria struggled in the chair. Her forearm muscles bunched and pulled, but her arms didn't move, as if her wrists were pinned to the arms of the chair. Maria's cheeks were wet with tears.

"We were outside. I couldn't see where because of the blindfold. All I could think of was wanting my brother. Where was my brother?

"Grans made me smell the bowl first," Maria said. Her voice was as flat as Alexandra had ever heard it. Alexandra waited. She watched the clock.

Two whole, very long minutes.

"He made me smell the bowl," Maria said at last. "It was like nails that had. . . that had been left in the rain for a long time. That was all I could think of."

Alexandra remembered her stomach turning then; still, she had waited.

"He gently pushed my head forward until I felt the bowl's edge against my lips."

For a long time, Maria didn't say anything. Alexandra prodded: "Then?"

"He took off my blindfold. The rusty smell made me look down."

Alexandra noted that the muscles in Maria's forearms were writhing and bunching again. Even more like her wrists were pinned to the arms of the chair and couldn't pull loose, no matter how hard she tried. Her cheeks were more wet.

"It was a red liquid. Thick." Maria bit her lower lip. "It made me hungry."

Alexandra sat up straight.

"He. . ." Maria sobbed, regained her composure. "He made me drink it."

That was when Maria began striking herself, much as James had done today. The same frantic beating and sobbing, the same one-sided protection.

26
Monday afternoon, October 4

Detective Watts slid the drawer shut, heard it click into its lock. Good enough. He stood up, hefting the folder in his right hand. He could take off for the day.

This should be enough to satisfy her, he thought. *It's as good as the original.*

It was amazing what computerized publishing was able to do these days: Collins had created this document on his laptop, and no one would ever be able to tell the difference. Watts was pleased.

However, he was less pleased with the weather. Still raining, but it looked to have slackened up a little. With any luck, it would be all finished before he had to leave for the day. Watts hated rain, and it seemed to him that the only time it wasn't raining in Morgantown, it was snowing.

He grimaced suddenly, the juices in his stomach flaring to an intolerable level. He gasped, his left hand gripping the edge of his desk. *Darned ulcers!* His forehead sweaty, Watts was pretty certain now that his ulcers had started bleeding again.

This darn case. Being forced to do things he didn't want to do was driving his stomach crazy. Not that he cared all that much about figuring out who killed the Anders girl. He had a pretty good idea at this point—not that he liked that thought either. His uneasiness was more about his lying to Chief Braxton. Basically, Detective Watts was caught between loyalties, something that had never happened to him.

The day before, he'd even done something he hadn't done in two years: He'd had a few drinks after work, down at Joyce's. He and Collins met there, and he ordered a shot of Cuervo without thinking. Over the next hour he had two more. He regretted it today—exactly the wrong thing to do for ulcers. His doctor claimed his drinking was largely responsible for the ulcers in the first place.

He set the folder down and fumbled in his jacket pocket, grasping for the pills the Family had given him. He mastered the child-proof cap and dry-swallowed a couple. Near-instant relief. The rumbling went down to a quiet murmur. He gripped the side of his desk, tried to steady himself.

There was a knock at his door. Watts straightened. "Come in," he said. It was Chief Braxton, and she wasn't smiling. He tried to head her off: "Morning, Chief. I've got the report from the Feebee medical examiner for you." He held the folder out to her.

"Good," she said, barely glancing at it. "Have a seat Detective Watts. We need to hash out a few things."

Watts set the folder on the desk, sat down in his chair. Chief Braxton appeared to be in a grim mood this morning. This wasn't going to be fun. Watts was glad he'd just taken one of his pills. "What about, Chief?"

"This Anders thing. A couple points bugging me. Toss them around with me, would you?"

Watts was relieved; maybe it wasn't going to be too bad, after all. When Chief Braxton had a minor criticism, she always delivered it as part of a "talk," just her and the officer, "tossing things around." It was something she'd picked up at one of those police management conferences she was always at. When she was really going to ream someone out, she didn't let that person talk, she made them listen. In those cases, she usually didn't scream. Not much, anyway.

He managed a smile. "There's a lot about it that's bugging me, too, Chief." He thought he caught a ghost of a grin pass across her face. "Nothing adds up."

"Talk to me, Detective. Tell me about your reports. What makes you so sure that this isn't connected to the Clawson case?"

"Clawson's in jail in Virginia, and he faces a 20-year sentence in Pennsylvania for three rapes, and two life sentences down here if he ever gets out."

Chief Braxton waved her hand dismissively. "You know what I mean. Why don't you think this is a copycat?"

"Lots of things." Watts rested his right elbow on his desk and held up a meaty fist. He raised a finger each time he stated a reason. "One: Clawson killed two girls at once. This guy just killed Anders—"

"So far."

"Okay, two: The Clawson coeds had both been raped, repeated—"

"The Anders girl was out there too long to know."

"True, but nicks in the upper thigh bones indicated stabbing in the vaginal area. Of course. . ." Watts cleared his throat. "There wasn't enough left to know exactly how. . . uh. . . *substantial* the trauma was."

Chief Braxton was nodding. "Point taken," she said. "Why didn't you mention the wax in your report?"

Play dumb. "I didn't?" He raised his eyebrows as if surprised. "I thought I put it in there. I guess, uh. . . maybe because it was late and I was tired, or. . ." He grimaced. Actually, he wasn't sure why he'd omitted mention of the wax, but Collins had also thought that it was deliberate. He'd already pointed out that Watts was stupid not to think of the other officers on the scene and what they had reported.

Watts shrugged. "I guess I'm not sure why."

"You usually don't make mistakes like that, Detective Watts. No matter how tired you are. It's not like you. Don't let it happen again."

It bothered him, too. Careless mistakes would be the surest way to get caught. "Yes, sir."

Still felt funny to him, calling a 'ma'am' a 'sir'.

Chief Braxton half-rose from the chair. "There may be a connection between this and the Clawson case. We know there are several similarities. Why don't you try going at it from that angle, Detective?"

Watts nodded silently. This would be the woodshed moment, if there was one.

Chief Braxton stood, picked up the folder with the autopsy report. She looked down at the seated Watts. "You're not thinking on this one, Darnell. If there's something outside of work. . ."

Watts shook his head. "No. Everything's fine. I'll be—" The phone buzzed. "I'll be more. . ." He let the sentence trail off, not sure of what he would be more of, and picked up the phone. Carol opened the door to leave.

"Watts," he said into it.

"Bunner wants to speak with you." It was Melanie in dispatch. "They've found another body."

Already? "Put him through." He held up his free hand to Chief Braxton, telling her to wait.

Wooshing sounds, cutting in and out, then, "Detective?" Bunner on a cell it sounded like, outdoors. The wooshing was cars passing.

"Yeah. Go ahead, Bunner."

"I'm up by Austin's Grocery?"

Watts kept calm. "No, Bunner. I mean, where is the *body?*"

Out of the corner of his eye, Watts saw the Chief look up from the folder sharply.

"Oh, that. Well, it's down near an abandoned house just off of Protzman. Kyle's there with it now. A kid found it when he was out in the woods, playing in the crick."

"Big old grey house, back in the woods? Kinda falling in on itself?"

"Yeah, you know it?"

"I'll be there in ten minutes."

"Sure thing, Detective."

"And Bunner. . . maintain radio silence on this."

Watts didn't hear what Bunner said in response; he'd already hung up.

"I'm going with you," the Chief said.

"Suit yourself."

He glanced out the window; the storm was picking up.

27
Monday afternoon, October 4

The rain came down in sheets, obscuring the late afternoon light, as if the day had suddenly become dusk. The rain was loud and relentless, forcing down the branches of the trees. It whipped into the empty windows of the ancient grey house that seemed to sag under the weight of the pounding water.

The man and the woman moved like shadows through the rain. They pushed through the heavy blanket of water, practically swimming the thirty yards toward where the other two officers stood, next to an adult and a small boy of seven or eight. As the man and woman drew close, twenty feet away, the man yelled, gesturing back the way he and the woman had come:

"Call for backup, Bunner! Get enough people out here to secure the perimeter!"

"But you said—!"

"Say that you have a domestic dispute and you need a couple of units! Do it!"

None of the people had adequate raingear, the fury had come up so quickly. It slapped into their clothes and bit their exposed skin. The woman walked with her head up, her forearm shielding her eyes; the man walked with hunched shoulders, his arms drawn close to his torso. Bunner hustled past them, back toward his car.

This body was much fresher than the other one. Her nakedness showed weather damage, but no canine scavenging. The heavy rain kept the smell to a minimum.

Her head was missing.

"Number two," the man shouted over the rain as he looked down.

Chief Braxton turned away.

28
Monday afternoon, October 4

Chase was walking down High Street, hands in pockets, shoulders stooped against the cold drizzle, eyes down and vaguely ahead. He'd walked all the way from the newspaper office, 45 minutes in this weather. He couldn't stop himself. Within a half hour of his encounter with Waters, he'd shut off his computer and left the building without a word to anyone.

In the two years since his demotion, he'd walked away from work twice. Never in the middle of a crisis or deadline—dissatisfaction always grew into moments of relative calm. Never a scene—he hadn't even been missed—and he expected it would be that way today. No one would notice that he'd walked away, left his car in the lot, walked away. . . And walked and walked. It worked for him, a kind of therapy.

He really did hate his job. Most of the time he managed to not think about that, but sometimes the awareness suddenly appeared, stark. A churning gut feeling. An anxious, restless urge. He had to move when it happened; he had to be outside, walking, somewhere, anywhere.

It had been raining hard when he got to the door to leave the newspaper building, something he hadn't been aware of since there were no windows in the newsroom. He tried to leave the building through the pressroom so he wouldn't run into anyone he'd have to talk to. Now he was stuck there, staring out at the sheets of rain. *The problem with spontaneous fits of petulance,* he thought. *You can't back out of them gracefully.*

It was coming down hard, but it couldn't last long; hard rains in these mountains rarely did. A meteorologist tried to explain it to him once at a party—something about the Appalachian range breaking up storm fronts—he couldn't remember exactly, because he'd been more interested in the woman on the other side of the kitchen.

The rain slowed, and Chase was out the door and walking before the rain had completely stopped. The clouds hadn't broken up and didn't look as if they would any time soon. In a town where it rained or snowed 200 days a year, clouds often stayed for days at a time. The meteorologist would probably tell him it was the Appalachians stalling the west-east storms.

At first, Chase hadn't thought about where he was going, but he wasn't in the mood to cut through people's yards or scramble up hills overgrown with blackberry bushes. He stuck to the two-lane in front of the *Dispatch,* which only offered a way to the interstate or into downtown. He turned toward downtown.

By the time he was getting close, the clouds were breaking up a little, one of those freakish autumn storms that promised doom at first—dark, low, heavy clouds and ominously still air that exploded in fury—only to abate for a while, clouds breaking up, still drizzling off and on, sunlight bursting through occasionally, and then exploding again with hard rain. Chase had come to appreciate these autumn storms, their dominance and crackling energy, their cleansing wash and electric afterglow.

By the time he got into downtown proper, Chase's clothes were soaked through. It was drizzling again, and he was hunched and shivering slightly. He was walking down High Street with his hands in his pockets. Not many people on the sidewalk. He passed shops with people standing just inside the doors, talking and waiting for the storm to pass. He wondered about them, about the lives they led that allowed them to be slowed down by the rain.

He'd only come to hate his job after he'd been transferred away from crime and politics and into the society pages, the restaurant reviews, the trivial minutia he now had to write about. How had that happened? Waters never would have transferred him, no matter how hard they'd feuded over Clawson. Waters was spineless, but he knew which of his writers were good and which were not.

The pressure must have come from above. From Loughery, or more likely, from someone to whom Loughery owed a political favor. Who—five years ago, when the crime was being investigated—who had an interest in seeing the killer of two college students apprehended quickly? Everyone. The whole town was frightened and wound tight. But who would have been upset by Chase's continuing insistence that Clawson was innocent? Who might have had Chase yanked off the story?

He ambled down High Street, toward the Courthouse Square. The guy at the new specialty coffee place—Slight Indulgence, wasn't it?—was cranking up his awning in anticipation of an end to the rain. The man and his wife were from Jersey, had come to town six months ago, so they wouldn't know that more rain would come soon.

What was it about the Clawson case that someone didn't want to have discovered? Did someone specifically want Clawson to take the fall? Or were they using Clawson's guilt to hide their own? There was no evident answer. Not enough data. Does not compute.

At the Courthouse Square, Chase stopped, looked around. The place was deserted. The winos that were Morgantown's most visible homeless were usually there begging change, but they were nowhere to be seen. Chase sat down on a bench, in the shadow of a small tree. The bench was soaked, but so was he, so it didn't matter. Most of the winos were probably in somebody's living room, down in one of the rowhouses under the South High Street bridge, Morgantown's closest thing to a ghetto. Chase had spent a few afternoons drinking beer and telling stories with them in a couple of those rowhouses when he first came to town. He was working for the paper, getting to know the town, having come from Fresno by way of Seattle.

At the time, he thought he'd only be here a few years. He'd been a golden boy, ace crime reporter at the *Seattle Times*. After three years at the *Times,* he figured that since he really wanted to go freelance, he'd better find a base from which to pursue that dream. His Seattle job left him little time, and that was what he needed most. The freelance road was long, but it offered the Holy Grail—choice of stories, no boss, good pay—but he needed time.

So Chase applied to several papers around the country: The *Ithaca Sentinel* in New York, the *Chapel Hill Messenger* in North Carolina, and Morgantown's *Herald-Dispatch.* He looked at small towns whose crime beat would be relatively undemanding. Eventually, he hoped to write books, either explaining some aspect of science in the lucid and succinct way that Stephen Jay Gould did or books that chronicled outre cultural phenomena, like Tom Wolfe and Hunter Thompson did in their earlier work.

Only now he found himself in Morgantown, West Virginia, sitting on a bench on the Courthouse Square after a rain, hating his job so much that he had fled. He'd accomplished nothing over the last five years. A few articles in minor publications, but nothing substantial. The worst thing was that he hadn't really tried. He'd squandered the free time he'd sought. He had betrayed himself, the worst thing a human being could ever do.

He looked around the Square. Wet and empty benches seemed to crouch low in the aftermath of the storm, the straight and tall young trees stretching toward the sky, their leaves nearly gone for the winter. Streaks of sunlight shooting down, coloring the bricks of the Courthouse with spots of light and dark.

He looked up at the parting clouds. *The eye of the storm,* he thought. *The rain'll come back any time now.* The waxing moon lay just over the horizon, like pitted, scarred bone.

Chase heard Shango before he saw him: "Snap out of it, Bwana!"

As Shango stepped toward him, Chase gave him the finger.

Shango laughed. "Tell me another one. You couldn't do it even if you wanted to. You *do* look like heck."

Chase wasn't in the mood. "If you don't have a quarter for an aging bum, you should just get your big butt on up the street."

"What are you doing here, Chase? You come to your senses and quit your job?"

"No." He tried to muster a sarcastic comment about doing a story on shelterless winos, but it didn't form. He didn't have it in him. "What are *you* doing here? Am I cursed, or what? I don't see you for months and then—WHAM!— you're there every time I turn around."

"You know I go where the action is. Why are *you* here, is the question. I figured you'd be up at the kill site about now."

Chase's breath caught. "What are you talking about?"

Shango slid on to the bench beside him. "Got a cigarette?" He looked Chase over. "A dry one."

Jeez! Chase had forgotten about his cigarettes. He felt his shirt pocket. He fished out a very wet pack of cigarettes. He tossed them at Shango. "Keep the pack."

Shango let them fall to the pavement. They landed with a slap.

"So there's been another one?"

Shango stood up. "C'mon. Let's go get you another pack, and I'll tell you all about it."

They crossed against traffic and headed up High Street toward the drug store.

"Yeah, they got called out about an hour ago," Shango was saying as they walked. "Musta found her a little before that."

"You already know it's a *her*?"

"Sure it's a *her*. I already explained all that to you. The other night. Or were you too drunk to remember?"

"No, I wasn't too drunk." Suddenly annoyed, Chase wasn't sure why. There was something he'd left undone that night, and it was still eating at him. Something he had forgotten. There was all the stuff Shango had said about the killer seeing Anders as his enemy, in a generic sort of way. "You said there would be more of—"

Chase snapped his fingers, stopped on the sidewalk. "That's what it was. That's why the FBI's here. This is part of some larger case they're investigating. Laana Anders was not the first with this MO. Not the first and not the last." He looked at Shango, who was staring hard at him.

"You just figured that out?" Shango turned and started walking quickly again.

Chase caught up with him. "You knew that?"

"No wonder you can't play chess."

Chase ended up paying for the cigarettes, but he'd expected that. He bought Shango a pack of the generics, too, even though Shango usually smoked OPC brand: Other People's Cigarettes. As they were coming out of the store, Chase was trying to convince Shango to go to the Omega with him.

"I'll call Waters. He's probably got Dumont out there. Maybe we can find out where it's happening." He wasn't sure why he wanted Shango along. Maybe just someone to bounce ideas off.

"Nah, I don't want to sit around while you make phone calls, and I sure don't want to go see no sliced-up dead body. I've had enough of that for one life."

"I'll buy the beers."

"Lead the way, Bwana. You can use my phone."

29
Monday afternoon, October 4

Her appointment schedule was light that day, and Alex managed to get away from the office early. If she hustled, she could get down to the police station on time. When she called earlier, she'd been told that a request like hers had to be filed by 4:30, or there wouldn't be anyone in to process it.

That surprised her at first, because she thought of the police station as being a 24-hour-a-day operation. Once she thought more about it, though, she realized that could only apply to emergency situations. The police department must have a million more mundane things to take care of—like taking in parking fines, typing out arrest warrants, filling in stolen property claims—that could just as easily be done in the daytime. No point keeping people in the middle of the night to process a request to tap the phone of a private citizen. She'd never had any interaction with the police, except that time in—jeesh, what was it—'82? '83? when she'd had to bail Craig out of jail on misdemeanor pot charges.

What a scene that had been: her crying, too shocked and scared about having to deal with the police to keep her head about her; Craig comforting her later, even though he was the one facing six months in jail, saying, "It's no big thing, baby—they're going to have to drop the charges, no Probably Clause." That's just what he'd said, too: "No Probably Clause." Even Alexandra knew that was wrong. But Craig hadn't cared. What's more, he'd been right.

Alex liked remembering what a naive child she'd been. Helped her realize how much better it was to be 40 than 20. Then she thought of the reason for her visit, how scared and helpless the midnight phone calls made her feel, and how the Laana Anders girl never had the chance to be 40.

She pulled into the parking lot next to the Safety Building at 4:15. Enough time to spare. She'd make her request, but she wasn't sure what they'd do from there. Would they have some uniformed guy follow her home? She wondered if they ever had to do that any more.

Alex saw the woman at the counter looking at her as she walked across the tiled lobby. She'd been gathering things on her desk; Alexandra could see she was getting ready to leave. Without missing a beat, the woman tucked some curly strands behind one ear and said, "Can I help you?"

When Alex thought of something concrete she could do about the mysterious caller, she'd felt better, calmer, more assured. Now she was actually in the police station, and she was nervous. She had to try to keep in mind that she was in police territory for help, not as a criminal this time.

"Yes. I called earlier about. . . uh. . . about having my phone tapped."

The receptionist's smile put her at ease. "Oh, sure. You're. . . Heyden, right?"

Alexandra was surprised. The call had been hours ago, and she must get dozens like them. "Yes, that's right. Alexandra Heyden." She held out her right hand, up and over the counter.

The woman seemed taken aback at first, then shook Alexandra's hand. "My name's Elaine," she said, smiling again. She settled back into her desk chair, opened a drawer and rifled through it, looking for something.

Alexandra had seen the same reaction before to an offered handshake, but only from women. She still found it odd that women strangers didn't have the same kind of codified greeting as men.

Elaine didn't find whatever it was she was looking for. She looked up at Alexandra with eyebrows raised, a what-did-I-expect expression.

"Okay, before we go any further, Ms. Heyden, I should tell you that nobody's here to process your statement right now."

"But I thought you said—"

"Wait, wait," Elaine said, holding up her hand. "I told you that one of the day detectives would be here if you came before 4:30. Which would normally be the case. But they were unexpectedly called away. They won't be able to get to it until tomorrow. In the meantime, I can take down some details and have them call you. I'm sorry, but that's the best I can do."

The woman did seem genuinely apologetic. Already, Alexandra was impressed with the department. Unexpected things came up, she could understand that. She didn't know if the rest of the staff was any good, but at least someone had the sense to hire a competent receptionist instead of officious paper shuffler.

"Okay, well, if that's the way it has to be. What do you need to know?"

"Just a second. I need to go see if I can find the right form. I usually don't do this kind of thing, but I'm supposed to have extras up here for times like this. Lemme go check Detective Watts's office. I'll be right back."

Elaine came back with several sheets of paper, stapled together. She walked into the lobby instead of the little room behind the counter. "Let's talk out here," she said, gesturing toward the chair-and-coffee-table setup over to the side of the lobby. "Randi's supposed to be here to take over in a second anyway." She looked at the clock on the wall: 4:35. "Actually, she was supposed to be here five minutes ago, but she's always late."

She leaned over the counter and grabbed a clipboard and pen, then motioned Alexandra over to the chairs.

For the next fifteen minutes, Alexandra answered questions while Elaine filled in the blanks. Name, Address, Occupation, Nature of Complaint, and so on. Elaine advised her on that last one, "Keep it simple. We'll get the details in a sec."

It was a long form. The top of the first page was labeled, TELEPHONE SURVEILLANCE REQUEST. Alex couldn't see exactly how many pages, but it was at least five or six. She wondered if all policework was this paper-heavy.

On page four, just after she had noted down the frequency of the calls, Elaine stopped writing. She set the clipboard and pen on the table and glanced at the clock. "Ms. Heyden. Listen, I don't mean to be discouraging. I mean, this sounds like a scary situation and all, but there's no way Detective Watts will okay this one."

Alexandra's stomach fluttered. "Why not?" Going through this had made the memory of the calls very immediate.

Elaine sighed. "I'll go ahead and finish filling this out if you want, but they usually have to have something more solid to tap someone's phone."

"What's not solid?" Alexandra heard her voice rising in pitch: shades of twenty years ago. "I've been getting these calls in the middle of the—"

Elaine cut her off. "Yes, ma'am. I understand that. But you've only gotten four of them."

"How many does it take?"

"It's more frequency than amount. We've got to be real careful with tapping phones. It usually only happens with excessive calls over a short period of time, or regular calls—you know, every Friday or Saturday night—or in the case of terroristic threats."

Alexandra was brought up short, blinked twice. "Terroristic threats in Morgantown?"

Elaine laughed. "Sorry. Not like that. That's what they call, you know, death threats, bomb threats, stuff like that."

Alexandra wondered at the kind of job that could make a young woman refer so casually to bombs and death.

"But you can still send it through?"

Elaine's voice was conciliatory. "Why not? Randi's not here yet, so whatever. I'll see if I can get Watts to do it." She smiled and picked up the clipboard.

30

Monday afternoon, October 4

The phone sang three, four times in Chase's ear as he looked across the table at Shango. The man was halfway through his first beer, even though this was only Chase's first call. Finally, someone in the newsroom answered.

"*Morgantown Herald-Dispatch* newsroom, Theodore Dumont speaking."

Chase was surprised. "Eddie? This is Chase."

"Hi, Chase. What can I do you for?"

Chase sighed; Eddie was in his one-of-the-boys moods. "What are you doing there?"

The line was silent for a moment. "How do you mean?"

"Why aren't you down at the Safety Building or somewhere?"

More silence. "Why should I be?"

Chase looked over at Shango, whose mug was empty. He was holding it up, motioning for Cory. "Let me speak with Waters."

"He's gone, Chase. Went home about a half hour ago."

"Okay, Eddie. . ." Chase rolled his eyes for Shango's benefit. "Connect me with whoever's covering the radio today."

"That'd be Adams. Hold on, please."

The phone went silent as Chase was transferred. Thank God it was Adams. He could count on the kid for some straight answers and no crap.

Suddenly, a voice: "Adams."

"Hey. This is Chase. I hear you're on the radio today."

"Yeah, what's up?"

"Can you tell me who went out on the body count today?"

"I haven't heard anything about it."

Chase found himself silent, staring past the phone at Shango, who took a big drink out of his mug. "Nothing on the radio about it?"

"Not since noon. They had some domestic disputes. A fight down at Cappellanti's. That's about it."

"Okay, uh. . . Thanks."

"Sure." Slight hesitation. "What's going on, Mr. Chase?"

"Just Chase. And nothing much. I gotta go."

"Hope I helped some on the nothing much."

"You did, Adams. Thanks."

"Sure thing."

Chase thumbed off: Why didn't anyone at the *Dispatch* seem to know about the homicide?

Shango looked over at him and lifted his mug in silent toast. Chase keyed ten digits on the cell. The phone rang only once.

"Jacobs." Chase was surprised that he'd answered.

"Paul, it's Chase. How's it going?"

"Fine."

How should he proceed from here? He blurted: "I was just calling to see how it was going today." Stupid. He was losing his touch for deception.

"How should it be going?"

Chase took a breath, hoping something would occur to him. Reporters were always suspicious, and besides, it wasn't as if he and Jacobs were really friends or anything. A "casual" call was bound to arouse suspicion, and Chase often forgot that, technically, Jacobs and the AP were in competition with the *Herald-Dispatch*. He was used to the delicate dance of it—reporters from different services sharing information, dropping hints whenever possible, in a complicated, unspoken etiquette. Might as well come clean. More or less.

"I just heard from a source. . ." He looked over at Shango again and added, "Not one I've used before, but I think he's pretty good. He told me the police were out on another murder call."

"Like the Anders girl?"

"Exactly, Paul. But the thing is, our radio monitor didn't hear anything."

Jacobs paused. "Well, neither did I. And I've been here all day."

"You didn't hear anything?"

Jacobs chuckled. "There was some kind of scuffle down at Cap's. Nothing serious. Three guys, from what I gather. It's Check Day."

The day people received their government checks, there were always fights in certain beer halls. Cappellanti's had been around for a century and still served dollar hamburgers. It was the center of action on Check Day.

"That's it?"

"That's it. I thought you weren't officially working on the murder story, Chase."

"I'm not."

Jacobs chuckled again. "But Dumont is."

"You got it."

"Good enough. Do me a favor?"

Chase knew that the request that was about to follow would have to be fulfilled, now that Jacobs had given him some information. That's the way the etiquette was danced.

"Okay, shoot."

"If you find out anything—unofficially, I mean—throw me a bone. It's really your story, but it could be big."

"You got it, buddy."

Chase had more questions than he had started with and put down the cell. Why didn't anyone seem to know about the second body? Except Shango. And how *had* he known? Chase remembered the way Shango had broken into his house a week earlier, had known Chase was down to the Safety Building and what he had gone down there for, and he suddenly saw what was going on.

Chase looked across the table at Shango and raised his glass to his lips: "So, who are you hitting down at the police station?"

Shango took a deep drink of his draft and smacked his lips. "Why would I hit dat?" He grinned.

Chase drained half his beer with one long slug. If Shango wanted to keep his sources quiet, that was okay. Chase could relate.

He should probably get over to the Safety Building right about now, anyway, although there wouldn't be much to find out. Both Watts and Carol would deny everything, like Shango just did. He might know they were lying, but without police confirmation of a second victim, there was nothing to print. Nothing but rumors.

It was still Dumont's story anyway. Technically. Chase had already decided to get it out of Dumont's clutches, but at this point, Waters would never allow him to work on it, especially not if the story was entirely heresay. Dumont should be the one to go. Chase'd be cursed if he was going to do Dumont's legwork for him.

"What do you say we pick up a six-pack," Chase said, "and go have a sit across the street from the station where we can watch some comings-and-goings?"

Shango took another drink. "I don't think it would be good for my reputation to be seen with you. They don't much like you over there. "

Chase drank more of his beer before answering. Finally he said, "They don't like you, either."

Shango laughed. "True dat. But I'm the Man's worst nightmare—a large, unemployed black man. I'm a black rattlesnake in a dark room. Anything can happen. You, on the other hand, are a huge and constant pain. That's worse."

True enough, Chase thought. *On both counts.* Maybe he should mosey over there after all. He took a sip of beer. Maybe later.

"You're sure your information is right?"

Shango held up open hands, palms turned toward each other. "One hundred percent."

"You know this means we may have a serial here?"

Shango shrugged. "What did I tell you?"

31
Late Monday afternoon, October 4

It had been a long, wet afternoon, with a long evening heavy on its heels. Detective Watts nodded to Randi at the reception desk as he and Agent Collins marched through the lobby, headed for the front doors. Watts thought briefly—as he often had before—of how he would like to jump her beautiful bones.

As the two of them passed out the station doors, he put the thought out of his mind. He and Collins still had things to discuss, and they were planning to go to Joyce's to discuss them. The case had taken a turn for the better. They'd managed to keep the press out of the loop, and Watts had plans to have a few drinks to celebrate. The heck with his ulcers.

Watts stopped on the top of the building's front steps, took a deep breath: Things were going well. Collins stopped with him stiffly, looking around. The light was fading from the fall evening sky—getting dark earlier and earlier—and Watts had been at it since four in the morning, but he felt good.

He and Collins started down the steps. They hit the sidewalk and turned left toward Joyce's. Watts didn't see the man sitting on the bench reading a book until they were next to him. The man looked up.

That blasted Chase.

Chase nodded at each of them: "Detective Watts. *Mayor* Collins." Chase had the audacity to smile!

They ignored him, although Watts would have loved to stop and smack the crap out of him. See if he smiled then.

"He's a reporter," Collins said quietly after they were about twenty yards down the street.

"He's the one I told you about," Watts said.

"Ah," was all Collins said.

Watts's stomach churned. His evening had suddenly turned sour.

32
Monday night, October 4

Devon holds each position for at least fifteen minutes. He uses standard hatha yoga asanas ordered in a manner specific to his needs, developed by himself and Yogi Shivananda more than ten years earlier.

He starts with the Stork: poised on one leg, the other tucked behind the opposite knee, arms held a little above shoulder level, elbows slightly bent, wrists flexed with all fingers drawn together and pointed toward the earth, spine straight, shoulders relaxed, eyes unfocused and forward.

Fifteen minutes.

He changes legs.

Fifteen more minutes.

Then he moves toward the Cobra. Each transformation from position to position is done very slowly, each taking over a minute.

Holding his weight on the one leg—which he changes every time, Mondays it is the right leg, Thursdays it is the left—he bends his knee, drawing closer and closer to the earth, his arms still out, Stork-style, until heel touches buttock. He bends forward, maintaining his balance, until his torso is parallel to the floor. His long arms swing down and forward slowly. They land, palms to the floor at shoulder-width, far above his head. From there he slides up, stretching out, his nose and belly less than an inch above the floor, until his head passes between his hands and then his spine arches, his arms straightening, his eyes sweeping up and across the ceiling, back, back, back until he is able to focus on the point where the ceiling joins the wall behind him.

He holds the Cobra position for fifteen minutes, just like all the others. From there he moves to Tiger, then to Spinner, Supplicant, Lilly, Mongoose, each in turn, ending with Monkey.

The exercise takes over two hours, and develops patience as much as physical well being. It is going well tonight: He can feel it, his body flowing effortlessly through the ritual, his mind as placid as might be expected under the circumstances.

The police scanner crackles softly in the background. The volume is turned down low enough to ignore the occasional talking, but loud enough that if the call comes through, he will hear it. Nothing yet.

He finishes the ritual and stands, shaking his limbs and lolling his head. It has been a long journey for him—strange at times, terrible at others—a search through the esoterica of the world for the eclectic mix that best suited him, and the road he traveled. None of the physical rituals he has learned has the kind of mentally clarifying effect that yoga has for him. Not even the Tai

Chi clears his head and calms him as much. Only the dervish exercises he learned in Afghanistan compare favorably, but they require so much preparation. And cannot be performed indoors.

He flashes briefly on the whirling he did in the desert: the polyrhythmic clapping of the allies, their watching and hooded eyes, the firelit shadows of the sand-dust kicked up by two dozen shuffling feet, the ecstatic groans of the other aspirant Sufis. Sometimes the rituals lasted for three days, three days of nonstop dancing and clapping, three days of ecstatic wandering.

Certain localities are stronger than others, more powerful. Devon has heard many reasons for this, but as far as he is concerned, none of them is a true explanation. What is indisputable: This region of the Alleghenies is among the most powerful in the world. Why, he does not know; he also does not care that much. What he does care about is that it is no coincidence that this thing is coming down here. Now. It has to be here.

Devon puts a big furry robe over his nakedness to relax in. Silk is okay, but there is nothing like terry cloth for comfort. He sits on the edge of his bed.

Why have the police not found the second body yet? It has been several days now since her. . . since the murder. *What is taking them so long?* It looks like he will have to give them a few clues earlier than he had expected. If the timing was not just right, this whole thing could get very sticky.

At the thought of stickiness, Devon's hands tingle with the memory of sticky-tacky drying blood. The body remembers things for a very long time. His mind remembers holding his hands up to his face. The sour, rust smell of drying blood. The sweet taste of it.

Devon stands and walks deliberately over to his free-standing chifforobe. Time for another cleansing ritual. And maybe it is not too early to start with the far-seeing exercise: The moon will be full in exactly three weeks. Full like bone.

33
Monday night, October 4

Collins walked down the hotel corridor slowly, not even turning his head as he passed his own room. He saw no light under the door, heard no sounds coming out, no signs of life inside. He stopped and patted his front pants pockets casually, as if he were trying to locate his key. There was still no sound from inside the room or from behind him.

To make sure, he turned abruptly: empty hallway. The fluorescent lights overhead buzzed. The otherwordly orange print of the carpet and the sickly yellow of the walls made his eyes hurt, but there was no sign of anyone following him. From all appearances, his hotel room was still secure. He walked back to the door.

Collins extracted the key card from its place in his inside jacket pocket, looking both ways as he fitted into the slot. The *snick* was harsh in his ears, but his hands only trembled slightly. All things considered, a good sign. The door slid open with the *hush* of wood grazing carpet, and a soft gust of stale air hit him in the face.

He paused again, listening, smelling the air, trying to determine if anyone had been in the room, or if anyone was still there. When he had checked in the week before, he'd left strict instructions that no maids were to clean the place; he'd take care of all that. The man at the desk had said the maids would be happy to skip a room, and so far Collins had had no problem with that. From everything he could sense now, his instructions had been followed.

He set the folder that Watts had given him on the desk and went into the bathroom to splash some water on his face. Even as he turned on the faucet and thrust his hands into the stream—the shimmering drops of water reminding him of humans, the way they seemed to move and collect and separate for no apparent reasons—Collins knew that he was just putting off the inevitable, the fulfillment that was to come.

But there were some things he had to go over first, two matters specifically. He left the bathroom, pausing in the entryway to make sure his door was locked, and walked into the main portion of the hotel room. King-sized bed, endtables, one long desk, a chair, a TV: There wasn't much to work with. His briefcase stood by his bed with all the information he'd brought with him about the case—the stuff he was able to commit to paper anyway—and his suits hung in the little closet. His suitcase with the other necessities was under the bed.

The first night he'd spent in town—this time around, at least—he'd pulled the chair over in front of the window, where he could sit with his feet propped up on the radiator. He had no use for the desk or the TV. Or even his notes, for that matter.

He opened the drapes so he could look out over the city. That was one of the advantages of an old downtown hotel. He could look at the lights of the town from eight stories up. From that angle, the view helped him imagine that he had some kind of overview of the operation.

Collins looked at the lights and thought briefly about the small and purposeless lives that scurried below. About how those people just didn't have a clue about the power and pleasure that was possible, and about how he had used to be like that, before. Before the Family had discovered him.

He gazed at the city lights again. There were two issues: Watts and Chase. He had his doubts about Watts—the man was, after all, nothing more than a foot soldier, a pawn in the game. If he followed instructions, things would work out.

Michael Chase, on the other hand—he was a wild card, and Collins was there to take care of exactly that kind of variable. What was Chase's interest? What was he up to? And what was he capable of? Those were the pertinent questions that Collins would have to deal with. Soon, apparently.

He stood abruptly. It was time, and he could allow himself now. He turned and pulled the suitcase from under the bed. After making sure first that the hair he had placed in its jaws was undisturbed. he opened it carefully.

He pulled out the disposable syringe package and tore open the paper. The syringe popped out. He removed one of the vials that had been neatly inset in the rack he'd built inside the suitcase, held it up to the light. Looked good, a pale fluid in an amber bottle. His mouth watered involuntarily; Collins didn't like it when his body responded without his permission, but he let it pass.

He knew that once he'd had his shot, he'd pass the night productively, reviewing records, looking for discrepancies, assessing Darnell Watts's commitment and deciding what to do about Michael Chase. He would sleep a couple of hours near dawn, having worked all night. A step ahead of the competition, as he liked to say; it was what made him a good agent, in line for promotion in the FBI, but even better, one of the Old Man's primary deputies.

The mix of amphetamine and heroin was fine—*horsefly* was what the junkies called it—the exact dose he requested, one shot a day. He set the point of the needle against the rubber top of the vial. He dipped it in, sucked up the nearly clear, slightly brownish liquid until the vial was empty.

As he unbuttoned his sleeve to roll it up, he noticed the splashes of water on it, now nearly dry. Not good. He'd been sloppy in his haste. He was reminded of how, when he first went to the Academy, he'd come home after a full day of classes, having put off the need to go to the bathroom until he got home, and as soon as he got there, the urge became overwhelming. It hadn't really bothered him before that moment, but as soon as he'd put his key in the door, it became intense. Collins had ultimately conquered that with discipline and denial, but apparently he was that way now about getting a hit, a mainline of his medicine. That would have to be mastered.

He placed the needle against the soft skin and bulging vein on the inside of his elbow, thinking about how he'd have to bring that impulse to haste under control. He broke the skin with the needle; he felt the point enter the vein. He pushed the plunger forward with his thumb and felt the liquid stream sliding up the vein of his bicep.

He smiled tightly as he waited for the rush that lead him to ever greater clarity and control.

II

"Satan's mark"

34
Thursday morning, October 7

Carol held down the button and spoke into the phone: "Elaine, could you bring me the Anders-Samosky files?"

"All of them?"

"If you would."

"Coming up, Chief."

Carol had expected more from Theron Davies's visit. She had believed the M.E. would be able to find more out from the Samosky woman than he had from Anders, if only because the evidence was fresher. But it didn't work out that way. The FBI medical examiner was as thorough and business-like as he'd been during his first visit; he was also just as condescending and sarcastic. Carol chose not to join him in the examination room this time, though, not wanting to know if he still had that creepy attitude toward corpses. Still, she hoped he would turn up something useful. Some skin from under a fingernail, perhaps, or traces of semen—any hard evidence would help. But he hadn't. Nada. Nichts.

There was a quick rap at her door before it opened and Elaine poked her head in. She held several folders in her hands, some of them an inch thick.

"Thanks, Elaine." Carol half-rose to take the file from Elaine.

"Sure," Elaine said before leaving.

She sat down and opened the top folder, the master, looking at the contents sheet. The file had expanded quickly after the discovery of a new body. The department had gotten lucky a second time, since Samosky, like Anders, had been a college student who was already reported missing, which meant they didn't have to waste time and resources trying to find out who the victim was.

The file hadn't quite doubled yet, but only three days had passed since the discovery of the body. Legwork took time. What Watts had found so far was that Samosky was much like Anders. A little wilder perhaps, more of a partier, several boyfriends, but very close to the Anders profile. They moved in similar social circles and might even have known each other, or had friends in common. That was a lead, however vague.

The Davies autopsy *had* given them one thing to go on. The young women were most likely victims of the same killer. Same MO: The fresher body showed more clearly the twine fibers imbedded in the wrists and ankles, the parallel and jagged slices of a kris, the stabbing in the vaginal area. Both were missing their heads. Both killsites had similar evidence of ritual behavior: droplets of red wax, twine on the wrists and ankles, and there were the same cleared places with the holes that had presumably held stakes— Something clicked. She thought it through: The first body had been found a month after the murder, the second body about 10 days after. Ten days was the MEs' best guess, both their own and the FBI's. They had both been found displayed in the middle of a ground cleared for a ritual killing.

But that couldn't be, Carol realized. The first body showed signs of being scavenged; one lower arm was even missing, and they still hadn't been able to locate it. It was probably devoured by now, and they never would find it. But the body was still in the middle of the circle, which wasn't possible. *Unless someone had moved it back there.* Someone had taken the time and risked discovery to move the bodies back to the centers of the circles, probably more than once. The killer had then cleared away the five spots where each victim had been tied down, the spots that formed stars.

Carol was sure now: A serial killer, or killers, was— She smacked her hand on the papers in front of her, angry with herself. *That was the FBI interest. These two weren't the first.*

Maybe she'd been too caught up in routine matters and her doubts about Watts to notice the obvious. She'd been taking on too much, perhaps. There had been no real need for her to be the one to notify Samosky's parents, for instance. Carol had begun to take this case personally.

Samosky was from upstate New York, and her parents had driven in the day before to ID the body. Carol used to think that would be the worst part of a police job, escorting the relatives through the morgue to identify the victim. She found out over the years that wasn't the case. Most people were grim and stoic when they stared at murder. She'd come to assume that they saved their grief for privacy. If anything, breaking the news to them was usually far worse.

It had been the opposite with Amelia Samosky's parents.

It was really more Watts's job, but Carol had been present when Watts informed family and thought him unnecessarily callous. She didn't hold it against him—a product of his nearly thirty years on the force—but she wanted to spare the relatives whenever possible.

She asked to speak with Mr. Samosky when she called. Men were always easier to deal with on this subject. He had answered the phone curtly: "Reverend Samosky."

Oh crap, Carol thought. "Ummm, Reverend Samosky. This is Chief Carol Braxton of the Morgantown, West Virginia, police department. I'm afraid I have some bad news." She could think of no other way to introduce herself.

She heard the Reverend sigh. "What's she done now?"

Carol was taken aback. "She. . . She hasn't done anything, Reverend. Your daughter's. . . She's been killed."

Carol braced herself, but nothing came across the phone. She could hear him breathing, deeply, regularly. Other than that, no sound, nothing. She waited.

Finally she said: "Reverend Samosky? Are you there?"

She heard him sigh again. "I suppose you'll need me to identify the body." It was not a question.

"As soon as it is convenient for you. . ."

"We'll be there tomorrow." The line went dead.

The Reverend Samosky and his wife arrived the next day. When they came into Carol's office, they looked like they'd driven all night. The Reverend had dark circles under his eyes and his wife's hair was tousled, as if she'd slept in the back seat. Carol took them to the morgue in an unmarked car.

As per Carol's instructions, the morgue had made specific arrangements for the identification. A cloth had been draped over the shoulders, held down by small weights, so that the Samoskys would not be confronted with the headless condition of their daughter's body. Still, it was obvious, the cloth concave where there should have been a head. Carol carefully drew the sheet up, revealing only Amelia's right arm, a Celtic triskele tattooed on the inside of the wrist. Mrs. Samosky saw the red, gold, and black design, three curls sprouting from a triangular shape.

"That's her," Mrs. Samosky nodded. "Some kind of Irish thing she—" Her voice cracked.

Carol was surprised she'd spoken so assertively, having said barely three words before that. Carol looked at the Reverend Samosky.

His eyes were wide and looking down at the sheet-covered form of what had been his daughter, his jaw set, his hands clenched. Carol saw that his eyes were locked between her shoulders, where her head should have been. He began to tremble, slightly at first, visible only in his fists and face—his jaw still clenched, his lips quivering perceptibly—but spreading up his arms to his shoulders, which shuddered as his chest heaved and he drew a huge, convulsive and rasping breath. His head jerked back suddenly, his eyes to the ceiling. He fell to his knees, tugging at the sheet, tearing it down and grasping his daughter's cold hand. "Jesus, Jesus," he whispered as he kissed and kissed her knuckles.

Carol was frozen for a moment, never having heard such resigned passion in a whisper. She tried to break the Reverend away, clutching at the sheet to pull it up. He didn't so much fight her as ignore her. He was much stronger and wouldn't let go of his daughter's hand. And the way he looked at her: grief-stricken, angry, accusing, his eyes brimmed with tears, but his cheeks dry.

"This is Satan's mark, the Devil's work," he said at last, looking away from his daughter's corpse toward Carol. He shook the meat and bone that had been his daughter's hand. "Satan did this." He let go, and Amelia's hand clunked against the side of the medical table.

Mrs. Samosky's eyes were fixed on her daughter's body, on the slices that the kris had made, on the medical examiner's crudely stitched Y incision that ran from pelvis to neck.

Carol flipped idly through the pages of the reports, not really looking, thinking instead about Reverend Samosky. He had no idea how close he was, actually, in terms of the ritual nature of the murders. Whoever was doing this might as well be Satan. Or one of His followers.

She came to Davies's report on the autopsy of Laana Anders. She glanced down, realizing she'd never really read it. Hm-hmm-hmm. It was what she had thought. Until she came to *Instrument of Trauma*: "Either a single blade drawn across the skin in several closely spaced cutting motions, or a single instrument fitted with multiple blades."

Almost word-for-word what the local ME had concluded. There was no mention of a ceremonial kris.

35
Thursday morning, October 7

Chase leaned back in his chair, looked around the newsroom. The Mid-morning Dead Zone. . . Reporters clacking away as far as the eye could see. He gulped his coffee, which was almost room temperature. It braced him.

He shook his shoulders to loosen them. The article was done as far as he was concerned, but he had to figure out how to slip in another few paragraphs to get it to 18 inches. As much as he wanted to see more computers in public school classrooms, he knew this story about the new iPads over at South Junior High was a real ho-hummer. He hoped Dale had gotten some good pictures to liven it up.

Truth was, he couldn't get his mind off the murders. He was now absolutely convinced that another body had been found. It had been three days since Shango told him about it, and so far, he hadn't been able to verify anything. He'd talked to Elaine and gotten nothing, although she seemed very nervous about his questions. He approached Watts and was told bluntly to go away. The most helpful response had come from Carol: "I can't comment on an ongoing investigation." No confirmation, but no denial either. He and Carol used to joke that politicians always said, "No comment" when they couldn't tell the truth, but didn't want to lie. Carol's "No comment" was practically an admission, although not one he could use in print.

Chase tried to tell himself it didn't make any difference, it wasn't his story anyway, he wasn't a crime reporter anymore. But he didn't believe himself. This was his story, by right, and there had to be a way. . . Nothing else interested him, especially not this thing about the new iPads at—*Oh, crap!* He looked up at one of the wall clocks. He had 45 minutes to get this story done and put it in the copy room's folder. Another two hundred words.

His notebook was open to the scribblings he'd made while out at the school. Probably a quote would do it. They were always good for 25 words at least, including attribution and brief commentary, and then he could talk about the quote for maybe another 75 words. He flipped a couple of pages, looking for some pithy words from the principal. He flipped some more pages. Unfortunately, it appeared the man hadn't said anything worthwhile that Chase hadn't already used.

Maybe a few words from one of the kids. Something he'd missed. Something cute. He scanned all ten pages of his notes—nothing there either.

This was ridiculous, trying to get a thousand words of copy out of what was basically a two-sentence story. Then again, if he wasn't so distracted by the murder story. . . Besides being interesting in their own right, the events had the potential to vindicate him, confirm what he had said all along: Clawson didn't kill those girls—he was framed. He was railroaded by a public demand for a culprit and by a prosecutor—Barnetti, the grandstanding demagogue—who was smart and able and knew how to play the sentiments of the jury. But Clawson—despite pending charges of rape and child abuse, and the discovery of child pornography in his two-room apartment in Philadelphia—didn't have the intelligence or inclination to pull off the coed murders.

He'd punched out of work at a warehouse in Philadelphia less than four hours before the girls were allegedly picked up. He had three witnesses. Philadelphia was six hours away from Morgantown by car.

But Barnetti managed to gloss over that in his closing arguments. He was a master at shaping the perceptions of jurors: "Maybe he flew, who knows. The defendant won't say how *he got here,* and it doesn't matter how *he got here.* What matters is that *he did get here.* " He emphasized the "abject, pathetic fear these young women must have felt" and the "perversion of this man. . . this Eugene Clawson."

Chase felt all along that evidence had been hidden. Probably by the police department. Probably by Watts, specifically. His insistence of this to Carol—late in the night, pillow talk—had played a role in their breakup. She had defended Watts and the department. He was sure she was wrong, and told her so.

As far as he was concerned, the murders were unsolved. They would start again: He had said so at the time. Those first two killings were ritualistic, and from every indication, so are these new ones. This time, he wanted to follow up. Searching the web, he'd found mostly sensationalism and unreliable reports, and he'd been about to go to the library to do some research on ritual murder in America when he heard about Clawson's arrest. The trip was long overdue.

If there was some way he could officially get on the story, he would have the time to make that kind of side trip. Or at least if he could get out from under his current obligations, most especially that cursed Morgan story.

Chase's eyes wandered up to the clock—35 minutes and 200 words to go. He thought about computers and classrooms and junior high kids. He thought about what it was like to be a kid and want to get out of doing homework. Getting out of any work, for that matter, whatever the adults had told you to do. He smiled and began to type into the middle of the story:

> The students will quickly realize the amount of work that
> computers can save them. . .

Three paragraphs later, Chase had his 200 words. It took seven minutes. He had to make up a quote about potential time savings— ". . . especially in English class, on rewriting. . ."—but he was sure that the principal would approve the whole quote. One phone call and the assignment would be done. Finally.

Chase was especially pleased because he'd also flashed on a way to trade assignments with Dumont. Waters would never do it willingly; he seemed to see changing his mind as a weakness. Dumont would never accept a trade if Chase proposed it, but Chase had figured out a way to get Dumont to propose it as if it were his idea.

Chase keyed into the main file server: It blinked ENTER USERNAME: at him. He went through the process and dropped his finished story into the copy department's computer in-box. All done. He logged off.

He was rising from his desk chair, about to step outside for a cigarette, when he became aware of a commotion at the entrance to the newsroom. He looked over and saw Shango passing the receptionist's desk and heard him saying, in that basso voice of his, "Don't worry about it. This'll just take a second. This is something he wants."

The newsroom was the last place Chase had ever expected to see Shango. The police station would have seemed more appropriate. Heads turned as he crossed the floor, a thick folder crimped in his huge right hand. He nodded to every desk he passed: "Good morning" "Sorry to bother you" "Hello" "Hi there." He came finally to Chase's desk and set the folder down, smiling broadly. *Basking in the scene he's causing.*

Shango spoke softly: "Sorry to bother you here, Chase, but I couldn't count on running into you."

"You could have broken into my house."

Shango laughed. "That's true, Bwana." He tapped the folder with his forefinger. "I thought you might want a look at this." He flicked open the manila cover to reveal the heading: *Anders-Samosky Investigation.*

Chase looked from the topsheet to Shango, and back.

"I didn't want you to think I was lying the other day," Shango said.

Chase picked up the folder; it was nearly an inch thick. He looked at Shango. "Perish the thought."

Shango grinned. "Good enough. I'll be in touch." Chase slipped the folder into the top drawer of his desk.

36
Thursday morning, October 7

"Yes!" Chase cried out, a little too loudly, and pumped his fist in the air in triumph. He sat back in his desk chair, furtively glancing toward Eddie's cubicle. Eddie had noticed, just as Chase had hoped. Step one, complete, Chase leaned forward again, staring at his computer monitor.

He hoped he'd chosen well, and he hoped that Eddie would take the bait. It was 12:15, and Eddie stood at his desk, gathering his things for his lunch break, as usual. Eddie's predictability would make him easy prey, if someone were ever to want to kill him. Not that anyone would bother. Chase went back to his list on screen, the list of story ideas he's kept on the back burner until they were needed.

> *Followup the fake id story with restaurant/ bar angle:* Talk to owners/ managers, see if any of them have been popped for serving to minors. . .

> *Current state of town/gown relations:* How are the two sides of Morgantown life getting along? Complaints about students from downtown merchants. . .

> *Homeboy makes good:* Successful people who came out of Morgantown and West Virginia; do the usual (Gates, Hickam, Kasdan, Knotts, etc.) but also. . .

> *Lifestyles of Morgantown's semi-rich and vaguely famous:* A series of profiles of local elite, where they live, how they live, what they do (if anything). . .

The last one was perfect. Absolutely perfect. Eddie would definitely go for this one.

Without looking in Eddie's direction, Chase brought up a new Word file and began keying in names:

Tycoon Mylan Puskar
Tycoon Millie Weintraub
Philanthropist Celine Roseamond
Philanthropist Marc Snyder
Author Andrew Paskins
WVU President Jim Clements

He was only six names into the list before Eddie was at his side, peering over his shoulder, just as Chase expected.

"What are you working on?"

"Nothing special." Chase didn't look up, keyed in another name.

WVU Coach Dana Holgorsen

"That's a serious list, Chase. Is this a story?"

"Just brainstorming." He tried to think of another name, but drew a blank. Movers and shakers on the Morgantown scene. People who got things done. People who had money. People who Eddie wanted to be.

"Seriously, Chase. I recognize the names, but what do these people have in common?"

Chase sighed heavily, pushed his chair back.

"Okay, I'll tell you. *If* you promise to go away." He studied Eddie's face and could easily read the raw eagerness. Like a puppy, this guy. "This is going to be so effing fascinating. . ." Chase let his voice trail off, afraid to give away his agenda; even Eddie might clue to the falseness if Chase said too much. He waited.

"What is it?"

"Well. . ." Chase spoke as if he were hesitant to reveal it. He glanced to right and left furtively. "I guess we're on the same team, Edward. Waters knows it's my story. Two things, really.

"Have you heard about the motion to disinter the bones of Haskell Morgan?" Chase said in a half-whisper. "I've been doing some reading about our town's founder. He wasn't quite the 'paragon of virtue'"—Chase made quote marks with his fingers—"that official history would have us believe. This is the kind of thing that's going to get people talking. Real investigative stuff."

"Oh, yeah?" Eddie tried to sound sympathetic, but he sounded bored.

"Yeah." Chase forced himself to sound enthusiastic. "I've been kicking this around for a while, but I haven't got the right angle on it yet. Guess I'm too close to it. I'm lucky it's not time sensitive. More a feature."

Eddie fidgeted with the lapel of his raincoat and looked at the ground. "I'd like to help, Chase, but—"

"No, no. Thanks, but the whole thing's about to break. It's a matter of time."

"Time?"

"Yeah. I'm supposed to have this done soon, but I've also been assigned this really cool series on Morgantown's elite. *That's* the story I really want to be working on. The Morgan story is like work, but this one is more like play."

Chase watched Eddie perk up immediately, then try to play it cool. He shifted his weight back to his heels. "How do you mean play?"

"Right now I'm starting to line up interviews. The way I thinking, I'll get to hang out with them for a while, talk to them, go to their homes, have meals with them, yadda yadda. See how the other half lives."

Eddie's weight shifted back to his toes. Chase could already see him considering the possibilities. "So how is that a problem?"

"Time, Eddie. Like I was saying. I don't have time to wrap up the Morgan story *and* start these interviews."

"You know," Eddie said after a moment. "Maybe I could help you out with that. I'm not too busy right now."

"Help how?" Chase tried to look suspicious, and he hoped that Eddie's eagerness would prevent him from sussing out Chase's actual motives.

"I wouldn't mind doing some of the interviews. Then you could take over when you've got the Morgan piece done."

"I don't know," Chase said slowly. "You know Waters doesn't much like his reporters to go trading assignments. Besides, aren't you doing that murder thing?"

"Yeah, but that's open and shut. Not much work there." Eddie laughed his one-of-the-boys laugh. He clapped a hand on Chase's shoulder. "What he doesn't know won't hurt him. You can sign the receipts for accounting."

"You think that would work? You'd have to spend a lot of time with them."

"Sure. It'll work fine." Eddie squeezed his shoulder in an effort to appear hale and hearty. "Leave it to me. I'll do the research, but you can have your name on the story. Uh. . . stories."

"Well. . . that'd really help me out a lot, Edward. That way I could at least do a few interviews. Hang out in some cool houses. Thanks a lot. But. . ."

"What? But what?"

"What if something comes up on the murder? I don't want you dropping this in the middle. That would leave me in some royal trouble."

That gave Eddie pause. He seemed to consider. "One hand washes the other. I'll take the heat off you, you cover me if anything comes up on the case. You can just be backup. Nothing will come up, so you don't have to worry about it taking much time, but that way you won't have to worry about me leaving you high and dry."

"Well. . ." Chase said, scuffing his feet against the carpet. "Might work. You're really saving my butt, Eddie. I owe you one. It's a deal."

He held up his right hand and Eddie, who was grinning ear to ear, reached for it—

"Except. . ." Chase said, touching his forefinger to his forehead. "Except, I've still got this Morgan story."

"So? You said you wanted to do it. You said it was almost done."

"I do, and it is," Chase assured him hastily. "But, uh. . . I guess I'm stuck. The research is done, the notes are made. What if I assemble them, and put them in order, and you just write up a rough. I'll take it from there."

Chase could see the conflicts racing through Dumont. On one hand he was being handed the opportunity to hobnob with the rich for a few days, maybe several days. On the other, he would have to take on more work to do it. But then, he would have unloaded that pesky murder thing.

Chase figured it was 50-50.

"I'll do it," Eddie said, finally. "Give me the notes. I'll write 'em up. Leave them on my desk and I'll pick 'em up after lunch."

Chase let a very satisfied grin flash. "Fantastic. I can't thank you enough. I won't forget this."

Eddie narrowed his eyes and pointed deliberately at Chase. "You *better* remember, Chase. You owe me."

"Like I said, man." Chase shook his head as he watched Eddie head back to his desk for his things. A jaunty, self-assured walk. The walk of a self-inflated man who had just gotten the better of a poor sap.

Apparently, Eddie had never read *Tom Sawyer.*

37
Thursday evening, October 7

The phone rang and Alex stiffened in her husband's arms. She felt his biceps flex. They were curled up on the couch, wrapped in each other's arms, watching *Sleepless in Seattle*. Jer had fixed a good tortellini primavera for dinner—al dente—and broccoli with baby onion cream sauce. Afterwards, sated, they'd settled into the living room couch for the movie that they'd both been wanting to see for years, but had somehow never gotten around to.

The phone rang right when Sam is dropping Victoria off at the airport, when he sees Annie for the first time.

"It's only 8:30," Jerry said. "It can't be him. Relax."

He hit pause on the remote and swung himself to a standing position.

"Yes?" he said when he picked up the phone. Alexandra watched him as he listened; his pleasant expression didn't change.

"No," he said. "We can work that out tomorrow." A few heartbeats passed. Jerry laughed. "That's really not the issue. I don't give a crap if the governor wants—"

His words were apparently cut off by the person on the other end of the phone.

"Okay, okay. Look, Lin. We'll talk about this tomorrow. . . Yeah, good. . . Yeah, goodnight."

Jerry slipped back onto the couch, trying to recover the position they had been in before the call.

"It's a good thing they didn't tap it," he said. "That call would be all they need. The governor has enough enemies as it is."

Alexandra wasn't so sure; she still hadn't been able to get the midnight caller out of her mind. She'd had a lot of strange calls since she'd gone into practice, but for some reason, the echoes of this one wouldn't leave her. There was something that she was not taking into account, she was sure of it.

But she had to let it pass, for tonight.

She snuggled against her husband, her head against his chest. "Let's roll 'em," she said, trying to put it out of her mind.

38
Thursday evening, October 7

Carol caressed her badge tentatively, her forefinger noting the ridges of the city seal, the feathers on the wing of the eagle. She stared at the closed door of her office. She had the sense she'd always had as a child when she swam in a lake: Huge, indescribable beasts moving beneath her in the depths, circling out of sight, waiting to rise and devour.

She didn't like the feeling. It came unasked, unwanted. Carol had always had a passing interest in psychology—wanting to determine what drove her to be the person she was, do the things she did—and she'd kept a journal since college. It helped her sort out her inner life. After going into the criminal justice field, she'd felt funny about introspection and had kept it private because other officers would give her a hard time. Still, the only thing to do was ana- lyze the images.

In her adult life, the images of water beasts circling beneath her often came to her when she was losing control of a situation. There was something she was missing, or ignoring. Part of her knew what it was—the subconscious part, the part that watches and judges—but the conscious part of her struggled to make sense of the feeling. So what was it? Why was she feeling out of con- trol?

She was in charge of herself, in charge of the department. She'd heard over and over, from veterans as well as rookies, about how she was the best chief the department could possibly have. A decorated officer, twice cited for bravery, a proven investigator, high marks in that FBI course two summers ago: She was the first female chief-of-police in the state, and she was deter- mined that nothing would slip by her. She was on the alert, always.

So what was the problem now? She sat back in her chair, hoping it would come clear, that it was not what she feared it was, what she was already sure it was. She closed her eyes, let her mind wander freely, trying not to let it land on anything specific, but she kept coming back to it, the same problems, the same issues:

Why didn't the FBI ME's report reflect what he had said to her in the au- topsy room? Which time had he lied to her?

Why didn't anyone besides her noticed that the bodies had been dragged back into the circles, probably more than once?

Why did Watts seem to be stalling on this one?

Where were the heads?

And what other sea monsters were waiting?

39
Thursday evening, October 7

Chase put the folder down on his bed and sat up. This was everything he'd wanted, and more. He wriggled his feet into his tennis shoes, which were still tied from when he'd kicked them off and flopped back onto his bed with the file. It was time to go out for a walk so he could clear his head. He had much of the story now and a lot of footwork before him. He left the bedroom, headed for the front door, headed for the neighborhood streets.

Outside, there was a hint of chill in the air. He thought of the cold Mared Malarik and Karen Ferrell must have felt that January night they were taken. It snowed that night, and they must have died in the dark, in the cold. Two girls, one night of murder. He wondered if they had been decapitated before or after they died. But Anders and Samosky had not been cold. They'd both been killed in the early Fall, when it was still warm, and they'd been murdered separately. And maybe the most telling difference: Malarik and Ferrell had been raped repeatedly, while Anders and Samosky showed "only" signs of vaginal stabbing. Similar, but not quite the same. Chase had begun to believe that these latest killings were *not* the work of the same man, Different, but related somehow.

He surveyed the street from his porch, the parked cars, the mostly dark houses, one or two with the eerie blue light of TVs coming through their front windows. This neighborhood was working class and went to bed early. The stillness of the scene helped quiet him, though he sensed that the racing thoughts didn't so much slow as submerge to some shadowy place beneath his awareness. Still, he felt a little more in control.

At the bottom of his porch steps, Chase stopped, craned his head back for a wide view of the sky. The autumn stars, glittering white and blue against the clear black of the night. Wisps of white curled in, very high, and there was an arc of light around the waxing moon. He remembered that a ring around the moon meant something, meant that some kind of weather was on its way, but he couldn't recall what kind exactly.

He lit a cigarette, trying not to think about the murders and barely succeeding, trying to decide which direction to walk. He looked toward the uphill direction of the street. Stillness. He breathed out smoke. As he turned his head to look down the street, a tremor shook his neck, a shiver that ran up his spine.

He turned slowly back toward the uphill direction, his eyes coming to rest on a white compact car. Hadn't he seen someone sitting in it when he looked out from his porch? The silhouette hadn't registered consciously because it hadn't been moving, but it registered now by its absence. He was sure no one had gotten out of the car. He didn't think he'd seen that car parked around here before, and since this wasn't a student neighborhood, everyone was familiar with the cars that should be parked around here. He stared for a moment more, his mind once again racing.

Chase had long known that he had a tendency toward paranoia, which wasn't such a bad thing for a journalist; it had helped him out, back when he worked the crime beat. It only got to be a problem when he automatically constructed complex notions around small events or perceptions. Like this one: It had already occurred to him that 1) there was someone in that car, and 2) whoever it was was hiding from him, because 3) they were following him.

Which was nonsense; he was just on edge. He decided that his racing thoughts had become paranoid in the brief moments that they had dipped below the surface of his mind. He decided to walk downhill, away from the car, just to prove that he didn't have to give in to his paranoia and go take a look inside it.

40
Thursday evening, October 7

Maria came in the front door all smiles. She felt very satisfied with herself, euphoric, in fact. She felt like she was walking on a blanket of air. This was the kind of mood that sometimes made Alex chide her playfully: "You're getting giddy, Maria. Come on back to earth."

She went into the living room and saw Don on the couch, staring at the TV. She could tell from his expression that he wasn't really watching, though, and that he was none too happy. *Poor Don. He takes everything so seriously.*

She crossed the room holding her package out in front of her, her arms straight and shoulder high. The package was big—2 by 3—and wrapped in a nice, subdued Christmas kind of wrapping, just like she had asked the store clerk to do it in. She held the package out in front of her and smiled slyly when her husband demanded to know where she'd been.

"I got you a present," she said, ignoring the accusation in his voice. "Open it."

Don sat up, accepting the package into his lap, although he didn't seem all that pleased about it. He tugged at the wrapping, cautiously it seemed to Maria, like he thought it might be a bomb. He worked his way down to a white cardboard box. The wrapping lay in pieces beside him and at his feet. He lifted the top. . .

. . . to discover a new briefcase. He lifted it by the handle. It was all leather—suede, actually—the soft, warm skin of baby cows. Maria liked the way it held the heat of her hand when she touched it, the way it darkened when she stroked it a certain direction. "Do you like it?"

Don's eyes were wide. His hands caressed the briefcase. He looked up at Maria, his eyes searching for something.

She knew what he was looking for.

"I'm sorry I've been distracted lately," she said. "Actually, the store's been doing better than ever, so I've been wrapped up in my needs. It's been driving me nuts trying to keep up with it all. This is just to say, 'Forgive me.'"

Donald smiled again. He drew her to him. "There's nothing to forgive."

Maria blinked twice in her husband's arms. For a second, she wondered what he was referring to. Tears started, but she held them back.

41
Thursday evening, October 7

Collins could have waited in his hotel room for hours, or days, or weeks, if it had been necessary. In one sense, he had been waiting for years—it was a perpetual state of mind—and it didn't make any difference to him where he was physically when he was waiting. There was no reason to wait here tonight, however, since he could get the report on Michael Chase tomorrow. No rush. He trusted his men to give him a top notch report, and it could wait until tomorrow.

The groundwork was all laid for the case to play itself out. As was usual for him, everything was in its place, ready to go. Collins was fastidious by nature—his training and the drugs only made him more so—and he disliked unpredictability of any kind. No, that wasn't true; it was only undesirable when he was caught by it. Utilized properly, unpredictability was extremely helpful as a device to disorient his opponent. Or his prey.

He stood up from the chair, looking out at the lights of Morgantown. He had been nearly motionless for the hour since his shot and noted with pleasure the familiar springy lightness that the horsefly gave him. It was always that way after the first rush of fulfillment, and it lasted him most of the way through the night. Buoyancy and sustained strength. When he passed the dresser mirror, he saw The Smile: a small, tight, upturning of the corners of his mouth. Yes, the shot was working its magic well tonight.

In his suitcase he kept what he brought in case he had any nights off. He changed into the jeans and flannel shirt, slipped everything else in the pockets of a windbreaker he'd modified himself: the regular pockets enlarged, two large pockets sewn into the lining. He could leave his gun in his room; no need for that tonight.

Before he opened the door to the hallway, he listened at it. Can't be too careful. A couple was going into a room across the hall and down a few doors, laughing as they went. Then silence. He unlocked his door and slipped out, looking both ways before walking down the hallway.

In the elevator on the way down to the lobby, Collins thought only of his upcoming night out. He had set the operation aside for tonight. The elevator had mirrors that ran from waist-level up on all four walls, and he was pretty pleased with the way he looked. His outfit always reminded him of his dad and his dad's working class buddies. He figured he could pass for working class tonight, if whoever was checking him out was drunk enough, or didn't look too closely.

He thought he'd hit the strip of student bars that he'd passed when he first came into town. He remembered them fondly from a few years ago, and figured that was where he'd have his best chance. He'd spot someone—male or female, it didn't really matter for what he had in mind—someone who had come there to get drunk, hang out. Maybe someone talkative, maybe someone depressed. Definitely someone young, like most of the students in those bars would be. Collins didn't drink, but he'd watch them get drunker. He'd buy them drinks until closing time. Then he'd take them home to their place.

But after they got home, Collins would have to be careful. Restrain his desires somewhat. He'd have to wait to get back to the city to completely let loose. He couldn't take the chance of attracting the attention of the police. Watts, he could count on to cover for him, but he didn't want to give Braxton any cause for more suspicion, and Collins knew that his erotic habits would invite nothing but unease.

When he stepped out of the elevator, he found himself whistling, "I'm in the Mood for Love."

*   *   *

The crescent moon rose higher in the night, an off-white that glared almost yellow down on the hills. The light it cast was the white of a bone that had been left out in the weather. Beneath the moon's eye, predator and prey stalked and skittered, pursuer and pursued.

The hour was late.

At the edge of town, the moon shone down on one particular street that still had some activity on it. Now and then people emerged from one of the bars, alone or in pairs or in loose staggering groups. One man, dressed in jeans and a flannel shirt, emerged from Mr. Sam's and walked up the street to Grand Central Station, where there was quite a crowd. The steam of breath and body heat beaded on the plate glass windows. The man went inside.

The moon was cradled in an arc of light that night. That meant a storm was coming.

*   *   *

The inside of Joyce's bar was always dark, even in midafternoon, which was just as well, because the place was pretty shabby. The paint, white once, many years ago, was a sickly yellow and peeling or gone altogether in many spots. Portions of the ceiling showed water stains and were starting to collapse.

It's almost as run down as most of its clients, Watts thought as he sipped at his bourbon.

A friend of his, visiting from England, had commented that American bars were like isolation tanks. People came to get away from life for a while.

According to his friend, English pubs were bright and lively, places for community. Watts didn't know it was true, the part about England, but most bars around here sure were depressing.

He recognized the few other men at the bar. They were too old and tired to cause trouble anymore, but he'd heard stories of their younger days. Smitty was there, known for beating up three cops at once, tossing one of them on top of his own cruiser. The patrolman had landed on his back on one of the lights, cracking a rib. And Will, who used to be the head pressman at the *Dispatch*, a disturber-of-the-peace only on weekends. And there were others. Now they were just barflys, nothing to do all day but nurse their beers.

Watts glanced at his watch as he ordered another. Collins was late. Again. The longer this thing carried on, the less and less Watts could tolerate feeling like a lackey. It was getting so that Collins was almost as much of a pest as Chase, and that was saying something. Watts didn't like being kept waiting, even if it was by a superior in the Family, which he wasn't even sure if Collins was. Besides, the longer he waited here, the more whiskey he would drink, and the worse his ulcers would get. The bartender set the whiskey down with an "On the house, Detective." At least there was one good thing about Joyce's.

Watts's morning had not gone well. This whole operation was beginning to unravel. It was taking longer than Watts expected, and the full moon was only two weeks away. He didn't know if he could sit still through another one. But that was the least of their troubles, and Watts knew it. The operation was beyond him now, and no matter what he thought, it would go on as planned.

One problem was that Carol Braxton. Watts was pretty sure she had figured out a few things she was keeping to herself, and he was positive she didn't trust him anymore. That would make things hard enough when this was over, but it could also have an impact on the operation in progress. But that wasn't the worst of it: The Family's most obvious trouble was Michael Chase. That meddler had some kind of hair up his butt. Watts hadn't been sure until the sonuvabitch had barged right into his office at 9:00 that morning.

Watts had been sitting with his feet up, trying to puzzle out how to best proceed with the investigation so as to keep up a good front while actually stalling for the time Collins had asked for, when Chase charged in, carrying a tape recorder and pulling a notebook out of his coat pocket.

"Okay, Watts, old boy. We've gotta talk." He closed the door behind him.

Watts stared at him. The stones on that guy. "Leave it open. You won't be staying."

Chase closed the door. "Sure, I'll stay. Thanks for inviting me, buddy."

"I'm not your buddy. Now get out."

Chase sat down. "Thing is, buddy, you need to talk to me as bad as I need to talk to you."

"The hell," Watts said, rising from his chair. "Now get out before I throw you out myself."

"Ooh, a threat." Chase sat down. Watts started to walk around the desk to get his hands on Chase. He'd show him it wasn't just a threat. He'd wanted to pitch this. . . this *gnat* out the door for years—

"Let's see," Chase said without moving; he was looking at the ceiling. "Two murders—Anders and Samosky. Both victims female, in their early twenties, college kids, smart, pretty."

Watts stopped moving.

Chase looked at him. "How'm I doing so far?"

Watts clenched his jaws, stared down at Chase.

"We'll consider that a compliment, Detective. Hmmm. . . Both victims slashed horribly, their heads missing. Sexual indications, but no direct evidence, since you people like to pretend that vaginal stabbing is not necessarily sexual in nature. Ritualistic overtones also."

Chase straightened in his chair. "Why don't you have a seat, Watts. So we can discuss this like gentlemen. I'm not really looking for confirmation, just a few answers."

Watts eased back into his chair. His stomach churned. Chase seemed to have a *very good* source. "Where'd you hear this?"

Chase waved his hand dismissively. "Doesn't matter. I just want to know, why all the secrecy?"

"It matters to me. I'm in charge of the investigation."

Chase thought this over for a moment. "Okay. Tell you what. I'm going to go to press with everything I've got unless you give me a good reason not to."

"You don't have any proof!" The words exploded from Watts.

"Sure I do. I talked to the Reverend Samosky on Saturday. Nice fellow. Very forthcoming. Says he and the wife have already been down to ID the body."

Where did he get this stuff? thought Watts. He narrowed his eyes and spoke slowly, more in control now. "So you know there's been another murder. Go ahead, print it, we won't stop you. But if you mention anything in more detail than that, it'll be your behind. It's all hearsay."

Chase laughed. "So what? I don't need proof. I'll just quote an unnamed police source. Then if you want to prove me wrong, you'll have to open up your records in court. Probably something you'd rather avoid. But you answer a few questions for me and I'll keep a few details out of the story so we don't tip off the bad guy or panic the citizenry. Quid pro quo."

Watts leaned forward. "If I answer your questions, you keep the whole thing out of the papers. For at least 10 days."

"No can do. I've gotta get at least a couple of paragraphs on the second victim. Look, it won't make any difference, Watts. Did I do you wrong with the Anders girl? You people are already talking to the victim's associates. How long you think it's gonna be a secret? The students have their own newspaper and radio station. You're better off if you let me feed them the story."

"What do you want to know?"

"Why the secrecy? Is it because of possible connections to the Clawson case? You don't want it to be known that you convicted the wrong man?"

Watts knew he had to step very carefully here. Chase suspected a lot, but Watts didn't think the man really knew anything for sure. But he was smart, and if Watts wasn't careful, he might unintentionally give away more than necessary. He needed time to think this through.

"What time do you go to press, Chase?"

"Midnight."

"Can you meet me someplace? Say around six? Will that give you enough time?"

"Why the delay?"

"I have to check some things on this."

"Okay, then." Chase stood up. "I guess that's how it'll have to be. I'll be at the Omega. But Watts. . . If you're not there by 6:30, I go with what I've got."

He opened the office door. "One more thing. Why did you pull your support on the Clawson thing? You knew as well as I did that he didn't do it."

"Close the door on your way out."

42
Monday afternoon, October 11

Watts finished his second whisky. He looked over his shoulder toward the front door for Collins, turned back and held up his glass to the bartender. "Another." It still bothered him that he'd let Clawson go to prison, but orders were orders. Besides, it wasn't like Clawson was an innocent man. He'd been arrested more than a dozen times in four states since the age of 12. At least six times for sex offenses. Who knew what he'd done that he hadn't been caught at. He deserved every day of his sentence.

What bothered Watts more was that he still didn't know *why* he'd been told to let Clawson take the rap.

Watts watched Collins put his glass down on the table. It seemed like that man always moved slowly, carefully, precisely, like he was overly conscious of every movement. Collins didn't seem too happy to hear about Chase and what he knew, but then he wasn't as upset as Watts expected, either.

"If worse comes to worst," the FBI man said, "we can just let him print whatever he wants to print. This will all be wrapped up in about two weeks anyway. If he prints, we sue—publicly and with great fanfare—and then after we catch the guy—before the case comes to court—we drop the suit."

Maybe Collins did have everything under control after all.

"I should remind you, Agent Collins, that we aren't going to get much fanfare when the same guy owns the newspaper and the biggest radio station. We still gotta see what we can do to stop the leak. We don't want Chase looking too closely at this."

"I'll take care of that. This afternoon."

The two sat in silence for a few moments, Watts draining the last of his fourth whisky, Collins holding his club soda—not drinking it, just holding the glass an inch or so above the table, staring at it and swirling the contents. He might have been a robot, for all the expression on his face. Watts still hadn't gotten used to Collins's blank, thousand-mile stares.

"So is that it then?" Collins said at last. "We finished here?" He stood up, looking toward the door.

Watts spoke hesitantly. "You said. . . Uh, you said *after we catch the guy*. So we already know who's doing this?"

Collins looked down at him and smiled with his mouth only. "Of course we know who's doing this, Detective. The Family does—not the FBI yet. They will soon, after I take care of a few loose ends. We'll take it federal. There is a man here in town who will receive the death penalty, if his case gets to trial.

He might end up getting shot trying to escape."

"Then what are we waiting for?"

"We need to secure the evidence, and he's a very smart and dangerous individual."

"How long?"

"Not sure. A week perhaps. Ten days."

"Then no more girls are going to die?"

"Probably not." As Collins turned to go, he slipped his hand inside his jacket breast pocket. He pulled out a small pill bottle.

"Oh, Detective. Your refill." He tossed the bottle to Watts, who caught it with a little effort, four whiskeys in an hour having slowed him somewhat. When he looked up, Collins was gone.

Watts held the bottle up, tapped the side of it. He was glad to get it; he'd almost run out.

43
Monday afternoon, October 11

When Collins left Joyce's, a slight drizzle had started. Or rather, the drizzle had picked up again: raining for days, now softly, now hard and fast. Not that Collins cared one way or the other; it always seemed to be raining in these mountains.

Despite the rain, he didn't go immediately to the Public Safety Building, even though it was across the street and down a hundred yards. Instead, he cut into the alley that slanted over to High Street. There was rarely any traffic in that alley—except for the occasional truck making a delivery—and there was a narrower slice of pavement that ran off the alley in behind St. Paddy's, a bar that fronted on High Street and on along behind other High Street businesses.

The track was too narrow for anything bigger than a motorcycle, and so had only foot traffic. It was a little trashed up and smelled faintly of urine. Collins had discovered it last time he was in town, and he went there to think sometimes. Only people he'd ever seen back there were Courthouse Square winos, come there to drink a six-pack, and a few solitary young people who walked past with their heads down. Primarily, the latter were wearing black.

Collins leaned against the brick back of St. Paddy's, under the shelter of the eave, his arms folded, his head down, but not so far that he couldn't see someone approaching from either direction. He was getting a little wet, but there were things to consider.

This Michael Chase was looming ever larger as a potential problem. Since last week, when he had started to be an issue, Collins's operatives had been tailing the man, but he hadn't done anything or gone anywhere of any real interest. The disturbing thing was that when Collins's men had gone into Chase's apartment—Thursday last, while he was out walking—they had found that he had a copy of the Anders-Jacoby file. That meant someone was helping him.

There was only one person Collins had any reason to suspect—Carol Braxton—but he was far from sure of it. She just didn't fit the profile. In fact, he had every indication—from Watts, from other people he'd talked to—that Braxton wouldn't feed anything to the media like that, least of all Michael Chase.

There was a missing element here, something or someone. Either Collins already knew what it was, but wasn't taking it into account, or he hadn't yet come across it. The latter was probably the case, since he had all confidence that once given the information, he could process it and find the connections that made it fall into a sensible pattern. He was sure there was something he didn't yet know.

But ultimately, that was all background. The important thing now was to slow Chase down. Frighten him a little. Collins felt The Smile curling the ends of his lips. It shouldn't be hard to do; the man was a journalist. He should scare easily. If Chase were out of the picture, this operation would go exactly as expected. And then, once that was taken care of, Collins could take another night off to enjoy the time he had left in this town. Maybe the night would be as fulfilling as it had been last week.

He started back down the narrow track toward the alley, where he would walk over to the Public Safety Building. He was whistling again, for the first time since last Thursday: "I'm in the Mood for Love."

44
Monday afternoon, October 11

The door to Carol Braxton's office was open most of the time. A little trick she'd picked up at a leadership training course she'd taken many years ago. A small gesture that said to anyone and everyone on the force, 'I'm here. Talk to me if you need to.' It cost her little in the way of privacy, since as long as she didn't look up from her desk when people passed in the hallway, few actually disturbed her.

What privacy she did sacrifice was more than compensated by the way it kept channels of communication open. Like most quasi-military organizations, a police department is rigidly hierarchical, and as in most hierarchical organizations, people tend to tell higher-ups only what they think the higher-ups want to hear. The Achilles heel of rigid structures: garbled and fragmentary communication. Open doors help minimize that.

Carol was looking toward the papers on her desk—sheets from the Anders-Samosky investigation—but she wasn't really seeing them. She was beginning to suspect that the investigation was suffering from a variety of severe communication problems. That could explain several things: The obvious fact that Collins and what-his-name, the FBI medical examiner, were not being up front with her; her sense that there were things going on that she didn't know about; Watts's apparent footdragging—

A sharp rap on her door snapped her train of thought. Agent Collins was standing in her doorway; Carol wondered how long he'd been there.

"Yes?"

"Do you have a moment, Chief Braxton?" He came in, closing the door.

"Come in," she said, waving to a chair. "You're wet."

Usually, she would have expected someone to say something like, "It's raining out" or even just "Yeah," but Collins didn't acknowledge her comment. She smiled. "You have good news of some kind for me, I hope?"

"I'm afraid not. Quite the opposite. We have a leak in the operation."

"I'm aware of that." Did he use the word *operation*?

Collins didn't even blink. "I expected as much. Why wasn't I informed?"

He was one cold customer. It would have been easy to assume that working in the Bureau's Behavioral Science unit—for she was convinced now that was where he was from—would turn anyone that way, but Carol felt there was something more to it than that. There was something. . . *missing* in the man.

Carol didn't take her eyes off his and smiled again, this time not so warmly. "I just learned of it a half hour ago. I got a call. How exactly did you find out?"

"Detective Watts told me. Some reporter harassed him this morning. He seems to know a lot about the investigation. His source is apparently very well placed."

"So it would seem. Tell me, Agent Collins, if Detective Watts learned this morning, and you talked with him after that, why didn't I know before a half hour ago when Michael Chase called me from the newsroom?"

"Didn't you and this. . . *Michael Chase* used to be. . . let's say, *involved?*"

Thrust—parry—riposte. "Please answer my question, Agent Collins."

She let her voice rise just a touch, her smile turn vaguely menacing. The one advantage she had as a woman—sounding like everyone's angry mother.

Agent Collins simply stared, unblinking, as if he had only a dead spot where the memory of his mother should have been. She felt as if she'd just wasted the biggest arrow in her quiver and wondered if he even *had* a mother. Time to shift gears.

"I'm sorry," she said. "I'm just exasperated with our lack of progress. And now we have this leak to deal with. . ." She let the sentence trail off, as if she were at loss for words, held hostage by trouble.

"Why don't you stop trying to con me, Chief Braxton," Collins said quietly. "It only makes me lose respect for you."

Carol sighed and leaned back in her seat, looked at Collins. Her voice level, she said, "You still haven't answered my question."

Collins made people edgy, expectant, mostly by coming across as edgy and expectant all the time himself. Carol couldn't put her finger on it, but it was like he was always *waiting* for something: He sat forward in his chair, or he stood poised on the balls of his feet. His eyes watched constantly. He spoke softly, making people lean forward to hear.

"It's not my job to—"

"I'm the case officer on this one, not Watts."

"True. But it was Watts's place to inform you. You'd have to ask him why he didn't. I'm telling you now."

Carol sighed. It wasn't an explanation, but it would have to do for now. "Okay, Collins. What is it you want?"

"You were involved with Michael Chase."

"Yes, but that was over two years ago. I haven't even spoken to him—"

"Except for a few weeks ago. When you introduced us."

"Except for that. I haven't spoken to him for over six months. Until today."

"Why only six months?"

Carol realized that Collins was not used to small towns. "You have to go out of your way to avoid anyone for longer than that around here."

Collins leaned back and steepled his fingers. He said nothing. Carol watched his face go absolutely blank for nearly thirty seconds—a long time if you're waiting for something to happen. He finally spoke.

"Maybe it's time that you spoke with him again. We need to put a temporary muzzle on the press around here."

Carol had no qualms about restraining the media. Free press was fine, in theory, but there were times when free press was potentially dangerous. It was the clash between the public's need to know and law enforcement's need to keep secret.

"Why all the secrecy, Agent Collins?"

Collins leaned forward; for the first time, he actually seemed eager. "Chief Braxton—"

"Look, if we're going to get through this, let's at least be on a first-name basis. Call me Carol." *I still have a few tricks left,* she thought. *And I still don't trust you.* "Go ahead." She leaned forward, too.

"Okay. . . Carol. You have no doubt been wondering what brought the FBI in on this so quickly. When you first reported the Anders girl's death to us—"

"Which is voluntary—"

"Yes, but SOP now over most of the country. When you sent in your report, our computer kicked it out. It matched a certain profile almost exactly. Something we've been watching for." He narrowed his eyes—which Carol noticed were looking inward—exactly as if he were watching for something. He continued.

"Do you remember what happened up at the University of Vermont in Burlington about ten years ago?"

It took him more than fifteen minutes, but when Collins was finished, and he'd left, Carol was convinced that she had to get Chase to spike his story. For the time being at least. This was bigger than she'd suspected, but at least now she knew what was going on. Mostly. There were still problems. Someone was talking to Chase, for instance, and Carol would lay odds it was Detective Watts.

45
Monday evening, October 11

Chase's attention snapped back to the Omega. He'd been lost in thought when he'd heard someone say his name. He casually turned on his barstool to look around the restaurant, scanning to see who might have spoken. Nothing. Probably he was just getting tired of waiting for Watts. Even though it was only 6:15, Chase had been here since 5:00, and he wasn't just sipping his beer. He was on his fourth.

He didn't feel bad about being there, as wet and nasty as it was outside. The sprinkle this afternoon had turned back to a downpour, like it had been much of the day before. The only thing to do was stay inside.

The last few days had been very good to him. He'd managed to get the murder story—although if Waters ever found out, that was probably the end of his job. He had determined that Watts was answering to a higher-up—the man gave new meaning to the word 'transparent'—who was either Carol or Collins. Probably Collins. And this afternoon he'd gone ahead and written the story; if Watts didn't show, he could send it over to the office in time for tomorrow's edition. He'd written the story 'modular fashion', so if he needed to remove certain parts, he could do so without weakening the integrity of the article. He'd use those bits later, that was sure. If Watts did show, he'd have the inside track for an exclusive down the line, when they caught the guy.

A good day indeed.

He heard the restaurant door open and turned to see Carol Braxton come through. She was smartly dressed, as if she'd just come from work. She shook off her umbrella and waved at Chase, made her way between tables over to the bar. She set her handbag on the bar. He thought she hated purses.

She pulled up a stool. "Heard you were here, Mr. C."

"Since when did you start carrying a purse?" Chase asked as she settled beside him.

"Aren't you gonna offer me a beer? You're forgetting your manners."

"I don't have manners." He took a drink of his beer. "When did you start carrying a purse?"

"You've been here a while, I gather." She caught Cory's eye and motioned him over.

"I've been somewhere," Chase said, then realized he sounded sulky. *Hope she didn't notice.* "Where's Watts?"

"Cheer up, jack. I'm his sub."

Before Chase could say anything, Cory was there and Carol was ordering a beer.

"On me, Cory," he said.

Chase hadn't seen Carol in months—except for that brief encounter on the steps of the Safety Building—and he hadn't really sat down with her for over a year. They were both silent while she waited for Cory to deliver her beer.

After it arrived, after she'd taken her first drink, he turned toward her. "What gives?"

She didn't say anything right away, and Chase felt some relief at that. Carol was trying to sound light, breezy. She'd never been good at that, even in her best moments. Something was bothering her. He tapped a fresh cigarette on the bar.

"You still smoke."

Chase stared at her as he lifted the cigarette to his lips. Lit it. Inhaled.

"That stuff'll kill you."

She was baiting him. Great. He was waiting for information, between police and reporter—a 'yes' or a 'no' at least—and she was playing games because things were still awkward between them. He was resigning himself to a very long non-conversation before she got around to talking about what she'd come to say.

"How 'bout them Pirates, huh?" Chase didn't know a thing about the Pirates, and Carol was well aware of that.

"They were out of it in July," she said.

46
Monday evening, October 11

Devon pulls the throw rug aside, revealing the pentagram underneath. He stands at its boundary, cards and reeds in hand. He is naked. He wants to build maximum redundancy into this reading; there is no room for error at this stage.

He wishes—not for the first time—that the various methods he employs were more precise, less dependent on interpretation. They have never failed him, but he has more than once failed them. The more he is affected by the situation, the less clearly he can see its outcome. Of course, that makes the tools least useful when they are most important. . .

He draws a deep breath; it is important not to doubt.

It is twilight outside and still raining. A little before seven o'clock now, it has been a long afternoon. Things are rapidly coming to a head. Today, this morning, nothing goes right. He misses every green light on the way to work and is forced to wait. He cannot parallel park where he usually does because someone has parked too far back, taking a third of his space. He gets held up by a girl who drops her papers just inside the rotating door at the entrance. Danger is everywhere. He must take care now, or the enemy would overtake him.

He steps into the circle, crossing himself as he does, whispering, "Ator, malkuth, ve-gevurah, ve-gedulah" at the appropriate points. He knows every motion, every ritual obeyed, is done for subjective reasons. But that is all there really is, is it not? Subjectivity. God is in the details. God *is* the details.

He decides to do the cards. It feels right. The Celtic Cross layout, choosing the King of Swords to signify himself for this reading. As he lays the cards, the Heirophant crosses him; the meaning of that one is obvious enough. He continues. The final card, the one at the top of the Staff of Wisdom, is the Page of Pentacles. The bearer of news. Wise news. It is time to communicate.

But how? What? To whom? he thinks as soon as he sees it.

Stop! There will be time to consider later. First, silence the thoughts, the questions. Finish the readings.

47

Monday evening, October 11

"Chase, you remember what happened at the University of Vermont ten years ago?"

"Can't say that I do." Chase was getting tired of humoring Carol's mood. He hadn't liked it when they were going out, he didn't like it now. They'd talked about the Morgan piece that he'd pawned off on Dumont, but that he was still responsible for and believed he'd still have to write. They'd gossiped about local notables, talked about city politics and about upcoming elections and about the way teens were wearing pacifiers around their necks as a fashion statement, blah, blah, blah. Almost an hour, and Carol'd had two beers in that time—which was a lot for her—and he still hadn't found out what he had come there to learn.

When Carol had leaned forward abruptly, cutting off the gossip, Chase was caught by surprise.

"Don't you remember the M.A.S.K. Protests? What started them?"

He lit a cigarette. "Oh, yeah," he said, almost to himself. He wasn't sure he did remember them. "I knew there was something I was forgetting. You think it's the same guy?"

"A copycat thing, more likely."

Then it came back to him: five women murdered in Vermont—killed and decapitated ritualistically. The perpetrator had never been caught.

"That's the secrecy? *That's* why you don't want any details to be published? You're afraid the news would spark off another series of M.A.S.K. Demonstrations." He shook his head and stared into his beer. "That's really lame."

"Not just that, but that would be bad enough."

"Wouldn't happen. Not the kind of thing locals get all worked up about, and as for the university population, this is WVU, not the University of Vermont. Oh, *please.* Look around—" He gestured to the mostly student crowd at the Omega. "These kids couldn't care less about that stuff. And these are the *intellectuals.* These are the ones who think of themselves as activists."

"Hear me out, Chase. You remember M.A.S.K. started off as a protest by women against violence against women. At first only a few hundred protesters, but more unsolved murders meant more and more people. Mobilize Against Sadistic Killers, remember?"

"Vaguely."

She lifted her beer and continued. "The mask was a symbol of women's degradation. . . . the anonymity of being a woman in this society. It was also meant to call to mind the executioner's hood, an implicit threat to fight back. But it was *also* supposed to remind people of the ritual nature of the deaths."

"And that the victims were headless. Anonymous."

"The murderer was a self-styled Satanist. That's what the FBI thought at the time, and that's what they still think. The last thing—"

"Clawson was no Satanist; what makes you think the new one is? In fact, what makes you think this *is* a new one? Satanism's just a bunch of hooey. Kids digging up graves and skinning black cats. Or crazy people imagining that they *are* Satan. One way or the other, it's nonsense."

"Fine, Chase. That's what you think, and that's what I think. But in the last two decades there's been a resurgence in hard-shell Baptist movement— especially in West Virginia—and that's *not* what they think. The feds believe things could get ugly. Apart from the killings themselves. And I agree, to a point. The last thing we need is a bunch of wackos agitating about everything from Satanic rock music to the evil books their kids are forced to read in school."

Chase leaned forward, his forearms resting on the table. "Chief Braxton, that's exactly the kind of dismissive attitude that gets them 'worked up.'" Chase made air quotes as he spoke the phrase. "They're serious people, Carol. You should take them seriously."

"Don't lecture me. I do take them seriously."

Chase chuckled. "You do not." He shook his head. "I don't know about violence, though."

"I'm not totally convinced, either. But I'm not alone on this one."

Chase considered. "Is Collins his real name?"

Carol shrugged. "As far as I know."

As they paused, Chase took another drink of beer. He was sure Carol was telling the truth—even the whole truth—as far as she knew it. And if it *was* the whole truth, there were good reasons to omit some facts from publication. Still, he suspected it was not the whole truth. Something was funny. He didn't trust feds, on principle, but that really wasn't germane. Was it?

"I hope you're watching your back on this one, Carol."

She sighed. When Carol had a couple of drinks, she was even easier to read. He could see it was bothering her, too, but she also didn't want him kibitzing on this one.

She covered his hand with hers. "I'm fine, Chase. It's you I'm worried about."

"Don't worry about me; I can take care of—"

She closed her hand, bending his first knuckles forward so sharply that he couldn't take his hand away. "Not your safety, schmuck. I'm worried that you're going to print something that'll screw everything up." Chase's pain was intense.

"Okay, okay! Le'go! I'll just print the stuff about another murder. I won't even say where the body was found. I'll hold off for a week on the rest of it."

"Ten days." She smiled at him and squeezed harder.

"Ten days! Ten days! Don't cripple me! I type with this hand!"

She let his hand go, and he rubbed it with the other. They met eyes, both of them smiling. "You're a hard case," he said. "You know that."

She smiled even wider. "That's why you like me."

48
Monday evening, October 11

Carol nodded curtly as she walked past Randi, who was working the evening shift. Carol knew that Randi—competent but none too bright—had been hired by the previous chief because she was thin and had an impressive figure. She'd once overheard two patrolmen joking about her. The memory made Carol queasy.

She took her keys out as she walked, wanting to duck into her office, gather up a few things, and get out, get away from there for the day.

It'd been some day; nearly 8:30 and it was not over yet. First sparring with Collins, then practically duking it out with Chase. He knew just how to get to her. She resented him for what he knew about her, for what he knew about this case, and she resented Collins for putting her through having to talk to Chase.

She opened the door, flipped on the light, and walked around her desk. She opened the top drawer: the Anders-Samosky file. If Watts wanted it, he'd have to come to her to get it. Still standing, she flipped it open, past the contents page, to the page that listed similarities in the two MOs. She stared at the paper blankly, not reading, not comprehending. She already knew exactly what was printed there and didn't need to see it again.

What *was* she doing here at this hour?

While talking to Chase, Carol had figured a way to trap Watts. She was certain he was the source of the leak. She'd mention the kris to Watts, something that was not in the files, and then see if it turned up in anything Chase said. If it did, she'd have Watts. He could forget pension, retirement, benefits. She'd be darned before she'd have officers breaking ranks.

Suddenly, she sank down into her chair. This was no way to run a department. Suspicion, distrust. No way to build morale, that was sure. Should she really be setting traps for her senior officers? But there was still the leak.

Carol heard a soft scratching noise on her door. Three scratches. Outside. From the hallway. She froze.

Again. Three scratches. On her door. *Scrikkkk—scrikkkk—scrikkkk.* She sat up straight, quietly opening the right-hand drawer for her gun. Her fingers closed over the handle. She pushed her chair back quietly and started to rise.

An envelope slid under the door.

Barely hesitating, ignoring the envelope, Carol leapt around her desk, gun in hand and flung the door open, then pressed her back against the door jam. She looked up and down the hall.

Nothing. No one. There was no sound, which was normal for this time of night.

She stepped into the hall, careful to keep her legs braced wide, ready to move in any direction, her head jerking back and forth, scanning it all.

But there was nothing to see. There were only two directions in a hallway. She thought she heard a scraping sound above her and fell against the wall, bracing her back, her gun pointed up, her eyes to the ceiling. She saw nothing, but *Did I see one of the ceiling tiles settle into place?*

Not likely. She waited. And heard nothing. She glanced at the envelope, which was lying just inside her office.

Stashing her gun in her shoulder-holster, she strode down the hallway towards the main lobby. She checked other doors as she went—all locked.

She slapped her hands on the counter. "Randi!" The poor girl looked sharply up from her magazine, startled half to death. "Has anybody been here in the last thirty minutes?"

She had no sooner said the words than she realized she should have tried to sound as casual as possible. Her voice sounded weak. She hoped Randi wouldn't notice.

"No one's come in since I came on. Except you." Randi looked scared.

Carol patted the counter lightly with both hands. "Okay. Yeah. I'm sorry. I didn't mean to startle you. Ummm. . . But I'm expecting someone. It's very important that I talk to him if he comes in." She tapped the counter, hoping she didn't seem too nervous. "Let me know, will you?"

"Sure. Sure, Chief Braxton." Carol noticed that the pages of Randi's magazine were jiggling slightly; the girl's hands were trembling.

"I'll be down the hall." Carol walked away, back to her office. She felt bad about having startled the girl.

When she got back to her office, she stepped over the envelope and went straight to her desk. In the top right drawer she kept several packages of latex free evidence gloves. She tore one package open and was pulling out a glove as she crossed back to her door. To the envelope.

She picked it up with her gloved hand. Her fingers caressed its ruffled gray ridges. Good paper, business-type paper. Using the glove she wasn't wearing to shiled the envelope against her fingerprints, she fingered open the unsealed envelope with her gloved hand. She took out the letter. The same fine paper, expensive. She read it as she closed the door to her office and walked across the room to her chair behind her desk. Her hands were shaking slightly.

There was no greeting, no signature at the bottom. Just words:

I call your attention to Lot's wife. She did not listen to authority.

She looked into hell's mouth. She was a courageous and admirable woman. Still, things did not turn out well. I fear it will be that way with you. She did not understand what she was up against.

Listen: This has happened before, many times.

Look: It is possible that Jack in Behavioral Sciences does not even know Collins is in your town. Find out. Do not trust Collins. Ask for another agent.

Keep your eye on Watts, too.

Last: You are not looking for one man only. These murders involve many people, none of whom live in this town, although it may appear otherwise.

Be very careful. Trust no one.

Now, what was that supposed to mean? The Biblical allusion was a rough fit with the ritualistic overtones of the murders. The letter could have been from someone who had guessed that these murders were similar to the ones up in Vermont ten years ago. But how would they know about Collins?

Something didn't fit.

And station security apparently sucked.

Carol scooped up the Anders-Samosky file and left the office, wondering if the case would end with her turned into a pillar of salt.

49
Thursday afternoon, October 14

The back of Chase's hand landed on the newspaper with a sharp *smack*. He paused on the walkway, savoring the front page of the *Dispatch*. It had taken two days, but Waters had run it. Below the fold, it was true, but at least his words were not in the *Metro* or *Lifestyle* sections. A three-paragraph story, only discussing the body found, who found it, how, without detailing anything. Just as he had promised Carol he'd do. He'd passed the abbreviated version along to Jacobs at AP, with hints there was more to come. The *Dispatch* had published his version—under the byline of Edward Dumont—rather than the AP rewrite.

Ahhh, satisfaction.

Chase swatted the paper with the back of his hand again and looked around at the students hustling along the sidewalks, looking nervous and pressed for time; at the big, arched, intentionally intimidating doors of Wise Library. What a name. It reminded him how infinitely glad he was not to be in college. He had little patience for undeserved pomposity and rigid hoops that only existed for jumping through. As far as he could see, the only sight that redeemed the landscape of a university was young women. The rain had finally quit, at least for a while, and it was too warm today for coats and other nuisances. The best time to visit a campus.

Chase had arrived in the vicinity of the main campus library about one o'clock. The sky was high and white, characteristic of certain days in late fall in West Virginia. He had done what he could using Google and some deep web searches; it was time to get the advice of a human being. He finished his cigarette and ducked in through the main doors.

The woman at the front desk was courteous, but not much more. She sent him to the Reference Room. *I could have figured that one out,* he thought. He'd hoped that she would be able to send him directly to someone who could help him. Maybe someone who knew a little bit about Satanism, the M.A.S.K. Protests, or the hard-shell Baptist revival—someone who could have guided his blind research. No go.

The man in the Reference Room was a little more collinsative. Chase explained he was doing an article on Satanism and didn't have time to start his research from scratch.

"Your best bet would be Devon, then. He may even be able to give you some direct quotes. He's got a masters in comparative religion." The man frowned, his eyebrows knit together. "Or anthropology. . . I guess I don't know exactly." He laughed nervously, then frowned again, as if concentrating.

This guy makes thinking look like a decathlon event. Chase had long since given up the illusion that librarians were any brighter than anyone else just because they were the priests of the temple, so to speak. He waited for the man to tell him where this Devon was, and he didn't, Chase said, "Hello?"

The man's mind came back from wherever it had been. "What? Oh. Yeah. He's up on the fifth floor. Special Collections."

Chase had never been in Special Collections, which was odd considering the number of times he'd researched stories. The background for his stories usually came out of periodicals, and the stories themselves usually grew from phone interviews.

The Special Collections room was not what he had expected. The air was cooler and felt drier than in the hallway. To help preserve whatever printed matter the collection had, he guessed. The light was fluorescent, but indirect, running in tracks near the ceiling and floor all the way around the room.

The area was small, with space for only three bare 4'x8' tables. A largish spruce desk at one end, with a stuffed chair behind it and one in front. A narrow bookcase ran floor-to-ceiling at that end of the room, and on each side of it there were doorways opening into dimly lit corridors. The rest of the walls were as bare as the tables. No windows. No pictures.

The place struck Chase as a mausoleum. *It is. A book mausoleum.*

"May I help you, sir?"

Chase jerked; he hadn't seen the man come in. Where *had* he come from? Chase had been looking in the direction of the desk, looking to see if there was a bell he should ring or something, and then suddenly the man was just there, standing behind the desk, as if he'd been there all along.

"Sorry," Chase said as he walked toward the desk. *Why am I apologizing?* "Maybe you can. I'm looking for a guy named Devon?"

"Are you not Michael Chase?" The man's voice had a strange, slithery quality. But familiar. Somehow. Chase was sure he'd never spoken with the man.

"Yes, I am." Chase stopped in front of the desk. "Guess you recognize me from the paper. My picture was in there recently; I did a story on kids making fake IDs."

"No."

The single word seemed to echo in Chase's head.

Chase had never seen anyone stand in quite that way: at ease, immobile and alert, waiting. His eyes weren't moving and didn't appear to be fixed on anything. Chase was reminded of the Navy Seals he'd once interviewed for an AP story, when he worked in Seattle. The Seals are the Navy's best warriors.

They stood like that.

A fist-sized solid glass globe with swirls of embedded color sat on the desk, and the man's hand rested on it. *Engulfed* would be a better word. The hand was huge, and the forearm that had sprouted it was gnarled and hard. His forearms reminded Chase of the manzanita trees on the west coast, the way their branches twisted and turned back on themselves, one side of every branch all rough bark and the other a hardness as slick as marble. He wore a white button-down over broad shoulders.

Why was the man so familiar?

"Devon Lancaster." The man was coming around the desk, holding his hand out. The movement startled Chase because it didn't seem to have any prelude—first he wasn't moving, then he was, suddenly, purposefully—Chase had an impulse to flee.

Instead, he let the hand take his. Engulf it. "What can I do for you, Mr. Chase?"

Chase had the impression that Lancaster was trying to be friendly, ac-commodating, but the aura of menace had not entirely disappeared. It wasn't even well disguised. The voice was still a whisper.

"Yes, well. . . umm. . . I'm doing some background work for something that I hope to turn into an article." He tried a wry smile; it felt more like a gri-mace. "If my editor will let me."

Devon's hand still encased Chase's, his dark eyes studying Chase's face. "Did you not work these details out beforehand, Mr. Chase?"

"Well, yeah, generally." He wished Devon would let go of his hand. He tried another smile and shrugged. "But sometimes you play a hunch."

Devon released him. "A hunch brought you here, then."

Suddenly, again without Chase being ready for it, Lancaster was walking back around the desk. Chase noticed that he had short legs, with a long upper body and those long arms. Why hadn't he seen that before? He thought of spi-ders again. *Like that song,* he thought. *"Spiderman is having me/for dinner/tonight."*

He tried to maintain the thread of conversation. "Umm. . . You could say that, Mr. Lancaster. I need to get up some information for an article proposal. They told me down in Reference that you might be able to help." *There it is again, that feeling of familiarity,* Chase thought as Devon settled into the chair on his side of the desk.

He held out his hand over the desk, palm up, indicating that Chase should have a seat. "What does the article concern?"

Chase had a sense that Lancaster already knew. "I'd like to do something on Satanism. Hasn't been much coverage of it lately."

Devon raised his eyebrows, and Chase had the distinct impression that the man was play-acting. No, that wasn't right. Every expression, every movement was *deliberate*. That he was very conscious of his own movements, his own facial expressions. He barely heard Devon's words. "You believe there should be?"

"Our readers do." It was one of Chase's stock responses.

Devon sighed and his lips tightened, as if he were disappointed with something. It seemed to Chase that it was Devon's first spontaneous expression. He didn't speak and Chase waited. He seemed to be considering something. At last: "Is that what you are made of, Mr. Chase? The small scurry of reader interest?"

The man can pack a lot of disdain in a whisper, thought Chase. But he was used to dealing with disdain. Even comfortable with it. Another stock response would cover this one. He let a sharp, chiding edge creep into his words. "If our readers are concerned with it, Mr. Lancaster, then *we* are concerned. You may not realize it, but many people rely on the *Herald-Dispatch* for information about the things that really affect their lives."

It wasn't until it was out that Chase realized what he had just said. It wasn't like him to be this behind himself; this Lancaster character really had him off balance.

Devon was laughing. A large laugh, from the belly, so genuine, so infectious, that it dissolved all trace of dread in the air. Chase felt it in his chest and began to chuckle as well.

"Um. . ." Chase tried, still laughing. "That—uhhh— That didn't come out right."

Devon caught his breath. "Sure it did. You said exactly what you wanted to say. You just did not *mean* it." He picked up the glass globe and began tossing it up and down with his right hand, throwing it a few inches in the air and catching it. He wasn't laughing now. "Tell me, Mr. Chase. How does Satanism affect your readers?"

Chase's snicker caught in his throat. He felt like crawling under the desk to get away from. . . what? This guy was weird. "I guess it really doesn't."

"Sure it does." Devon caught the globe and didn't toss it again. He leaned forward, rested his forearms on the edge of the desk. "It affected at least two of them."

50
Thursday afternoon, October 14

Detective Darnell Watts leaned back in his Lazee-Boy, fingered his drink glass. He liked to think of himself that way: Detective Darnell Watts. It gave him a sense of accomplishment.

He was going to have to go in to work soon, but he was putting it off as long as possible. He was due this half-day, and God knew he needed it. The job was pressure enough normally, but this latest thing. . . Collins got on his nerves. Watts was even drinking again, which was not a good sign. He thought he'd conquered that little problem. His ulcers were acting up, too, no surprise. Good thing the Family supplied him with a better medicine than what Dr. Crane was pushing.

Without moving from his reclined position in the chair, he flicked the remote until he found a program he could tolerate. "Body Beautiful" or something like that. He chuckled. These people pretended they were doing an exercise show, but everyone and his brother knew what they were doing was T & A.

He took a drink of his whiskey as he stared at the screen. *That's the thing. It's all an illusion. The whole world is like that.* Shakespeare had said that, and everyone thought he was so great.

Darnell had enough sense to know that all a man needed was a worthwhile job, to give him a sense of purpose, a willing woman, to give him some sugar every now and then, and an enemy to fight, which was kind of the same as a sense of purpose.

The problem with the modern age is that you can't have a job that you feel good about all the time, and too many women think they're here for something besides strange. He took a drink of his scotch. *Feminazis.*

The "athletes" on the program were still gyrating away when Watts picked up the newspaper he'd brought in earlier. He'd always had the feeling when he took weekdays off that something terrible would happen. But he knew that wasn't likely to happen with this case. This wasn't something the Family could take a chance on. The illusion had to be perfect.

Watts knew how perfect the Family's illusions could be. He knew better than anyone. Ever since he'd found out how that first ritual had been faked, he'd vowed never to take any of them seriously again. It was only now, thirty years later, that he'd begun to suspect how much he had missed.

The first thing, they'd thrown a hood over him. He was naked and when the hood was thrown, he was trembling. He was scared. They'd said, "Once you are one with us, you are one of us for life. There is no turning back. You will bear our mark throughout eternity." That part didn't get to him. He knew some guys it did, though. But talk like that usually made him roll his eyes.

Still, Watts had shivered when he felt the hand on his genitals. He didn't cry out like a girl; his grandfather wouldn't have liked that.

"Are you, Darnell Lancaster Watts, supplicant and neophyte, standing before us with your eyes open but shrouded in darkness, aware of the present and in awe of the future, ready and willing to receive your Calling Mark?"

He had memorized the words. "Yes, I, Darnell Lancaster Watts, supplicant and neophyte, standing before you with my eyes open but shrouded in darkness, aware of the present and in awe of the future, am ready and willing to receive the Calling Mark." He could feel the heat of the iron next to his flesh. He held his face impassive, even though no one could see it.

"Darnell Lancaster Watts, you are one of us. . . NOW!"

He gasped and his knees buckled; the red-hot brand dug into his most tender flesh. It burned so! He gagged back the reflex as he smelled burning meat, burning flesh, his flesh. His head swam.

Later, he was proud of himself because he had managed not to pass out.

He slept a long night and avoided looking at his genitals.

That morning, there had been no brand on his penis, just a small red mark, almost a stain, right where he had felt the brand.

He found out the secret when he reached the next level in the organization: He had been branded with 'hot ice'; the smell of burning meat came from a beef filet and a well directed Bunsen burner.

He picked up the newspaper that sat on the small table to the right of the overstuffed recliner. He snapped it open. He scanned the whole page, ready to move beyond it, but— There it was, *Second Victim Found*. He skimmed the article: no definites, only generalities. The byline was Dumont's, but the story was obviously Chase's. Chief Braxton had managed to minimize the damage, but for how long?

Not good. The feces was going to hit the fan now.

51
Thursday afternoon, October 14

Chase held his breath and didn't say anything. Neither he nor Devon moved.

"You are here about the murders."

"No, I'm—"

Devon dropped the glass globe with a *crack* to the desktop. Chase jerked in his seat, startled. Devon stood up suddenly. It was the third time the man had drastically changed his position without first telegraphing it. That's what it was: Usually when people sat or stood or walked away, they gave some indication with their bodies before they actually began to move. Maybe they tilted their heads, or they unconsciously led with their hands, or they took a deep breath. Devon did none of those things. He simply. . . moved.

Devon was pacing back and forth behind the desk, slowly, his head bowed, his right hand holding his left wrist behind his back.

"You do not give much credence to the topic, do you Mr. Chase?" Devon had stopped pacing.

"The murders?"

"Satanism."

"Let's just say I've heard the questions too often. 'Is your teenager moody, depressed? Is he uncommunicative? Does he wear black? If so, he may be killing neighborhood blonde children in his spare time.'"

"You should not be glib." A ghost of a smile passed over Devon's face. "It is not all so frivolous."

"Good. Fine," Chase said, his little ramble having loosened him up. "Tell me why not. Help me out on this."

After a moment, during which Devon stared hard at him: "Okay, Mr. Chase." Devon sat down again. He opened the top center drawer of his desk and took out a small notebook. He lifted a pen from his shirt pocket and scribbled on the paper. Tore it out of the notebook. Held it up for Chase.

Chase took it and looked at the three titles and their LC numbers.

"You will find them in the stacks on the eighth floor. Get back to me after you've read them."

Chase folded the sheet once and tucked it in his shirt pocket. "Thanks."

Devon nodded. "Also, you should look into the Burlington incident."

52
Thursday afternoon, October 14

The sky was high and clear and the sun shone down with its autumn white light: the eye of the storm. The shadows cast by the autumn sun were thin, insubstantial. A haze in the air, a humidity that no one feels because the air is not hot enough, humidity that is a thickness, beneath awareness, preventing visible shadows.

On the campus below, students and faculty and staff walked in their summer clothes. Many smiled, enjoying the sun, the relief from the rains. It might be the last sunny day before the snows came.

Cars traveled slowly through campus, past Woodburn Circle, past the student union, past Wise Library, stopping every so often—very often—to allow people to cross in front of them. A great number of pedestrians crossed the road in that part of campus, especially on the hour and the half-hour, between classes.

One particular car, a white Nissan, passed in front of Wise Library several times. Again and again for the last couple of hours, since about noon. The driver would look left, toward the library, every time he passed, his eyes narrowed as if watching for something. He scanned the long, sloping lawn that stretched from the library down to the road.

On the passenger seat beside him was a 9 mm Glock semi-automatic. It was loaded.

53
Thursday afternoon, October 14

Chase leaned against the brick wall outside the library and enjoyed a long drag on his cigarette. He'd been in the library for nearly five hours, most of the time lost in the stacks. Online research was *much* easier, and Chase hated spending so much time in the library. The leaden scents of old leather and dust and decomposing paper had filled his morning and spilled into his early afternoon. Some people considered those smells romantic, calling them *rich* and *earthy* and *musty*.

They may think that's romantic, Chase thought. *But it smells like dead things.* He hadn't even missed the cigarettes.

As much as he disliked libraries, Chase had long ago come to the conclusion that they had documents and information that he couldn't get online. But even in the library, he couldn't find what he was looking for, nothing that could document the hard-shell Baptist revival Carol had talked about. Nothing. In fact, just like the online sources he'd seen, several library sources had noted exactly the opposite, pointing out the declining influence of religious organizations. There did seem to be more people who professed to be 'born-again', but they were a scattered and unorganized bunch. One source had noted that, so far, the only issues they'd been able to organize around were abortion and gay marriage. No mention of interest in Satanism.

He breathed in another hit of his cigarette and looked around. It was still a sunny and warmish fall day. The female students still had on shorts and thin dresses, and their hair still scattered in the occasional gust of wind. At least there was that. It wouldn't be long before the sweaters and coats came out for the next few months. Campus would become that much less inviting.

He took another drag, and with his cigarette almost gone, he thought about Devon Lancaster. It had been an unnerving encounter. In the canvas bag that sat on the grass next to him he had the three books that Lancaster had recommended: *Satanism in America, The Twenty-First Century Evil,* and *The Satanic Bible.* The books weren't what Chase kept coming back to, though. It was the encounter.

He flicked the cigarette away, into the grass that stretched down the gentle hill to University Avenue. He looked at the traffic, thirty yards away, which was inching along as usual, slowed to a turtle's pace by the flocks of students who crossed the road between classes, choosing their crossing places at random. The city was going to have to do something about that. He pulled his cigarette pack out of his shirt pocket, tapped out another one. Two in five hours wasn't so bad.

There was that sense of danger with Lancaster. Chase'd experienced it before, besides when he interviewed the Seals. He'd spoken with that guy in solitary in Seattle, the one who had killed his family and the babysitter with a screwdriver. Chase had been there at the murder scene, and he would never forget his first glimpse of the wife's twisted body, her contorted face, the handle of the screwdriver poking through the hair on the side of her head. That killer had the same aura of menace around him that the Seals carried, but unlike theirs, his was uncontrolled.

Lancaster's felt like controlled menace. That he knew something about the current murders was clear. What was it he had said in reference to Satanism and its effect on *Dispatch* readers? "It affected at least two of them."

There was something else nagging about the encounter. It had to do with familiarity. That sense that Chase knew him, had seen him before. But he was sure he'd never laid eyes on the man. What was it?

Everything Lancaster said, everything he did—especially at first—seemed to remind Chase of something else, made him conjure images, imaginings. Chase was staggered by the weight of related experience. Time had seemed to stop.

He turned his head to the side, eyes downcast, and felt somehow ashamed, like Devon had abused him. The more he thought about it, the more he realized that the librarian had manipulated him from start to finish. He stared at the patterns of the bricks of the wall. *Like a rat/in a maze*, he thought, remembering the Simon and Garfunkel song, *The path before me lies/And the pattern never alters/Until the rat dies.*

He cast the cigarette away, even though it was only half done.

Suddenly, the brick wall exploded. It happened in the same stop-time he had experienced with Devon. A crater a few inches wide and an inch deep appeared, spraying small fragments of brick. A sting on Chase's cheek, blood started.

And then again: a percussive *pumpf!* and another niche appeared in the wall, this time within a foot of his head. He looked around wildly, unable to move with any speed. No one had seemed to notice. What was happening! He saw a woman under a nearby tree turn a page in a book she was reading. She moved in a slow-motion dream. Another student, her skirt fluttering up then down slowly as she walked along the path toward University Avenue.

Again: *PUMPF!* the bricks exploded, this time the crater less than six inches from his head. A piece of brick shocked his forehead; he could feel it draw blood and he knew—

He was being shot at. He caught a glimpse of a white car—was it the same Nissan he'd seen the other night?—on University Avenue that had stopped traffic, its driver holding something long and thin and black out the window, and the next thing he knew, he was tumbling down the hill *toward the car*, thinking, *This is crazy!* and seeing a chunk of sod tear up and fly away and knowing another bullet had hit.

He piled against the woman who was reading next to the tree—rolled over her. Before she had seen him coming, he was tumbling into her, rolling up against the tree, yelling, "Down! Down! Lay flat!"

The woman immediately sat up.

A bullet tore up the turf by her thigh. Chase looked up: She looked confused, and he knew the bullet must have gone right over his shoulder.

Down on University, the white Nissan was pulling away. Chase saw the window sliding up.

He looked around again, and still no one had seen anything.

He was on his feet without thinking, sprinting after the car. Down the hill to University, then following the traffic flow. He watched the car take the big left turn onto Willey. . . .

Darnit! He smacked the wall that stood on his left side, the border between campus and town. He'd lost them.

He fell back against the wall, breathing heavily. *I've got to quit smoking,* he thought.

Then he took out a cigarette with trembling fingers and lit it.

54
Thursday afternoon, October 14

"But Maria, you must have known what I would say about that," Alex said. She was trying not to treat it too lightly. "You know there's nothing wrong with those feelings."

Maria smiled and looked down, playing with the buttons on her blouse. "Yeah."

Alexandra noted the affect, the word Maria used and she wasn't encouraged. The whole gestalt was of a young person, a teenager. She wasn't sure how to get around that. She decided to stall, try a different angle, see what might come up.

"Maria, are you attracted to older men?"

"I don't know, Dr. Heyden. It seems like it lately." She continued to fiddle with the buttons on her blouse.

It was the use of the address *Dr. Heyden* that bothered Alex the most. Out of hypnosis, Maria usually called her *Alex* or *Alexandra*. For some reason, Maria had retreated into a kind of teenage state—she seemed semi-hypnotized—and it was up to Alex to find out what that was about as quickly as possible.

"What is it that you find attractive, Maria?"

Maria stretched unselfconsciously, raising her arms high above her head and clasping her hands together so her breasts swelled. Alex recognized the gesture.

"They're so sophisticated," Maria said. "They know so much about you." She giggled. "They know everything."

Alex saw an opening there. "Are you attracted to that, Maria? To the power of knowledge that they have?" Alex was sure as she said it that she was leading things back to target.

"Oh, yeah," Maria said. "You got that right." She stretched her hands above her head again.

*   *   *

Maria shook her head, clearing it. She noticed her hands were above her head, and she lowered them. She realized that for the last hour Alex had been talking to her about her. . . urges. Her unseemly, inappropriate urges. And gradually, she'd come around to Alex's point of view, as she'd known she would when she'd decided to bring them up. Even though she'd known what Alex would say, it had helped to hear it from an authority. It had helped a lot.

"You are transferring, Maria," Alex had said. "You know better than I do that most of the problems we've discussed in your therapy are based in your relationship to your grandfather. He dominated you—"

"He smothered me," Maria interrupted.

"And he didn't let you explore anything?" Alex prompted.

"He didn't let me explore anything that should have been normal for a teenager."

Maria sounded petulant, even to herself. Alex let her be quiet for a while after that. Alex was so wise.

"Okay, Doc. I get it. I'm sorry. We've talked about it before. There's a fine line between love and dependence—"

"It's not a fine line, Maria."

"Okay, okay." Maria laughed. "It's a big, fat, thick line." Maria could tell from the brightness she saw on Alex's face when she said that she was saying the right thing. "But we often fall for the same figures that controlled us when we were kids. Right?"

Alex smiled.

Maria spoke with assurance: "Right. I think I get it now, Alex. Thanks."

The two of them smiled at each other, and Maria knew that Alex felt something had been achieved, or broken through, which it had, Maria was also sure, but there was still the problem of the apartment that Maria had rented, and the keys to it that she had mailed somewhere.

Where had she mailed those keys?

55
Thursday afternoon, October 14

Chase finally got back to the newsroom a few minutes before four. He had spent two hours on the lawn of Wise Library, re-creating the events of the crime for Watts and that new kid, Dale Whatshisname. Two uniformeds searched for bullets and found two: one still imbedded in the wall and one at the end of the furrow it had dug in the grass. The other was nowhere to be found. The shells turned out to be 9 mm. Probably. Tests would have to be done. It was also too soon to tell the make of the gun.

When Chase reported the incident, Watts seemed to find it funny, even calling Chase paranoid. That set Chase off. "Get down here, spit-for-brains, so you can see the craters my paranoia blew out of the brick wall in front of Wise."

"Okay, Chase. Relax. We're on our way. Make sure the other witnesses stick around."

"That's *your* job." He slammed the phone down.

Chase did keep the woman there, though. She seemed to be the only other person who had noticed what was going on and that was only because he had rolled into her. She seemed to be taking it well, though: "The police are coming? Cool. I've never been shot at before. This is definitely way cool." She ran her fingers through her hair.

Chase lit another cigarette and looked away. He'd never been shot at either, but he didn't think it was too cool.

"Why do you smoke cigarettes?"

Chase didn't answer.

Chase could tell Watts didn't find it so funny once he'd gotten down there. He and the Dale guy asked the girl—Melina, as it turned out—a few questions, then turned her loose. They asked Chase all the usual questions: No, there wasn't anybody else standing anywhere near him when the shooting started; no, he had no idea who would want to kill him; no, he didn't see the shooter clearly enough to ID him; no, he had never seen Melina before today.

At one point, Deputy Dale spoke up. It came out like he was talking to himself, which he probably was: "He wasn't no good with a gun."

Watts tried to silence him, "Detec—", but Chase cut Watts off.

"How do you figure—uhhh—Dale?"

"How could he miss from the road there? It's only 30, 40 yards."

"Detective Culberson!"

"Just thinking out loud, boss."

"Save it."

145

Watts turned back to Chase. "You got a partial? And he had a sticker on the plate?"

"Orange and white. Virginia, I think." Chase gave Dale the license numbers he'd been able to see.

"We'll check, Mr. Chase," Deputy Dale said. "But it won't do any good. If it was a rental, he probably didn't rent from around here."

Watts stared at his junior officer, who swallowed hard, but didn't say anything more. *That should do it,* Chase thought. *He'll really shut up now.* But he was right, and Chase wished he'd thought of that. That's two obvious points he'd missed. Getting shot at could really screw up your head.

By the time Watts released him, Chase had begun to recover. There *was* someone who might be ticked off enough to take some shots at him—maybe even two someones—although Chase didn't think either of them would be stupid enough to try it. It wouldn't make any sense. There wasn't that much riding on the Anders-Samosky case, was there?

As he drove out to the paper, he tried to think it through, but he found it hard to focus for long enough to really follow a thought to its conclusion. His mind kept drifting off in circles, usually coming to rest on Devon Lancaster. How did he figure into this? There just wasn't enough to go on there.

Surely Watts hadn't shot at him. He wouldn't have had time to get back to the station to take Chase's call. That would be easy enough to check anyway; he'd just ask Elaine. It would be harder to check on Collins, but it was still do-able. Probably.

And if it wasn't one of them, which it almost surely wasn't, that leaves Lancaster, Chase thought. Which was even more ridiculous, on the face of it. Why would he have done it? There was no reason; he seemed to actually want to be helpful. He probably couldn't help it that he scared the bejeezus out of people. That weird birth defect, or whatever it was, that made his arms too long and his legs too short.

But he would have had plenty of time. In the time that Chase had spent in the stacks, Devon could have even driven to Pittsburgh, rented a car, and driven back. No sweat. But the whole idea was silly, and was even less likely if the car was the same one Chase had seen outside his house last week. Best table the notion. For now at least.

The rest of his drive to the paper was made of scattered thoughts, images of brick flying in slow motion, and a cold sweat on his forehead. Blood had crusted there and on his cheek. Had to hit the washroom before he went up to the newsroom to enlist Waters's help. Chase had an idea.

Waters was annoyed at Chase for some reason Chase couldn't put his finger on. He had looked Chase up and down stonily when he came in, and although the grass stains were still on his pants, his cuts were cleaned up. He didn't want to tell Waters why he was at Wise Library.

"What do you want, Chase?"

"Easy, Chief. I just need to ask your advice about something." Chase could feel himself returning to form, which was lucky, because this would be tricky.

Waters put down the edition of the *Dispatch* he was looking at. He didn't say anything.

"Okay, Chief. I've come up with an idea that'll really add something to a story. But I need a computer hacker."

Waters didn't say anything. Chase knew that Waters did that whenever he wanted a reporter to keep talking, to dig their own grave, so to speak. He took the bait anyway.

"See, it's best if you don't officially know anything about this. Plausible deniability, and all that."

Waters still didn't say anything.

"But I figured, though, that we had one on the payroll—more or less— someone you could tell me about without, you know, actually telling me."

"Why would we have a computer hacker on the payroll?"

"I don't know, you know, investigative reasons. The same reason you have that PI on retainer. Stuff like that thing last year with the mayor and what's-her-name."

"Mr. Hare is an insurance investigator. He just does little odds and ends for us."

Chase smiled. "Yeah, Chief. Like that."

"Chase. Even if we had a computer hacker on the payroll—which we don't because hacking is illegal—which story would it help you with? The Bistro review? Or the Morgan piece?"

Jeez, Chase thought. *The Morgan thing.* He'd have to check to see how Dumont was coming with that. "Umm. . . The Morgan thing."

"Speaking of which, Chase, you said you'd have it in this week *without fail.*"

"I know, I know. But I hadn't come up with this other angle then. Trust me. Have I ever let you down before?"

"Last week." Waters glared at Chase. "How is a hacker gonna help you on a piece about a dead person?"

"The researcher's not dead. Besides, like I said, you shouldn't hear about this. Need to know, and all that."

"Humor me."

That's it, Chase thought. There was no way he'd get any help here, not without telling everything. As it was, he'd probably already blown his chance to use the *Dispatch* phone lines—if he could even find a hacker.

"Screw it, Chief. Forget I asked." He turned to go.

"Chase."

When Chase turned back around, Waters was holding up the paper.

"Dumont didn't write this."

More bad news. Chase tried to look confused. "What?"

Waters read from the article: "'According to police department spokesperson Nolan Davis, no second body was found. But the *Herald-Dispatch* has learned that there was a second body located, also within the city limits.' Don't say he did, Chase, because we both know that Dumont can't investigate himself out of an unlocked meat locker."

"An 'unlocked meat locker'?" Chase had never heard that one.

Waters shrugged. "Figure of speech. I have an idea of what you guys have done, and this time—because of the nature of this case—it's none of my business."

Chase started to speak, but Waters cut him off.

"But officially, *officially*, plausible deniability and need to know and all that, the story assignments stay exactly as I made them."

Chase started to speak again.

"Which means, Chase, that your writing might appear with Dumont's byline." He paused for effect. Chase waited for the other shoe. "And more to the point, *his writing appears with your byline."*

Chase was suddenly queasy. He hadn't really thought about that. After a moment, he said, "Okay, Chief. Fair enough. Thanks." He turned to go again.

"And Chase. You might talk to Adams about the hacker business."

Bingo. Of course.

56

Thursday evening, October 14

Chase lifted his glass, held it out to Shango. "Here's to survival, big man."

Shango chuckled. "Yeah. Good enough reason to drink." He clinked glasses with Chase.

They were back in the Omega. The place was not at all crowded that evening, only four tables with diners. No one else sat at the bar, so Chase and Shango had Cory's full attention.

Chase had made a point of searching Shango out: It wasn't easy to track down a man with no fixed address, who had no job and no schedule to conform to or place to check in every day, who knew everyone but had no known associates. Chase had walked through downtown, leaving messages everywhere: "Meet me at the Omega at eight. Urgent."

"I sense skepticism," Chase said.

Shango's eyes went wide. "Moi?"

"Asshat. You've been shot at enough times. It's kinda new to me."

Shango shook his head. "You weren't shot at. Unless there's a jealous husband in your life that you're not talking about—or maybe a blind man was driving that car—whoever shot at you only meant to spook you." Shango laughed. "As if you weren't already enough of a spook."

"Spare me the racism, boy." Chase took another drink. "Deputy Dale said kind of the same thing. Only he got it backasswards."

"Dale Culberson's a yokel. He's just up from Buckhannon. What does Country know?"

"Maybe you're right. You're the chess player. Say someone shot at me, but he didn't mean to hit me. Why, do you figure?"

Shango shrugged. "How should I know? I don't know what you're into."

"It's got to be this thing with the murders. There's nothing—I mean *no-thing*—else going on in my life. Nada."

Shango finished his draft, held his glass up for Cory. He looked at Chase. "Consulting fees."

Chase flipped the back of his hand at Cory. "My tab." He looked at Shango. "Somebody rented that car. And I can't count on the cops in this one."

"Watts?"

Chase nodded. "He didn't ask what I was doing at the library."

Shango raised his eyebrows. "That is strange. They always ask about that kind of thing. What about the Braxton chick?"

Chase stared at the contents of his glass, swirled it. He had considered that, but there was no way. "No. She's good to go."

Shango laughed as Cory set a full glass in front of him. "You sure you're not lust-blind?"

Chase said, "I'm sure," but he wasn't. Not entirely. Sometimes it was hard to tell with these things. "I don't think so."

"What now, then?"

Chase turned on the barstool to face Shango full on. It wasn't much of a plan, but it was all he had. He hoped for the best. "That's where you come in. I need your help with something." When Shango looked skeptical, Chase added, "I'll pay you two hundred bucks for the first two hours' work. Then a hundred bucks a day after that, if necessary." Chase was hoping he could get the paper to cover expenses.

Shango didn't answer, but he tilted his head toward the door of the Omega. Chase looked. Carol was crossing the restaurant floor toward them.

She reached the bar and set her bag down next to Chase. "Thought I'd find you here, Chase."

"Am I that predictable?" Chase noticed that Shango was studying Carol with the same wariness—only more so—that he had for all cops. It was still hard for Chase to think of Carol as the Chief of Police.

"Yes." Carol smiled. She looked at Shango for the first time. She nodded to him. "Mr. Amirdentay."

Chase noticed that her greeting served two purposes: politeness and official notice that she knew exactly who he was. No, three purposes: She didn't approve. Chase knew it wasn't lost on Shango.

"Miss Braxton." Shango bowed his head formally. "Can I buy you a beer?" He motioned for Cory.

"Thank you, sir." Carol pulled a stool over so she could sit between them and a little back from the bar.

This is getting thick, Chase thought. He nodded to Cory so the beer would go on his tab.

"Detective Watts seemed to think the attempt on your life was a real hoot," Carol said.

"He would." Chase and Shango exchanged glances.

"You think it was serious?" Carol asked.

"No. I think I don't want to talk to you about it at all."

Carol got her full glass from Cory. She sipped. "Why not?" She raised her eyes to meet Chase's.

"Because there is no hard-shell Baptist revival in West Virginia. Or anywhere else, for that matter."

Carol looked surprised. "Why do you say that?"

Chase shrugged. "If there is, nobody else's heard about it but you."

Carol looked genuinely confused. "But I—" The words caught in her throat.

Shango stood up and drained his glass with a flourish. "I really do have to go. It's been nice chatting with you, Mr. Chase."

Chase put his hand on Shango's arm. "Wait. Just a second." He fished in his pocket, pulled out a twenty and his keys. He handed them to Shango. "Why don't you get some beer and go back to my place? I still have to talk to you. Full consultant's fees plus expenses, half on acceptance."

Shango looked at Carol, then back at Chase. "Okay. I'll see you when you get there. Miss Braxton." Shango bowed his head again. Chase admired the way that Shango could get sarcastic with a head-bow.

After Shango was gone, Chase turned toward Carol, who had moved to the stool Shango had sat on. "What gives?"

"Can't a lady seek out the companionship of an old friend and business associate?"

"You ain't no lady, lady. What's wrong?"

"Nothing," she said, a little too quickly. "I just needed to get out of the house. I do that once in a while, you know."

Chase waited; she obviously had something on her mind. They both sipped their beers. Eventually:

"Chase, if I talk to you about something, will you promise not to write about it?"

"No."

"Chase, I'm serious."

"I'll tell you what," he said. "I won't quote you, and I won't use anything you say without getting independent substantiation."

Carol studied him over the rim of her glass. "I guess that'll have to do. I need your help. Chase, I can't trust Collins. I don't trust feds, and those Behavioral Science types are creepy."

"So they're creepy. So what?"

"I think he's stalling on the investigation. He's shutting me out. I'm frustrated with the whole thing. Collins won't give me a thing, not even the stuff from Burlington that never got published. I need that research done. Also— here's the kicker—and you have to promise me you won't print any of this."

Chase shrugged. "You'll just have to trust me."

Carol looked at him for a long time. He knew she was looking to see how much of the old feelings were still there. He had been wondering much the same thing lately.

She took a piece of paper that was folded like a business letter out of her purse.

"I gave the original to Collins to send to DC for a better analysis than we could give it here."

She wiped the bar dry with the heel of her right hand and spread the paper out. Chase started reading:

> I do not think you understand. I call your attention to
> Lot's wife. . .

57
Thursday evening, October 14

When Chase finished reading the letter, he asked, "Who do you think wrote this?"

Carol looked at him like he was an idiot. "Whoever killed those girls."

Chase considered. There really wasn't much reason to make that leap of logic. "The author knows something, but I don't think you can say that—"

"Sure you can," Carol said impatiently. Chase noticed her hands were trembling, whether with strain or excitement he couldn't tell. "It's exactly the kind of thing these people do. Notice the grandiose wording. The way it attributes great power and skill to the killer. The Biblical reference. It's all consistent with delusional thinking."

Chase nodded, looking at the letter. It made sense. "So how do I fit into this?"

Carol leaned forward. "You don't have to do anything that you aren't already. Just go on with your investigation. Dig a little. Nothing you hadn't intended to do anyway. But let me know what you come up with."

Chase snorted in disbelief. "Why would I want to let you in on what I come up with? You've already lied to me. . . what? Three times on this case? You extorted a ten-day publication delay—"

"Extorted?" Carol raised her eyebrows.

"You almost broke my knuckles. That's assault. You probably would have if I hadn't agreed."

Carol chuckled. "Yeah, I probably would have."

"Now you want me to turn over my files—"

"Okay, okay. That's not what I'm talking about. In fact, I'll turn over the Anders-Samosky file to you. Tomorrow, if it'll help."

"I already have it."

Carol sighed; her shoulders slumped. "I figured as much."

Something's very wrong in Copville. "Out with it. What else is there? What're you not telling me?"

Carol was looking down at the bartop, her forefinger tracing something in the wet rings left by her beer mug. "Things are not working right with this case," she said without looking up, "but I can't put my finger on why. It's like someone doesn't want us to do this right. It's like the Clawson thing, only there's no Clawson to pin it on."

Chase very carefully didn't say, 'I told you so.' But there didn't seem to be anything else to say, so neither of them said anything. He ran through it in his mind: At least two girls dead, investigation going exactly nowhere, and a

very active force blocking the investigation. And Watts, the acting senior officer, overtly hostile for some reason. Chase had been shot at; and now the Chief
of Police was coming to him for help. The frame of an explanation was forming. . .

"Chase, I can't trust Watts."

Carol's statement hung in empty air. Somewhere behind them a glass fell
off a table and shattered. Chase saw a waiter scurrying towards the table,
heard babbled apologies. He looked at Carol, who was still looking at the bartop. The worst feeling: a commander who couldn't trust her troops. If she
couldn't trust Watts, there was no one—maybe some of the younger cops, or
possibly the women, what few there were—but he knew in this instance most
of the guys would go to Watts, innocently or not, and they would trust a thirty-
year veteran *male* before they trusted their appointed chief.

"Okay, Carol," he said quietly. "What now? Do you deputize me, or
what?"

Carol looked at him. "You watch too much TV."

"What then? What do you want me to do?"

Carol narrowed her eyes. "You've got a conflict of interest here. If we ex-
change information, I've got to know what you're going to publish and what
you're not."

Chase had a brief moment of paranoia. The whole thing could be a setup.
The cops had some reason to suppress publication, and this was the way to
do it. He even thought of how easily Waters had acquiesced to the trade with
Dumont. The whole thing suddenly stank.

But then, ironically, his paranoia came to his rescue. If it did turn out to
be a setup, then it was an agreement made under false pretenses. It was null
and void. He could make the promise and break it in good conscience, if necessary. Either way, he would benefit, even if the *Dispatch* didn't. He could publish the bare bones updates for local interest, and then, if this turned out to be
as spectacular as his instincts suspected, he could sell the whole thing to a national.

"You got it," he said. "I get an exclusive, and I'll clear everything with
you. I'm on your team."

"Great, Chase. It means a lot to me." She smiled at him; it was a smile
that reminded him of old times. She held up two fingers to Cory and touched
her nose. "What next? Which way are you going with this?"

Chase's antennae went up again. He thought of Shango and Adams and
what he had in mind. "You probably don't want to know."

Carol looked at him sharply.

He smiled. "I'll tell you if I find out anything."

Carol cupped one of his hands in hers. "Thanks." It was a gesture that reminded him of the times when they had been closer. And it reminded him again of her trick with his knuckles the last time he had offered to help.

"'Thanks'? That's all I get?" *She's relieved,* he thought. He was wrong.

Carol raised her eyebrows. "Who do you think you are, Chase?"

Good question. I might be drunk, he thought, but he said, "Apparently I'm your knight in shining armor."

Before she could take him too seriously, he added, "How come you and I didn't work out, Carol Braxton? What happened?"

Carol straightened her back and looked at him with feigned shock. She fanned her face with one hand, but she didn't let go of his hand with the other. "Besides the fact that you're a lying, procrastinating, drunken bum with no apparent ambitions or aspirations?"

Then she patted his hand patronizingly.

"Besides that," he said.

58
Thursday night, October 14

Collins eased the needle out of his arm and set his works down carefully on the stand beside his chair. He leaned his head back and looked at the flickering lights of the city through slitted eyes. He could feel the Smile on his face.

He was good for more reasons than the drug, though. That was important to him. He had to feel—as he always has—that he was using the drug rather than vice versa. The drug could never use him; as soon as he suspected that it was, he would quit.

He felt good because things were coming to a close. He would be able to leave with another successful operation under his belt: a serial killer captured for the FBI, a nuisance eliminated for the Family. The job couldn't have been executed more precisely, and Collins was sure that the Old Man would take notice. It was time for him to name a successor, and with this job, Collins was in line. First in line.

He also felt good because he had received an okay on Michael Chase. Collins's operants would do it quick, an in-and-out. No risk to themselves or the Family.

The best thing was that Collins could take another night off now. It had only been a week since Collins's last night off, but he already felt the growing urge for more. He'd managed to avoid going too far, prevented police involvement in the last one. The boy had apparently been feeling too unclean and guilty to complain to the police. Collins counted on that, and it usually worked. His only cost had been the clothes he wore, which had to be destroyed, lest the boy complained.

He'd try the same method tonight; maybe this time he would find a girl to take home. Girls were even less likely to complain.

59
Monday morning, October 18

Chase paused in the corridor before opening the door to the Special Collections room. He took a deep breath. *Why does this guy make me so nervous?* There was really no reason for it. He could understand the way he'd felt after the last encounter, and the way his feelings of dread had been magnified by the attempt on his life, but the feelings really seemed silly now, distant and dream-like.

The books Devon had recommended were a bunch of crap. The worst one was LeVay, the self-styled head of the Satanist Church. Either the man was dumb as a fencepost, or he thought his followers were.

"Welcome back, Mr. Chase," came the half-whisper from behind him.

Chase started, his eyes widened, but he managed to control the reaction before he turned to face Devon Lancaster.

Devon stepped past him. "I take it you have finished the books," he said as he unlocked the door to the Special Collections room. He stepped inside. Chase followed him, with the distinct sense of following a spider into the lair. He mentally shook himself, trying to throw off the melodrama.

Devon threw on the overheads and glided toward his desk. Once again, Chase noted the controlled ease with which the oddly shaped man moved. Uncanny.

As an antidote, Chase tried to concentrate on how stupid the books were. When Devon had gotten behind his desk, Chase said, "Yeah, I'm finished with the books." He stepped farther into the room. "How come you wanted me to read books that you knew were BS?"

Devon settled into his chair; he held out a palm for Chase to sit as well.

Chase moved to within a few feet of the desk. "I'll stand, thanks."

Devon shrugged. "So you think they are nonsense?" He put his elbows on the table and clasped his hands.

"Nonsense. Crap. Whatever." Chase realized he was taking the aggressive pose he sometimes took when he was intimidated. "LeVay's an obvious megalomaniac, and whathisname, Shockly, the guy who wrote *The Twenty-First Century Evil*, is a hack for the Baptists or somebody. Who knows? Who cares? *Satanism in America* might make some sense, if you didn't know anything about early American history."

Chase stopped talking; he realized he was breathing heavily. "Why'd you give me that, Lancaster? You knew what it was worth." He still sounded on edge. This wasn't going well.

Devon laughed, but it wasn't like the last time: It was a dry rasp of a laugh. "Things have changed since the other day, Mr. Chase. You are not working for the paper this time. You are working for Carol Braxton."

Chase couldn't speak.

Lancaster laughed again. This time it was thick and booming. "You are a deer caught in my headlights."

Chase shivered. His face was rigid. "No. . . I'm really not."

Devon steepled his fingers. "Yes, you are, Mr. Chase. Do not tell me that. Tell me instead that you drew some useful conclusions from your readings."

"Besides the fact that Satanism's a load of horsecrap?"

Devon shook his head. "You disappoint me, Chase. You are not thinking this through. That is not like you."

"How would you know?" Chase began to pace in front of Devon's desk. His feeling of menace from Devon had disappeared, but curiously, it had been replaced by a sense of being *tolerated,* and he couldn't stand that. He was suddenly in the role of the feeble-brained student.

"Because I know you, Michael Chase." His words were the hiss of a snake.

Chase was snapped into sense: Where *had* he seen Devon before?

"Think, Chase," Devon whispered. "The books I gave you were nonsense. They are also the best-selling authors on the subject. Do they not confirm your suspicion that the whole subject is a 'load of crap', as you would say. That means that the children who want to get into this are going to read crap. A pity, really. What does all that 'crap' focus on? You said it before, but you did not know it."

"I've had enough games, Lancaster. I—"

"No, you have not. Think of it as a dance."

Chase felt like spitting. On the floor, in Devon's face, anywhere. He wished he could just walk out. He wished he'd gotten more sleep the night before. He sighed, suddenly deflated, and sat down in the chair Devon had offered him. He closed his eyes and rubbed them with thumb and forefinger. When he looked up again, Devon was still sitting there, watching.

"What do you want from me, Lancaster? Told you yesterday I came up here on a hunch. I was just looking for some information and was told you might be able to help me. Now I get the feeling that I've stepped into some kind of private joke you're having at my expense." He waved his hand as if pushing away objections. "Not even that, necessarily. Maybe I'm just intersecting with a joke you're playing on someone else. I don't care."

Devon smiled; the smile reminded Chase of Shango's. "You are closer than you realize, Mr. Chase." He leaned forward, expectant. "Tell me, do you play chess?"

Chase blinked. That was some coincidence: No sooner had he thought of Shango than Lancaster mentioned chess.

"Or Go, perhaps?" Devon asked.

Chase had heard of Go, the Chinese game of strategy, but he didn't play. He knew it was played with small round stones on a board with a grid pattern and winning had something to do with surrounding your opponent's stones with yours, a few stones at a time.

"I play some chess. Not very well, I'm afraid."

"That is unfortunate. You are very intuitive, and you could probably be quite good, especially at Go, if you learned some strategy."

"Look, Lancaster. I'm still not interested in games. Or dances. I just want to know why you're stringing me along like this. Yesterday, you gave me books that were nothing but a—"

Devon interrupted, his voice forceful but still barely above a whisper. "We have to circle around this very carefully. This has to be danced just right. Otherwise, you will not understand anything." He closed his eyes for a moment, looking to Chase for all the world as if he were listening to something. He opened them again after a couple of very long moments. "Chase. Monstrous crimes have been committed." Devon spoke very slowly, very quietly, very precisely. "Now that you are working with Carol Braxton—"

"But I'm—"

"Sh-sh-sh. . . Do not demean yourself by insulting me. There are indications that. . . these crimes. . . were of a ritual nature. I do not think you know what you are up against."

Chase's sense of Devon's familiarity was back. That phrasing. . .

"I had to show you those books so you could see what most people think Satanism is. And what it actually is, most of the time. As you said the other day: 'Is your teenager moody, depressed? Is he uncommunicative? Does he wear black? If so, he may be killing neighborhood blonde children in his spare time.'"

Now Chase's sense of menace was back as well. As far as he could tell, Devon had quoted him exactly.

Devon laughed softly. "You should not underestimate the number of children—by which I mean teenagers—who have lost or never had any. . . compass for life, and they actually do wear black and chant and dance and kill cats in graveyards. Add to them more than a few adults who think by aping LeVay's silly rituals they can gain power over those around them, and you have described 95% of the self-proclaimed Satanists in America. Mostly they cause minor trouble—sometimes a murder or two, but those result from paranoia more than anything. That kind of Satanist enclave is no more disruptive than any other church."

"A murder or two is not disruptive?" Despite himself, Chase felt himself drawn in by Devon. He supposed that a fly might feel the same distracted pleasure as it was wrapped in shimmering threads.

Devon smiled. "Not necessarily a church-sanctioned thing, but it is no different than any other fledgling church. Remember, the Sons of Dan, the official paramilitary wing of the Church of Latter Day Saints—the Mormons—killed the governor of Kentucky in the late 1800s. Minority religions tend to get a little tense, especially when they are just starting out, and they are based on false premises."

Chase hadn't heard that about the Mormons, but he supposed it was true—he didn't really care if it was or not; he had caught Devon in an error.

"Satanism's been around since at least the Middle Ages. The *Malefactoria* even talked about it as an excuse for burning witches in France." He felt good about being able to cite a work that he had heard about during his brief college flirtation with anthropology. Devon didn't have a corner on the historical market.

"That is not the same Satanism. Not at all. America has spawned its own simplistic version. That is the Satanism you read about last night."

"It's bull."

Devon nodded. "Mostly."

60
Monday afternoon, October 18

It was 12:30, and Katie had to get to her stats class by one. There had been no sign of Maria since 9:30. She said she'd be back by noon. It wasn't like her to be late—not without calling anyway—but Katie wasn't really worried. Not yet.

There was no one in *Chuckles* at the moment, and Katie walked around aimlessly, occasionally straightening merchandise on the shelf. It had been a slow morning, as it usually was on weekdays, and Maria had asked her to watch the shop while she went to an appointment. Her boss hadn't said so, but Katie had assumed it was a therapy appointment. Maria seemed to have a lot of those lately.

It must be hard to be a middle-aged woman these days, if you had your eyes open, anyway, which her boss definitely did. Katie and Maria had talked about it a lot. For twenty years, your whole life was kids, but then they turned 18 and you turned 40, and you had 25 or 30 or 40 years of an empty house to look forward to. Not a happy prospect. Sounded lonely. No wonder she was in therapy.

Katie knew that *Chuckles* had been a product, more or less, of those therapy sessions. The store was something Maria could find value in. She'd noticed that Maria often used family-type words when she spoke about the business, phrases like "gave birth to *Chuckles*" and "nurse this thing along" and "can't wait till it grows up." Katie was glad she grew up when women were encouraged to find their own niche.

She was going to, too. If she passed stats anyway. Which she would have no trouble doing if she made it to the review today: The mid-term was coming up. 12:40. Where *was* Maria?

61
Monday afternoon, October 18

"Then why are you wasting my time with it, if it's all bull?" Chase turned his head away. He had that frustrated, ugly feeling that he got when he was caught in a verbal wrestling match.

Lancaster didn't deign to answer his question. Chase thought about what had been said so far. "Ninety-five percent. You said 95%. What about the other five percent?"

Devon sat back. "We will make a chess player of you yet."

"A friend of mine says the same thing. He's as full of crap as you are."

Devon ignored him again. "What are you made of, Chase?"

Suddenly, Chase knew: Devon's familiarity—Chase had dreamed him. Those dreams—the apelike arms, the glass globe, the phrasing. . .

Devon was laughing. "You are doing your deer imitation again, Chase." Before Chase could speak, he continued. "Consider this. Modern Satanism is a meager replication of the real thing. The same way that the people—mostly women—who call themselves witches today really have no concept of what the real *wicca crafte* was about. Think analogically now, Chase.

"In the same way that modern 'witches' are trying to recapture what the true witches of old enjoyed, the modern Satanists are chasing shadows. Modern witches seek empowerment, influence, respectability. The *wicca* assumed it. It was a part of their society, nothing strange. So they could focus their energies elsewhere, on much more. . . arcane pursuits. Modern witches cannot conceive that status, for the most part, and they waste their time pursuing it.

"Likewise, most modern Satanists seek a power that they do not understand, and they try all the silliest things they can imagine to get it. That is the 95% I was talking about. Whatever their ages, they are children playing god."

Chase waited for Devon to say something more. It didn't come. Once, years ago while working on a story about common con-games, Chase had interviewed a bait-and-switch man who worked the streets of Sacramento, near the capital. He felt the same now as he had then when he had pushed the conman's plant aside, and—even though he knew the woman who had just won was a plant—had thrown down a fifty, certain that he could pick out the ace of spades from the three cards the conman threw around.

"What about the other five percent? Are they playing God?" he asked.

Devon picked up the crystal paperweight. He tossed it up and then caught it. "No," he whispered. "Think about it. America is the perfect society for a real Satanist, as well as a fake one. The lack of community ties encourages formation of outsider groups and makes it possible to commit horrible crimes and go undetected. The antiauthoritarian bias and the lack of clear and demonstrable outlets for religious affiliation, coupled with a history of religious concern and an intense need to feel religious. All of this makes America perfect for cults and anti-Christs. The focus on money and sex—what could be more perfect?"

Chase felt like he'd been ripped off. He said so. "Bull."

Devon smiled what Chase now saw as his conman's smile.

"You should not be so sure, Michael Chase. Real Satanists have the power to invade your dreams."

III

"Wrong place, girly"

62
Monday afternoon, October 18

At 12:45, Katie decided she had to do something. Maria hadn't come or called. She tried calling the Redmanns' house. No answer. She left a message, and as she hung up the phone, she thought of the apartment she'd rented for her boss.

Was it possible? Katie chuckled at the thought of matronly Maria having an affair. But that must be what the apartment was for. Her boss had been especially secretive about her need for the apartment. She had pretended to be confused when Katie asked about it, but Maria's confusion was a little too exaggerated to be credible. Too much wrinkling of the forehead.

The more she thought about it, the more Katie was convinced that was where Maria was. She'd lost track of time, forgotten her responsibilities in the midst of her illicit affair. Katie entertained the notion of letting Maria's indiscretion go. She could enjoy some gentle teasing and a one-up on her boss. It sure wouldn't hurt job security.

Then she remembered her stats test. Two days from now. She needed all the help she could get, since she had been focusing on her other classes, knowing that stats was not all that tough and that she could catch up easily. Only now it was down to the wire. She couldn't afford to miss the review.

Katie made it to the apartment in less than five minutes. She'd taped the sign to the doorway of *Chuckles*—"Quick take-out lunch/Back in ten minutes"— and rushed out of the store and up the street. She'd never done that before, but she figured that since the store had been empty for a half an hour and Maria hadn't called. . . . She could dash up the street to the apartment.

She heard voices inside, male voices. Two of them. They sounded casual, not at all what Maria had expected to hear. Her imagination had run away with her. She knocked.

The voices stopped abruptly. After a moment, she heard footsteps. The apartment was a second floor walk-up in an old building, above the "Plant and Pet Shoppe." Katie could hear slow footsteps on a hardwood floor. Creak-creak.

The door opened a little, and Katie focused on the gold chain across the gap. An old man's eyes peered out.

"Yes?"

She could hear a lot of phlegm in his voice; Katie knew the dangers of a life of too much dairy products. Probably a smoker, too.

"Is Maria here? I'm working down at the—"

"What're you saying? You got something all messed up, missy."

"I'm sorry. I thought—"

"You got the wrong place, girly."

The door closed.

Maybe Maria had let the apartment go. But then, where was she?

Katie felt sorry for old people. Especially the ones who were alone. But she'd heard two voices inside: The old man wasn't alone. He was just rude.

63

Monday afternoon, October 18

Chase dropped the books on his desk and flipped on his computer terminal. He looked around the newsroom without really seeing the other people working or hearing the soft clack-clacking keyboards. His head moved in circles that were even tighter and crazier than the track he'd been on the day he'd been shot at.

What are you made of, Michael Chase? When the words came to him, they were more outloud—like someone was whispering them in his ear—than they were like his own thoughts. He blinked and looked around for their source. They were the words that Lancaster had said to him in a dream. And in the Special Collections room.

Chase had decided he didn't like Devon Lancaster one bit, respected him maybe, intrigued definitely, but he didn't like him. Not that that made any difference to Lancaster. Lancaster was like very few people Chase had met; he didn't give a crap whether he was liked or not. Most everyone wanted to be liked, and some—like Shango, for example—had a perverse urge to be disliked, but very few people really didn't care one way or the other.

Chase became aware that Eddie Dumont was aware of him. He'd only gotten to the newsroom a few minutes before and had been hoping to get in and out quick. He wanted to confirm with Adams, check something on his computer, and go. Now Eddie was glancing furtively up from his computer as if he wanted to come over to talk. Chase was careful not to meet his eyes. He sat down quickly, calling up his email to pretend he was busy. Maybe Eddie would leave him alone.

Lancaster. He had to keep focused on Lancaster and try to ignore Dumont. No matter how valuable a source Lancaster might prove to be—or not, the jury was still out on that one—Chase didn't like games being played with his head.

What was that crap about real Satanists invading dreams? As soon as he had said that, Lancaster had essentially terminated the discussion, although not before he'd brought out three books for Chase—*The Cather Revolution, Whispers of Heresay*, and *The Steel Gods of Ur*. More dead ends, Chase had no doubt, and he resented the fact that he'd have to spend time reviewing them.

Maybe they would explain something about whatever game it was that Lancaster was playing. Maybe. He knew something about the murders, Chase was sure of it. He caught a flash of movement out of the corner of his eye, his shoulders tensed up. He was even more on edge than he thought. The movement was just Eddie, closing in on Chase's desk. *Crap.*

"I read the crime reports today, Chase. How come you didn't say any-thing about the attempt on your life?"

Chase counted to ten before taking his eyes off his computer screen.

"I, uh. . . Just a sec." He hit the ESC key and flashed back to the main menu, his email no longer visible. Nothing there today anyway. He swiveled his chair to Eddie. "There was nothing to say. Police don't think it was a seri-ous attempt. Someone just wanted to scare me."

"Scare you off what?"

Chase laughed. The look on Eddie's face told him that, for once, Eddie was asking a question he already knew the answer to.

"Apparently, there's a lot more to this murder thing than we thought. That's how I figure it, anyway."

"Well. . ." Eddie began and Chase could tell that he'd thought this out and it wasn't easy to say. "If you want to—" He lowered his voice to a whisper. "I mean, this switch we made was not exactly your idea, and if you want to switch back. . . ."

Chase was caught by surprise. This was the last thing he'd expected. He didn't know what to say. He gave Eddie's forearm a squeeze. "Thanks, guy. I appreciate that. But there's nothing to worry about. Really. Thanks, though."

Chase smiled and Eddie looked relieved. He obviously really hadn't wanted to take the story back, but Chase was very impressed by the offer. Maybe there was more to this guy than he'd given him credit for.

Chase didn't even have the heart to bring up the Morgan story, which he knew for sure that Eddie was getting nowhere with. Waters would want that one by the end of the week.

64
Monday afternoon, October 18

Maria was going for the door when the phone rang. She ignored it and opened the door. She was late getting back to the shop. It kept ringing. *Blasted answering machine.* It should have kicked in on the fourth ring. She glanced over at it, and the light was off, indicating the machine was off, too. Funny, she didn't remember turning it off.

She'd come home for lunch, a luxury she rarely afforded herself, because things had been going so well for her lately. Alex seemed pleased about the progress in therapy, and Maria felt like she was coming to some kind of resolution. Maybe her problems were not all that deep after all. Maybe the last year and a half of therapy had been all that was needed.

The phone rang again. *That sound really cuts through a person,* Maria thought. In the old days it was more possible to ignore a ringing phone. Now—something about the electronic tone and pitch of the new ringers— even the neighbors could hear it ring. And you sure couldn't ignore it easily anymore.

Setting down her handbag, she answered the phone. "Redmann residence."

A dry voice said, "Darnok."

Maria stopped. She wasn't thinking anything at all and her head was completely empty.

65
Monday afternoon, October 18

Carol touched the lit button on her phone console. "Yes?"

"Michael Chase here to see you, Chief Braxton."

"Send him in."

Carol closed the file she'd been looking through. It had been something to distract her for the moment, the open-and-shut case of Mrs. Levinson stabbing her husband to death. The department had done a thorough job—Polinsky being the senior on the case—and Carol's review had found all bases covered, no loose ends.

The case was not that open-and-shut really, not in the broader sense, because now that it was coming to trial, the woman claimed the stabbing was in self-defense after years of abuse. Carol knew—had known—the couple, and she privately suspected that the woman was telling the truth, but that was for the courts to decide. The police department had done their bit. At least the case was at least a lot cleaner than the Anders-Samosky thing.

There was a tap at her door. Chase always tapped like that.

"Come on!" Carol realized she sounded irritated. She didn't like the fact that she'd brought Chase in on this; it had been a matter of necessity. He was good, once he got going, even if he was far too aware of that. Part of her even hoped he'd come up with nothing and was just slinking in to tell her so.

He opened the door, and Carol was surprised at what she saw. When they'd more-or-less lived together, she'd seen him before in all kinds of conditions: tired, depressed, drunk, feeling sorry for himself, hungover. . . every down space. She'd never seen him as worn and haunted as this.

"Chase, um. . . Have a seat."

"Thanks, Braxy." He collapsed into the chair that sat on the other side of her desk. Carol clenched her jaws; he hadn't called her Braxy in two years.

"You look like you could use a drink."

"Nahhh," he said. He waved his hand in a way that made her realize that he wasn't interested at all. "I'm fine. Listen, I been doing some checking. I think I have something for you." Chase flicked his hair back off his forehead and glanced out the window. "You need to check it out anyway."

"Okay." She leaned forward. "What's up?"

"Guy named Lancaster. He's over at Wise, Special Collections. I've been talking to him. A little. He's. . . very strange. I asked at the front desk and he's only been there a couple of years. I have a hunch. Can you check to see who was working at the Burlington library ten years ago? Maybe get a list of employees or something."

"Is this what you were alluding to the other night? The thing you couldn't tell me about?"

Carol thought a smile crossed Chase's lips, but if she hadn't known him so well, she wouldn't have seen it. Maybe she was imagining it. Hoping for too much.

"Nahhh. No, not at all. Believe me, Carol, you don't want to know about that."

Carol thought she knew how Chase's mind worked. She could make a guess or two as to what he was planning. Right then, she also hated Chase's need to be mysterious. That was how he kept control of his world.

"Are you planning to check this information out yourself?"

Chase did smile now. "If there's time."

"That's illegal, you know." She felt a duty to say something to that effect.

Chase snorted. "Yeah. Thanks. I'll let you know what I find out."

Chase got up; Carol thought his movements looked tired.

"Do you think this Lancaster guy is the one? Did he do it?"

Chase shook his head like she'd just said something incredibly stupid. She *really* hated when he did that. "You know the saying, Carol. Nobody's innocent. It's more a matter of who's guilty."

66
Monday afternoon, October 18

Katie almost had to physically bite her tongue when Maria came waltzing into the store at 2:17.

"Hey, kiddo," Maria said, dropping her handbag on the counter. "Everything copascetic?"

"Mmm," Katie said, unwilling to produce a yes.

"Oh. Sorry this is late, but some things came up. Hope it wasn't any trouble. What time is it anyway?"

"Quarter after two." Katie straightened and looked toward the back counter. Her backpack was there with her books in it.

"Okay, kiddo. Get lost." Maria made shooing motions with her hands. "If your profs say anything, they'll have to answer to me."

That was small comfort to Katie; she'd already missed most of the review. She wanted to say something, but she felt right then like Maria, her boss, her friend in a way, was someone she'd never met before. Someone she didn't want anything to do with. She didn't want to say anything unpleasant that might lose her job, so the best thing was to get out of there. Right away.

"I'll see you next week, Mrs. Redmann."

67

Tuesday night, October 19

Chase looked up sharply from *The Cathar Heresay*. A sound on his porch had caught his ears. He looked out from his kitchen table, his eyes squinted past the space of illumination that his porchlight gave, trying to peer into the darkness beyond. Nothing. No movement, nothing.

It must have been his imagination. Or his eagerness. This was a quiet neighborhood and disturbances were few. He must want this more than he'd admitted to himself. Shango and Adams should be here any minute, and the book had gotten him on edge.

Why had Devon given him this particular book? A history of the Cathar movement that had caused the Catholic Church a lot of trouble in the twelfth century. Chase had read some about it years ago, but this book really made it clear why and how the Cathars had caused so much difficulty.

Chase laughed and took a sip of bourbon. His own difficulties working for the papers he'd worked for, his urge to go freelance—he felt they were similar to the impulse behind the Cathar movement: individual interest, self-interest. The Cathars emphasized personal knowledge of the divinity, something the rigidly hierarchical Catholic Church could not put up with because it would have weakened their political influence.

The knock startled him because he hadn't heard any steps on his porch. He looked up from the book again. Adams's face was framed in the window of his kitchen door. He motioned the kid in. Adams opened the door, blinking rapidly at the light.

"Come on in," Chase said as expansively and calmly as he could.

Adams held two briefcases, which he set down carefully in one corner of the room. He straightened, looking to Chase apologetic and childlike.

"Make yourself at home. You want a beer or something?"

"No thanks."

"Sit, sit," Chase offered. Adams shook his head. "You get what you needed?"

"I got a few things."

"Great. We're set then. Shango should be here soon. Then we can get started. We have to wait for the muscle, though."

Adams's eyebrows went up. "The muscle? What do we need muscle for? I've been in and out of there a hundred times. I've got everything we need, Mr. Chase."

"Just Chase." Chase thought he had said that to Adams before, but he wasn't sure. He stood up and stretched; it might be a long night. "I've got a hunch is all." Seemed like he'd been saying that a lot lately. He didn't want to worry the kid.

"I'm still not clear about why we can't use the lines at the paper, Mr.— uh—Chase." Adams was pacing. "Even if we get tapped, too many people have access. You worried about implicating the paper?"

Chase laughed. "Not at all." He got the impression Adams had used the paper's lines to hack before. "But if we're seen there, we'd be implicating ourselves, eventually. Waters already has an idea of what we're up to."

Adams frowned and kept pacing. "Could I have a cup of coffee?"

"Instant okay?" Chase asked as he grabbed the kettle off the stove. "All I got."

"Sure." Adams looked at the kettle in Chase's hand, then looked around the room. "You can't nuke it?"

"No. Microwave went out a few months ago." He set the refilled kettle back on the stove, flipped on the burner. "I never really used it, anyway."

Adams looked disbelieving. "You mean you *cook*?" Coming from him, the question sounded like an accusation.

"Every chance." Chase got a cup and the coffee out of the cupboard and turned back to his guest. Adams looked at the floor, shaking his head.

"I've got a thought here, Chase. Why don't we just tie in to the file server at the newsroom from here if you're worried that someone will see us? It'd be a heck of a lot easier. Not to mention the fact that we could be more thorough. We could take all night if we had to." Adams started pacing again.

"We wouldn't be breaking so many laws that way either, eh?"

Adams smirked. "Well, s'pose so, yeah. That's not really it, though. Guess I was just hoping that while we were at it, I could take care of a couple other things, but we'd need time."

"Not tonight, okay Adams? This might get a little tricky on its own."

"You think the shooter's coming back, don't you?"

Chase shrugged.

68

Tuesday night, October 19

Carol decided to wait until tomorrow to call Chase. Nothing could be done about it now, anyway; might as well call it a night. She flicked off the office light and locked the door. Her footsteps echoed in the empty corridor. She rarely failed to be struck by the differences between the nighttime and daytime in Public Safety Building. On her way through the lobby, she nodded at Randi, but didn't say anything.

After so many weeks, they might have actually gotten a break today. She'd followed up Chase's hunch, calling the University of Vermont's library system and asking them to run a personnel check, and just like that, they had their lead. Ten years ago, UV at Burlington had employed a man in the reference library by the name of Devon K. Lancaster. *Bingo*, as Chase would say.

She had Lancaster's file faxed down, and it had been there within the hour. Seems he had started there two years before the first killings and had quit without notice less than a week after the last one. He'd left no forwarding address and had never picked up his final paycheck.

Unfortunately, the library had no real background on him, besides the vita he'd sent when he applied for the job. Carol had passed that on to Lieutenant Simmons, who was the best researcher they had on staff, to see what he could dig up. He also wasn't working with Watts at the moment. If she'd had to, she would have gone to a less skilled researcher, just to avoid bringing Watts into the loop. She'd have his report the next day, and if he hadn't turned up anything useful, she'd talk to Watts and Collins.

It was premature to arrest Lancaster, probably a mistake to even question him yet, but that afternoon, Carol had sent another officer over to keep a discreet eye on Lancaster. "Just watch him," she'd said. "Make sure he doesn't see you, but stay with him. He might be dangerous. I'll leave instructions for Kyle for when he comes on."

The night was crisp and Carol could feel the first chill of winter coming on. It *smelled* like winter. There were no clouds, and as Carol unlocked her car door, her eyes found the moon, just rising over the I.O.O.F. building across from her office. It was nearly full again.

69
Tuesday night, October 19

"It's getting *cold* out here," Shango said as the three of them hustled across Wiley Street. "It's going to start raining again."

"Quit whining." Chase was more nervous than he expected, probably the most nervous of the three of them. Adams had done this a hundred times, by his own account, and seemed to view it with the same relish Chase looked forward to the verbal tussle of an unfriendly interview. And Shango had, well. . . Chase wasn't sure what Shango had done before, but he was sure a little unauthorized entry was no big deal.

The big man sprinted across the street and now stood jumping up and down on one foot then the other to keep warm, even though he had what looked like a good fall jacket on. Adams walked briskly, carrying two laptops, his long trench coat making him look taller and more dour than Chase knew him to be. He hadn't said a word since they'd left the house. That kid could get awful serious, like there was a right way and a wrong way to do things, and he preferred to do them the right way.

Once they were across the street, they headed up the alley that Adams had directed them to. It was the alley behind Kent Hall, the WVU chemistry building.

"Bad juju," Shango said, still moving as if he were trying to keep warm, his voice reverberating off the high walls on either side of the narrow alley. "This may be okay for you cavepeople, but it ain't for me, I'll tell you that."

"Would you keep your voice down," Chase said. "We're almost there."

"What's he mean, 'cavepeople'?"

"Shango thinks that white people are a genetic mutation that originated in deep caves in northern Europe. An unfortunate mutation."

"That's not *my* idea. That's Elijah Mohammed."

"Who?" asked Adams.

"A noted biologist," Chase said sarcastically. He really didn't feel like going into it right then.

The trio walked another fifteen yards.

"This is it," Adams said as they reached the cul-de-sac that ended at the back of Appel Hall. His voice lowered to a whisper as he pointed to some bushes that stood just past the edge of the turnaround, a few feet away from the back of the building.

"Behind there?" Shango asked. His voice was also quiet.

Adams nodded.

Chase was looking around to make sure no one was nearby. He was very nervous now. "You sure now's the right time?" he asked, but when he looked back, both Adams and Shango were stooped over behind the bush. He covered the distance in time to see Adams dropping into a hole in the ground. Shango lowered Adams's laptops down to him. The way Shango and Adams worked together, Chase could have sworn they'd done this together before.

"In you go, Bwana," Shango said. A large manhole cover leaned against his left forearm. "I'll wait up here, in case of visitors. Don't play with yourselves down there."

He helped Chase down the ladder that led into the opening.

Chase had expected it to be dark in the tunnel, but of course maintenance tunnels had to be well lit. Made sense. Except for the egress to the surface world, which was about seven feet over their heads, the tunnel was only about six feet tall, which meant that Chase would have to slouch a little to walk. On both walls ran a complex network of different colored pipes and cables.

Adams was standing beside him, leaning forward on the balls of his feet. "You ready, Chase?"

"Lead the way."

From right where they had dropped into the tunnel, it fell away gradually to either side of them, sloping down both ways for about forty feet before both reached T-intersections and split at right angles.

Adams said, "It doesn't really matter which way we go. They all link up. It's like a huge maze that runs under the whole campus."

"Even up to the coliseum and the arts center?" Chase asked. The campus of WVU was really two campuses, separated by about two miles, although it seemed like they were drawing closer all the time as the university grew. It amazed him that he'd been in town so long, and even worked at the newspaper, and never knew about these tunnels.

"Oh, sure. I've seen maps, but I've never been up there," Adams said.

"How come it's so warm down here?"

"Steam pipes, mostly. This is how the university buildings get their heat. Let's go this way. There's a patch down here I've used before." He led Chase off to the right of where they dropped in. "Watch your head."

Chase was grinning as they walked. "Adams. You're an honest-to-God hacker."

Adams looked at him. He smirked like he had back at Chase's apartment. "Spose so."

"We could do a story on you. Anonymously, of course." Chase enjoyed the irony of doing an exposé on a hacker who actually worked at the *Dispatch*.

"I don't think so."

"Sure. It'd be great. Look, I know you guys are not the demons that you're made out to be. Most of you are just having fun."

Adams was shaking his head. "That's the number two myth about hackers. We're not criminals—most of us aren't anyway, we don't eliminate our credit card debt or any of that—but we're also not really pranksters either. Chase, I've been doing this since I was about seven. A lot of people have. We're like a big virtual family."

They drew near the T-intersection, and Adams directed them: "Down here a little ways." They kept walking in silence for another couple of minutes, until Adams said, "Okay. We're here."

Adams had his left hand up under a thick black cable near the top of the wall, feeling between it and the cinder blocks. "Got it," he said. He pulled down three sections of wire, each one about as thick as a finger, each forming a kind of a V-shape, with larger versions of those colored plastic caps that electricians use on wire splices composing the bottom of the V. The caps were green.

"Green is for 'go'," Adams said. "A little joke."

Chase had the distinct feeling that the joke was Adams's own doing.

"Get the laptops out," Adams said, pulling the caps off. He reached inside his coat and produced the smallest needle-nose pliers Chase had ever seen. "We've got about forty-five minutes before the guard comes around again, but we should hurry anyway."

Chase opened the laptops and booted them up. He uncoiled the various wires that Adams had jacked in the side pouches of their cases. He plugged in the wires he could. Meanwhile, Adams was working the overhead wires he chose to work.

"The trick is," he was saying through teeth clenched around two green caps, "to use different lines every time, so they can't track the physical location. If they do that, it's a big pain. Each of these three holds dozens of lines that go to different buildings on campus. Which means that totally different departments end up with the bills and any tracers that happen."

He held out his hand to Chase for one of the cables that came now from the computers. Each cable had a specialized connector at the outer end that Chase had never seen before. A completely new world for him.

"Thanks," Adams said. He used a different tool to attach that cable, then held out his hand for another. "You do this once," he said as he connected the cables one by one, "and there's *no way* they'd figure out where it came from. A few times, and it's possible, but it would take a computer to pin down all the specific points of intersection from which the calls might have been made. And that assumes everyone involved shares information and collinsates, and that ain't gonna happen."

As he finished speaking, he finished connecting the cables.

"Let's see what we've got now." Adams turned both computers on. Chase could see Adams's excitement. He thrived on this. Adams keyed in a string of numbers and letters too fast for Chase to catch, and they didn't appear on the screen. He hit *enter*, and then typed in another sequence on the other, hit *enter*. He pulled out his wallet and shuffled through a collection of business cards, one eye on the computer screens. "I keep all these numbers I get in a notebook, but I didn't get a chance to write these in today. Here we go."

A flashing message lit up first one screen, then the other: WAITING:. "Okay," Adams said. "We're online."

"What just happened?"

Adams's answer was disjointed because he was typing in one of the numbers from the back of the business card as he spoke. "Got on the system. Called up. . . a diagnostic. Got the modem. Make sure made all the connections right."

"All that with just a few keystrokes?" Chase was thinking of what it took to get into the system at work, username, password, and all that.

"Wrote a macro."

Chase knew that a macro was a sort-of mini-program that made it possible to run routine operations, even fairly complex ones, with a few simple commands. "Could you do that at work?"

"Already have." Adams looked up. "Chase, could we save the questions for later? I might have to move quickly on some of this."

"Okay." He'd have to contain himself, which wouldn't be easy. "At least tell me the basic plan."

"Fair enough. As soon as I tell it to, it'll call the Virginia Department of Motor Vehicles so we can see what car that license plate belongs to. Since it's a rental it'll be registered."

"If not?"

"Don't even think it. We'd have to try other state DMVs, and I've only got numbers for about fifteen of them. If that didn't work, we'd try all 57 of the car rental agencies that I wrote down. The big ones are nationwide, so they should be quick, but the smaller ones I got out of phone books." Adams ticked the phone books off from memory. "Pittsburgh, Wheeling, Wierton, Charleston, Huntington, Beckley, Fairmont, Clarksburg, DC, Baltimore, Philadelphia, Richmond, Cleveland, Columbus, Cincinnati, Lexington. Everything within about a six- or eight-hour drive. Let's hope we don't have to check all of them."

"That'd take some time."

"More than we have. Better hope the car is registered in Virginia."

Chase thought for a second about what Adams had just said. "Isn't it tricky, tapping into a DMV computer?"

"Not really. The system registers your call and where it's coming from, but unless a very alert sysop—uh, systems operator—is working, nothing else happens. Maybe if they do a thorough audit a year down the road, they find out that an unauthorized call was made and that it came over one of WVU's lines. That's it. Dead end from there."

"But if that's it, if that's all that happens, then people could be getting in and out of government computers all the time."

Again that wry grin from Adams. "Basically, they are." Before Chase could say anything, Adams added, "The more secret stuff, like the Pentagon and NORAD, has plenty of protection these days. Some very aggressive defenses have been developed." Adams hit *enter*. "Lemme work now; we talk later." Adams watched the screen.

"Couldn't the police do this just as fast?"

"Sure. But you want to know who rented it. They can't do that part as fast. Now, shhh. . ." His fingers worked the keys. He waited.

"We're in," he announced.

70
Tuesday night, October 19

Maria Redmann came through the front door and tossed her handbag on the table. She kept the package in her hand, meaning to take it up to her and her husband's room. She stopped short when she saw her husband sitting in the living room.

"Hi, baby," she said. She was trying to sound cheerful, though she didn't feel that way. She was glad to see him though.

"How'd shopping go?" Don asked. "You're back pretty late."

Maria thought he seemed sullen. "I'm sorry, honey." She stooped to kiss him, thinking at the same time that she wasn't sure why her trip to the mall had taken as long as it had. At one point, she'd found herself staring into the window at the Vanity Shoppe, looking over the bridal gowns. They were so white, and the color had seemed wrong to her. *Bridal gowns should be red,* she'd thought. An image of her grandfather came to her then, sitting in his reclining chair in front of the fireplace, laughing.

It crossed her mind that maybe she should get back on her therapy sessions again.

"I've got a surprise for you," she said, trying to shake off unpleasantness. She heard her voice and was a little surprised at how steady and sure it sounded. But she was pleased, although unsure why.

She tossed the package lightly onto the coffee table and drew herself up onto the couch with her husband. Her knees lay in his lap. She kissed him.

After the kiss he said, "Let's see it." He reached for the package.

"No, no, no. That's not the surprise." She intercepted his hand. She wanted to save the bridal veil for later, for sometime when they were in bed, perhaps, when it would have the most effect.

"Next Monday, honey," she said. "That's the surprise." She smiled because she was feeling very good. She felt right for the first time in a very long time.

71
Tuesday night, October 19

"Now it gets a little trickier," Adams said. "We've been fairly lucky so far."

As far as Chase could tell, they'd been extremely lucky, but this hacking business still looked like magic to him. It might as well have been, as unreal as it seemed. In the last fifteen minutes, according to the computer screen they had been in the registered vehicles list of Virginia's DMV, where there were only three rental cars with L5T as part of the plate number and only one white Nissan, and in the national systems files of a major car rental company based in Delaware, where, according to Adams, they had accessed the file that contained passwords.

"Can you do that at work?" Chase asked.

Instead of answering, Adams typed, NO SWEAT, HYEENA. The computer, still tied in to the rental company's mainframe answered, ERROR. RETRY, CANCEL, ABORT? The computer didn't understand, but Chase did.

"You snake."

Adams was grinning as he hit R and the message PASSWORD? reappeared.

"The reason this is slightly tricky is that we have to go through the right terminals for the passwords to work. We're going through the Seattle office where there's this person, H. Hawkins, who uses the password 'alias'"

"Alias?"

Adams shook his head. "Not smart. A lot of people use it. Here we go." He keyed in the password. A few seconds passed. "We're in," he said again. Chase figured it must be a reflex statement for hackers, like "We have to cut the deficit" was for politicians.

Adams was typing again, off to the races. He sent a message, the computer in Seattle responded, he sent another. It went that way for a few more seconds. Then: "Okay, let's see. . . ."

Chase looked at the screen, where the history of the white Nissan was displayed. He watched the lines scroll slowly by.

"That's it," he said. "Stop." The car had been rented on October 3rd, two days before, in Bristol, Virginia, by a Mr. William Abbot and returned to Bristol the same day. Bristol was in western Virginia, right on the Tennessee line.

Who is *William Abbot?* Chase was at a dead end.

"What now?"

Adams was scribbling numbers on the back of the same business card he'd gotten the other numbers he'd used from. He clicked his pen and put it back in the pocket inside his coat.

"Now we check the credit card company."

* * *

Since she couldn't sleep, Carol decided to try Chase's house after all. She scrunched up on her pillows and pulled the phone from the night stand. It only rang twice.

"You have reached MC's private secretary. Whatever you say will be remembered and possibly used against you."

Carol wondered if this was Chase's way of saying that he expected her to call. "Chase. Just wanted to say that I followed up on what you suggested. Don't go see him again until we've talked. This is important." She started to add "Call me," but decided he'd figure that out. "Bye."

She looked at the clock, which read 12:07. She knew he was still out doing whatever it was he had hinted at this afternoon. It was probably not a good idea for her to puzzle out what that be, because she would probably then have to try to stop him from breaking the law in some way. Chase wasn't a criminal, exactly, not in the sense that he'd ever intentionally hurt someone or disrupt society, but he did seem to ignore laws he found inconvenient.

That might be the worst kind of criminal, she thought groggily as she drifted off.

* * *

"Our luck is holding, Chase," Adams said. "But I'm afraid this is where the tedium sets in. I'll need your help on this." He was working the keyboard again, so Chase didn't say anything. After a minute: "Okay."

Chase saw the screen showed a ready menu for the credit card company, and underneath it read, USERNAME:. There was no cursor.

Adams turned away from the screen and pulled his pen and a folded up piece of paper from his inner jacket pocket. "Without going into the details, there's no way I can break into the company's most secret files—card holders, credit histories, stuff like that. I'm not good enough for that. But I can get into the outer layer of the system—which I've done—and then use this neat little program. What it does is simulate the screen that shows on some employee's terminal. Like a spy glass, like you're looking over the employee's shoulder. Then when they type in their username and password, you can see it. *Then* we can get in."

"You lost me." Actually, Chase thought he had it, but he wanted to hear it another way to make sure.

"I picked out a specific terminal in New York—mostly because I thought one there might be used a lot—and now we're, like, spying on it. As soon as someone uses it, you write down their name and password. But do it quick, because as soon as they enter it, we're booted out of the system."

"And they're up there right now, in New York, at work?"

"Right. This is realtime work. The most tedious hacking you can imagine."

"What if it takes them an hour to enter anything?"

"Then we miss it, 'cause we got about 20 minutes before the guard gets here."

Chase stared at the screen. He had just discovered that hacking was like any other job: Hurry up and wait. But something bugged him. "How come I can see it? Isn't it blanked out like it is at work?"

"The program I have subverts that. Don't worry about it. While you're doing that, I'm going to try the other stuff you wanted, but I'm not making any guarantees. Keep your eye on the screen and be ready."

72
Tuesday night, October 19

Collins sits in his car in the university parking garage, the one nearest the student union, Wise Library, Appel Hall. He doesn't expect to be there long. On the seat beside him is his windbreaker, its pockets holding the silk ties, the blindfold, the blades. He anticipates another night out tonight, after the small annoyance named Michael Chase is taken care of. He has given his people the go-ahead; another hour or so and Chase won't be around to play the wild card.

Chase has decided to do a little hacking in the tunnels beneath the university, and Collins couldn't have come up with a more convenient place to stage a hit if he had been asked to. If both Chase and the hacker have to die instead of just Chase, that really makes no difference. Collins's people are professionals, and nothing will be traced, nothing will be discovered.

Collins is sure that once Chase is out of the way, he can bring this operation to a successful conclusion, despite the doubts he's been having about the Old Man and his leadership. The Old Man is falling apart.

He still has genuine appreciation for the Old Man, who spotted him as a prospect back when Collins was in the FBI Academy. That discovery had blessed Collins in ways that he has only gradually come to appreciate. But the Old Man is getting older, and Collins worries that he's beginning to slip. The Old Man can't last forever, and some day—possibly soon—the entire northeastern seaboard organization will need a successor.

Collins has studied history, and he knows that it is often mundane error that brings down the powerful. That looks to be possible in this case. The Old Man hadn't counted on Chase, but one pesky journalist shouldn't be this much trouble. It is more than that.

The operation's been a little trickier than the one the Family staged here a few years ago. Entirely different, in fact. They didn't start this one, and as far as Collins can determine, the Old Man wants two people out of the way this time. Neither of them will be easy. All Collins can do is his part, which is one of the reasons he waits in the dark car, in the dark parking garage, tonight. Besides waiting for word on Chase and that hacker, he is waiting for the deaths themselves.

Two deaths are better than one; he knows that from experience. He'd never been able to figure out precisely what purpose the deaths of the WVU students had served in terms of the Family—or the Old Man's Dark Art—but he knew how much their spirits had helped him. He'd do it again, given the chance. That is why Collins has decided to be nearby when tonight's killings occur. He is performing his own experiment—based on the principles of the

Family, to be sure—but an experiment he feels is sound nonetheless. He hopes that the deaths are as good as the other ones he's experienced, even though they are not proper, not ritual.

Collins smacks his hands against the car seat: That is not his concern right now; his concern should be the operation, his place in it, and its successful conclusion. One of his people will tell him when the hit has been successfully completed, and Chase is dead, and then Collins will feel okay about going out on the town tonight.

In the mood for love.

*   *   *

The waxing moon hovers, its light covering the mountains. The moon's light is especially brittle this night, maybe fragile from the chill. Maybe held in suspension by the water in the air, maybe the light is held in stasis by the earthy force of the mountains themselves.

Whatever the reason, the light seems frozen on the leaves of the trees, frozen to the sides of buildings, frozen to the top of the parking garage. As if the heavens and the earth are holding their breath. As if nature has been suspended, as if the world has stopped.

73
Tuesday night, October 19

Adams looked up from his keyboard. "How's it going, Chase?"

"Nothing so far." Chase looked at his watch and looked immediately back at the screen. "We haven't got much more time."

Adams nodded. "About ten more minutes." He went back to entering data. Chase had glanced at his screen a couple of times, but it was all gibberish to him. Not the neat little user-friendly windows he was used to, just lines of code that were entered by Adams or spit out by the machine. The only thing Chase understood was Adams's occasional curses.

"You're right, this is tedious," Chase said. "How long did you say I'll have between the time a name is entered and the point this screen goes blank?"

"Depends. Maybe less than two seconds." Adams hit return and sat back, staring at his screen. ACCESS DENIED blinked on and off. "Crap. Well, Chase. There's no way I'm going to get past the outer layer of this system. The FBI's system is a little more complex than a rent-a-car company."

"I thought you said you had a number or a code or something."

"I can do a read-only of certain batch files and sysdocs. That's it."

"In English."

"I can look at certain. . . uh larger, more general files. Tables of contents, sort of. And the ones that control the way the system operates. But all I can do is scroll them from beginning to end, I can't really move around in them or open anything."

"Which ones?" Chase said without taking his eyes off his screen.

"Let's see." Adams asked the computer for a list. "'Cm103cng', that might be—and I'm guessing—'Communications with the 103rd Congress'. Umm. . . 'Cmexbrnc', maybe 'Communications with Executive Branch'. 'Cmjdcial'. That's probably—"

"Okay, okay." Chase realized Adams was trying to tell him they didn't have the time to do it like this. "See if they've got anything that lists a Collins, in any way. Something about the Behavioral Science unit. Or a list of agent ranks, maybe." Chase was trying to think and watch his screen at the same time. "Or— Hold it. Here we go."

A name appeared on his screen one letter at a time, but quickly, as if whoever was typing it in did it often. Chase wrote it down as it materialized. CBO-SIO. Then a password: SLVRSRFR. *That's a good one*, Chase thought. *CBosio, the Silver Surfer.* "Got it," he said aloud. His screen went blank. He looked over at Adams, and he could see the hacker smiling.

"I might have it, too. How about, 'Acdutoct'? Maybe 'Active Duty: October'? Let's try it. Watch here, Chase. We can't do anything with that one for now anyway. The system won't let two people log on with the same password at the same time."

Adams called up 'Acdutoct' and suddenly lines of letters materialized:

ChristopheraadlandAngeliaabateEdwardabbadiniDavidabbitKennethabb
ottJessicaabbuhlFadiabdouJessicaabbediDavidg.abelDavidk.abelJohnaber
soldCarlablesBrianabrahamCharlesabrahamsonJoselleabreuAnthonyabr
uzinoLancasterabsherDavidabstenMichelleacardoJohnacheeBenticeache
nbachFrancisackersonJameskleyLeighannaacordTracieacksAllenac

It took Chase a few seconds to recognize them as names.

"Will this help?" Adams said.

"Beats me. See if you can find the name Morton Collins."

Adams began to scroll the list. Lines of letters flashed up the screen:

nyammarDaniealammonsAlbertandersonAugustandersonBarbaraande
rsonClarenceandersonEricandersonJacobandersonLeeandersonChasea

It wasn't easy to read the names as they scrolled by, all run together like that, but about the time Chase noticed the first 'B' names, the screen went blank and the names were replaced with a message. The message was a full paragraph, but Chase only caught part of it.

YOU ARE TRESPASSING ON THE PROPERTY OF THE. . .

"What's happening?"

Adams punched something into the keyboard. "They've noticed us. They're tracing the call." The names reappeared:

aricebishopMarshallbishopWillisbishopAllenbissetEarlbitelyScottbitting
erWilliambjorkmanGarybjorndahlBruceblackJoelblackLillianblackDoug

"Shouldn't we get off?" Chase asked. There was an edge to his voice.

"We've got a couple minutes." Adams continued to scroll the file. In seconds, however, the message reasserted itself. This time Chase caught more of it:

YOU ARE TRESPASSING ON THE PROPERTY OF THE UNITED STATES
GOVERNMENT. THIS IS A CRIMINAL OFFENSE PUNISHABLE. . .

"This is not good, kid."

"Be quiet. Do you want this stuff or not?" Again, Adams made the names reappear:

obertcanterburyCarloscantisBernardcantoniDianacantuWilliamcantwell
KaimingcaoLewiscapannaManuelcapeltyScottcapelleJonathoncapicolaGi

Suddenly, the message was back:

YOU ARE TRESPASSING ON THE PROPERTY OF THE UNITED STATES
GOVERNMENT. THIS IS A CRIMINAL OFFENSE PUNISHABLE UNDER
STATUTE 67.15 OF FEDERAL PENAL CODE #187. EXIT SYSTEM OR IDEN-
TIFY YOURSELF IMMEDIATELY TO AVOID. . .

Those specifics made Chase very nervous. "If they're telling us to go, then we'd better—"
"Just shuttup."

lescomerThomascommodariDarnellcommodorCliffordcompAlbertcom
ptonJasoncomstockMelissaconawayPatrickconnerAlexcopaxoneEugene

The scrolling stopped on those lines.
"Okay. Stop," Chase said, even though Adams already had. There was no Collins listed.
"None too soon," Adams said. Just as he touched the keys to exit the system, the message flashed up again. Then it disappeared. Adams had reached behind the portable and disconnected the cord.
"What could have happened?"
"A lot of things I suppose, if they'd had time to trace the call." He started to coil the cord. "I'm glad that's over. I don't like poking around in government files." He tucked the cord into the case and looked at Chase. "I hope you got what you wanted."
"I'm not really sure." Collins hadn't been listed on active duty. That could mean many things: There was a slip-up at the data entry end in DC; 'Collins' was not his real name; the mission was too secret to be listed in this file; a million other things that didn't occur to him right then. There would be time to think about it later. Right now, they only had a couple of minutes before the guard came around.
Adams was already at the other keyboard. With the paper on which Chase had recorded the username and password, it only took him a minute or so to access the credit card files. Chase watched over his shoulder. Working the credit card menus was much easier than reading lines of letters in a read-only mode. It was menu driven. Adams only had to type in the name of

William Abbott, his credit card number, and the address, place of employment, credit history, and other background of William Abbott materialized on the screen.

Chase scanned it. "Looks like there's a second card user named."

"Theron Davies," Adams said. He looked at Chase. "You know him?"

Chase shook his head. "Never heard—"

Chase stopped speaking. He held his breath. Footsteps in the tunnel, around the bend away from them. He turned his head instinctively toward the sound, which was coming from the direction opposite that which they'd come. The guard, walking slowly, humming slightly, but coming their way. They had run out of time.

He looked back at Adams, who was already yanking the computer connections free of the university's lines and tucking the splices up between the thick cable and the wall. Chase started to stuff the computers in their cases, not worrying about proper placement of the cables and other such delicacies.

It was hard to gauge distance by sound in the tunnel, but Chase could tell they weren't going to get packed up before the guard rounded the corner. He grabbed Adams's upper arm and motioned down the corridor, away from the guard, toward the exit. Adams was gathering the cord from the second machine; his mouth was tight as he shook his head, 'No.'

Chase rushed to stuff the laptop into its case. *What the hell is he—*

"Psssst, asshat," came a whispering voice.

Chase and Adams both froze. The footsteps had stopped, still around the corner, out of sight. It took them a second to realize that the voice was not directed at them.

A loud *POP!* echoed through the tunnel, and what sounded to Chase like a large laundry bag being dropped to the floor. Then, no sound at all for a heartbeat. The *POP!* still echoed in Chase's head—a handgun with a silencer.

Adams's whispered "Crap" broke the silence, and before Chase knew it, Adams was running down the corridor toward the corner around which the exit waited, one of his computers under his arm. Chase was right behind him, the other computer in his grip. He thought he heard the slap-crack of hard soles on the pavement behind him.

As he rounded the corner, he saw that Adams was at the ladder to the surface. He also saw that Shango was standing next to him, hoisting him up, practically lifting him with one arm, a dark shape that looked like a gun in the other hand.

"Go! Go!" Shango's big voice boomed as Adams was up the ladder and out. Chase reached the ladder, and he felt Shango's grip on the back of his coat, forcing him up. He had a flash of Shango the Marine in the sands of Iraq as he went up the ladder. It was a scary flash, Shango's lips pressed tight against his teeth, his eyes narrowed, nostrils flared.

As he scrambled up and out, he heard Shango shout, "Surprise, cracker!" followed by the percussive roar of a large handgun.

Chase rolled away from the opening, laying down, scrunched against the side of Appel Hall. Shango emerged next, his torso and head out of the hole. Adams was only a vague shadow behind the bushes. Chase heard another *POP*, slight this time, now that there was several feet of ground between him and the shooter. Shango groaned and rolled up and out of the hole.

The rain had started again, and Shango cursed at the sky. He rolled the iron cover back over the hole. He had set his gun down in the dirt between the bushes and the building, and he was chuckling. "Let him come up now. Scumdog." He looked at Chase and smiled his toothy smile. "Smile when you say that."

Chase let go of the computer and it dropped the inch or so to the ground. "You idiot," he said to Shango as he sat up. "You're supposed to be watching our backs."

"I can't help it there was more than one entrance. He won't risk coming up that ladder 'cause he's not sure if we're up here or not. Now, consolidate your feces you two, we're outta here. Hyup, hyup!"

Chase had enough sense to be quiet then. He and Adams got up, lifted their computers, and followed Shango back down the alley. On the way, Chase noticed that Shango's right calf was bleeding.

"Don't worry about it, Bwana. I got a nurse friend."

"We should get to the emergency room," Chase said as he unlocked the car.

"Just take him home," Shango said, his thumb jerking toward Adams in the back seat. "We'll go see my friend tonight. You shouldn't go home anyway. He'll be okay. They won't know anything about him."

"Yeah," Adams said. "Can you take me home now?"

The rain came down harder.

74
Friday afternoon, October 22

As Chase walked up the front steps of Wise Library, he thought about how Shango gritted his teeth as Larae—his nurse friend—cut his pants leg away from the wound and smoothed on the salve. Shango was right about it being a flesh wound; no bullet to remove, just skin to be soothed. Salve, a wrap-around bandage, a couple of pills and Shango was asleep in no time. Chase had stayed the night, too, exhausted, stretched on the couch, but he didn't sleep much.

He climbed the steps slowly. He just couldn't shake the belief that Devon knew who'd killed those girls; in fact, he'd come to suspect that Devon was the one who'd done it. Although that didn't explain who had killed the guard in the tunnel, or who had tried to kill him—maybe twice.

The attempt on his life the week before *could* have been Devon. The car had been rented in Bristol, after all, and although the name Abbott didn't match, the name Davies was not entirely unlike the name Devon. But that was tenuous at best. The shooting the night before was entirely unconnected, at least directly. The shooter was a white male—no way Shango would miss that—and he was over six feet tall and normally proportioned. Definitely not Devon.

Once inside the library, Chase headed for the Special Collections room. He was off his game, his intuition silent. There was something he was missing, and he was getting tired of being in the dark. After the computer hacking and the shooting, Chase had stayed awake another four hours, checking into those books Devon had loaned him. *The Cather Revolution, Whispers of Heresay*, and *The Steel Gods of Ur*. What those had to do with Satanic cults in America, Chase just couldn't figure out. He'd seen relation to his own freelance work and Adams's computer hacking in the first two, but nothing that connected to Satanism.

What was Devon trying to tell him? Chase ran it through what he knew of the psychology of murderers and criminals in general. Maybe it had to do with the glorification of the do-it-yourself attitude. *I Did It My Way* could be the anthem of certain sociopaths; maybe that was what Chase was dealing with.

Many serial murderers gave information to people who were near authorities, although not necessarily the authorities themselves, and that was often seen as a desire to be caught. But Chase didn't see it that way. He believed they were more often interested in matching wits than getting caught. They wanted to outsmart the police. Devon wasn't cut out to be a victim, not even of himself.

Chase opened the door to the Special Collections room, trying not to listen to the blaze of his beating heart. He glanced quickly around the room: nobody home.

"Good afternoon, Mr. Chase." And abruptly, Devon was there, his voice a whisper. Standing behind his desk, as if he'd been there all along. It was just like the first time Chase had come to see him. "I suspect you have read the books? You are most diligent. I am impressed. Come in, come in."

Chase couldn't force himself to meet Devon's eyes; he went through the door anyway.

"You seem nervous, Mr. Chase. Did you have a rough night?"

*   *   *

Carol cradled the phone; it was ringing on the other end. Enough was enough. She'd already left a message with the newspaper and two of them on Chase's answering machine. She had to be sure that Chase wasn't doing what she thought he was doing, or that if he was, he was okay. Someone picked up the phone.

"Wise."

"Put me through to Special Collections, please."

The phone went into that dead silence that meant she was on hold. Carol missed the old days when you could hear the clicks as the call was transferred. At least then you knew there was something happening. She hated not knowing.

"Special Collections."

The voice caught her off guard. The way Chase had described it, she'd expected a feathery, more gender-neutral voice. Instead, she found Devon Lancaster's voice to be sensual and very male. It shook her.

"Yes. . . I'm looking for a Mr. Michael Chase, and I was told that he might be there this afternoon?"

"Yes, Chief Braxton. He is here. Hold on."

The phone went silent except for a muffled, scratchy sound, like it had been smothered by a palm. Then:

"Carol?"

"Chase. I've been trying to reach you." Now that she heard his voice, she felt silly about calling at all. "I left messages with your secretary."

"My—Oh, yeah. I didn't check. It was a late night. Look, why don't I call you later. I'm right in the middle of something."

"Sure. I just wanted to make sure everything was okay." Chase was silent after she said that, and she knew right away why: He didn't appreciate being checked up on, not even if there might be good reason.

"I've checked out Devon," she said in a rush. "And he *was* in Burlington during the killings. In fact, he disappeared just after the last one. I think he's a very dangerous man. I can't do anything yet, but I have a tail on him, and I should have a report on his history any time now. Just thought you should know. Do me *and you* a favor and call me or come by today after you leave there."

There was a pause before he said anything. Carol had a mental image of him sitting there, next to Lancaster, trying to think of exactly what to say.

"Yeah, Carol. That sounds great. I'd like to see you again. Maybe next week would be a good time. Maybe dinner at Casa. I'll call you."

When the line went dead after that, Carol was pleased: Chase had gotten the message and taken it seriously, despite the echoes of old business in the way it was delivered. Now there was one other precaution she could take. She punched up Elaine.

"Yes, Chief Braxton?"

"Patch me through to Greathouse." Robert Greathouse was the man this shift who was assigned to Devon. His cruiser would be sitting outside the library, and his cell would be on if he was in the library itself.

*   *   *

"What did Chief Braxton want, Mr. Chase?" Devon said as Chase hung up.

"She wanted to know that I was all right." Chase let the truth slip out before he thought about it. He should know enough to pay attention when he was talking with Devon. He was surprised by Devon's reaction:

"Thank you." Devon's eyes crinkled. Chase wanted to know what he meant by that, but Devon waved him off and stood up.

"We do not have as much time as I had hoped, Mr. Chase." He walked to the edge of his desk, played the glass globe in his hand. "Time is very short, in fact. I am going to have to lead you through this to the end. Do you have any objections?" His voice rose above a whisper and took on a sing-song quality. "We will lose all the subtlety."

Chase was reminded of the times he had interviewed psychotic patients—the same sing-song intonation.

"I'll live."

"You should watch the sarcasm, Mr. Chase. It has a way of sowing seeds that are exactly the opposite of the plants you want to nurture." Devon tossed the globe up and down as if feeling its weight.

"Thanks for the warning."

Devon shook his head sadly but with amusement, as if Chase was an errant child. "Let us proceed then. I assume you got the message implied by two of the books. The third one then, *The Steel Gods of Ur*, requires explication." He set the globe down very deliberately on his desk. "What did you get from that?"

Chase thought for a moment; he had only skimmed that one.

"The high priests of Ur sacrificed children to what they considered the high gods," he ventured uncertainly.

"And they sacrificed them how?"

"By throwing them in the furnaces."

"The steel-making furnaces."

Chase nodded, although he wasn't sure this was the case. Devon was pacing now, and he seemed agitated. Chase felt as if he didn't dare say anything.

"The parents did not want the children sacrificed," Devon said, his voice a controlled whisper even though his pacing and his hands had become suddenly twitchy and vibrant. "But the priests did. The government backed the priests. What choice did the parents have?"

Chase shrugged. "None?"

"Exactly. The parents had no choice but to collinsate with a very evil state of being. The evil—and the people knew at the time it was evil—was backed up by the power of government and the power of technology—the newly discovered methods of steel-making and the furnace required—which was associated with that evil."

Chase's stomach heaved. Even his body knew he was in the presence of evil, although his mind called it *insanity*.

Devon leaned over the desk, his face inches from Chase's. "And what kind of evil would we call that today?"

Chase made a guess, but he knew the guess was what Devon was looking for. "Satanism?"

"Exactly." Devon began to pace again. His path was wide now, sweeping back and forth in great swaths behind the desk. Suddenly, he stopped behind his desk again. "But the problem is, they *do* get power from the deaths of innocents. Power you cannot imagine as an uninitiated person. You are but human, so you do not understand this easily. That is why I wanted you to come upon it on your own. But one gains personal power—many powers, and they are not simple—from torturing and killing the unsuspecting. If it is done properly."

Chase knew this was everything short of a confession. *Now what?* He stood up. Slowly. He watched Devon turn his head and look. He fixed his eyes on Chase. "Do not go yet," he whispered.

Chase wanted to leave, but he didn't move, and he wasn't sure he could have if he tried.

"This may be our last conversation, Mr. Chase, and there are still two more points I want to make."

When Devon didn't say anything further, Chase tried to speak, but the words caught in his throat.

Devon smiled slightly. "The first point: A large and influential organization must be very close-knit to remain secret from the general society. You no doubt know that the existence of the Mafia was not even acknowledged until the early 1960s. La Familia, they called themselves, because they *were.*"

Chase didn't know what to make of this. He still wanted badly to get out of there, but he somehow felt he'd be safer if he waited until Devon gave him some kind of sign that he was free to go. He nodded to signal Devon to continue.

Devon smiled. "Think about it. It will come to you." He sat down in his desk chair. "One more thing. Do you know what comes out after a body is cremated?"

Chase shook his head.

"Mostly, salts. You put a body on a slab and slide it into an oven, and mostly what comes out is salt. A row of salt. You might call it a pillar."

Chase thought about the note Carol had received, and the hair on the back of his neck stood up.

75
Friday afternoon, October 22

An hour later, Devon Lancaster is thinking about his conversation with Michael Chase. He is not pleased, not sure his message got through; Chase left looking more frightened than enlightened. Maybe it would sink in, eventually. Hopefully.

His hand caresses the glass globe on his desk. Maybe this whole thing is getting out of hand. He is not sure whether it was best to involve the journalist. Too late, though; that is the Way. And a police tail—one man working alone, a different man on different shifts. Probably Chase tipped Braxton, who ordered the surveillance, but there is no way of being certain. Uncertainty is bound to be a feature of this Work.

The doorknob to his Special Collections room turns. Devon likes the fact that this door still works on the old-style latch, instead of the newer, automatic slide-back doors. He does not much care for technology, except insofar as it adds to the aesthetics of an event.

The doorknob continues to turn.

Devon has time to contemplate such things. Time moves in slow motion for him, when he wants it to. More precisely, his mind works on fast-forward according to his desire, and perception of reality is relative to the state of mind in the perceiver.

The door opens. Devon freezes.

He knows that as long as he does not move, the man will not see him. The secret of invisibility. Every animal knows it instinctively. Humans are aware of it, too, when they bother to pay attention to what their bodies know.

The man is Morton Collins, and he has come to make an arrest. His gun is out. Devon hopes that he has not miscalculated the timing too drastically on this Work. It is apparent now that he is somewhat off. The full moon is not until Monday. It comes down to who set the policeman to trail him. If it was Braxton, the Work should still go smoothly.

He is going to miss this library.

Devon watches Morton scan the room, notes that he does not see anyone. The fed's eyes passed right across him. He wonders if Morton knows yet with whom he is dealing. Probably, yes, to some degree: Konrad must have told him.

"Can I help you, Morton?"

Collins looks toward the place where Devon has thrown his voice.

The glass globe flicks across the room, fired by Devon's powerful forearm.

* * *

Carol ignored the blinking light as long as she could. Might as well keep 'em waiting. She picked up the phone.

"Yo, Braxy." It was Chase.

"Where have you been?" Carol wasn't as angry as she sounded, but she decided to let it stand. She was leaning back in her chair, trying to catch a moment of relaxation.

"What are you talking about?"

"You were supposed to call me after you left the library."

"I'm calling you now."

Carol sighed; she hadn't wanted to say it: "I've been worried."

"Because you love me?"

"Screw you." She *knew* he would say something like that. "Just because we're on better terms doesn't mean that you can—"

"Woah, woah. You can ream me out later. I got something for you."

"This better be good, Chase."

"Okay, check this out. The thing is, someone else tried to kill me the other night. And the guys who rented the car before go by the names of William Abbott and—."

"We know that."

"What about Theron Davies?"

Carol's breath caught. She couldn't say anything.

"You know him?"

Even though it was a lie, she managed to choke it out. "No."

"Here's the thing, Carol. Lancaster definitely wrote that note."

Carol sat up straight, her eyebrows raised. "Why do you think he wrote it?"

"I just came from there. I spent the afternoon with him. He knows a lot about Satanism. He's very educated. His speech patterns are odd, archaic somehow. And grandiose. He also talked about pillars of salt. And he's crazy as hell."

Carol didn't say anything for several heartbeats: It sounded like they had him.

"Do you have probable?"

"No."

* * *

Carol told Chase and the two officers to wait in the hallway for five minutes before following her into the Special Collections room. She wanted Lancaster at ease when he realized what was happening. In plain clothes, she had a chance of doing that, but once he saw the uniformed officers, that chance would be gone. Although if Chase was right, this character was never what you could call at ease.

She didn't feel too at ease herself. She could arrest the man, but based on what? The word of a journalist with a hunch? Judge Wheeler didn't like her anyway; he'd love a wrongful arrest ruling.

"Charge him with withholding evidence," Chase had suggested. "Then all you have to do is prove he wrote the note."

The question became moot once she opened the door. Collins was the only one in the room. He stood behind a large wooden desk; he appeared to be rifling its drawers. He looked up sharply, and Carol caught surprise, and—she thought—a flash of guilt pass over his face.

"Where's Lancaster?" she asked, looking around the room.

Collins straightened and began rubbing the base of his skull with his left hand. "Ms. Braxton. It's about time you got here. He's gone. About 20 minutes ago, nearest I can tell."

It's about time. . .? Carol thought. This guy was really beginning to bug her. "What exactly are *you* doing here?" She opened the door to the hall: "Come on in, folks."

"Following up on that note you gave me. Didn't Watts talk to you? I called in to let you know what was up. You were in some kind of meeting." Collins looked at the two uniformed officers and then at Chase. He jerked his head in Chase's direction, then winced and rubbed again. "What's he doing here?"

"Don't worry about it, *Agent* Collins," Carol said. "You were supposed to report to me. That was our arrangement." The officers took positions on either side of the door. Chase leaned back against the wall and crossed his arms.

Collins came around the table. "Look, *Chief* Braxton. I was doing my job as a member of a *federal* agency. I didn't have time to wait around to tell you *personally* about every move I make. I told *your* Supervising Detective. We've been through this before. A communication problem among your people is not my concern." Collins kept looking back and forth at Carol and Chase as he talked.

He's right, of course, thought Carol. She'd ream Watts out later for this little embarrassment. But she'd be darned if she'd apologize to this. . . goon. "What happened here?"

"The man nearly killed me, *that's* what happened." Collins was looking at the floor and rubbing his head again. "I came down here to talk to him. Find out what he knew about the note. He got real defensive, real fast. Said if I ever tried to talk to him again, I'd better have a warrant. I don't think he's screwed on too tight. He got pretty abusive." Collins looked up. "Braxton, if you didn't talk to Watts, what are *you* doing here? And why the backup?"

Carol glanced over at Chase. Back at Watts. "It looks like Lancaster is rapidly becoming a suspect in these murders." When she said that, Carol thought she caught a ghost of a smile in Collins's eyes. "But what else? What do you mean he tried to kill you?"

Collins shrugged. "I turned to go, the next thing I know, I felt a sharp pain in back here—" He indicated a spot at the base of his skull. "—and then. . ." He shrugged again. "I guessed I passed out."

"He hit you?"

He shook his head. "He wasn't close enough. He threw something at me. I don't know what, though."

There was a moment of silence, in which Collins looked down. Carol glanced at Chase, who was looking at Collins, one eyebrow raised. Chase was thinking about something; he *knew* something. *Later, later.*

76
Saturday evening, October 23

Chase saw Carol as soon as he arrived at the Omega. She sat in a booth facing the door, and she lifted her chin in greeting. Chase wasn't late—6 o'clock on the dot, in fact—so she must have gotten here early. That surprised him, because Carol was never early for anything. She also had a half-empty beer mug in front of her, which was another surprise.

As he walked across the restaurant floor, Carol caught the eye of a waitress and motioned for her to bring two more beers. She was apparently planning to put a few away tonight.

Chase slid into the booth opposite her. "You sure you should be drinking tonight, Braxy? Aren't you on call or something?"

Carol took a long, deliberate pull on her beer before changing the subject. "You didn't go home last night, did you?"

"Jealous?" Chase had expected her to be on edge, what with the prime suspect still at large. "Stayed with a friend of a friend."

"That Shango person?"

The waitress arrived with the beers. Chase noticed she brought bev naps for them, something none of the wait staff did when they were bringing him beers.

"Yeah," he said as he raised his head. "A friend of his."

Carol looked at him silently for a second, considering something.

"At least you'll be safe with that thug. Relatively. That is, if he can get out of bed. How bad did he get shot?"

Chase feigned surprise, but as soon as he did, he knew they both knew it was an act. Still, there was no reason to come clean, and every reason not to. Even if she didn't turn him in, she would be put in the position of concealing evidence in a homicide: The guard in the tunnel where they had been hacking had died on Thursday without regaining consciousness. Whoever had come after them hadn't been just trying to scare him this time.

"What makes you ask that?" he said carefully.

Carol leaned forward in her chair. "Two other people were shot besides the guard who died. One person bled a lot, and there was more than a little blood on some pipes near one of the street-level exits. Traces of blood on the surface, too, behind the bushes by Appel Hall."

"Why didn't you tell me this yesterday, Carol?"

"There really wasn't any time. After we left the library, I expected you to meet me down at the station, which you didn't do. So I left that message for you to meet me today. There's a few other things we need to go into, but let me finish with this.

"Whoever was the one who was shot bad was the one who killed the guard." Carol held up her hand as Chase started to protest. "I don't think it was one of you guys, but I want to know who it was. I need to talk to Shango."

"How do you know him, anyway?" Chase decided not to tell her Shango was right outside in the alley, shadowing Chase like he'd been paid to do. Like he'd been doing since Tuesday night. Chase felt a lot safer with Shango watching his back.

Carol smiled tightly. "You should probably ask Elaine about that one."

Elaine, huh? Chase thought. So she was Shango's police station connection. At least he had taste. "Why do you think it was Shango?"

"There had to be three of you in that tunnel Tuesday," Carol said. "You, because it was your idea. Someone did the hacking, which was how you came up with Davies's name. And since hackers are not notoriously proficient with firearms, I think that's what you had Shango along for."

"Okay, Carol. Suppose that was where we did the hacking—if we actually did any, that is—and suppose that Shango was there with us, and suppose that he got a good look at the shooter—"

"That's what I want to talk to him about."

"Wait, wait. My turn now. Suppose he saw the shooter and can absolutely confirm that Devon is not our man. What then?"

Carol thought about it, took a drink of her beer. "I guess you never actually said that you thought he was the killer we were looking for."

"I said he was crazy, which he is. I think." Actually, Chase was beginning to wonder about that. He'd been thinking more. . . He'd had those dreams, and Devon seemed to know about them. Maybe what he had said about powers. . . "But I'm not so sure he's the one."

"He did try to brain Collins."

"So Collins says. But it doesn't fit, not the way he told it, at least. I can't see Lancaster suddenly getting abusive like that. It's not consistent with the man I met. That man was *in control*. Besides, why didn't he kill Collins if he's a murderer?"

"He only kills women. Ritualistically. Some kind of power trip. You said yourself he was talking about some kind of powers he thinks Satanists get from killing women."

"People."

Carol looked up. "What?"

"People. Lancaster said they get power from ritualistically murdering innocent people. Not just women."

"Whatever. You know as well as I do that translates mostly into killing women."

Chase couldn't argue with that. For one thing, he didn't know enough about it. For another, he suspected she was right. He decided to let it pass; there were other things to get to. "I think Lancaster was trying to help in some twisted way. Remember how in his note he warned you not to trust Collins?"

"Which is just what he would say if—" Carol stopped talking abruptly and looked off to her left, thinking. "There must be a connection between the two of them."

Chase was nodding. He let her keep talking. It had occurred to him, too, but he couldn't come up with anything. Maybe if Carol talked it out. . .

"That's why you were looking at Collins when we were in Special Collections? You were wondering how he'd known to come after Lancaster."

Chase nodded again, took a sip of his beer. He made a rolling motion with his hand to encourage her line of thinking.

"He couldn't have found out from me about the background check I'd run, and other than that, Lancaster's name has never come up." Carol paused again, looking off to her left; Chase remained silent. "So Lancaster knew about Collins, and Collins knew about Lancaster." She looked at Chase. "Chase, this is more than just a serial murder case."

"I agree." Chase had come to that conclusion when he'd realized that Lancaster and Collins knew each other—it was nice to hear that Carol also believed that. It was good to know that his essential paranoia was not totally misguided in this case. "What did you find out about Lancaster?"

Carol began to root around in her briefcase. "Order me another beer, would you?"

Chase thought he'd seen this mood in her before, but only a few times, and those were years ago. He flagged the waitress.

Carol found what she was looking for and pulled a file folder. She opened it and smoothed it on the table in front of her.

"There isn't a lot, Chase. The most surprising thing we were able to track down is that he's a doctor, although he's never practiced as far as we could tell."

"An MD?" The waitress set Carol's beer on the table and then disappeared. *They never give me that kind of service.*

Carol was nodding. "Boy genius, too, apparently. He got into Princeton at 16 and was through the whole program by the time he was 25. His instructors noted that he seemed to be indestructible. He breezed through his internships, and those things are nearly impossible as it is. But he never took any boards or applied for a license as far as we can tell. He also didn't mention his medical degree when he applied for the job at Wise."

Chase frowned. "Why not?"

Carol shrugged. "No idea. Probably afraid of being overqualified. He came close to it as it was."

"How could he have been overqualified, since he had no Library Science degree. Did he?"

"No. But after med school, he disappears entirely from any records in the U.S., unless maybe he's on the IRS files. We couldn't get access to those." Carol smiled knowingly. "Although maybe your buddy could—"

Chase waved his hand and cut her off. "Forget that. What next?"

"His Wise application gave references in Italy and the Mid East. We checked them out and they seem legitimate. He worked as the curator of a private museum in Italy for seven years. That started about four years after he graduated. I called the museum personally, and whoever answered the phone—in Italian, I should add—confirmed that Lancaster had worked there as curator. When I asked, he said the museum was devoted to—quote—the preservation of religious artifacts—unquote. He wouldn't go into any more detail."

Chase had nothing to say to that. There was a lot more to Lancaster than met the eye, which was consistent with his impression of the man he had spoken with. He wondered what such a man was doing in Morgantown, West Virginia. "So what about the Mid East stuff?"

Carol took two big gulps of her beer. She wiped her lips. "He worked sporadically for a library in Oman that professes—according to our calls—to be interested in recovering the works that were created during the glory days of Islam. You know, the original works that concern the invention of algebra, astronomy, bronze, steel, the sixty-minute clock. . . ."

Chase didn't feel it was necessary to correct her: Everything but algebra had been invented long before Mohammed, but there was no use going into it. Instead, he brought the discussion back to the case they were involved in.

"What's he doing here, Carol? Why here?"

Carol shrugged. "Beats me." She took another gulp of her beer.

77
Saturday evening, October 23

Alexandra was laying back on their couch reading *The Sociology of Crime*. She was rubbing her feet together slowly while Jerome held them in his lap, one hand on them, the other holding up his book: *Alfred's Muse*, a long and, to Alex's mind, tedious novel. Someone had given it to her last Christmas, and she'd tried to read it but found it about as interesting as doing laundry.

It occurred to her that this was an example of one of her favorite moments: relaxing in the evening with her husband, reading in front of a robust fire, warm and snug and secure. To top it off, rubbing her stocking feet together was one of her favorite things. She'd had a whole day to cleanse herself of the demands of her clients, a quiet day puttering around the house letting the concerns of other people drop away. Only a small tickle still worried the back of her mind, practically a physical sensation.

Despite her apprehensions, Alexandra hadn't heard from the midnight caller for almost a month. He'd never gone this long before. Maybe it was over, and apparently the police had been right not to bother tapping the phone. Still, she hadn't quite been able to get him out of her mind. She felt he was still out there and was waiting for the next call, the knock on the door, the shadowy figure waiting for her in the parking lot late one night.

"You okay, lady?" Jer asked. She sighed: He'd noticed that she'd stopped reading.

"Yeah," she said lazily. "I'm just feeling really happy." She'd decided not to mention worry. She looked over the top of her book. "I love you, Jer."

"Mmm," he said, patting her feet. "I love you, too, Alex." He sat up. "You know, this book's getting on my nerves. Why don't we go upstairs?"

"But it's only 8:30, mon amor."

"I know that," Jerome said. He winked.

78
Saturday evening, October 23

Chase finished his beer and was about to order another. He glanced at Carol, who was downing the last of hers. She nodded, raising her eyebrows. Chase signaled the waitress.

"This is a switch," he said. "Instead of too few suspects, you have too many."

Carol wiped her mouth with the bev nap. She shook her head. "Actually, that's the way it goes a lot."

Chase tapped the tabletop with his forefinger. "Okay, what have we got? There's Lancaster and Collins, who both figure into this somehow, but we've got no idea how. And whoever it was who took the potshots at—"

"You sure it wasn't either of them?"

Chase shook his head. "No way. Shango saw the—" Chase stopped abruptly, aware that he'd said something he didn't mean to. He was on his third beer, and his tongue was getting loose.

Carol smiled and waggled her finger at him. "I've got to talk to him. The sooner, the better."

Chase wondered how many beers she'd had before he got there. He'd never known Carol to waggle her finger before at least five beers. Since she almost never had that many at one sitting in all the time they'd been involved, he'd almost never seen her waggle her finger. She must be more upset than he'd realized.

"I'll see what I can do," he said lamely. There were a lot of reasons he couldn't call Shango in from the alley, not the least of them being that he still wanted his back watched and he didn't want to present Shango with a fait accompli when it came to talking to the cops.

"You do that," Carol said. "Now, go ahead."

"Umm. . ." Chase stalled, trying to remember where he was. "Yes. Uh, we have at least those three, and probably the Theron Davies guy, although he might be the same guy as the shooter." He stopped; Carol was shaking her head.

"No. Well, maybe, but I know who that is. Was the guy who Shango saw in the tunnel an African-American?"

"I don't think so." He'd thought that Carol recognized the name when he told her, but he hadn't pressed it. Now was the time. He held out his hands, palms up, and raised his eyebrows. Carol got the hint.

"Davies is the ME that the FBI sent us. He's good, but he's creepy."

"Creepy how?"

Carol swirled her beer. "He seems to have an affinity for dead bodies."

Chase leaned forward. "Carol, are you sure the FBI sent him?"

"As opposed to what? He had his ID."

Chase shook his head, trying to clear it. No use, the beers made it hard to think. "Carol, I don't know how to say this—and I don't want to pre-empt you in any way—but is there some way you could find out who sent Davies?" He sighed. He took a drink of beer. He had wanted to avoid this. "I'll tell you something, but if I'm ever asked, I'll deny I said it. That way, neither of us will get in any trouble. Think of it as the source-to-journalist thing, only in reverse."

Carol leaned forward. "I never heard it from you."

Chase noticed her eyelashes and remembered how they felt against his cheek, which didn't make it any easier.

"Collins's not on the active file at the FBI. He's not listed. I didn't know to look for Davies, but it could be that this is a renegade operation of some kind. For sure it isn't on the up-and-up."

Carol surprised him by laughing. She patted his hand patronizingly, breaking his thought. His hand flinched away, remembering the pain from a couple of weeks before.

"What?" he asked, feeling sulky.

"Chase, the FBI doesn't jerk around like that. There must be a reason."

That was where he had her. "What is it? Can you come up with one plausible explanation?"

Carol's face changed from gloating surety to uncertainty. At last, she ventured: "This is a top secret operation."

Chase snorted his disgust. "Why exactly? Something's wrong here, and you know it. I'm not just being paranoid."

Again, Carol smiled. "Not you."

Chase ignored her comment. "Can you check it out? Can you see if Collins or Davies was officially assigned?" He sat back in the booth, took a drink of beer. "If not, what are they doing here?"

Carol started to speak and then stopped. Thought better of it, apparently.

"It's not so simple this time, is it Carol?" Chase knew that she would take his comment as a dig at her about the Clawson case, which was exactly what he intended it as.

Carol spoke hesitantly, and she chose to ignore his verbal dig. "Chase, you know that I think you're paranoid." He started to speak, but she held up her hand. "We both know you are, so that's not really the issue. You may be right this time, and I can see what you're saying. The only thing is, I think, if you're going to insist on a paranoid worldview here, then you ought to include Watts in the whole equation."

Chase noticed she was choosing her words carefully, and she was enunciating more precisely than usual. She was definitely drunk.

"Somebody's responsible for a false report that ostensibly came from Davies. I don't think—whatever side he's on—that he's dumb enough to try to fake it the way he did. He mentioned something to me when I talked to him in the morgue, and it wasn't in his report. Somebody faked it, and I think it was Watts."

Chase sighed deeply; he leaned against the back of the booth. He looked at Carol, trying to think of her as 'Chief Braxton' and not the woman who had shared his bed for more than a year. He wasn't succeeding.

"So where does that leave us?" he asked.

Carol sat up straight and motioned for the waitress. "I think that leaves us with the fact that you can't stay at your place tonight."

When she said that, Chase's first thought was that this was his chance. He hadn't liked the way things had ended between them, didn't like the *fact* that they had ended. This was his chance, his first thought. But his second thought was that this moment, this rekindled connection they felt tonight. . . "Carol, I don't know if that's such a good idea."

"Shhh," she said. "Where else are you going to stay?" It wasn't a question. "Shango can just shack up with his friend. You'll be safe at my place." The waitress brought the check, and Carol gave her a twenty.

When the waitress brought her change back, Carol pocketed it, leaving a five-dollar bill as a tip. Chase thought that was extravagant, but he didn't argue.

He couldn't help but feel a little self-conscious about the sequence of events. Carol gripped his hand and tugged him toward the door. On the way out, he saw the old man who had been sitting in the next booth—the man smiled and crinkled his eyes.

"Wait, wait," he said as they passed through the Omega door and stood at the bottom of the steps that led up to the alley and away from there. It was still raining.

"Carol, you know I'm easy when I've been drinking," he shouted over the rain.

"That's what I'm counting on," she yelled.

"But I can't. Not tonight." He looked away so he wouldn't see if she was disappointed. Or pleased.

79

Saturday evening, October 23

Maria was shouting: "Darnit, Don! There's nothing wrong! Okay! Okay? Just let it go." Sometimes she wished her husband wasn't so aware of her moods, that he didn't care so much.

"No, I won't let it go, Mar. It's been going on too long. It's not like you. Something's going on that you're not telling me."

But there isn't! The voice in Maria's head screamed it; she wanted to scream it, too. But she didn't. "Don, honey," she said instead, trying to keep her voice steady, "There's nothing going on. Now, would you just drop it?" Despite her efforts, she heard her voice rising in pitch.

Don reached across the bed and touched her bare stomach. He spoke quietly, carefully. "Maria. You've been denying it for two months now. Why don't you just say it, bring it out, so we can talk about it?"

"That's it," Maria said sharply. She rolled, pulling away from his hand and moving her feet out of the bed and onto the floor. "I'm tired of this crap." She stood and walked to the bedroom door. There was nothing wrong—Alex had cleared her up on the attraction to older men thing—and if Don wasn't going to leave her alone, she was just going to have to leave him alone until he came to his senses.

"I'll be downstairs," she said. She didn't look forward to spending the night alone, on the foldout, especially since it seemed like she'd been doing that a lot lately, but if her husband wasn't going to come to his senses. . .

*   *   *

Thrashing in tangled sheets and the smell of sweat: That's what Chase woke up to. He instinctively felt for Carol, but he was in his own bed, and she wasn't there. He lay his head back, remembering the dream, his dream: He'd seen Lancaster standing there, on the roof of a high building—he didn't know what building or where because he couldn't see the building or landscape beyond it—and Lancaster was tossing the globe up and down with his left hand.

"It will come down to this, Mr. Chase," the Lancaster figure had said. "You are the only one. *What are you made of, Michael Chase?* A full bone moon is coming. Less than 48 hours. Make sure there is a strong police presence at Woodburn Circle. Be ready. Look for me behind the exhaust stack."

Chase's dream froze after that, a freeze frame like one provided by a DVD, like a still photograph. The freeze broke and moved into slow motion. He looked around and spotted Lancaster peering from behind an aluminum smokestack, on top of a raised portion of whatever rooftop they were on. Lancaster waved at him, actually fluttering the fingers of his right hand. And then he laughed. Words echoed through Chase's dream: "Full bone moon." And then Lancaster disappeared.

80
Monday evening, October 25: Full bone moon

She is still a hundred yards ahead of his position, but Devon sees her well enough. After two weeks, the rain has finally stopped, but Devon is not surprised. *Nature respects the real storm,* he thinks, his eyes still glued on the young woman. He is pretty sure she is the one from his vision: brown hair, short, slender, her bookbag slung over her left shoulder, her thumb out. She is waiting for a ride, and as soon as a few more cars get through the stop sign, he will be there to give her one. His hands grip the wheel.

If only she knew.

He is positive it is her. Unlike last time, he feels the ache at the base of his skull, in back, right above where it joins his neck. His palms itch, too, which is the sure sign of success, the sign he missed in last month. And the months before. . .

He takes a hand off the wheel and rubs his broad forehead. Not too much sweat. Temperature high, but that is to be expected. He had not expected it to be so difficult to get right, but he should have known. He is really reaching this time. Not overreaching, he hopes. If there was only some way to be sure. The Opponent is better than guessed.

Only five cars between her and him now. . . . Traffic started up, then stopped again. This should be a sure thing, unless Chase had taken his warning seriously. If so. . .

Four cars now. . . Start and stop. Three. . . Start and stop. Two. . . *Dang it!*—a car is stopping and picking the kid up. Too late. This close, too!

He grinds his teeth. His hands grip the steering wheel and twist. If the wheel was one of those plastic ones, it would torque loose. But it is steel. It holds.

He considers following the car—recent model, bright red, West Virginia plates—but decides that would be futile. He should go back home, perform a ceremony. Perhaps he can do something from there.

The full moon is rising in the evening sky. He imagines he can hear it whisper: "Ator, malkuth, ve-gevurah, ve-gedulah, le-olahm."

He scans the area for police presence, sees none. No, wait. Those three, on the bench to his right, they are too old to be students. He looks left and right at three other men now loping across the street; they are reaching in their jackets. In his rearview mirror, he sees that the two cars that had been sitting in front of the student union are now pulling into traffic, their lights come on as he watches.

Devon surmises two things: his warning had gotten through to Chase, but in the worst way; and he is beaten on this move—one more pawn down. This is it.

Suddenly the passenger door to his car rips open—it is what he asked for; what should he expect?

"Stop right there, big boy. Keep your hands in sight!"

The officers surround his car, three on his left and three on his right. Devon freezes and puts his hands on his head so they would not get nervous, do something he might regret. He can only hope the rest of his warning got through to Chase, and that Chase was able to arrange with Braxton to get the thing covered.

He could only hope.

As they take him out of his car, Devon lapses into a deep meditation, the way he had been taught in the desert. He had known the skill would come in handy some day. . . .

. . . which was just what his mentor had chided him about. "You still think in terms of—what is the word?—'utilitarianism'. You think about this world. You think it matters. You think that you are doing things instead of the fact that things are done *through* you. You are the instrument and not the handler."

As the hands grip under his armpits and throw him against the hood of his car, Devon decides to be the handler and not the instrument. He wills it. He feels his eyes roll back in his head, his body go limp against the trunk of the car, his spirit ranges out, searching for Chase or Braxton or any of the principles in this affair.

He only barely feels the handcuffs.

*   *   *

Katie opened the door to the car that stopped for her, happy to see Maria for the first time in a week. She was kind of surprised though, because even though she hitched from here three times a week, every Monday-Wednesday-Friday, Maria had never picked her up before. Usually, her boss was tending to *Chuckles* at this time of the evening.

"Hey, Boss," she said, mostly because she knew Maria liked to be called 'Boss'. "Going my way?"

Maria didn't turn her head, only stared out the front of the car. She put the car in gear and started forward. Katie wondered what that was all about, why Maria was being so cold, but she figured it must be because of the way she had acted the week before, when Maria had been late.

"Hey, I'm sorry about the other day. Really. I just got upset because I have that stats test coming up." She laughed and looked out the window to her right. "It's got me really freaked out."

Katie didn't look back in Maria's direction, but she listened and heard only silence. She figured Maria must be really angry. Instead, she looked over her right shoulder, behind her, out the back window of the car. She saw the flashing police lights and six men running up to one car.

"Look at that!" Excited, she turned back to Maria. Her boss was still staring straight ahead; she didn't even look in the rearview. Katie wanted to get out then, go back and see what was happening, but she was even more concerned with Maria's attitude. She decided to stay focused on what was happening in the car.

"Maria? Boss?"

Maria didn't answer. She turned the car right, up a side street that would lead up a steep hill, a windy back route up to Austin's Grocery. It wasn't the way Katie wanted to go, and she knew Maria knew that.

"What's up? Where are you headed?"

It was then that Maria finally turned to look at her. There were tears in her boss's eyes. "I'm sorry, Katie."

Katie had a second of short-circuit. She couldn't think anything, and it was a moment before she managed to wonder just what Maria was sorry for. "What are you—uummmph!"

Katie felt the wet cloth cover her nose and mouth from behind. She wanted to breathe, she tried to breathe, but she drew harsh, chemical-scented air through her nostrils. She tried to choke, but the rag or whatever it was, smothered it. The scene out the window, in front of her eyes, was turning dark and she realized that the smell must be chloroform and she panicked about her stats test and she thought about how she hadn't fed her cat.

IV

"No choice"

81
Monday evening, October 25: Full moon

Watts picked up the phone because he was tired of the flashing light. "Yeah?"

He couldn't help but sound irritated because that's what he was. He looked at Collins, who was starting to leave, caught his eye and silently told him to hold off, into the ceilingwait a second, they would continue the discussion in a moment. Things were down to the wire now, and with everything going just on schedule, Watts didn't want to end what might be their last conversation before he had his say.

But when the caller spoke, Watts froze inside; he recognized the raspy, whispery voice on the other end. "Give me Collins."

"Wait a second. What makes you think Collins's—"

The Old Man interrupted with a bark: "Now!"

Watts held out the phone, motioning Collins over to it. Watts's stomach churned, and Collins must have seen it on his face, because he grimaced then and looked at Watts questioningly. Watts nodded. *It's him.* He heard Collins mumble something incoherent.

Collins took the phone.

Collins said, "Agent Collins," then listened. Watts imagined he could hear words slithering through the phone.

After a while, Collins said, "Yes, he's in custody."

Pause, while Collins listened.

"No, sir, it's not. We can tie him to the case, but—"

Collins waited, apparently interrupted. After a few seconds:

"No. But we have a search on his apartment, and we can use all that—" Collins twisted the phone line. Watts was thinking that it was the first sign of nervousness—of *humanness*—that he'd seen in Collins.

"I know it's circumstantial, sir, but we also have the letter. We had to move—"

This time Collins was interrupted, Watts saw his jaws clench: another sign of humanness, human qualities. But then, he shouldn't be surprised that the Old Man inspired such fear. It occurred to Watts that such things shouldn't be: No one should go along with another unquestioningly. It wasn't right.

Collins stiffened abruptly, his whole body going rigid. "What?" Collins closed his eyes as he listened, as if in frustration, or pain, or. . . "There's no way to stop it?" he said at last.

Watts figured they were talking about another death, and he didn't want to be a part of it. He didn't know where these thoughts were coming from, but he knew what they meant. He watched Collins listen, before saying:

"This is not a good—" Collins was interrupted again. He listened some more.

Watts noted that somehow Collins managed to nod his head *yes* and shake it *no* at the same time. He imagined that Collins was now the one with a churning in the gut.

"Okay, sir," Collins was saying. "Okay. We'll find a way. . . . Yes, sir. . . Yes, here he is."

Collins reached out the phone to Watts, his hand cupped over the mouthpiece. He was shaking his head. As Watts took the phone, Collins silently mouthed the words, "He's really screwing up on this one," shaking his head as if it were a shame.

Watts took the phone, slightly shaken. It took him a second to lift it to his ear. The Old Man had never screwed up before, and he found it hard to believe it was happening now. The Old Man had always known everything, and he knew it before anyone else.

But there were implications about this case he found difficult to gloss over, and he knew that the press and public would find them even harder to swallow. It hadn't been conducted the way that the Clawson investigation had, and Chase would be even harder to throw off this time. He held the phone to his ear.

"Darnell, you there yet?"

"Yes, sir."

"When they bring him in, let him go."

That was not what Watts had expected. He phrased his words carefully: "I can't do that, sir. There's too many people that know."

"Let him go. Let him *try* to escape."

Watts hesitated; he sighed heavily. "We discussed that before, and we decided that it would be too—"

"Don't worry." The Old Man cut him off. "Not what we were talking about before. It's over now. Let him go; we've finished him. He'll disappear. Collins knows what to do."

Watts decided; he couldn't go along with it unquestioningly: Those days were over.

"I can't do that," Watts said, and even as he said it, he knew that the Family thing was nearly at an end: He just couldn't let it go any farther.

He remembered the sacrifices he'd participated in, how he had thought them faked the same way the Family had faked the burning of his flesh, and how now he knew that none of it was faked. None of it. Those girls had died on the alter, and now he knew it and now he would no longer collinsate: There was no excuse he could see or feel for slaughter, not even for the supposed powers it conferred.

He shook his head. It wasn't like him to doubt like this, to question. He had put his trust in the Family years ago, and it had never let him down, and he had never let it down and it didn't matter that he was still a boy when he decided to join and he didn't know what he was doing and he wasn't responsible for his decision because it was made under duress and—

He held the phone away from his ear for a second, confused by his thoughts. They were swirling in spirals and he felt almost like there were two competing voices in his head and they were saying different things and they were making him think about what he didn't—

"Get a grip, Watts!" The raspy voice on the phone snapped him out of it. "You can't do this," the whispering voice said. "For lots of reasons. The main thing is we're your Family. You can't leave us behind." The voice stopped, and Watts could hear the labored breathing of an elderly person, and that brought him up short. He'd never thought of the Old Man as *an elderly person*.

"You have to follow this through, Watts. You have no choice."

Watts said nothing in protest, because he thought it was the truth.

82

Monday evening, October 25: Full bone moon

Devon comes out of his meditation, and he is lying on a cot. He realizes this dimly through the receding echoes of his trance-dream. As is usually the case, his dream memories are vague and hazy; in the past he has likened his recollections of them to watching a Balinese shadowplay done with a very diffuse light source while he was very drunk and then trying to remember the characters in the morning. But he *knows* things after the trances, and even if he cannot be sure where the knowledge comes from, it always proves to be accurate. He has learned to trust it.

Without opening his eyes, he knows that it is a prison cot. He opens his eyes a crack, sees the bars across the front of the cell, the bars that cover the one window that would let in the daylight, although at the moment, it only lets in the streetlight and the nightview behind the light. That leaves two exits.

His best choice is to wait until someone brings him food. That is when he will act. That decision made, Devon allows himself to slip into a light sleep.

Sometime later—he canot be sure when—a small clatter in the hallway awakens him. Devon is still lying on the cot and sees the whole, unfolding action through slitted eyes. A guard. The officer unlocks the cell door gingerly, and he is carrying a tray. Devon smells food. Hot roast beef, mashed potatoes, and something green. Food at midnight? Devon is sure that this is a setup. But how? He is sure they are not going to shoot him, that this is not that kind of trap, but equally certain that it has been arranged: He can all but smell the breath of the Old Man, hovering. He is suddenly certain this is one of the things he learned in the trance-dream.

He watches the officer place the tray on the cement next to his cot, apparently careless of the prisoner. They must have told the man that Devon was drugged and no threat. Devon realizes that this is the opportunity being provided. The question is whether to take it. The Old Man obviously wants him to escape, but maybe it would be better not to.

No: Everything clicks into place in his head. It is the last full moon before the Celtic new year, the full bone moon, the time when the veil is thinnest. There will definitely be a sacrifice tonight, if there has not been already, and they need him out so there is someone to take the fall. Wait. *Not just that.* They are letting him go because it is not only him they are after. Not this time.

He decides: He can do more outside these walls.

He takes the chance: As the officer turns to leave, Devon explodes off the cot. The officer has no time to react beyond a startled, "Oh!" as Devon crooks his arm around the man's neck, cutting off blood flow through the carotid artery—a sleeper hold. In seconds, the man relaxes and drops, a sack of loose bones.

Devon looks around as if the exit choices had multiplied, maintaining calm, making certain no one is in the hall. He pauses to still his heartbeat. They will be expecting him to go out the front door, so he will not do that. He steps into the corridor: To his left is the door that leads to the main holding area—sure to have cops, even at this hour—to his right is the dead-end corridor.

Stop. Think.

He looks at the ceiling all along the corridor. He lopes down to the end—the dead end—to where he sees the drop ceiling tile he wants. He jumps up, his fingers punching the Styrofoam tile up, grabbing the slight aluminum supports, bracing his heels on the cinderblock wall. He moves so quickly, his heels taking much of the weight of his body, that the aluminum does not even have time to bend.

He walks straight up the wall, into the ceiling.

*   *   *

The full bone moon is high over the clearing, shining liquid silver down on the three figures. Two are standing, covered in black silk robes that drape from shoulders to feet. The feet are bare.

The light of the moon blankets the treetops that surround the clearing, glimmering in the *shush* of a gentle wind through the leaves. This is not far from town, but the quiet and the dark spirit of the woods could be a thousand miles from human habitation.

The third person is lying on her back, tied down in the dirt that has been cleared of leaves, her arms out and elevated slightly above her shoulders, her legs spread in a perfect 45 degree 'V'. She is tied to the five points of a star.

Around her, a circle has been traced in the dirt. A star has been etched as well. There are red candles at the five points. They are not yet lit.

The two standing figures are outside the circle. The man is old, and he stands slightly bent, angling his torso away from the woman. The woman holds a wavy blade that shimmers in the moonlight.

"Does it have to be her?" the woman is saying.

"She was there, she fits the specifications." The man shrugs. "Besides, she saw me." He walks away from the woman, then turns and walks back.

The woman who is tied down starts to move her head, and groan, as if she is waking up.

"She knows me," the Old Man says to the younger woman. "It is not co-incidental that she was hitchhiking where she was." He bows his head. "Blessed and whole, what Bringer of Light provides."

When he raises his head, he grabs the woman by the shoulders, his hands like striking snakes, shaking her slightly. "You know what to do, Maria."

The woman in the robe stands with her head bowed for several seconds. The naked woman in the circle groans. The standing woman holds her arms slack at her sides. She nods.

"Good girl," the man says, shaking her shoulders again. "I'll be in the specified place."

Without another word, the man walks over to the woman who is tied down, stands next to her head, careful to stay out of the circle. He leans over, taking something from inside his robe: It is a .45 semi-automatic. He places it next to the captive's right hand. Straightening and turning, he begins to pace very careful and measured paces that run in a straight line away from her head. He goes twenty steps before he disappears into the trees at the edge of the clearing. He keeps going.

The woman waits for nearly five minutes, not moving, her head bowed, the kris in her left hand, which is limp at her side. Then she draws a huge, shuddering breath.

From inside her robe, she removes five wooden matches and a small block of flint. Careful to stay out of the circle, she steps to the candle that is planted above the woman's head. As she strikes the match, she cries, "Mhalo-el!" She lights the candle.

She moves to her right, to the candle nearest the captive's right hand. As she strikes the match, she cries, "Haludeg-ev!"

She moves to her right again, to the candle nearest the captive's right foot. As she strikes the match, she cries, "Haruveg-ev!"

She rounds the circle to the candle nearest the captive's left foot. As she strikes the match, she cries, "Htuklam!"

She completes the circle with the candle nearest the captive's left hand: "Rota!"

She moves to the captive's head, completing the circle, and faces the inside. She bows. She steps into the circle.

She straddles the waking, naked woman. She raises the kris high above her head, holding it with both hands. "Htuklam rota!" she says loudly, bringing it down slashing to her right, cutting into the woman's left arm, drawing blood. The woman jerks and cries out.

The arc continues until it reaches its limit, the robed woman's arms outstretched and down to her right. She brings the blade up swiftly then, slicing to her left, ripping across the skin that covers the captive's collar bone and spilling fatty tissue from her left breast.

The captive screams at the same time that the robed woman yells: "Harubeg-ev!"

One hundred and sixty nine paces away, in the woods, the Old Man sits cross-legged in the woods. The first words sound and he smiles.

The first scream comes and his eyes roll back in his head.

83

Tuesday afternoon, October 26

Carol looked up from her notes when she heard someone come in the door. It was Chase, and he looked depressed.

"I'm sorry, Braxy," he said, setting his notebook down on her desk.

She clenched her jaws, relaxed them. "Yeah, well." She tucked the notes into one neat pile. "So am I."

"Do you know how it happened yet? I'm not asking as a reporter."

Her smile was weary. She did know that Chase wouldn't take advantage of their relationship—whatever it was at the moment—to get an article. He'd never done that, and she didn't think he ever would.

"Yes and no. Someone left Greathouse a note instructing him to take the food at eleven and telling him that Lancaster was drugged and insensible, that he'd wake up hungry in another half hour. The note had Darnell's initials on it, but he denies any knowledge of it."

Chase raised his eyebrows and rubbed his cheek. Carol noted he hadn't shaved that day. He fiddled with the edges of his notebook, looking down, and Carol could see that he wanted to say something, but didn't want to be overeager and press the issue.

At last he said, "So I assume that you have a dragnet out. Or whatever."

Carol shrugged. "Sure. We have men at his apartment collecting evidence right now, but he's not going to go there. His car's impounded and we have alerts at the local rental agencies and the airport, the bus station. He has no known acquaintances, so there's nothing to watch for there. We have men all over town working double shifts, but something tells me that he won't be found if he doesn't want to be."

She noticed that Chase carefully waited until she was finished. Then he said, "But that's not what worries you."

"No, Chase, of course not. Watts is what worries me. And Collins. And that Theron Davies character. I've been undermined here." She reaches her hands toward Chase, palms up. "I don't know which of my officers Watts may have gotten to and which ones I can still trust."

Chase's eyes widened. "That's bad."

Carol covered his hand with hers. "That's very bad."

* * *

Sounded like every alarm is the house was screaming as Don Redmann came in the front door. He smelled smoke, saw it, too—thin yet, but rapidly thickening.

Darn it!

He'd had a nagging feeling all morning that there was a serious problem. He was needed at home. Which was crazy, on the face of it. Adrian should be at school, Danielle in class, his wife at the shop: No one should be here this time of day on a Tuesday.

He'd ignored it, at first. *I've been worrying about her too much,* he'd thought. He came to terms with the feeling.

But it had persisted into the afternoon. He was in the home office, filling out the time cards for his crew, and it had nagged and tugged at his mind. He'd been in the bathroom shaking the last drops off when the voice came: *Get home! Maria needs you! NOW!*

That was all he needed. It was crazy—like a thought, but like a voice at the same time—but it was enough. He had the seniority to leave on his own word. He'd never had a voice like that before, and he didn't ask himself where it'd come from, but darned if it didn't sound like her brother.

Don had seen the smoke as soon as he'd opened the door to the house. He rushed in. It was not thick yet, but it was obviously growing. There was a helluva fire somewhere. He saw smoke pouring around the frame of the kitchen door. Thick brown smoke, with swirls of grey.

He remembered to touch his hand to the door first, to feel if it was hot, to learn whether there was a fire just on the other side. The door was warm, but not hot. No fire in the kitchen. Probably.

He pushed the door open. Smoke made his eyes tear.

He waited for the smoke to clear. It didn't exactly, but it thinned. He went into the kitchen, his hand waving in front of his face, crouching low. He was looking toward the stove, but nothing seemed to be on fire there.

That was when he heard the voice. It was deep and throaty, a man's voice. It came from the basement:

"...tuklam, rota ... mal-oel, halu-degev"

Don Redmann's hand trembled as he opened the door to the basement. He forgot to check it first, to see if it was hot.

"... haru-vegev, tuklam, rota ... "

Hot smoke hit him, stung his eyes. The chant—

"...mal-oel, halu-degev, haru-vegev..."

He made his way down the steps.

"...tuklam, rota ... mal-oel, halu-"

He stopped on the bottom step. The chant was not coming from a man; it was coming from his wife. A shiver shot up his spine, like an electric shock.

"-degev, haru-vegev, tuklam, rota ... "

The fire was burning in front of her, in the center of a circle. The circle surrounded a five-pointed star, and Maria stood naked at the edge of the circle, at the top point. She held a long, wavy blade straight over her head. She was bleeding from cuts on her biceps and thighs.

It was unreal; what he saw couldn't be true. He couldn't move.

". . .mal-oel, halu-degev, haru-vegev, tuklam. . ."

Maria chanted on, oblivious of Don. Her voice was rising in volume and pitch now.

He was so hypnotized by the scene that several heartbeats passed before he saw the girl who lay bound and hooded over in the corner of the basement, naked, with dried blood coating her body. She wasn't moving.

". . .rota . . . mal-oel, halu-degev, haru-vegev. . ."

Maria's voice got louder and stronger. Her head lolled back, and Don noticed that he could only see the whites in her eyes. Her face twisted itself into a masklike horror that Don didn't recognize as his wife's.

A fat black handgun lay on the cement floor in front of his wife.

". . .haru-vegev, tuklam, rota."

The chanting ended. Maria stood very still. Don stared, unable to move as Maria shifted the blade in her hands so that it pointed down and inward. His eyes were wide as she bent over, positioning the point so it aimed up between her legs. He saw her forearms knot as she drew the blade out slowly away from her to the farthest point of an arc that Don could see would end when she thrust the knife up between her—

"MARIAAAA!!!" Don screamed as he leapt off the steps toward her.

84
Tuesday afternoon, October 26

Alex suddenly sat up straight on the couch, the book she had been reading clutched stiffly in her hands. Her thumbs crinkled the pages. Jerry peered over his *Wall Street Journal* at her. A fire crackled in the fireplace.

"What's up?" he asked.

"I don't know." Alex shook her head. "Something is happening." Even as she said it, she was aware of the way it echoed the words of the mysterious caller, the implied melodrama. But she was absolutely certain that there was something very wrong.

Jer laughed softly. "Not much is happening here," he said. "All's quiet on the Heyden front."

Alex shook her head again, unable to rid herself of the certainty. "Not here. Somewhere. Something's happening with one of my patients."

Jer set his paper aside, leaned over and touched her thigh. "What makes you think that?"

"I don't know. Just something. A certainty. I *know* it."

"Can you pin it down any more than that? Do you know who?"

Alex shook her head. "No." She closed her book and rose from the couch. "I'm going to lay down for a while, Jer."

"Is there anything I can do?"

Alex could see that he was concerned, but this wasn't something he could help with. "No. No. Just wake me up in about an hour, if I'm not up already."

She headed for the stairs, sure he was watching her with those concerned eyes of his, sure something was wrong that she couldn't do anything about, sure that a nap would help.

*   *   *

From the outside, it was a nice suburban home. Smooth driveway, red compact parked in front of a two-car garage. Chase guessed that most people would be surprised to learn what had happened here, that it had involved a respectable family who lived in a place like this. But then, most people didn't stop to consider the fact that most everyone could be called *nice*. They all had secrets. He had learned that much as a journalist, if nothing else.

He'd sat quietly in Carol's cruiser on the way over as they had been filled in on the situation. As a journalist, he was fascinated by what happened; he'd never ridden in a police car. "Go to code," dispatch had said. Carol held the steering wheel, guiding the car through traffic, as she leaned forward and punched an orange, plastic button on the radio.

"What's happening?" he'd asked.

"Dispatch just went to scramble." She looked at him as she sat back. "If I don't go to code too, all we'll hear is gibberish. That way, curious people who happen to have police radios can't hear what's going on. We rarely ever use it, but when we do, people know something big is happening."

He had worked the radio before, but it had been a couple of years; they didn't have this when he was covering the crime situation. "You don't want people to know?"

When Carol looked at him, Chase was sure he'd asked a stupid question. Of course they didn't want people to know everything, it made sense. Some information might cause what the police called *citizen interference*—at best—or a panic at worst.

Through the scrambled police band, they heard the whole message, and Chase could see why the department didn't want people to know: Distraught husband, wife taken to Ruby Memorial Hospital. Fire department on the scene. All the ugly details and their implications. Carol translated the police codes for Chase as they came over the air.

Carol's presence got them through the police cordon and into the kitchen of the house. The kitchen floor was splashed with muddy footprints from the firemen. There was a thin veil of water on the floor. A door that looked like it led to the basement was thrown open. The tracks were heaviest there.

Chase spotted Watts standing next to a man who Chase presumed was the husband. Watts had his notebook out. He saw Chase and frowned slightly. Carol went over to Watts and Chase followed.

"The subject's been taken to Memorial, Chief," Watts said. Chase noted that he said *subject* and not *victim*. "She's okay, more or less. Her husband managed to deflect the blade so that it didn't hit the femoral. She's pretty cut up, though."

"What about the other woman, Detective?"

Chase looked at Carol; he hadn't known there was another woman. He managed not to ask, though.

Watts looked at Chase pointedly. "Do you think the press should be allowed in just yet?"

"He's working as an advisor, Detective."

"Right."

The sarcasm was thinly veiled. They stared at each other until Watts flipped open his notebook.

"The other woman is Katie Shaver. She's an employee of Mrs. Redmann's at Chuckles, the toy store down—"

"How *is* she, Lieutenant?"

Watts shrugged. "She's alive. They've got her under sedation in the ICU ward at Memorial. She's cut up pretty bad—lost a lot of blood—but they think she'll be all right. You should see what's downstairs, Chief."

Carol turned to the man who'd been giving a statement to Watts. "Are you Mr. Redmann?" She put her hand on his shoulder. Lightly. "I'll need to speak with you in a few minutes."

"Of course," Don Redmann said. His voice quavered. He ran his hand back through his hair nervously. "I don't see how she could have done this. Maria couldn't have done this."

"In a few minutes, Mr. Redmann, if you don't mind. Now if you'll excuse us. . ."

Chase felt bad for the man. He obviously had no clue as to what this was about. The implications. He was probably right that Maria couldn't have done it unless she was a lot bigger and stronger than Chase surmised. She couldn't have done it without help anyway. Chase started to follow Carol and Watts downstairs. He looked back at Redmann leaning against a kitchen counter; he tried to smile reassuringly, but what came out was a grimace.

The basement was as bad as dispatch had said. The intense smell of smoke and dampness made Chase want a cigarette. What he saw made him want a drink.

Mrs. Redmann had had a bonfire going right in the middle of her basement. The coals had been scattered by the firehose, but the charred spot on the concrete still showed. The water pressure had pushed most of the coals against an old oak dresser nearby. From the style, Chase guessed that the dresser had been handbuilt, handcarved, a real antique.

The dresser, and the boxes on either side of it, had also been burning, at least by the time the fire department had gotten there. The dresser's front was charred and the edges of the boxes had burned away. Chase spotted the remains of what he thought was a wiffle ball bat and what looked like the edges of board games. The accumulation of family.

"Here's the thing, Chief," Watts said. "The Redmann woman was unconscious when they took her out. About a half hour ago. I wasn't able to talk with her. She was unconscious, in shock, but the EMS guys say she'll be all right." Watts looked away for a second. "It was close."

Chase looked again at the place where the firehose had wooshed the coals against the dresser, against the boxes. On the floor he saw a large wavy blade with dark grit coating it. Suddenly, he felt himself freeze. His eyes drifted up to a shelf above the coals and the blade and the detritus. Two skulls, all traces of hair and skin and muscle gone, sitting side by side. The left sides of both were blown out.

If the skulls belonged to Laana Anders and Amelia Samosky, someone had done a very thorough job of cleaning them.

Carol didn't say anything, her eyes also locked on the skulls.

Chase felt an ache when Watts said it: "I think we found our killer."

85
Tuesday afternoon, October 26

Watts felt intimidated in his own office, which had never happened to him before. He wished he was behind his desk, at least, so he would have that security and intimidating factor between him and the raging Collins. But he wasn't; he stood in front of the desk, Collins only a couple of feet from him.

The man was really on a rampage. Watts almost preferred the soulless behavior he'd seen from Collins in the past to this frothing anger. "How the hell did this happen, *Detective* Watts?"

Watts shrugged, trying to remain calm. "You'll have to ask the Old Man about that one. I think this was all part of his—" Watt hesitated. "His arrangements."

"He's blind, that's what it is. He's losing it. He's so set on saving himself that he's gonna screw everything up for the rest of us."

86

Tuesday afternoon, October 26

Chase said, "You know it's not over."

Carol downshifted as they approached the stop sign. She looked over at Chase. "Where does Lancaster fit into this?"

"Yeah, that's a problem all right," Chase said. "But I was thinking more about Collins. How does he fit in? After I didn't see him on the active duty roster at Quantico, I asked around. It's not even normal for the FBI to send people out on a case like this."

Carol looked out of the corners of her eyes. "It is if the case is part of a national pattern. Who told you that anyway?"

"You're not the only one I know at the department. Didn't you think it was strange the way he showed up? And Davies—have you ever worked on a case where an FBI medical examiner was involved? Do they even have medical examiners?"

Carol was stuck on that one. She never had worked with one, but she'd been to their forensics lab in Quantico, Virginia, and it had been an impressive collection of equipment and technicians. They must have MEs, but now that Chase mentioned it, she had never met one.

"So what, Chase? I faxed a copy of the report of the first killing to Quantico, and Collins showed up the next day. Nothing strange about that. Get to the point."

Chase laughed. "You know where this is going as well as I do."

Carol wanted to hit him. He was such an *arrogant* SOB, and she was getting frustrated: with the case, as well as with the traffic and Michael Chase. "I don't know anything of the kind. I don't know who Collins and Davies are, but they *are* FBI agents. I checked them out. I don't know who tried to kill you, and I don't know how Lancaster fits into this yet, but right now I'm pretty sure we caught our killer. Isn't that enough? We can chase down the loose ends later." She amended that. "Tomorrow."

"Someone trying to kill me is not a *loose end*. Neither is the question of Collins's legitimacy. You don't know if he's here officially or not, do you?"

That was the last straw. "Who do you think you're talking to, Chase? I talked to his supervisor two weeks ago, and Collins's here on assignment."

"Then his supervisor's in on it, Carol. Don't you see the implications here?"

Carol started to say that Chase was letting his paranoia get away from him, but she was cut off by the words:

"You are quite right, Mr. Chase."

She froze. The words hadn't come from Chase *or* her. They sounded like they came from the cruiser's dashboard. The words were a whisper. Instinctively, Carol reached her right hand toward her inner jacket pocket.

"If you touch that gun, Ms. Braxton, I will have to hurt you."

This time the voice came from behind her. The back seat.

"Lancaster," Chase said.

Devon Lancaster was in the back seat. She wondered what he held pointed at her spine.

"Pull over up here," the voice said. "I have to talk with both of you."

Carol did as she was told, pulling into a pickup loop in front of a campus building, just off Woodburn Circle. The clock tower looming overhead: 5:30.

"Thank you," Lancaster said. "Please do not turn around. At least until we have had a few words. I want to tell you both a story. I will make it as brief as possible. I went to Maria's house because I knew you would both come. Even if you didn't show up, Mr. Chase, I knew that you would, Ms. Braxton."

"Get to the point." Carol glanced in the rearview, but Lancaster was not there. A muscle in her neck twitched. She looked over at Chase; he stared straight ahead.

A dry laughter came from the back seat. "Tragedy is what you are about, Carol Braxton. Surely you know the true definition: The hero, or *heroine*, makes all the right decisions, but is still faced with something that is terribly wrong. When your mother was murdered on her way home from her volunteer work—when you were 15 years old—it was tragic."

Carol swallowed; her throat was dry. Who was this guy?

"And you, Chase. Who are you? What are you wearing on the various sleeves in your wardrobe? *What are you made of?*"

The dry laughter came again. Carol shifted in her seat, leaning onto her left buttcheek, freeing her right arm. She glanced at Chase; he appeared to be frozen in place.

"Ms. Braxton. Maybe it would be best if I held your gun for a while."

Carol felt a hand sneak over her right shoulder. Briefly, she saw a very large, well-muscled forearm and then it disappeared behind her again. With her gun.

"Just listen. Both of you. I know this will not be easy for you to believe, but maybe I have already given you enough reason to believe that I know things that are. . . not common knowledge. Brace yourselves.

"Maria did play a part in the killing of those girls, but she is not responsible. In fact, the only reason Katie Shaver is still alive is because Maria was able to break with her conditioning enough to come to her assistance."

Carol was trying to think of a way to call for backup, a way to stall for time. She started to speak, but Lancaster cut her off.

"Do not call yet, please. Let me finish. I do not want to harm you. There are some things you should know."

He continued, still whispering. "Maria also did not act alone. She had one direct accomplice and several people who both helped and benefited from the deaths. She had no choice in the matter. I do not know what else Agent Collins told you, but I did knock him out. He came to kill me, and I had no choice. In a way, I suppose Collins had no choice either. He is under the influence of a very powerful man."

Carol could feel Chase bridling beside her throughout Lancaster's brief speech. She saw what happened next as if it were in slow motion. Chase started to turn—

—a gigantic hand cuffed his left ear—

—Chase fell forward in the seat.

"Look," came the whispery voice from the back seat. "This is not an excuse to be a hero. My sister and I have lived with this our entire lives. We witnessed things that would put the Old Man away forever. Murder and suicide—we saw it all before we were twelve. I do not want to hurt you but I will. The Old Man must be stopped."

Carol made the leap first, while Chase was still shaking the stars out of his head. "Maria is your sister?"

"You do not understand what this is you are dealing with," came the voice from the back seat. "I have been after the Old Man for as long as I can remember. You people laugh at psychic activity, but that is the battleground."

Carol suddenly remembered the old man she and Chase had seen in the door of the Omega the night they had too much to drink. She hadn't really seen him then, but she saw him now. A shiver ran through her.

"I think maybe you have seen him, Chief Braxton. And although I doubt you spoke to him, I suspect something about him made you very uneasy. You are highly attuned that way. So are you, Michael Chase."

Carol glanced at Chase, saw the grimace on his face was almost a sneer. She knew that he had even less tolerance than her for talk about psychic phenomenon. And she didn't have much tolerance.

"Hear me out," Lancaster said. "Just a little more. There are some things you can check out.

"I am from a small, exclusive Vermont community called Oak Circle. There are only maybe two dozen families there, all old money. My father was William Eugene Lancaster and my mother was Colleen Maria O'Shaunassay. They had three children: Colleen Raime, Maria Elizabeth, and myself, in that order. Maria and I were born a year apart, but Colleen was 15 years older. Our mother was very young when Colleen was born.

"Colleen was raised by our grandfather, Konrad Eugene, to be the Heiress, but she ran away at the age of 15. Unfortunately, she chose West Virginia as her hiding place. She had no way of knowing that these mountains act to focus energy, the way that a magnifying glass focuses sunlight. By running here, she was certain to be found eventually.

"But not for a while. She met a man here and they married; they moved to Morgantown. A year later she had a son; he was given the name Darnell Lancaster. She eventually committed suicide because she could not stand the fact that our grandfather had found her and recruited her husband into the very things that she had been running from."

Lancaster apparently leaned forward, his head between her and Chase, because Carol could hear his words from inches away.

"Listen," he whispered. "There is much more to this, but we do not have the time now. Check out those facts." He repeated the names slowly. "Oak Circle, Vermont. William Eugene Lancaster. Colleen Maria O'Shaunassay. Colleen Raime, Maria Elizabeth. Darnell Lancaster. You will find I am telling the truth.

"The main thing now is that we have to act. These things are far more advanced than you understand. This is an *old* battleground. Chase, how do you think I know what I know? I *planted* those dreams. I need you both."

There was a long silence after that. Very long. Carol didn't dare say a word, and Chase seemed to be examining the buttons on his shirt.

Finally Carol spoke: "What is it you want?"

A whisper came from the back seat. "They are going to try to kill Maria. They will do it tonight. Grandfather, Collins, and Watts. Maybe Davies. We have to stop them."

87
Tuesday night, October 26

Devon draws back against the door, shrinking from the open corridor, trying to avoid being seen. The nurse who is pushing the cart down the hall passes by at first, then stops a few feet past him. She turns her head toward him.

"Can I help you?" she says.

He recognizes her. "No," he says. "No, thank you. I thought this was my friend's room, but I guess I was wrong."

She smiles, and Devon realizes—as he had not the last time he had seen her—that she is very young. She must not be a real nurse, but some kind of nurse's assistant. "What's your friend's name?"

"Konrad Lorenz," he says. She tilts her head, apparently thinking.

"I don't think Mr. Lorenz is on this floor. You sure he's in ICU?"

Devon tries to look embarrassed. "This is ICU? I am very sorry. I thought I was in the cancer ward."

She smiles again. "That's the next floor down."

"Thank you very much." Devon turns as if to go.

"Don't I know you?" the woman says.

"I do not think so."

She stares at him for a moment, cocks her head again. Slowly, a smile spreads over my face. "Sure, I do. You picked me up hitchhiking a couple of months ago."

"I did?" Devon says, even though he knows the truth.

"Yes, you definitely did." She holds out her hand for a handshake. "My name's Shannon. I may even owe you a thanks."

Devon shakes her hand. "Why would that be so?" he asks, although he knows why.

"I don't know if you meant to, but you scared the hell out of me. I don't hitch anymore. What with what's been going on in town, it's probably a good thing."

"It is. Please excuse me, I need to find my friend." He turns as if to go.

*   *   *

Shannon pushed the cart to the end of the hallway and glanced back over her shoulder. The strange man was gone. He'd really given her a scare a couple months before, and she hadn't been sure whether he was doing it intentionally or not. He might have let her out a few hundred yards past her parents' house just to scare her. She thought at the time that maybe he'd just chickened out on whatever sick game he was playing. Now she felt he'd had her welfare in mind.

Jeesh, she thought. *When it rains, it pours.* She turned left at the end of the corridor, wheeling her cart down toward the door where the policeman sat. First they bring in this woman who was apparently psycho or something, cops and lawyers and stuff everywhere, then she runs into that weird guy. What would be next?

Actually, she liked this job. She'd never expected it to be so exciting, but it sure beat working as a waitress, which was what Staci was doing tonight. Shannon would have to remember to call Staci and tell her all about this shift when she got off. No way she'd believe it!

She brought the cart to a stop outside the psycho woman's door. She saw the cop who was guarding the door look up when she got there. She ignored the other guy, who was leaning against the wall, a few feet down. The cop was a young guy, kinda cute.

"This is for whenever they're done in there," Shannon said. She smiled at the police officer. She was pleased that he smiled back.

* * *

Chase leaned against the wall, worried about the next few hours. Sometime soon, Maria Redmann's room would empty out, the brief mental hygiene hearing having come to its expected end. He was no psychiatrist, but from everything he'd heard in the last few hours, he was sure that the unfortunate woman would be confined to Baker's Ridge Hospital for some time to come.

Not that he necessarily believed everything that Lancaster had said, but the man had apparently been on the mark with at least part of his story. After he'd finished his say in the back of Carol's patrol car, he'd taped their hands together with duct tape—Chase and Carol's four hands joined—and then he'd slipped out the door. It hadn't taken them long to radio for backup, but it took much longer than it took Devon to disappear around the corner of the student union.

Carol had cursed, but Chase was resigned. Lancaster had escaped again, but Chase wasn't so sure that was a bad thing. While they were waiting, Carol radioed for a check on the names and facts that Lancaster had provided: They'd all checked out. Carol hadn't liked that much better.

Chase hadn't seen why until she explained: "Lancaster mentioned his older sister's son, Darnell Lancaster—Detective Watts is Lancaster's nephew."

That explained a lot about why this case had so many convoluted twists.

"Now we know how Lancaster and Watts fit in," Carol had said. "So what about Collins. And Davies."

Chase didn't say anything at first, reluctant to jump in with what he thought was the obvious. Carol would just think he was being paranoid. They could see the backup approaching, a hundred yards away.

Carol leaned back in the seat the best she could with her hands still taped to Chase's. Her eyes closed. "What do you think of his claims about a conspiracy, Chase? As if I needed to ask."

Chase didn't say anything.

Carol sighed. "I think they're really going to try to kill Maria. Tonight, probably. I doubt we'll be seeing Collins again either."

"I think you're right, Braxy."

She sighed again and looked over at him. "Thanks, Chase. This whole thing would've been too weird if you weren't around."

Chase laughed and shook his forearms, rattling Carol's along with them. "What's that supposed to mean?"

Carol was laughing, too. "It means you're a lunatic, and if it wasn't for your presence, I would have to have myself committed for listening to Lancaster."

The backup patrol car pulled up alongside them. As the two officers got out, Carol said to Chase, "Do you think he's right? About the psychic stuff?"

Chase just grunted and shrugged. If it had been anyone else but Lancaster, he would have said 'no' right away, but he'd seen too much of what that man could do.

He honestly didn't know.

88
Tuesday night, October 26

Judge Polander was first to leave Maria Redmann's hospital room. Carol Braxton watched him open the door and walk into the hallway. She'd never quite figured out which came first: a judge's upright and regal bearing or the respect accorded the office. She'd decided that, on balance, the bearing came first, because she'd seen a few judges walk as if they'd just robbed a convenience store.

She stood just inside the room and watched the assembly file out: Maria's lawyer, retained by Don Redmann; Rita Kavakian, Morgantown's district attorney; Officer Wilson, who had been first on the scene that afternoon. Don Redmann stopped at the door: "Thanks, Chief Braxton." He looked at the floor.

Carol wished she could say something to make it easier on him, but nothing came. Instead, she tried a feeble smile and the words, "I wish there were more we could do, Mr. Redmann."

He looked up. "Do you think she'll have to go to jail?"

"That's not for me to speculate, Mr. Redmann." She couldn't say anything more at this time, but the fact was, she was pretty sure Maria would never stand trial.

She wished she could question him about the things that Lancaster had said, but knew it just wasn't the time. Before Lancaster had left the patrol car, he'd said that Mr. Redmann didn't know anything, and telling him would only disrupt events unpredictably. Carol had assigned an officer to keep an eye on Mr. Redmann, and that would have to do for now. She could question him tomorrow.

Carol turned back to the hospital room and Maria's psychiatrist, Alexandra Heyden. Her mouth was tight as she watched Ms. Heyden check Maria's IV. Carol didn't know exactly how to start this. She cleared her throat.

Ms. Heyden looked up. She didn't say anything at first. It was apparently only after seeing that Carol wasn't going say anything that Ms. Heyden spoke: "Is there something else, Chief Braxton?"

Carol looked down. This wasn't easy. "I was wondering if you could answer a few questions, Ms. Heyden."

"That depends. I'm afraid that client confidentiality prevents—"

Carol held up her hand. "I respect that. I want to talk to you as a therapist. I won't ask you to violate any confidences. It's just that we have a difficult situation on our hands."

"If you want to know whether or not my client could have—"

"Wait, wait." Carol took a breath. She wanted to get to the bottom of this, and there was an adversarial relationship to transcend. How to do that. . . She took another breath.

She decided to stretch the truth a little. "We have a statement on record from Mrs. Redmann's brother. Turns out he's been living here in Morgantown for several years." Carol could see the surprise on Heyden's face. She decided then to press on. "He alleges certain abuses in Maria's background that are responsible for her actions. What I need to know from you, Ms. Heyden, is whether or not these allegations have any basis in fact. From your client's point of view."

Carol watched Heyden turn away from her, run her hand through her hair. She walked over to Maria's bedside, patted her unconscious hand. A moment later she turned back to Carol.

"Maria's been through a lot. Over the last few years we've uncovered a lot that's been helpful, but I've always thought there was more there that I hadn't touched. Just a sense, you understand, nothing I would stand behind, but I've always thought there was something deep and disturbing that even hypnotherapy couldn't reach without some pressure on my part. Which I never dared to apply."

Carol watched the woman draw herself up, come to a decision. She wished she'd met Ms. Heyden under other circumstances: She seemed like someone she woud've liked as a friend.

"Tell me what you've found out, Chief Braxton, and I'll tell you whether I can help you or not."

*   *   *

Alexandra watched the way Maria sat in the bed, and she knew it was as bad as the chief had said. Worse, in fact. It was a good thing no one else was in the room; this situation would be hard to deal with if it came to court.

Maria stared straight ahead, her neck rigid, her back straight. Her eyes were gazing on people and activities that were not occurring in this room. Alex had suspected it, but she'd been afraid to check. Afraid, basically, to probe deep enough.

Alex knew for certain now that the calls that she had received had been about Maria. She suspected now that whoever the old man was—likely Maria's grandfather—he'd been frightened, terrified of being discovered. Alexandra swallowed and clenched her teeth; she braced herself. "Go ahead, Maria. What's happening now?"

"He's cutting her," Maria whispered. "Cutting her bad." Maria coughed, choked. "There's blood everywhere!"

"Who's there, Maria?" Alex asked.

"Me," Maria said. "And my brother. I'm scared because his eyes are gone.

They're all gone! There's blood all over her skin! Everywhere!"

"What do you mean, his eyes are gone?"

"Gone, gone. White where his eyes should be."

"What else is happening now? What about the girl?"

Maria was crying; Alex watched the tears roll down her face. "She's almost dead; she's almost dead. Now Grans is—" Maria choked.

Alex clenched her teeth. "Go ahead."

"He's sticking his thing inside her! She's screaming! He's moving his thing back and forth, and she's screaming and he's untying her right hand and she's screaming and. . . He's putting the gun in her hand and he's whispering in her ear. . . Now she's. . . She's putting the gun next to her head. . ."

That was enough. Alexandra decided to stop it there. "Stop Maria, stop now."

"She's gonna shoot herself!" Maria screamed. "She's gonna—"

"Maria, this is Alex! Stop now!"

"I . . ." Maria trailed off with a sigh. She lay back against the pillows.

Alexandra jumped up, took Maria's pulse. It had been even worse than she had expected. She'd failed Maria; maybe if she had the courage to probe deeply earlier, this might not have happened. She held the woman's wrist; the pulse was getting stronger. Maria would sleep it off. Alex would give her a few days rest, but her and Maria's work was really just beginning.

She opened the door to the hallway and saw Chief Braxton leaning up against the opposite wall.

"Well?" Chief Braxton said.

"I hope you're satisfied," was all that Alex could manage, even though she knew Braxton didn't really deserve it.

89
Tuesday night, October 26

Agent Collins didn't like being in the waiting room for so long. He didn't much care for hospitals anyway, and he felt it was too much of a risk for him to be lounging around like this—too exposed, too much chance someone would come along who might recognize him. When he'd brought that up, he'd been told: "The best place to hide a murder victim is on a battlefield; the best way to hide the fact that you are waiting for me is to sit in a hospital waiting room."

Collins pretended to be leafing through a *Sporting Life* while he waited. Now and then he glanced at his watch, or up at the large clock on the wall. *This is no way to run an op* kept running through his mind. This should be run like any other black op, like the Company would do it. What was taking the Old Man so long?

He had had a bad feeling about this ever since he had received the call to come down here to West Godforsaken Virginia. He had gotten the initial call at home in the evening, and it was not until the next day that his division chief—his direct boss—had called. Agent Collins had acted properly surprised and he was sure that his chief had not suspected a thing.

*   *   *

Detective Watts examined himself in the bathroom mirror, making certain the bag and hose were securely fitted under his shirt. He was pretty sure no one would note the extra bulge on one side of his hip. The sports coat covered most of it; besides, nobody ever looked too hard at a middle-aged man's spare tire. He should know.

His stomach was churning and his tongue felt like sandpaper. This job would not be easy for him. He'd heard this kind of thing referred to as *wet work* and knew it had been called that for hundreds of years. He had no idea why, didn't much care either. All he knew was that it went against everything he had always thought a policeman's job was. His stomach gurgled.

Darnit! he thought. A good shot would steady his nerves. Even if it would make his stomach feel worse, he wouldn't care as much. It was a good thing he'd gotten a refill of the pills today. They were everything he'd been told: They calmed him, made him more alert, and settled his stomach. If only the doctor knew about these, but they were another one of those secrets—Family secrets. It was a good thing he had gotten more before tonight. He dry-swallowed one.

If he was going to go through with this, he was going to have to keep re-

244

minding himself that this was the woman who'd killed all those girls. She deserved whatever happened to her. He stepped out into the hospital corridor.

*   *   *

The Old Man finishes changing and stuffs the clothes into the locker. By the time they are noticed he will be long gone. He glances in the mirror: No question he will pass for a doctor. He had purchased the uniform at a costume shop in DC the week before. *Foresight. The Bringer of Light brings foresight first and foremost.*

He doesn't need to check his bag; he is sure the IV pouch is inside. The Old Man also doesn't need to look at his watch; He is certain Watts is almost finished. He goes out the door, turns right, walks at a measured pace. Collins is waiting for him. He smiles and begins to whistle tunelessly.

*   *   *

Detective Watts looked down the corridor and saw Officer Briggs seated in front of the last door on the right. Maria Redmann's door. Briggs was reading a book. Watts's stomach still churned, but not nearly as badly. He felt light-headed, but clear. Strong, he felt strong.

When he was halfway down the hall, Watts thought, *Christ,* he thought, *They call this security? He still hasn't even looked up, yet. It would be bad news for her if I was coming to. . .* His thoughts trailed off as he realized that was *exactly* what was happening. *How did it get this far?*

"Okay, Briggs," Detective Watts said. The man hadn't looked up until Watts was nearly on him. "You can go home now."

"But Captain, I just—"

"We'll deal with it tomorrow, Briggs. Anderson will be here in fifteen minutes. Go make out your report. I'll take it from here." Even under the circumstances, sloppy policework annoyed Detective Watts.

"Yes, sir."

After Briggs left, Watts looked down the hall to make sure it was empty, then he went into Maria Redmann's room. Only, he had stopped thinking of her as *Maria Redmann,* and started thinking of her as *The Suspect.*

*   *   *

Agent Collins looked up when he heard the name called.

"Stan Connell." It was the name they had agreed on.

The Old Man looked like a doctor, and Collins didn't think that anyone noticed that he followed the "doctor" into a hallway that didn't lead to the examination rooms. It led to the elevators.

90
Tuesday night, October 26

The first thing Watts did once he was inside the Suspect's room was lock the door. A low nightlight near the head of her bed gave off enough light to work by. He wanted to get this over with as quickly as possible. In fifteen minutes he wanted to be outside, waiting for Anderson, the officer who was due to replace Briggs.

The suspect was on her right side, facing away from him, toward the window. The IV tube stretched down under the blanket to her left arm. Bandages covered the entire left side of her face and head; he hadn't known the bullet wound was so severe. She'd been lucky—

He bit his tongue. He couldn't think like that and still do this job. It may not be pleasant, but it was required, and Watts had always done what was required. Although when he had joined the Family, he never imagined that this would be required of him. It had taken a couple of years before he had attained the rank that allowed him to see the stranger ceremonies and experience more deeply the power of... what? He still doubted that power. What had he seen? Nothing but stage magician's tricks, he'd thought at the time. He wasn't so sure now.

Membership in the Family helped out his career in the Force. He was also able to purchase things he could never have afforded on his salary. Suddenly he could travel to just about anywhere, practically for free. . . . And women. There had been plenty of women.

He untucked his shirt and pulled the tape, got the bundle free. As he fixed the bag to the top of the IV stand, or tree, or whatever they called it, he had a last moment of hesitation. If he was going to stop this madness, it had to be now. There would be no other chance.

He heard again the whisper in his head: *We will not kill you. You will be left an invalid. You will not be able to move or talk. You will still know what is happening around you, but all you will be able to do is drool.*

His stomach churned. He couldn't refuse. His hands shaking, he detached the clamp that held the IV tube that dripped fluids into Mrs. Red—the Suspect's hand. He attached the tube that led from the bag he'd brought. His chance passed.

Detective Watts watched the first drops of fluid trickle down the tube. The Old Man had not told him what was in the bag, only that it would be enough. Watts clipped off the original bag and disengaged it from the stand. He tucked his shirt in, holding the bag in his lightly clenched teeth. Not worried about concealment at this point, he sealed off the bag and dropped it into the pocket of his sports coat.

"*Detective* Watts."

Watts looked up, startled.

Chief Braxton was standing in the entrance to the bathroom, both hands on her service revolver. He could practically look down the barrel. His shoulders sagged.

"I hope that isn't what I think it is."

He had nothing to say. She knew exactly what it was. He was resigned.

"Chase," she said levelly. Watts watched as "The Suspect," "Mrs. Redmann," rolled onto "her" back and peeled the bandage off. He saw Michael Chase there in the bed, propped up on his elbows. He grinned at Carol.

"Is that all there is to it?" he asked.

"We got lucky," she said. "Watts. . . Turn around. Against the wall." He did as he was told; Watts heard Chief Braxton say, "Chase. Pinch off the flow. We'll need that later for evidence."

91
Tuesday night, October 26

Agent Collins and the Old Man arrived at the door.

"They don't even have a guard?" Collins said. He still wasn't sure the Old Man was right. Was she actually in here?

"They think they don't need one," the Old Man said. "They think we are fools. Wait outside. This will just take a second."

92
Tuesday night, October 26

"You. . . *cretin*," Chief Braxton was yelling. "You've. . . Your life in the toilet. . . Did you think. . ."

Detective Watts had never heard her this angry. Her voice strangling on her own words. It was odd, but he felt sorry for her, in a way.

"How did you think—What were you going to do? How were you were going to get away with. . ."

Chase's voice cut across her words at the hesitation. "Carol."

"*What!*"

Chase was sitting on the edge of the bed, scratching his chin. "That's the thing. *How could he get away with it?* He couldn't. He was never meant to."

As soon as Chase said this, Watts figured it out, too. *I was never meant to.* Even if I had killed her. . . the Suspect. . . Mrs. Redmann, it would have been clear who had. . .

Chief Braxton shook her head, looking worn down, like someone who's just finished a long and complicated logic problem. "Cuff the animal."

Just then, Watts felt sharp pains rip through his innards. It felt like he was bleeding; he didn't know how he knew that, but he was warm all through his insides, a trickling warmth. *The pills*, he thought. *The old man screwed me!*

The last thing Watts heard was Chief Braxton yelling, "No!" and the tinkle of keys flying through the air.

93
Tuesday night, October 26

The Old Man fits the IV bag onto the stand. Atropine—she would die in seconds, blood vessels in her brain bursting, neurons flashing and flickering like summer lightening.

The thought makes him tired.

She sleeps so deeply, unknowing. He strokes her cheek. It has come to this. *You were such a cute little one,* he thinks. *You were perfect. Everything could have been yours.*

*   *   *

Carol arrives a little too late. The door to Maria's room is just closing. Agent Collins looks up as he sees her round the corner. His gun is coming up. . .

*   *   *

The Old Man is taking his time. Who can say—he can't even say—if he regrets his actions. He hears a shot in the corridor. He reaches up to start the flow of atropine.

*   *   *

Michael Chase has come up the back way, two flights up, three steps at a time. He bursts through the door in time to see Collins crouching over Carol's still form, his gun to her head. A small pool of blood has collected under Carol's torso, and Chase sees the jagged edges of her jacket where the bullet entered her right shoulder. Collins cocks his pistol.

"Nooo!!" Chase yells as he launches himself at Collins.

Collins looks up, startled by Chase's shout; his hand jerks up as he raises his head, the gun discharging as Chase's body slams into his. The bullet grazes Carol's head and ricochets off the hard white tile. The gun skitters away and the two of them tumble hard against the hallway wall.

The impact separates them, and they roll apart, both dazed. Chase thinks he hears hard-soled footsteps, many feet, running, toward them as he pushes himself up. He is uncertain where Collins is, where he has landed, and he lurches to his feet, staggering like a drunk.

He sees Collins: back to the hallway wall, bracing his feet, looking for Chase, finding him. Collins smiles: "Nice try, Chase."

251

A gunshot from inside Maria's room makes them both stop for a second. Chase hopes everything is in control in there, but there are other things for him to deal with out here. He knows he has no chance one-on-one against this man. Still, he has no choice.

"Would you like to dance, Mr. Collins?" He braces his feet.

Collins smiles but says nothing, takes a step toward Chase, who is maneuvering to stay between Collins and Carol's still form.

Then the running steps round the corner. Chase doesn't look, but he hears, "Freeze, both of you. We've got you covered."

Chase would have figured it could only be Deputy Dale saying something that inane, even if he didn't recognize the man's voice. He turns toward Dale Whathisname, making sure to move slowly. "Where've you been?"

* * *

"I don't think so, scheisskopf." Shango steps from inside the bathroom, surprised that this is so easy. One old man standing beside an IV bag. Shango sends a bullet through the bag, punching a hole, making it lose all its pressure to shoot whatever into the arm of the Redmann woman. "Guess again."

He is taken by surprise when the old man turns to him, his hands out.

"My son," the Old Man whispers. "You know not what you do."

Shango frowns, cocks his head to the side, wondering what he is up to. *Crazy old cracker.*

The Old Man takes another step forward. "You are one of us already, my son." He steps another step.

Shango frowns. "What the—? Stop there."

The Old Man only smiles again, staring at Shango. Shango starts to feel himself lost in the man's eyes. Deep eyes. Grey eyes.

"Give me the gun, my son," the man says. He is reaching inside his jacket—

Shango's awareness comes to a point then, just for a second: "Screw you, you spook bast—"

The Old Man is unbelievably quick. Before Shango can shoot, the Old Man has thrown something at Shango's feet. It explodes in a *puffff*, smoke billowing up. *Contact explosive*, Shango thinks. *And something else.* Whatever it is, it makes Shango's eyes tear, his hands shake, his vision undependable. He thinks he sees the Old Man throw a chair through the window right before he passes out.

* * *

It's not until they see smoke pouring from under the door to Maria's room that Chase is able to convince Deputy Dale to open the door. Dale's partner—Chase thinks his name is Greathouse—guards Collins and Chase while Dale opens the door. Smoke billows out, and Chase ducks his head, pulling his shirt up over his mouth. He spits into the cloth, his mind filled with the instructions of what to do when there's a house fire.

Dale takes the force of the smoke full in the face. He sways momentarily, then collapses. Greathouse swivels, looking alternately in the room, then back at Chase and Collins, unsure of what to do. Chase ignores him, looking into the room as the smoke clears, trying to make out what is inside.

He sees Shango prostrate next to the bed. He also quickly takes in the hanging IV tube, the way it doesn't connect to Maria, and the large hole in the bag itself. And the window—broken out glass, a rope with knots dangling just outside.

As he turns back to Greathouse, he is already trying to figure some way to get it across to the man that—

Collins makes a break for the stairs. Startled, Greathouse yells, "Hey!" but when Collins doesn't stop, Greathouse aims and fires. The bullet catches Collins in the thigh and Chase sees him go down.

Chase knows that now's his chance. He runs to the window in the room and sticks his head out. The sidewalk is more than eight stories away, but the rope only dangles a half a dozen feet. That means the Old Man went up.

94
Tuesday night, October 26

Chase hits the roof out of breath. *Blasted cigarettes,* he thinks. He'd thought it was bad to get shot at—now he knows there are worse things. Cigarettes, for one. It had only taken him a few seconds to convince Greathouse to let him go up to the roof. Carol had already briefed Dale, Greathouse, and a few other officers about Watts and Collins. Hopefully, Greathouse was radioing for help.

He looks toward the side of the building where he'd expected to see the Old Man—if Chase was lucky—emerging over the edge of the roof. It had to have taken him longer to climb hand over hand than it'd taken Chase to run up one floor. No such luck.

He looks around, extremely nervous. He knows he's in over his head. He finds himself there only out of necessity: Carol, down; Dale, down, Shango, down; Greathouse guarding Collins—Chase is the only one to follow up. He doesn't like it, but it's the way it is. He has the gun he took off of Shango, but he isn't sure he can use it. He swivels his head, unsure of why he is here.

The roof has two levels: the square raised portion in the middle with the smoke stack, the upraised portion off the main roof that probably houses the mechanical necessities that make the hospital run, and the primary one, the one he is on. That's when he sees the helicopters.

The whole rooftop is lit brightly by the moon—just past full—in the cloudless sky, and an eerie silver light casts sharp shadows from everything that stands up from the roof.

There are two helicopters, medical emergency helicopters, used to fly the critically injured in from highway accidents and areas in the West Virginia mountains that are too remote to reach quickly by car. *And they're the perfect escape vehicles,* Chase thinks. He starts to walk toward them.

He wonders if maybe there were three of them on the pad a few moments before; maybe the Old Man is already gone. Within dozen yards, he sees a body stretched out on the blacktop, face down. He sees the Old Man standing next to the body.

The Old Man waves. "Chase." It is a whisper that carries. He crooks his arm, waving for Chase to come closer.

Chase stops. He recognizes the Old Man he'd noticed in the Omega the past Saturday.

"You gave us a run for it, Chase," the Old Man says as he takes a few steps toward Chase. Chase can see his hands are empty, but he still doesn't trust him to be any closer.

"Stop now," Chase says. His gun is up and pointed. The Old Man stops.

Chase has a sudden sense he isn't going to get out of this. He feels tired, alone, futile. He tries to shake it off: "I did my best, slick. I could tell you wanted someone to keep a little pressure coming."

"You did very well, Mr. Chase."

The Old Man takes two steps forward. Chase doesn't want to shoot him—isn't sure he can, in fact, not having shot a gun more than twice before—but he doesn't want the Old Man any closer.

"STOP!" he yells. His voice sounds a little hysterical, even to him.

The Old Man just smiles. He looks like everyone's kindly grandfather. "You're not going to shoot me, Mr. Chase." He starts walking again.

"Yes, I am," Chase says. He cocks the gun and sets his jaw.

"No," the Old Man says. "No, you're not. Look behind you."

Chase is momentarily confused by the Old Man's words, as if the trick was too old and too tired to be attempted. The Old Man is ten feet away, still walking. Point blank. This is it—

"Just put it down, Mr. Chase." The voice comes from behind him, not more than two feet away. Chase has no idea who it is, but it's a strong voice.

He freezes.

"That's a good start. Now put it down."

Chase lowers his gun; that's when it hits him: Davies. It must be.

"Let it go, Mr. Chase. Drop it or I'm going to have to shoot you."

Chase lets the gun fall to the tar roof, where it lands with a dull thud. He turns slowly and sees a man with a raised gun approaching him. The gun is pointed at Chase's face. The barrel comes to within inches.

"I'm going to have to shoot you now anyway, Mr. Chase," the man says. He licks his lips, and Chase could swear the man looks forward to it.

Chase tenses for the shot, but it doesn't come. He bites his tongue and waits.

He hears a *shuck* and that's it: An arrow—the shaft sticks out of Davies's right temple, the point protrudes three inches from his left. Davies crumples to the tar roof in front of him. His eyes are wide with surprise.

Chase looks around wildly and sees the Old Man climbing into the helicopter. The engine turns over. The blades start to rotate.

He looks up—the only direction the arrow could have come from—and he sees a hunched figure who stands just beside the smokestack. The figure holds up an implement in its right hand; Chase sees it silhouetted in the night: It looks for all the world like a crossbow. The figure is Devon. Devon raises his left hand and twiddles his fingers, then disappears behind the smokestack.

The helicopter lurches, rising slowly. There is nothing Chase can do from here. It's over. The helicopter is twenty feet above the pad when its nose dips and it eases out across the roof, away from Chase, moving slowly over the vast open field to the east of the hospital, away. He sinks to his knees as he watches it go.

Then movement from next to the smokestack catches his eye. Devon is out again, his crossbow up, taking aim at the helicopter. Chase sees the arrow arch up and out, and he thinks he sees something long and fine, shimmering, trailing. . . Another arrow, another trail. And another, they follow faster than Chase can catch.

Then he sees the helicopter roters slow, stall, as if something is wrong. The powerful motor sputters. Then the helicopter is going down, crashing, exploding, flames everywhere. The percussion hits him before Chase hears it.

He looks up toward the smokestack, but doesn't see Devon.

He watches the flames, half expecting to see a fleeing figure burst from the wreckage, but nothing comes. No one could have survived that. He watches the flames burn in the moonlight, and he hears from far away their crackle, the whisper of the fire under the moon.

95

Wednesday evening, October 27

"You look like crap, Carol," Chase said as he stood at her bedside, patting her hand. He kissed her cheek.

"Screw you, Chase."

He had trouble understanding her because she had to mumble. Bandages swathed her head, covering the place where Collins's bullet had grazed her.

"Hey, it's not my fault you're stuck in here." He pulled a chair over by the bed. He took her hand again. "It could be worse."

"I know, Chase." Carol sounded very tired. "I owe you one."

Chase laughed. "You don't owe me anything. In fact, it's me that owes you."

"What's that mean?"

He laughed again. "Nothing. Listen, while I have you here—" He took out his tape deck and notebook.

"Very funny." Carol winced. Chase knew she had probably refused any painkiller stronger than a Tylenol; she was like that, didn't like to be "drugged up", as she put it. Which he thought was silly, because she was missing out on all the fun.

"Really," he said. "Do you feel up to talking a little? I still have an article to write—even if it'll appear under Dumont's byline—and you owe me an exclusive."

Carol grinned. "Ever the reporter."

Chase felt the words as a putdown. "That's what I do, Carol."

"I know. I'm sorry. What is it you want to know?"

"Okay." Chase crossed his legs and flipped on the recorder. "I just have some questions to clear up."

"Shoot," Carol said. She winced. "Figuratively speaking, I mean."

"Okay. Let's see." He flipped back through the notebook, looking at a few things. He flipped forward again to the blank page. "Let's start at the end. What were you able to find out from the remains of old man Lancaster?"

"There were none." Carol's were even more muffled than the bandages would have caused.

"Come again?"

"There were none."

Chase thought for a second before he said, "The fire was too hot, then. Nothing survived?"

"No. Plenty survived. There was no body."

Chase shivered. "Not even teeth?"

Carol shook her head. "Nothing. Best they can figure, he wasn't in the 'copter when it went down."

Chase didn't believe that. "But he had to be. I saw him get in; I saw him fly away."

Carol's voice was sharp. "You must have missed something, Chase."

Chase didn't believe that for a second. He's seen what he'd seen. He also didn't want to believe that the Old Man had gotten away. The sharpness of Carol's words told him that she didn't believe it either. She didn't like loose ends, and she had faith in Chase's observation skills, and she was frustrated. Believing that Chase had missed something was preferable to believing that old man Lancaster had flown away like a bird.

He decided to let it go, for now. Time to figure that out later.

"Okay, then. What about the crash itself? How was Lancaster able to bring the 'copter down?"

"You can't print this."

Chase sighed. Even though Carol was laid up in bed, she was as sharp and insistent as ever. "Depends on why."

"Because we don't want every crazy bozo with a kite trying to bring down helicopters!" Carol was so vehement that she tried to sit up: not a good idea.

"Okay, okay. Easy. I won't print it."

"Thanks, Chase." Carol eased back into her pillows. She took a deep breath. "He used something the Afghani rebels used to take out Soviet helicopters. If you shoot a couple of strong, thin wires into their blades, things get all tangled up. The rotors don't turn right." She made a cutting motion with her hand. "End of 'copter flight. The Vietnamese did the same thing to us, only they used stationary kites."

Chase made a note to check that as soon as Shango resurfaced. He hadn't liked being in the hospital and he'd disappeared one night. Down the steps, out the door.

"Wouldn't the turning blades cut the wires?" Chase asked.

"Not if they're weren't attached to anything. The blades just wrap the wires tighter."

Chase leaned back, thinking. No law agency would find Lancaster now; the man was probably in Europe or somewhere anyway, now that his grandfather had been taken care of.

Chase amended his thought: *probably* taken care of. He shivered again. He shook himself and brought his mind back to the present.

"So what happened, Carol? What was the motive?"

"As near as we can figure, the motive was basically what Lancaster said it was: There is a group of Satanists who believed they gained personal power from the slaughter of young females, especially if they did it on the night of the full moon, and especially if the full moon was near the end of the year as they counted it." Carol paused. "And who knows. They might really have gained something."

"You don't believe that, do you?"

Carol shrugged the best she could in the bed. "Beats me."

"I noticed you spoke in the past tense. Do you really think the group is broken?"

Carol hesitated, drew a breath. "I don't know, Chase. I don't see how it could be." She pointed a finger at him. "You can't print that, though."

Chase shrugged. She hadn't said it was off the record, which was standard procedure if someone talking to a reporter didn't want something printed. It was a rule of the game, a rule that reporters didn't violate because they wanted to maintain their standing. Most officials knew that if they didn't say "off the record" before a statement, then it was fair game. Chase knew Carol knew that; he wasn't sure what he would do. He'd worry about that later.

"What was Devon's role? Why was he picking girls up at Woodburn Circle?"

"I've been in here for two days, so I haven't been able to follow up, but from what the other detectives tell me—and they've been conducting a search and review sweep, interviewing everyone, students mostly—Lancaster picked up more than 23 students over the last three months, mostly on full moon nights. He scared the hell out of all of them. I think he was conducting a one-man campaign to get students to stop hitchhiking. He was trying to eliminate the easy prey."

Chase found that hard to swallow. "By himself? No one reported him?"

"What's to report?"

Chase had to concede that point. To an undergraduate college student, it would mostly be an occasion to gawk to friends with a good story: "You'll never guess the freak that picked me up today!"

He thought the whole thing through, as he had every night since Tuesday. The mechanics of the crime itself. He had one major question: "You've determined that it was Maria Redmann in every case?"

Carol sighed. The thought obviously hurt her. "Yes. Every victim was picked up at Woodburn Circle, and we have witnesses to place her car there every time. Alex—that's Alexandra Heyden, her psychiatrist—has been helping us out on this as much as she can.

"She's really torn, Chase. She wants to help her patient, and she also wants to get at the people who are really responsible. She trusts me, and she's told me things that violate doctor-patient confidentiality, strictly speaking." Carol shrugged again. "But like I say, she trusts me."

Carol looked at Chase. She looked at him hard. He recognized The Stare, having been on the receiving end of it often enough before. "And I don't want you printing any of this without my approval."

That one he could accede to. "You got it, Chief." The last thing Chase wanted to do was screw up someone's life, or someone's psychiatric practice. "I'll run it by you before I even show it to Waters."

"Good enough." Carol looked at him again, tenderly this time. "I trust you, Chase. You know that."

Whatever he hadn't already been convinced to keep quiet about, that did it. There was nothing more binding to him than an admission of someone's trust. He motioned for her to continue.

"Maria was always driving, so the victims got in without a second thought. Slightly frumpy middle-aged woman—why not? The Old Man was lying down in the back seat, out of sight. At some point he would sit up and slap a cloth filled with chloroform over their mouth and nose—We found one of those cloths in the Redmanns' basement.

"Once the victim was unconscious, they bound her with duct tape and gagged her. They put her in the trunk. Then they drove to some predetermined place—always at his direction—and that's where they did the ritual. Maria conducted it, but according to Alex's sessions, Maria was under some kind of deep programming that the Old Man had instituted when she was a little girl. Later, after the killings, she didn't even know that she was doing it—a multiple personality case. Some kind of hypnotic state that involved the use of the grandfather's name—Konrad—his name backward as a trigger."

Chase sat up. "Like *The Manchurian Candidate*. I've heard that was based on actual experiments."

Carol was nodding. "Just like that. Although we'll never know if that was a description of something already in use, or if the Old Man copied it from that. Doesn't really matter, I suppose."

"That's really—"

"There's one thing that bothered me," Carol interrupted. "The bodies were both found in the middle of the circles. The one, after a month; the other, after a week and a half. Come to find out that they believe that the body has to stay in the circle in order for the magic to be totally effective. For the magic to take, as it were. That's why. Old man Lancaster came back every day and dragged the bodies back in the circle, arranged their limbs just so."

"One crazy..."

Carol bit her lower lip. "I can't tell if there's something to it or not, Chase. Because of the way that Katie Shaver survived. Maria cut her bad, but not bad enough to kill her. Bad enough for the Old Man—who waited nearby but out of sight—to hear her screams. Maria says he could also feel her spirit dying. When Katie was nearly unconscious, Maria shot the gun in the air and punched Maria in the face, knocking her out. The Old Man was fooled, thinking her dead. Late that night, Maria drove out to the site and bound Katie and threw her in the trunk. It's a wonder the girl didn't die of exposure.

"That was when she says she knew that someone had to die in order for the Old Man to feel the strength of the spirit leaving a body. That was when she knew she had to kill herself rather than kill Katie. It was only her tie to her friend and employee that broke this whole thing."

"How much of this do you believe, Carol?"

Carol shook her head. "I'm a cop, Chase. I've heard a lot of strange things." Chase watched her eyes swivel left, toward the window, out at the gentle rain that fell. She sighed. "I don't know. I still can't figure out how Lancaster knew about my mother. Her official cause of death was listed as a hit-and-run accident. He would have had to know someone to know that it was deliberate. I don't know."

Chase waited before asking his last questions, but he felt like he knew what the answers would be. Silence filled the hospital room. Outside it was dark, the rain coming down slow, silent, relentless. Finally he said, "What about Collins? And Davies? And the other guy—possibly Abbott—the one who shot at me?"

"We don't have a clue about Abbott yet. As for Collins and Davies—the FBI denies they were on assignment; they deny that Davies is one of them, in fact."

Chase wasn't too surprised. "The same guy you talked to before, Carol? The guy who confirmed Collins?"

She nodded, but didn't say anything.

"You know what that means, Carol."

Her voice was sharp again. "I don't need any of your paranoia, Chase. It's not appropriate."

Chase laughed. "Appropriate paranoia? Come on, Carol."

He could see that Carol was very tired. "Look, Chase. I'm not ready to discuss it."

"But you are doing something?"

"There's this guy. Never mind his name. But he works in Behavioral Sciences and I met him at a conference ten years ago or so. We've kept in touch. He's going to follow up on some things for me. Some profiles, some compilations of similar crimes."

"Like what?"

Carol cocked an eye at him. "Never you mind. Not yet anyway."

Chase closed his notebook and switched off the tape deck. "Don't tell me as a reporter, Carol. If there's some kind of Satanic conspiracy going on, I want to know what's up. I've done some checking, and if you scratch the surface, there's a reality out there that no one's ever pinned down. Like the whole thing with psychiatrists treating patients of abuse who are lately claiming Satanic influence on their parents. Listen, tell me because I'm curious. I won't print anything till I clear it with you."

"Okay, Chase. Listen up," she said, and she proceeded to tell him things about organized Satanism for the next two hours.

96
Wednesday evening, October 27

"You've been here an awful long time without smoking, Chase. What gives?" Carol said after she finished.

"I quit."

Carol snorted. "Yeah, right."

"No, I did. It's just not worth the trouble." He laughed. "Although it took getting shot at to realize it."

There was a long silence; Chase could tell that Carol was having trouble digesting the news. "Hope it sticks," she said at last.

"It will, Carol. You know me. When I'm tired with it, I walk away."

There was an even longer silence then; Chase grew uncomfortable. He thought it was time to be leaving. He stood. "Well, thanks, Chief. I think that's about it. Thanks for your help."

"Chase." He stopped, waiting. She continued: "Chase, about the other night—"

"I know, Braxy." He patted her hand. It could never work out between them, mostly because neither one of them really wanted to be with anyone, not on a full time basis, at least.

"I care for you a lot, Chase."

"I love you, Braxy," he said as he leaned over to kiss her cheek. He really did, too; that was the amazing thing.

Epilogue
Friday afternoon, October 29

Chase tosses the Morgan story on Waters's desk. "Here it is, Chief. It may not be as hot as you wanted it, but I think it'll do."

Chase feels okay about it, though. He knows it will run as a light feature in the Sunday edition, the same edition that the 4000-word, hard news piece on the background of the murders will run, which he has written over two days in a fever of words. When he had finished, the opening to the Morgan piece had occurred to him, and he knew it would work, because it would run at a time when every reader's mind was turned to murder. He wrote it in a two-hour, 1500-word rush:

> Haskell Morgan thought he spoke with God on a regular basis. In his day, many people apparently believed him, too. He founded a town—Morgantown—with the followers he brought from the east, who came from states like Vermont, Connecticut, and Massachusetts. According to records from the time, he also very nearly succeeded in founding the religious order that he had intended from the beginning of his sojourn in what is now West Virginia.
>
> Was Haskell Morgan onto something, communing with a God that most of us cannot hear? Or was he insane, perhaps the victim of a bizarre illness that is only now beginning to be understood?
>
> Today, as many people put their faith in science as in religion, and scientists hope to be able to solve the leftover riddles from our collective past. Science may never be able to answer the first question, but recent advances in genetic analysis make it possible to investigate the second. Forensic science is a burgeoning field, and its tools and methods can do much to shed light on the mysteries of the past.
>
> Forensic scientists can determine the cause of a person's death, as well as some of the circumstances leading up to it. Bodies that have lain undisturbed for decades, or even centuries, can reveal facts that may shake preconceptions of. . .

Waters looks up at Chase. "It's not hot because it's three weeks late. I may not even run it. The city already decided to give the kid permission."

Chase smiles. Maybe the lack of publicity has actually allowed something to get done, in this case at least. "Well, good." He fingers the edges of the papers. "I should probably re-do this, though, so it's actually up to date."

Waters slaps his hand down on the story. "Don't touch it. Adams will revise it. I take it there's a file in the copy in-box he can work from."

"Right as rain, Chief. It's all his."

Waters sits back in his chair. He picks up that day's edition of the *Dispatch* and snaps it open. "Chase, did you see this piece Dumont did on the Lancaster killings?"

Chase knows when he is being baited, but he doesn't care: He has come to a decision of his own. He just smiles and nods. "Sure did. It's kind of amazing the way he got in on the investigation like that. Never thought he had it in him."

"Neither did I, Chase. It looks like when they catch him—if he's not already dead—he'll be doing a lot of time." Waters leafs through the paper. Chase is silent, waiting. Might as well let Waters have his final dig.

At last Waters comes to the Metro section. "And over here," Waters says, "We come to your announcement of the Sunday preview of a series on the lifestyles of Morgantown's own rich and famous."

Chase rocks back on his heels, tucks his thumbs under his arms, doing his best imitation of a proud parent. "It's gonna be great, Chief. You'll love it. Best stuff I've ever done."

"Yeah, right." Waters looks up from the paper. "That's why I wanted to talk to you. I think—" Waters gulps and swallows, looked down again. Chase knows it is hard for him to admit he'd been wrong, but he doesn't step in. This is what he's been waiting for two years.

"You should take over the crime beat again, Chase. What do you think?"

Now it is Chase's turn; he wants to milk it. "That's something I wanted to talk to you about. I don't think I'd be appropriate for that."

That catches Waters by surprise. He sputters. "W-why not?"

"Because, Chief. As of today, I quit. I'm outta here."

Without waiting for Waters to respond, he turns and leaves the office. He is surprised at himself: He should have wanted a cigarette. After all, it has only been 72 hours since he quit, but he finds the urge just isn't there. He has no desire for one. He is too filled with the vision of his first big freelance project, tentatively titled, *The Hacker Underground: Real Life Equalizers*.

He figures that'll be a good warm-up—take a year or so, during which he can sell serial excerpts to a few nationals, before he goes after the story he really wants to investigate: *Satanism in America: How Real? How Widespread?* Maybe he'll be able to find Lancaster again and get him to help out.

He leaves the building without even cleaning out his desk.

Afterword

I was nine years old when Mared Malarik and Karen Ferrell, two West Virginia University freshmen, disappeared. They had been hitchhiking back to their dormitory after seeing the movie "Oliver" on January 18, 1970. Three months later, on the morning of April 16, their headless bodies were found ten miles south of Morgantown.

The crime, which came to be known as The Coed Murders, had a huge effect on Morgantown generally and on me in particular. I was in high school in 1976 when the man who had confessed to the murder-decapitations, Eugene Paul Clawson, was first tried. I skipped school with my girlfriend to attend the closing arguments of his trial. After hearing the summations, both Sarah and I thought there was no way Clawson had committed the crime. We were stunned when he was convicted.

Although *Full Bone Moon* was inspired by the actual crime, the tale told in this novel is purely fictional. All events, characters, and descriptions are imaginary. The story in *Full Bone Moon* was built on rumors about the crime that have floated around Morgantown since 1970; I breathed life into those rumors with stories I'd read about Satanic abuse and murder, and with actual experiences related to me by people who claimed to have encountered such phenomena. In *Full Bone Moon*, however, Mared Malarik, Karen Ferrell, and Eugene Paul Clawson are just names, and the crimes described herein never occurred. In using the names, I meant no disrespect toward the actual people to whom those names also referred, or to the surviving families of the actual victims of the actual crime.

As it turned out, since writing *Full Bone Moon*, I have learned much more about that actual crime. For instance, I was shocked to discover how much of what is "known" about the crime by the public is completely false. The real Mared Malarik and Karen Ferrell were last seen hitchhiking on Willey Street that night of January 18, 1970, but they were neither raped nor sexually abused. No indication of a ritual component to the crimes exists, nor is there any indication of truth to the rumor that was (and still is) common in Morgantown, that the murder-decapitations were carried out by a member of a prominent Morgantown family and covered up by a conspiracy of the police and town leaders.

The story in *Full Bone Moon* corresponds to what actually happened in one sense: Eugene Paul Clawson, the man who confessed from his cell in a New Jersey prison, does not seem to have killed Mared and Karen. Clawson drew most of his confession from an article that appeared in a December, 1975, edition of Detective Cases, a lurid "true" crime magazine. He "confessed" in

January of 1976, a little over one month later. Every detail Clawson cited in his "confession" also appeared in the article. In fact, six facts in Clawson's confession and in the article were true, while seven facts cited by Clawson, identical to the "facts" in the article, were not true. In other words, Clawson's confession precisely paralleled the magazine article, even where the article got the facts wrong. Nevertheless, Clawson was convicted of the crime. He died in West Virginia's Mount Olive Correctional Complex in August of 2009.

I am currently considering writing a true account of The Coed Murders and the investigations of 1970 and 1976, as well as the much more fruitful investigations that occurred later, but I wanted to assure readers that *Full Bone Moon* is pure fiction, more akin to a yarn meant for campfires than to a true crime account. I hope *Full Bone Moon* was entertaining and chilling, but at the same time, I want readers to remember that the thrills of a fictional story should never be substituted for the real horror of two headless bodies found in the dark woods south of Morgantown, West Virginia.

Rest in peace, Mared and Karen.

The author can be found on FACEBOOK under Geoffrey Cameron Fuller. He can be contacted by email at geoff@gcfuller.com. His website is www.gcfuller.com.

* * *

Photography incorporated in the design of the cover of *Full Moon Bone* used by permission of Taryn Lee Pyle. with Born Barefoot Studios, TarynLeePhotography. See www.bornbarefoot.etsy.com or www.TarynLeePhotography.com. You can also find Taryn at Linked In: www.linkedin.com/in/tarynlpyle. Email: TarynLPyle@cox.net.

Other Great Book Titles
From Woodland Press, LLC

Mountain Magic
Spellbinding Tales of Appalachia
Edited by Brian J. Hatcher

Stories from the Hearth
Heartwarming Tales of Appalachia
Edited by Brian J. Hatcher

The Tale of the Devil
By Dr. Coleman C. Hatfield and Robert Spence

The Feuding Hatfields & McCoys
By Dr. Coleman C. Hatfield and F. Keith Davis

Shadows and Mountains
By Jessie Grayson and Ellen Thompson McCloud

Legends of the Mountain State
Ghostly Tales from the State of West Virginia
Edited by Michael Knost

Legends of the Mountain State 2
More Ghostly Tales from the State of West Virginia
Edited by Michael Knost

Legends of the Mountain State 3
More Ghostly Tales from the State of West Virginia
Edited by Michael Knost

Legends of the Mountain State 4
More Ghostly Tales from the State of West Virginia
Edited by Michael Knost

Writers Workshop of Horror
Edited by Michael Knost

The Mothman Files
Edited by Michael Knost

www.woodlandpress.com

CPSIA information can be obtained at www.ICGtesting.com
Printed in the USA
BVOW030655081011

273098BV00002B/1/P